For all who serve
Military, Law Enforcement, First Responders.
Your commitment and sacrifice inspire every page.

Author's Note

The S.E.A. began as a feature film screenplay written by Kris Michael McKenna and KA Plouffe in 2011 and registered with the Writers Guild of America (Registration #1464812). The screenplay was developed as a military science fiction thriller exploring the dark intersection of Cold War human enhancement experiments and modern geopolitical conspiracy.

This novel represents a complete adaptation of that screenplay into traditional prose fiction. While every scene, character, and plot beat remains faithful to the original script, the novel form allows for expanded internal perspectives, the visceral horror of biological transformation, and the kind of psychological depth that only literary fiction can provide.

The story you're about to read is the same one I wrote for the screen—complete with its supersoldier revelations, moral compromises, and that final confrontation in the Norwegian Arctic. But now you'll experience it the way novels let us experience stories: from the inside out, with full access to the thoughts, fears, and transformations of those who volunteered to become something more than human.

The title carries three meanings that reveal themselves as you read: the Soldier Enhancement Adaptation program that created these warriors, the *sea* creatures whose biology became the foundation for human augmentation, and the vast ocean of ethical questions that come with rewriting what it means to be human.

Welcome to a world where the Cold War never ended—it just went biological.

—Kris Michael McKenna, 2026

Contents

PROJECT CODE: SEA-19.5

FILE DESIGNATION: *BIO-STRAT INTERFACE / UNAU-THORIZED MATERIAL REVIEW*

ACCESS LEVEL: OMEGA/BLACK

DATE: 04 APR 20██

HANDLING RESTRICTIONS:

DoD Reg. 5220.78 — Deviation constitutes a federal offense.

Unauthorized duplication is prohibited.

Portions of this document have been redacted for program integrity.

SECTION I — PROGRAM ORIGINS (REDACTED)

The Soldier Enhancement Adaptation initiative (SEA) began as a feasibility inquiry under the Office of Naval Research (ONR) after multiple anomalous biological resilience reports among marine fauna aligned with deep-water extraction operations in the Norwegian Basin.

Informal intelligence flagged correlations between observed attributes (resistance, regeneration, cognition irregularities) and an unidentified civilian research interest predating official funding channels.

A review of CONUS academic institutions identified **one individual** (Name: ████████████, Status: ACTIVE) whose private work aligned with previously classified ONR data from Project KELP-9 (terminated 19██). The individual's early developmental history indicates **high-risk psychological indicators** matched to patterns from the aborted MK-Orchid trials.

Detailed profile unavailable.

Redacted by directive: DRN-04.229.

SECTION II — OBJECTIVE SUMMARY

SEA-01 seeks feasibility of *non-invasive* biological integration models capable of:

Augmenting warfighter survivability in hostile aquatic or semi-aquatic environments.

Enabling cross-domain adaptability (neurological, metabolic, and systemic).

Developing non-weaponized interfaces for reconnaissance operations.

Assessing potential for emergent traits not predicted in initial modeling (flagged by DARPA, 02 FEB 20██).

Initial assumptions regard Phase-I adaptations as **behavioral and peripheral**. Internal speculation suggests potential for systemic-level alterations; this remains unverified.

SECTION III — INCIDENT REPORTS (PARTIAL)

Berlin Archive 20██-B

Civilian environment. Unauthorized biological sample extraction.

Several items offcially recorded as "missing" despite documented chain-of-custody.

Northern Sector Acquisition (Case R-17)

Acoustic recordings reference rhythmic mechanical patterns.

No device recovered.

Classified under PSYOPS anomaly storage.

Data Cluster: SEA/CORE/OBS-03

Behavioral imprinting patterns observed in lab fauna inconsistent with conditioning protocols.

Possible cross-domain mimicry event.

Investigation suspended.

SECTION IV — SUBJECTS OF INTEREST (SOI)

SOI-1: ███████████████

Training file indicates above-average intellectual metrics + irregular empathic responses.

Notable fixation pattern referenced in multiple juvenile case logs (foreign origin).

Correlation between SOI-1 behavioral patterns and SEA Phase-I experimental goals deemed "statistically significant" by analytical staff.

Psychological Evaluation: *Unresolved dissonance. Predictive models flagged elevated determination under duress.*

Recommendation: Limited oversight; maintain compartmentalization.

SOI-2: Assigned codename: "KORT"

Physical aptitude exceeds baseline per age cohort.

Unverified incident suggests high tolerance for environmental stressors not matching medical history.

Cross-reference with SOI-1 prohibited under Addendum 12.

SECTION V — RISK ASSESSMENT

Threat Probability: UNKNOWN

Operational Yield: HIGH

Containment Difficulty: ELEVATED (due to biological unpredictability).

DARPA internal memo references:

"Adaptation is not linear. It is opportunistic. We may explore one capability and inadvertently unlock a different, unrequested trait. SEA-01 carries inherent risks of emergent behavior not aligned with program intent."

(Originating agent unidentified; line removed from archived version.)

SECTION VI — PROGRAM VIABILITY

The majority of SEA-19.5 remains in pre-deployment analysis.

Projections indicate:

18–24 months required before Phase-II trials. ███████

Psychological stability protocols remain unresolved.

Budgetary evaluation approved only on condition that all biological modeling remains black-compartmentalized and tied to foreign threat justification.

Multiple reviewers have expressed concern regarding the "foundational source material" (wording preserved from original).

Attempts to identify the source have been unsuccessful.

File included in this packet is incomplete and ends abruptly.

SECTION VII — FINAL NOTE

Per directive OMEGA/BLACK:

This dossier shall precede all SEA-related material for internal review.

All personnel are reminded that **this program does not officially exist**.

"Observe without interference. Record without interpretation."

-- DoD Oversight, Unattributed Signature Block

END OF FILE

One

Echoes of Destruction

Berlin, 1945 – The Fall of Berlin

The clocks in Frau Austerlitz's apartment breathed with a rhythm that defied the chaos outside. Nineteen timepieces in total—each wound, set, and positioned with mathematical precision. Grandfather clocks stood sentinel in corners. Cuckoo clocks adorned the kitchen walls. Pocket watches rested in velvet-lined boxes on the hutch, their brass cases gleaming even in the dim afternoon light filtering through dust-covered windows.

Six-year-old Filibert Austerlitz moved among them like a priest tending his congregation. His small fingers traced the Roman numerals on a mahogany wall clock, then reached up—standing on tiptoes—to adjust its minute hand. A quarter turn. The soft tick-tick-tick resumed, perfectly synchronized with its neighbors.

"Filibert!" His mother's voice cut through his ritual. "Come away from the window. *Jetzt.*"

He didn't move immediately. Through the kitchen window, beyond the war-damaged street, he could see the church tower—his reference point, his anchor. Parts of the steeple had been blown away by artillery three days ago, but the clock face remained visible, still marking time even as the world collapsed around it.

Half past one, the tower read.

Filibert's finger traced a small circle in the air, point-ing toward that distant timepiece. His lips moved silently, counting the rotation. Once. Twice. Three times.

"Filibert! *Sofort!*"

This time he obeyed, but only because the next clock re-quired his attention. A Black Forest cuckoo clock hung near the doorway to the living room. He checked his mother's position—she was pulling the sofa away from the wall, her movements sharp and purposeful—then wound the clock's mechanism with careful turns of the tiny key.

The apartment was small but had once been comfortable. Two rooms really: the kitchen that opened into a modest living area, and a bedroom beyond that Filibert rarely en-tered now. The walls were water-stained, the plaster cracked from nearby explosions. But his mother kept it clean, kept it ordered. And she had allowed him his clocks.

Outside, the sounds of war drew closer. The rumble of artillery had become so constant that Filibert barely noticed it anymore—it was simply the bass note in the symphony of destruction that had played for weeks now. What did catch his attention were the changes in rhythm: the sharp crack of nearby rifle fire, the deeper boom of tank cannons, the screaming.

Always the screaming.

His mother had moved the sofa completely away from the wall now. Filibert watched with curious detachment as she inspected the hiding place she had previously created using a kitchen knife to cut into the back of the upholstery. She'd worked on this project for two days, in-between other preparations, carving out the stuffing, creating a hollow space. A hiding place.

"*Es ist halb zwei, Mama,*" Filibert announced, checking the cuckoo clock against his internal count.

Halfway to two: One-thrity.

"*Ja, ja,* my darling." Frau Austerlitz didn't look up from her work. She was young still—barely twenty-five—but the war had aged her. Her blonde hair, once lustrous, now hung in lank strands. Her hands, which had played piano before the bombing of the concert hall, were raw and calloused.

She reached into her apron and pulled out several wrapped parcels—bread, hard cheese, a jar of preserves that had cost her two days' worth of ration coupons. These she placed carefully inside the hollowed sofa, tucking them into the corners.

Filibert returned to his circuit. The grandfather clock in the corner next. Then the small wind-up alarm clock on the side table. Each one required checking, adjusting, winding. Each one needed to show the correct time.

He understood, even at six, that time was the only thing left to control. His father was gone—killed in France, though his mother had tried to shield him from the details. Their food was rationed. Their movements restricted. The city itself was dying, street by street, building by building.

But time? Time could be measured. Time could be set. Time could be made to obey.

The building shook as something exploded several blocks away. Plaster dust drifted down from the ceiling like snow. One of the pocket watches on the hutch fell over with a tiny clink.

Filibert rushed to it, checking for damage. The crystal was intact. The mechanism still ticked. He set it upright again, adjusting its position until it sat at precisely the same angle as its companions.

"Filibert, *liebling*, I need you to listen." His mother had finished with the sofa and now knelt before him, her hands on his narrow shoulders. "Do you remember what we practiced?"

He nodded. "If the soldiers come, I go behind the sofa. I stay quiet. I don't move until you tell me."

"*Genau.* Exactly right." She kissed his forehead, her lips dry and chapped. "No matter what you hear, no matter what happens, you stay hidden. *Verstehst du?*"

"I understand, Momma."

She pulled him into an embrace that lasted three seconds—Filibert counted—then released him and returned to her preparations. She pushed the sofa back against the wall, not quite flush, leaving just enough space for a small body to slip behind.

The afternoon wore on. Filibert continued his rounds, though with increasing frequency he found himself drawn back to the kitchen window and that distant church tower. The light was fading now, the weak winter sun already beginning its descent.

Still half past one, the tower clock read.

Unless—

Filibert squinted. Was the minute hand moving? It was difficult to tell from this distance, through the haze of smoke that hung over the city. He pressed his nose against the cold glass, his breath fogging the pane.

A sharp knock at the door made him jump.

His mother froze, a dish towel clutched in her hands. They waited, neither breathing.

Another knock, more urgent. Then a voice, young and female: "*Frau Austerlitz! Bitte!*"

His mother rushed to the door, opened it just wide enough to see. Helga stumbled in—a neighbor girl, fifteen years old, barefoot and wild-eyed. She slammed the door behind her, pressing her back against it as if she could hold back what was coming.

"*Die Russen*," Helga gasped. "They've broken through! The soldiers—" She couldn't finish, her words dissolving into panicked breaths.

"How close?" Frau Austerlitz's voice was steady, but Filibert saw her hands shaking.

"Two streets. Maybe less. Frau Getman—they shot her in the street. She was holding her baby—" Helga's face crumpled. "*Sie haben beide getötet.*"

They killed them both.

Frau Austerlitz moved quickly then. She grabbed Helga's arm, pulled her toward the sofa. "Get behind. Both of you. *Schnell!*"

"No!" Helga shook her head violently. "There's no time. They're right behind me. I heard them—"

The door exploded inward.

The hinges didn't break cleanly—that would have been too merciful. Instead, the door hung crooked on one remaining hinge, swinging drunkenly as three Russian soldiers pushed into the apartment. They were young, Filibert noted with the same detachment he applied to observing his clocks. Seventeen, perhaps eighteen. Boys in men's uniforms, their eyes carrying the weight of things boys should never see. Not weary eyes though, not like their uniforms, disheveled and soiled from the fight with nearly spent supplies. Filibert blinked slowly, assessing, sinking into it; a few remaining RG-42 grenades dangled from twisted belts, a shovel missing from one soldier's cover, and ammo bags sagged near empty. Filibert went back to the eyes—not exhausted, but still hungry, still filled with dark intent.

"*Shlyukhi!*" the first soldier barked. Whores. He pointed at Frau Austerlitz and Helga with the barrel of his rifle, gesturing for them to move away from the sofa. "*Nemka shlyukhi!*"

Filibert's mother raised her hands, palms outward. "Please," she said in broken Russian, one of the few phrases she'd learned in the past weeks. "*Pozhaluysta.* The boy—"

"*Zamolchi!*" Shut up.

The first soldier—his uniform identified him as a corporal, though Filibert wouldn't learn this detail until much later—shoved Frau Austerlitz hard. She stumbled, catching herself against the wall. Helga started to move toward her, but the second soldier grabbed the girl by her hair.

"*Kakaya molodaya,*" he laughed. So young. "*Ot kakaya svezhen'kaya.*"

The third soldier, the youngest of the three, looked uncomfortable. He kept glancing at the door, as if hoping someone would call them back outside. His hands trembled on his rifle.

Frau Austerlitz righted herself from the stumble, pushing off the wall, turning so slightly towards Filibert, trying to conceal her face from the soldiers. "Filibert," his mother's lips formed the words, "behind the sofa. *Jetzt.*"

He wanted to obey. His feet wouldn't move.

The first soldier crossed the room in three strides and backhanded Frau Austerlitz across the face. The sound was sharp and wet. Blood sprayed from her nose and mouth, spattering across the wallpaper that featured tiny yellow flowers.

Helga screamed.

That broke Filibert's paralysis. He darted toward the sofa, squeezing into the narrow space behind it just as he'd practiced. The hollowed-out section pressed against his back. He could smell the preserves his mother had hidden there, the sweet scent of strawberries incongruous with what was happening just a few feet away.

Only the younger third soldier noticed the little boy scurry behind the sofa. The other two oblivious, fixated on their prey.

Through the gap between the sofa and the wall, Filibert had a clear view of the kitchen window and the church tower beyond.

Still half past one.

"*Ne soprotivlyaysya*," one of the soldiers said to Helga. Don't fight. "*My prosto khotyat nemnogo udovol'stviya.*"

The girl was crying now, struggling as the first soldier pushed her toward the sofa. He sat down heavily on the worn cushions—Filibert felt the vibration through the sofa's frame—and fumbled with his belt.

"*Na koleni*," the soldier ordered. On your knees.

Helga fell to her knees in front of him, her face level with his groin. The soldier grabbed her hair with one hand, his pistol in the other, pressing the barrel to the nape of her neck.

Behind the sofa, Filibert's finger began to move. A small circle, tracing an invisible path in the air. His eyes fixed on the church tower. On the clock face that refused to advance beyond half past one.

The boy perseverated a mantra he dared not speak into the world: Go back. Go back to half past one. Before the door. Before the soldiers. Before.

On the floor near the sofa, the second soldier had forced Frau Austerlitz down. She wasn't fighting anymore. Her eyes had gone blank, staring at the ceiling as the soldier tore at her dress. The third soldier stood by, his young face twisted with disgust at what he might be made to do, but would do nevertheless.

The sounds that filled the apartment were sounds Filibert's mind refused to process. The grunting. The sobbing. The rhythmic impact of violence masquerading as something else. His finger traced circles faster now, his inner voice entering the world as a whisper, barely audible:

"*Geh zurück auf halb zwei. Geh zurück auf halb zwei.*"

Go back to half past one—halfway to two.

The third soldier could not stand the brutality anymore. He walked toward the sofa, his boots heavy on the wooden floor.

"*Chto eto?*" What's this?

He peered over the back of the sofa, looking down at Filibert with eyes that held a kind of broken pity. The boy was so small, so still, making his little gestures in the air like a child conducting an invisible orchestra.

"*Mal'chik,*" the soldier said softly. Boy.

Frau Austerlitz's head snapped toward them. She saw the soldier approaching her hidden son, and something in her broke in an entirely different way. With a strength that shocked everyone, including herself, she bucked the second soldier off, her hands scrabbling at his jacket.

"*Nein!*" she screamed. "*Bleib weg von meinem Sohn!*" Stay away from my son!

The first soldier turned, his attention pulled from Helga. He leveled his pistol at Frau Austerlitz and then at the sofa.

"*Otoydi,*" he said to the third soldier. Move away.

Helga saw her chance. While the soldier's pistol was pointed elsewhere, while his grip on her hair had loosened, she lunged forward and bit down hard on the exposed flesh of his inner thigh.

The soldier's scream was high and animal. Blood—arterial blood, bright red and spurting—sprayed across Helga's face. The pistol discharged wildly, the bullet catching the third soldier in the neck. He dropped instantly, clutching at the wound, blood pumping between his fingers.

The second soldier scrambled away from Frau Austerlitz, reaching for his own weapon. The first soldier, still screaming, kicked Helga away from him and shot her in the face. The back of her skull exploded across the floor, fragments of bone and brain matter sliding toward the baseboard.

Frau Austerlitz was on her feet now, backing away toward the kitchen. Her dress hung in tatters. Blood streamed down her legs. But her eyes—her eyes were clear and focused in a way they hadn't been since the soldiers entered.

The first soldier advanced on her, limping, one hand pressed against his bleeding thigh. *"Ty umresh', suka!"* You'll die, bitch!

The second soldier was right behind him, his face twisted with rage and something else—fear, perhaps, at how badly this had all gone wrong.

Frau Austerlitz's hands were behind her back. When she brought them forward, she held a small object. Her fingers clenched around it, knuckles white.

A grenade pin.

The second soldier looked down at his jacket, at the grenade that hung from his belt, its safety pin removed. His eyes went wide.

"Khuy—"

The explosion was deafening in the small apartment. A bright flash, then a concussive wave that slammed Filibert against the wall behind the sofa. The blast shredded the three bodies, turning them into meat and bone fragments that painted every surface.

Then silence.

Not complete silence—Filibert's ears were ringing too badly for that. But a relative silence, punctuated only by the crackle of small fires catching on fabric, the distant rumble of artillery, and a soft tick-tick-tick that he gradually realized was coming from the clocks.

The clocks that, impossibly, were still intact.

Filibert stayed behind the sofa for a long time. Minutes, maybe hours—his sense of time had fractured along with everything else. He stared through the gap at the kitchen window, at the church tower beyond, at the clock face that was finally, finally, beginning to move again.

The minute hand crept forward.

Twenty-five minutes to two.

Twenty minutes to two.

When he finally emerged from behind the sofa, stepping carefully around the pieces of what had once been human beings, he went directly to the grandfather clock in the corner. His mother's blood had sprayed across its face, obscuring the numbers. He wiped it clean with his sleeve, his movements mechanical and precise.

Then he went to the next clock. And the next. And the next.

He wound them all. Set them all. Synchronized them all.

Every single one was set to half past one.

Outside, the battle for Berlin continued. The Reich was falling. The world was ending.

But in that small apartment, surrounded by death and the smell of cordite and worse things, a six-year-old boy learned the most important lesson he would ever learn:

Time could be controlled. Time could be stopped. Time could be made to go back to before the bad things happened.

If you were strong enough.

If you were smart enough.

If you were willing to do whatever it took.

Filibert Austerlitz sat on the floor, surrounded by his carefully synchronized clocks, and began to plan. The seed of an obsession had been planted—watered with blood, fertilized with trauma, destined to grow into something the world would never forget.

The clock struck half past one.

And would continue striking half past one, in Filibert's mind, for the rest of his life.

TWO

Brothers of Circumstance

European Orphans' Refugee Camp, The Bronx, New York – 1946

The church bells tolled across the wasteland that had once been a YMCA recreation yard. One-thirty in the afternoon, the sound echoing off brick buildings that still bore scorch marks from a fire three years prior. The bells were cracked—damaged during the same fire—and their tone carried a discordant quality that most people found unsettling.

Filibert Austerlitz found it perfect.

He sat cross-legged on the cracked asphalt, surrounded by his artwork. Dozens of clocks drawn in colored chalk, each one rendered with obsessive precision. The Roman numerals perfectly spaced. The hands positioned at exact angles. Every single one showing the same time: half past one.

The other children gave him a wide berth. Forty-three orphans called this place home—or at least, called it the place where they waited to find a home. Children from Germany, Poland, France, Russia, Hungary. Children whose parents had died in camps, or in bombings, or in the confused violence that followed the war's end. Children who spoke different languages and ate different foods and prayed to different gods, but who shared the common currency of loss.

Most of them had formed small clusters, nationality-based alliances that provided comfort and familiarity. The Polish children stuck together. The French children kept to themselves. The German children—there were only three, including Filibert—were generally avoided by everyone else.

Filibert didn't mind. The other children were noise, interference in the careful calculations he was always running. Numbers were clean. Numbers were predictable. Numbers, unlike people, always behaved exactly as they should.

He reached for the yellow chalk and began drawing another clock face. His movements were methodical, measured. First the circle—one continuous line, no breaks, no irregularities. Then the twelve numbers, each one placed with geometric precision. Then the hands, angled just so.

Half past one.

Always half past one.

"Crazy Nazi," someone muttered in Russian. The words were meant to carry, meant to provoke.

Filibert didn't look up. His finger traced a small circle in the air, pointing toward the distant church tower. Once around. Twice. Three times. The rhythm soothed him, helped him think.

The sound of footsteps approached—multiple sets, deliberately heavy. Filibert could identify five distinct gaits without looking up. Three boys, approximately ten to twelve years old. One girl, older. One adult, probably Ms. McGhee, the primary caretaker, though she was maintaining distance.

"Hey, Nazi!" The voice was closer now, more aggressive. "Why you drawing clocks? You crazy? All Germans crazy like cuckoo clocks?"

Laughter from the other boys. Filibert continued his drawing, adding minute marks between the numbers. Precision was everything. If the marks weren't evenly spaced, time itself might become unstable.

A foot kicked through one of his chalk drawings, scattering yellow dust across the asphalt. Filibert watched the destruction with clinical detachment, already calculating how long it would take to redraw. Approximately four minutes, assuming no additional interruptions.

"Look at him," another boy said. "Doesn't even care. Probably doesn't understand Russian. Probably too stupid."

"Not stupid," the first boy said. "Crazy. Crazy Nazi who draws clocks all day."

A hand shoved Filibert's shoulder, knocking him sideways. He caught himself with one palm, careful not to smear any of the remaining drawings. The yellow chalk rolled away, coming to rest against the shoe of the girl in the group.

She picked it up, examining it like it might be something valuable. "What you draw these for, German boy? What they mean?"

Filibert looked up for the first time, making brief eye contact before his gaze skittered away. Direct eye contact was difficult, uncomfortable. Eyes moved and changed expression and carried too much unpredictable information.

"Time," he said simply, his German accent thick around the English word. "Es ist halb zwei."

"He speaks!" the first boy—Dmitri, Filibert's memory supplied—crowed. "The Nazi speaks! What's he saying?"

"Halfway to two we say. In English—half past one," Filibert instructed, enunciating carefully. "It is always half past one."

"Always?" The girl—Katya—tilted her head. "That doesn't make sense. Time moves. It's afternoon now. Half past one was hours ago."

Filibert's finger traced its circle again, faster now. "No. It's half past one. It's always half past one. If we go back, if we make it stop, then nothing bad happens. We go back to before."

The children exchanged glances. Even at their young ages, they recognized the words of trauma, of a mind trying to process the unprocessable.

"Before what?" Katya asked, her voice softening slightly.

But Dmitri had lost interest in conversation. He grabbed Filibert's shoulder again, this time harder, pushing him fully onto his back. "Crazy Nazi. Drawing crazy clocks. My uncle said Germans killed my whole family. Said they put them in trains and sent them to camps and nobody came back."

He kicked at another chalk drawing. Then another. His friends joined in, systematically destroying the artwork that had taken Filibert all morning to create.

Filibert watched from the ground, his mind already calculating. Thirty-seven clocks destroyed. Approximately two hours and twenty-eight minutes of work erased. The yellow chalk was now broken into three pieces, scattered across the playground.

His finger continued its circular motion, pointing toward the church tower. If he could just make time go back far enough—back to before the kicking, before the taunts, before the boys approached—he could preserve his work. He could keep everything organized, everything in its proper place.

"Leave him alone."

The new voice cut through the destruction, calm but carrying an undercurrent of something that made the other boys pause. It was in Russian, but accented—not Dmitri's Moscow dialect, but something from further east.

Filibert tilted his head back, looking at the world upside down. A boy stood a few meters away, bigger than the others, maybe seven years old but built like he was older. His face carried a smile that seemed impossibly out of place in the refugee camp, like he'd somehow missed the memo that they were all supposed to be miserable.

"This doesn't concern you, traitor." Dmitri growled in Russian, puffing up his chest.

"Traitor?" The big boy's smile widened. "That's funny. We're in America now. Who am I betraying?"

"You're Russian. You should stay with your people, with us. But I always see you with others. I hear you speak English. You have no Russian pride! That makes you a traitor."

The big boy—Kort—switched to heavily accented English. "We Americans now. It good to practice the English. Yes? It good to make friends with everyone. We all Americans now."

Dmitri spat on the ground. "Traitor. After I beat the Nazi, I'll beat you for being a traitor."

He turned back toward Filibert, raising his foot to deliver another kick, when Kort moved. It wasn't a wild swing or a clumsy charge. It was a single, precise strike—a fist to Dmitri's nose, delivered with the kind of technique that spoke of training or natural talent or both.

Blood erupted from Dmitri's nostrils, shocking in its sudden brightness. The boy howled, clutching his face, stumbling backward into his friends.

Ms. McGhee came running now, her earlier distance abandoned in the face of actual violence. She was a plump woman in her early twenties, hair already graying from the stress of managing forty-three traumatized children.

"What happened here?" she demanded, her voice sharp with the authority of someone who had learned to control chaos through sheer force of will.

The boys all started talking at once, voices overlapping in a mixture of Russian, Polish, and broken English. Ms. McGhee held up a hand for silence, then knelt beside Dmitri, examining his bleeding nose.

"Who did this?"

The boys fell silent. Some unspoken code prevented them from directly identifying Kort, though their eyes kept sliding toward him.

Kort stepped forward, his smile never faltering. "Excuse for me, miss," he said in his careful English. "We play tag. He ran and fall down."

Ms. McGhee looked skeptical, but Dmitri was already nodding, seeing an out that would let him save face. "Yes. Playing tag. I fell."

"You fell and broke your nose?"

"Tripped. Hit face on... on ground."

Ms. McGhee clearly didn't believe it, but she also clearly didn't want to deal with the paperwork and government inquiries that would come from admitting there was violence in her facility. She sighed, standing up.

"Come inside. We'll fix you up." She pointed at the other boys. "The rest of you—clean play. No more roughhousing. Understood?"

A chorus of "Yes, Ms. McGhee" followed her as she led the bleeding Dmitri toward the building.

Kort waited until they were out of earshot, then turned to the remaining boys. He said something in rapid Russian that Filibert couldn't quite follow, but the tone was clear: a warning and a dismissal. The boys scattered.

Only Katya remained for a moment, looking between Kort and Filibert with an expression that might have been curiosity or might have been concern. Then she too walked away, leaving the two boys alone in the playground.

Kort approached Filibert, who was still lying on his back, staring up at the sky. He held out a hand.

"You can get up now. They're gone."

Filibert ignored the hand, sitting up on his own and immediately beginning to assess the damage to his chalk drawings. Most were destroyed. The yellow chalk was broken. He would need to request new chalk from Ms. McGhee, which meant filling out a requisition form, which meant interacting with the supply clerk, which meant unpredictable variables.

Kort picked up the three pieces of broken chalk and held them out. "You can still draw with these. Just have to hold them different."

Filibert took the pieces, examining them. The largest was approximately 4.7 centimeters long. Still usable, though the grip would be awkward. The other two pieces were too small for effective use.

"Thank you," he said formally, the English words carefully pronounced. His mother had taught him English. She'd said it would be important for when the Americans came to save them. But the Russians had come first and—

Mind blanked.

Then restarted. Once clandestine organizations had gotten him and other children of Berlin smuggled out to American safe havens, before Berlin was locked down by the Russians, his knowledge of English was a blessing. She'd been right about many things.

Kort regarded with interest the boy's brief lapse of awareness. "You speak English good," Kort observed, squatting down beside Filibert. "And Russian too, yes?"

"Yes. And German. And French."

Kort let out a low whistle. "Smart. Smart people in America are rich, you know. Get big houses. Drive cars. Have lots of food."

"I don't care about money."

"No?" Kort looked at the chalk drawings scattered around them. "What do you care about?"

Filibert considered the question seriously. "Time. Making it right. Going back to before."

"Before what?"

But Filibert had already returned his attention to the drawings, beginning the process of reconstruction. He started with a fresh patch of asphalt, drawing a new circle. Perfect. Smooth. No irregularities.

Kort watched for a moment, then picked up a piece of white chalk that had been lying nearby. "Can I help?"

Filibert paused, his hand hovering over the asphalt. Collaboration introduced variables. Other people made mistakes. They drew lines that weren't straight, circles that weren't round, numbers that weren't properly spaced.

But Kort had helped him. Had defended him. And there was something in the bigger boy's face—an openness, a lack of judgment—that Filibert had rarely encountered.

"You must draw exactly," Filibert said. "The circle must be perfect. The numbers must be evenly spaced. The hands must point to exactly half past one."

"Why half past one?"

"Because that's when time stopped. When everything was still good. Before the bad things."

Kort nodded as if this made perfect sense. "Okay. I will draw exactly."

He began sketching a circle on the asphalt. It was rough at first, not quite round, and Filibert felt his anxiety rising. But Kort paused, studied Filibert's example, and tried again. This time the circle was better. Not perfect, but acceptable.

They worked in silence for several minutes, Filibert drawing his precise clocks while Kort did his best to match the style. The church bells chimed—a quarter to two now—but Filibert didn't acknowledge them. In his mind, in his drawings, it would always be half past one.

"What's your name?" Kort asked eventually.

"Filibert Austerlitz."

"I'm Kort Sokolov." He finished drawing the clock hands and sat back to examine his work. "In Russia, before war, I lived in small village. Very small. Everyone knew everyone. My father was... I think in English you say 'blacksmith'? He made things from metal."

Filibert added numbers to his latest clock. "Where is he now?"

"Dead. Germans—Nazis—came through our village. I was hiding in forest. When I came back..." Kort trailed off, his perpetual smile dimming slightly. "Everyone dead. Germans burned everything."

"I'm German," Filibert said flatly.

"Yes. But you not Nazi. You didn't burn my village. You were just a baby."

"I was not baby," he protested. "I'm seven and I remember Nazis."

"Da? Me too. I'm seven like you. Still too young to burn villages." Kort winked, his smile returned, though it carried a melancholy edge now. "Besides, Russians came through Germany too. Did bad things also. War makes everyone do bad things. Makes everyone сумасшедший."

"Crazy," Filibert translated.

"Yes," Kort nodded, his smile visited a sneer for a moment, "much crazy."

Filibert's finger traced its invisible circle again. "I'm not crazy."

"I didn't say you were." Kort studied the chalk drawings around them. "But drawing same clock over and over... that's a little bit crazy. Yes?"

"It's necessary. To keep time correct. To make sure it doesn't move forward to when the bad things happen."

"But time already moved forward. Bad things already happened. We're here now, in America, in this place. Can't go back."

Filibert's hand stopped mid-circle. He looked directly at Kort for the first time, really looked, making eye contact despite the discomfort it caused.

"Not yet," he said quietly. "But I will figure it out. I will learn how to make time go back. I will learn how to fix things."

Kort held his gaze for a moment, and something passed between them—an understanding, perhaps, or a recognition. Two boys who had lost everything, who had survived when they shouldn't have, who carried wounds that would never fully heal.

"Okay," Kort said finally. "You figure out how to fix time. And I will help you. Yes?"

"Yes."

"Good. But first, we should learn more English. Ms. McGhee says American families want children who speak English. If we speak English good, maybe someone adopts us. Takes us to house with food and beds and—"

"I don't want to be adopted."

"Why not?"

"Because then I would have to leave my clocks. And someone might make me stop drawing them. And if I stop drawing them, time might move wrong, might skip ahead to more bad things."

Kort considered this logic with the seriousness it deserved. "Okay. Then we make sure whoever adopts you lets you draw clocks. Deal?"

"Nobody will adopt me. I'm German. Everyone hates Germans."

"I don't hate you. And I'm Russian. Russians and Germans supposed to hate each other most of all." Kort stood, dusting off his pants. "Come. I show you something."

He started walking toward the far end of the playground, not looking back to see if Filibert would follow. After a moment's hesitation, Filibert gathered his chalk pieces and trailed after him.

Kort led him to a corner of the yard where a group of older boys were playing some kind of ball game. He watched them for a moment, then said something in Russian. One of the boys tossed him the ball.

"This is mathematics," Kort said, holding up the ball. "You understand mathematics, yes?"

"Yes."

Kort rocketed the ball back to one of the boys, his natural athleticism evident.

The boy caught it with an *OOF*.

"I understand physical. But mathematics is universal. Numbers same in all languages. Bodies are not. So we speak mathematics together. Watch."

He drew a simple equation in the dirt with a stick he'd picked up: $2 + 2 = ?$

"Four," Filibert said immediately.

"Yes! See? You are smart. Very smart." Kort drew another equation: $5 + 7 = ?$

"Twelve," Filibert answered dryly.

"Good, good. Now harder one." He drew: $8 \times 6 = ?$

Filbert rolled his eyes. "Forty-eight."

Kort laughed, delighted. "So fast! You don't even think about it. How you do that?"

"Numbers are easy for me. This is easy—for babies. Like throwing ball or running is easy for you. Numbers always work the same way. Not like people."

"Yes. People are complicated. But mathematics... mathematics is clean. Pure." Kort handed Filibert the stick he'd been using to write in the dirt. "You try. Make a hard one for me."

Filibert thought for a moment, then wrote: $12 \times 13 = ?$

Kort's face scrunched up in concentration. His lips moved as he worked through the calculation. "Um... one hundred... fifty..."

"One hundred fifty-six."

"You sure?"

"Yes."

"How you know so fast?"

Filibert shrugged. The answer had simply appeared in his mind, complete and whole, the way answers always did when numbers were involved. Explaining the process was harder than doing the calculation.

"Just... know."

Kort shook his head in amazement. "You are very smart, Filibert. Smartest person I ever meet. If you can learn mathematics so easy, you can learn anything. You can learn how to fix time."

"Maybe."

"Not maybe. Definitely." Kort put a hand on Filibert's shoulder, his grip firm and warm. "And I will help. We will be brothers. Not by blood, but by choice. Brothers help each other. Yes?"

Filibert considered this proposition. He had never had a brother. His mother had spoken of having another child before him, but that baby had been stillborn. He had been alone for so long that the concept of partnership seemed almost foreign.

But Kort was different from the other children. He didn't mock or avoid Filibert. He didn't seem bothered by the clock drawings or the circular gestures or the difficulty with eye contact. He simply accepted these things as part of who Filibert was.

"Yes," Filibert said finally. "Brothers."

Kort's smile could have lit the entire playground. "Good! Now, we practice more mathematics. And English. And maybe I teach you how to fight, so next time boys come to bother you, you can break their noses yourself."

"I don't want to hurt people."

"Not hurt. Just defend. Is different. You must be able to protect yourself. Protect your clocks." Kort's expression turned serious. "World is dangerous place, Filibert. Even here, in America, in place that is supposed to be safe. Bullies everywhere. People who want to hurt you because you are different. You must be strong."

"I'm not strong. I'm small."

"Small now. But you will grow. And strength is not just muscles. Is here." He tapped his head. "And here." He tapped his chest. "You have strong mind. Very strong. That's good kind of strength."

They returned to the chalk drawings, but now they worked as a team. Kort would start a clock, and Filibert would finish it, adding the precise details that Kort's rougher approach missed. Their drawing styles were different, but together they created something that neither could have made alone.

Ms. McGhee found them there an hour later, surrounded by dozens of clocks, all showing half past one.

"Filibert," she said gently, "it's almost dinner time. You need to come in and wash up."

"Not finished," Filibert said without looking up.

"You've been drawing clocks all day. How many do you need?"

"All of them. Every clock, everywhere. They all have to show the right time."

Ms. McGhee sighed, exchanging a glance with Kort. The bigger boy stood, dusting off his knees.

"Come, Filibert. We draw more tomorrow. I promise. But now we must eat. Cannot fix time on empty stomach."

Filibert wanted to protest, but the logic was sound. His stomach had been growling for the past thirty minutes, though he'd been ignoring it in favor of his work. He carefully arranged his chalk pieces in a neat line—largest to smallest, sorted by color—and stood.

"Tomorrow?" he asked Kort.

"Tomorrow. Every day. We are brothers now. Brothers stay together."

As they walked toward the building, Filibert looked back at their artwork. Dozens of clocks, all frozen at the same moment. In the fading afternoon light, they almost seemed to glow.

Half past one.

The moment before everything fell apart.

The moment he would spend the rest of his life trying to return to.

That night, after dinner and before lights out, Ms. McGhee called Filibert to her office. Kort followed behind them in the shadows at a close distance, moving with the stealth of a big cat. It was a small room, cluttered with paperwork and files representing forty-three young lives waiting to be sorted and cataloged and, hopefully, given new starts.

"Filibert," she began, her voice kind but firm, "I've been asked to evaluate your... condition. The doctors want to know if you're adjusting well to life here."

Filibert's hands found each other, fingers interlocking in a complex pattern that helped him think. "I am adjusting."

"You spend all your time drawing clocks. You don't play with the other children. You don't eat in the dining hall—you take your food outside so you can be near your drawings. That's not... typical behavior for a six-year-old."

"I am not typical."

"No, you're not. And that's okay. But the doctors are concerned. They think you might be suffering from—from what you saw in Berlin."

Filibert's fingers tightened. "I do not wish to discuss Berlin."

"I know, sweetheart. But we need to help you. We need to make sure you're healthy. Not just your body, but your mind too."

Kort, who had been standing quietly outside the door, stepped forward into the room and into the light, giving Ms. McGhee a start. "He is healthy, Ms. McGhee. He is very smart. Smartest person here. He just... thinks different. Is okay to think different."

Ms. McGhee smiled uneasily, her heartbeat calming from the sudden appearance of this confident boy. "It's sweet that you want to defend your friend, Kort. But this is a serious matter. The doctors think Filibert might need special help. Maybe a different facility, one designed for children with... with challenges."

"No." The word came from Filibert, sharp and final. "I will not go to a different facility."

"It wouldn't be forever. Just until you're feeling better."

"I will not feel better. What happened will always have happened. Time does not erase. It only moves forward. Unless someone learns to make it go backward."

Ms. McGhee rubbed her temples. "Filibert, time doesn't work that way."

"Not yet. But it will. I will learn how." He looked at her directly, his eyes carrying an intensity that was unsettling in someone so young. "I will learn how to fix time. I will learn how to make things go back to before the bad things. And then everyone can be safe. Everyone can go home."

"Oh, sweetheart..." Ms. McGhee's voice cracked slightly. "You can't go home. That home doesn't exist anymore. Not for any of the children here. You have to make a new home now."

"Then I will make a new home where time works."

Kort moved to stand beside Filibert, his hand on the smaller boy's shoulder. "We will do it together. I promised to help. Brothers help each other."

"Brothers?" Ms. McGhee looked between them. "You've only known each other for one day."

"One day can be enough," Kort said simply. "If it is right day. If it is day that matters."

Ms. McGhee studied them for a long moment—the Russian boy with his impossible optimism and the German boy with his impossible dreams. Two children who had survived things no child should survive, now clinging to each other like shipwreck victims sharing a piece of driftwood.

"All right," she said finally. "I'll tell the doctors you're making progress. That you've formed a social connection, which is good. But Filibert, you need to try to do other activities. Draw other things besides clocks. Play with other children. Can you do that for me?"

"If I must."

"You must. And Kort, you need to make sure he does. Can you do that?"

"Yes, Ms. McGhee. I will take care of my brother."

After they left the office, walking down the dimly lit hallway toward the dormitory, Kort leaned close and whispered, "Don't worry. You can still draw clocks. Just draw other things too sometimes. Draw... I don't know. Dogs. Houses. Anything. Then they won't send you away."

"I don't know how to draw dogs."

"I will teach you. I draw very good dogs. And cats. And horses. My father taught me, before..."

He didn't finish the sentence. He didn't need to.

They reached the dormitory—a long room with twenty bunk beds lined up in rows, each one shared by two boys. Kort had claimed a lower bunk near the window. Filibert slept three beds away, on an upper bunk above a Polish boy who cried in his sleep.

"Tomorrow," Kort said, "we draw clocks in morning. Then we draw dogs in afternoon. Then maybe we learn more mathematics. I want you to teach me big numbers. Numbers with many zeros."

"Why?"

"Because if I learn mathematics from you, and you learn fighting from me, then we will both be strong. Strong in different ways. And nobody can hurt us."

Filibert climbed into his bunk, pulling the thin blanket up to his chin. Through the window, he could just barely see the church tower, its damaged, inharmonious bells mercifully silent in the night.

"Kort?" he said quietly.

"Yes?"

"Thank you. For stopping those boys. For not letting them destroy all the clocks."

"Is nothing. Is what brothers do."

"We're not really brothers."

"Not by blood. But by choice. And choice is stronger than blood. Choice means you pick someone. Means you decide they are important. Blood—you don't get to choose blood. You just stuck with it."

Filibert considered this philosophy. It made a certain logical sense. Choice implied intention, decision, agency. Blood was merely biology, random genetic lottery.

"Then I choose you too," he said.

"Good. Now sleep. Tomorrow we fix time together."

But Filibert didn't sleep. He lay in his bunk, staring at the ceiling, his mind running through calculations and theories. Time was a dimension, like space. If you could move through space—forward, backward, left, right, up, down—then theoretically you should be able to move through time as well.

The question was how.

Energy, perhaps. Time and space were related to energy, weren't they? Einstein had proven that. $E=MC^2$. And what about Planck's quantum equation of $E = hv = hc/\lambda$ that energy exists in discrete packets rather than a continuous flow?

Filbert paused his musings at the thought of his countrymen—German physicists dominated the field and he felt pride in sharing that heritage. He was grateful for the weekly outing to the public library—yet another reason he didn't want to get adopted out. While the orphanage staff and librarian shushed the disinterested children, others worked on learning English by sounding out words about a hapless boy and his dimwitted sister chasing a dog called Spot. But Filibert devoured the books in the mathematics and science sections where the other children wouldn't venture. Today the giants of science were his mentors, but he visualized, clearly, the day he would surpass them.

He smiled at the thought and then returned to the matter at hand—If you had enough energy, enough power, could you bend time? Push it backward?

And if you could push time backward, you could return to moments before tragedy struck. You could save people. Prevent disasters. Make the world safe.

You could stop the Russian soldiers before they burst through the door.

You could stop the bombs before they fell on cities.

You could stop the trains before they carried people away to camps they would never return from.

All you needed was enough power. Enough understanding. Enough control.

Filibert's finger traced its invisible circle in the air, pointing toward the distant church tower.

Half past one.

Always half past one.

From the bunk near the window, Kort's gentle snoring filled the dormitory. The Polish boy below Filibert whimpered in his sleep, crying out for his mother in a language Filibert didn't fully understand.

But he understood the pain. The longing for a past that couldn't be recovered.

Not yet, anyway.

But someday.

Someday, with enough knowledge and enough time and enough determination, he would find a way.

He would make time obey.

And everyone—everyone—would be able to go back to before the bad things happened.

The church bells remained silent, but in Filibert's mind, they chimed endlessly.

Half past one.

Always half past one.

Forever.

Three

Expelled

Columbia University, Department of Biological Sciences, New York – 1961

The hallway smelled of formaldehyde and broken promises.

Dr. Lawrence Henderson walked with the measured pace of a man who had rehearsed this confrontation multiple times in his mind, trying out different approaches, different tones, different combinations of words that might penetrate the peculiar armor of Dr. Filibert Austerlitz's psyche. His leather portfolio—Italian, expensive, a gift from his wife on their twentieth anniversary—felt heavier than usual, weighted with the documentation of academic heresy.

The biological research wing of Columbia's Schermerhorn Hall had been built in 1897, and its corridors still carried the Victorian grandeur of that era: high ceilings, ornate molding, tall windows that let in the weak March sunlight. But the grandeur was undercut by the smell—that perpetual laboratory smell of preservation and death, of specimens suspended in chemical baths, of the violent intimacy between science and mortality.

Henderson paused outside Laboratory 7, gathering himself. Through the frosted glass window in the door, he could see movement—the silhouette of a man among what appeared to be dozens of vertical shapes. He checked his watch: 2:17 PM. He'd deliberately scheduled this for an odd time, hoping to catch Austerlitz off-guard, though Henderson suspected the man was never truly off-guard. He lived in a state of perpetual vigilance, always calculating, always three steps ahead.

Or three steps into madness. Henderson was no longer certain there was a difference.

He knocked—two sharp raps that sounded too loud in the empty corridor. Most of the faculty were in classes or meetings. Henderson had made sure of that. This needed to be private.

"Enter." The voice from inside was accented—German, though softened by nearly two decades in America. Precise. Emotionless.

Henderson opened the door and stepped into what could only be described as a museum of nightmares.

The laboratory was large—thirty feet by forty—with the high ceilings characteristic of the old building. But every vertical surface had been colonized by Austerlitz's collection. Glass specimen jars lined shelves that ran floor to ceiling on three walls, each one containing something preserved in amber-colored formaldehyde. Marine life, primarily, but marine life that seemed wrong somehow. A lamprey eel with jaws too large for its body. An octopus whose arms appeared to have been modified, segmented in ways that natural evolution would never produce. Something that might have been a sea cucumber but had developed what looked like primitive eyes.

In the center of the room stood Filibert Austerlitz himself, a man of twenty-two, a genius who had puzzled the faculty as he rocketed into his PhD years ahead of his peers. And now, conducting his own lab research. His face was unlined, almost boyish, but his eyes carried a weight that spoke of sleepless nights and obsessions pursued past the point of reason. He wore a white lab coat that had seen better days—stained with chemicals, the left sleeve slightly scorched from some past experiment. His dark hair was meticulously combed, every strand in place, controlled.

He stood before a large aquarium tank, his hand pressed against the glass, watching something inside with the intensity of a parent observing a sleeping child.

"Dr. Henderson," Austerlitz said without turning. "You are seventeen minutes later than I calculated you would be. Traffic on Broadway, or did you stop for coffee?"

Henderson blinked. "How did you—"

"Know you were coming? Please. The department secretary has been avoiding eye contact with me for three days. Dr. Morrison changed his usual coffee break time to avoid encountering me in the lounge. And you have been carrying that portfolio with you constantly, clutching it like a talisman." Austerlitz finally turned, his pale blue eyes fixing on Henderson with uncomfortable precision. "The only question was when you would work up the courage."

"This isn't about courage, Filibert."

"No? Then what is it about?" Austerlitz moved away from the tank, walking to one of the specimen-lined walls. His fingers traced the glass of a jar containing what appeared to be modified muscle tissue. "Control? Propriety? Fear?"

"Ethics." Henderson set his portfolio on a nearby lab bench, careful to avoid the clutter of equipment—microscopes, dissection tools, something that looked disturbingly like a primitive centrifuge. "Your research crosses boundaries that are non-negotiable."

"Boundaries." Austerlitz's lips curved into something that wasn't quite a smile. "Interesting word. Implies artificial limitations. Lines drawn in sand by people who are afraid of what lies beyond them."

"Those lines exist for good reason."

"Do they?" Austerlitz pulled a specimen jar from the shelf—a lamprey eel, its mouth frozen mid-gape, displaying rings of razor-sharp teeth. "This creature has existed, largely unchanged, for 360 million years. Do you know why?"

"This isn't the time for—"

"Because it adapted perfectly to its environment. But adaptation requires change. Requires crossing boundaries. If life respected boundaries, we would all still be single-celled organisms floating in primordial soup."

Henderson opened his portfolio, pulling out the first document. "Unauthorized human tissue samples. You've been collecting them from the university hospital. Blood, skin, even bone marrow from patients who never consented to their use in research."

"The samples would have been discarded. Medical waste. I simply gave them purpose."

"That's not how consent works, and you know it."

Austerlitz set the lamprey jar down on a cluttered workbench. Around him, the laboratory was a study in organized chaos—everywhere Henderson looked, there were experiments in progress. Petri dishes growing cultures that looked like they shouldn't exist. Diagrams pinned to walls showing cellular structures that seemed to blend organic and inorganic materials. A small aquarium containing what appeared to be genetically modified crabs, their shells displaying unusual geometric patterns.

"I know exactly how consent works," Austerlitz said quietly. "I know that no one consented to being born into a world where their body can fail them. Where disease and injury can destroy everything they are. Where human potential is limited by the arbitrary constraints of biology that evolved for a world that no longer exists."

"You're not God, Filibert."

"No. God makes mistakes. I don't." Austerlitz walked to a filing cabinet, pulled open a drawer, and retrieved a thick folder. He dropped it on the bench next to Henderson's portfolio. "Three hundred seventy-two experiments. Documented. Methodical. Each one building on the last. Do you know what I've accomplished?"

Henderson didn't open the folder. "I know what the ethics board knows. Human tissue grafting. Attempts to bond artificial materials with living cells. Proposals for biological modification that read like something from a science fiction novel."

"Science fiction." Austerlitz's voice carried an edge now, the first crack in his controlled demeanor. "Do you know what science fiction was fifty years ago? Satellites. Penicillin. Nuclear power." He snickered to himself and added, "*Die Fertiggerichte*."

Henderson scowled, unsettled by the snicker and the foreign word—and at the heated feeling he was the brunt of a joke.

"The TV-dinners. The line between fiction and fact is just a matter of resources and will."

He opened the folder himself, pulling out a series of photographs. Henderson couldn't help but look—the images showed what appeared to be human skin cells under extreme magnification, but interwoven with the cellular structure were threads of something else. Something fibrous and artificial.

"This is a synthetic polymer bonded at the cellular level with human dermal tissue," Austerlitz explained, his voice taking on the tone of a teacher with a slow student. "It provides structural support without rejection. The immune system doesn't recognize it as foreign because it's integrated so completely that the body reads it as self."

"And the applications?"

"Soldiers who can't be killed by shrapnel. Firefighters who can walk through flames. Construction workers who can survive falls that would shatter normal bones. Eventually—everyone. Humanity upgraded. Humanity perfected."

Henderson pulled out another document. "Your proposal to the Department of Defense—unauthorized proposal. Sent without review or permission from the University, utilizing research done at Columbia. Creating what you call 'enhanced soldiers' with adaptive biological armor, regenerative capabilities, and—" he had to check the document to make sure he was reading it correctly, "—'controlled aggression protocols.' Heaven knows who else you've sent proposals to that we don't yet know about."

Filibert provided no reaction to the accusation. Henderson was fishing for information and Filibert knew it. Instead, he steered the conversation back to his agenda. "The military understands necessity. They understand that war is coming—not the small wars we've been fighting, but something larger. And when it comes, we will need more than brave men with rifles. We will need soldiers who can survive anything. Who can adapt to any environment. Who can complete their missions regardless of the obstacles."

"You want to turn people into weapons."

"I want to give people the tools to survive." Austerlitz pulled out another photograph—this one showing a cross-section of what appeared to be modified muscle tissue. "Look at this. Cellular density increased by forty percent. Response time improved by sixty percent. And the subject reported no pain, no rejection, no complications."

"What subject?" Henderson asked, though he already suspected the answer.

Austerlitz rolled up his left sleeve, revealing his forearm. The skin looked normal at first glance, but as Henderson watched, Austerlitz pressed a scalpel against his own flesh. The blade should have cut easily, but instead it skidded across the surface, leaving only a faint white line.

"Jesus Christ," Henderson whispered. "You've been experimenting on yourself."

"How else would I know it works?" Austerlitz rolled the sleeve back down. "I've been refining the process for three years. The integration is nearly perfect now. No scarring. No immune response. The modified tissue behaves exactly like normal tissue in every way except durability."

"That's—that's insane. You could have killed yourself. Infection, rejection, systemic failure—"

"Calculated risks. I ran thousands of simulations. The probability of complications was less than seven percent."

"Seven percent!"

"Acceptable margins." Austerlitz returned to the large aquarium tank, pressing his hand against the glass again. Inside, a large octopus stirred, its limbs unfurling. "Do you know what this creature can do? It can change the color and texture of its skin in milliseconds. It can squeeze through openings a fraction of its body size. It can regenerate lost limbs. It has distributed intelligence—if you cut off an arm, that arm continues to hunt and feed independently."

"What's your point?"

"My point is that nature has already solved the problems we're trying to address. Adaptation. Regeneration. Survival. We just need to learn the language. And once we do, we can rewrite the human form using nature's own alphabet."

The door to the laboratory opened without warning. Henderson spun, startled, but Austerlitz didn't react—he'd clearly been expecting this.

Kort Sokolov entered the room with the confidence of someone who belonged there. He was twenty-two, same age as Filibert, but where the scientist was pale and slight, Kort was built like what he was—a soldier. Six feet tall, broad-shouldered, moving with an economy of motion that spoke of combat training. His face was weathered, scarred along the left cheekbone from some old injury. He wore civilian clothes—work pants, a plain shirt—but he carried himself with military bearing.

"Is there problem?" Kort asked, his Russian accent still thick after all these years in America. His eyes moved between Henderson and Austerlitz, assessing the situation with professional detachment.

"No problem," Austerlitz said calmly. "Dr. Henderson explained that my research needs to be terminated."

Kort moved to stand beside Austerlitz—not threatening, but clearly present. A statement.

Henderson felt his authority slipping. He drew himself up, trying to reclaim control of the situation. "Mr. Sokolov, this is a private academic matter. I need to ask you to—"

"Kort is my research partner," Austerlitz interrupted. "Anything you need to say to me, you can say in front of him."

"Research partner? He's not even a student here. He's—" Henderson checked his memory, "— he works as a trainer at that, that weird Jap place in Queens."

"Isshin-Ryu karate," Kort dead eyed Henderson. A smile quickly replaced the warning and he said simply, "I also test doctor's theories. He makes something, I try it. I tell him if it works."

Henderson's stomach dropped. "You're both conducting unauthorized human experiments. On each other. Do you understand the legal implications? The ethical violations? This isn't just grounds for dismissal—this is criminal."

"Criminal." Austerlitz's voice was flat. "Like the experiments conducted in camps during the war? Like the radiation tests performed on unwitting patients? Should I count the number of syphilis and cancer studies in this country alone using non-consenting subjects—killing non-consenting subjects?" He shook his head. "Don't lecture me about ethics, Dr. Henderson. I know exactly where the ethical boundaries lie. I also know that every major breakthrough in medical science has required someone to cross them."

"That's sophistry."

"That's history." Austerlitz moved to his desk, pulling out a different folder—this one newer, the papers crisp. "I've been offered a position. NATO Research and Development. Project 19.5 has been approved for funding. Fifty million dollars over five years. They want me to create a prototype—a team of enhanced soldiers who can operate in conditions that would kill normal humans."

"NATO?" Henderson felt the ground shifting beneath him. "You've been negotiating with foreign governments?"

"International military alliance," Austerlitz corrected. "And yes. Because unlike Columbia University, they understand the value of pushing boundaries. They understand that the next war won't be won by who has the most soldiers, but by who has the best soldiers."

Kort moved to one of the specimen jars, studying a modified lamprey with clinical interest. "Doctor is right," he said quietly. "I fought in Southeast Asia–places the government won't tell you about. I saw men die because their bodies failed them. Because flesh is weak. Because human limits are too small." He looked at Henderson. "If doctor can make soldiers stronger, make them survive when they should die, then he should do this. Is not criminal. Is mercy."

"Mercy." Henderson tasted the word, found it bitter. "You want to turn men into monsters and call it mercy?"

"Monsters?" Austerlitz laughed—a short, sharp sound without humor. "Humans are already monsters, Dr. Henderson. We kill each other with remarkable efficiency using entirely natural abilities. All I'm proposing is to give the good men—the ones trying to protect others—the tools they need to survive the encounter."

Henderson picked up his portfolio, his decision made. There was no reasoning with this. No middle ground. "The university cannot continue to employ you, Dr. Austerlitz. Your tenure is revoked effective immediately. NATO be damned! You have one week to clear out your laboratory and return any university property in your possession."

"I see." Austerlitz showed no emotion, though Kort's expression darkened. "And my research?"

"Belongs to the university. All documentation, all samples, all equipment. You'll sign an agreement acknowledging that any work produced during your employment here is university property."

"No."

The word was quiet but absolute.

"This isn't negotiable, Filibert."

"You're right. It isn't." Austerlitz walked to his desk and pulled out a small device—a tape recorder. He pressed play.

Henderson's own voice filled the laboratory: "—I'll give you six months to clean up these experiments. Make them presentable. Get proper consent forms backdated. I can bury the ethics complaints if you make this right—"

Henderson's face drained of color. "When did you—"

"Three weeks ago. When you first approached me about concerns from the ethics board. You offered to help me cover it up in exchange for being listed as co-author on my publications." Austerlitz stopped the recording. "I have seven more conversations documented. Including one where you discuss selling my research to pharmaceutical companies without my knowledge."

"That's—you can't—"

"Can't what? Protect my own work? Document academic corruption?" Austerlitz's voice remained calm, but his eyes were cold. "Here's what's going to happen, Dr. Henderson. You're going to revise your recommendation. You're going to state that I'm resigning voluntarily to pursue opportunities in the private sector. You're going to provide a glowing reference letter. And you're going to forget you ever saw any of my research."

"And if I don't?"

"Then these recordings go to the dean. To the board of trustees. To the New York Times." Austerlitz tilted his head slightly. "How long do you think your tenure would survive that scrutiny?"

Henderson stood frozen, caught in a trap he hadn't seen coming. Around him, the specimen jars seemed to watch with their preserved eyes, witnessing his humiliation.

"You're insane," he said finally.

"No. I'm careful. There's a difference." Austerlitz pulled out a prepared document—of course he'd prepared it in advance—and set it on the desk. "Sign this. It states that I'm leaving voluntarily, with no findings of misconduct, and that all my research is my personal property, not subject to university claims."

"I can't—the board will never—"

"The board will accept whatever you tell them to accept. You're the department head. Your word carries weight." Austerlitz's smile was thin and humorless. "Unless, of course, they find out you've been embezzling grant money. That's on the tapes too."

Kort had moved to stand between Henderson and the door. Not threatening, but present. A reminder that this conversation would end only one way.

Henderson's hands shook as he picked up the pen. "You'll never get away with this. Someone will stop you. Someone will see what you're becoming and—"

"Becoming?" Austerlitz laughed again. "Dr. Henderson, I've been this way since I was six years old. I've just gotten better at hiding it." He watched as Henderson signed the document, witnessed the precise moment when a man's career was traded for his silence. "The world only understands power. I learned that in Berlin when I watched my mother die. I learned that in the orphanage when bigger boys tried to destroy my work. I learned that in every laboratory, every classroom, every interaction where someone tried to tell me that my vision was impossible."

He took the signed document, checked it carefully, then filed it away in a drawer that he locked with a key on a chain around his neck.

"The world is about to change, Dr. Henderson. And when it does, people like you—people who are afraid of what comes next—will be left behind. But people like me? We'll be the ones writing the future."

Henderson stumbled toward the door, his portfolio forgotten on the lab bench. Kort stepped aside to let him pass, but as Henderson reached for the doorknob, the Russian spoke:

"Doctor Henderson?"

Henderson paused, not turning.

"If you try to stop Filibert, if you talk to anyone about this—" Kort's voice was gentle, almost kind, "—then I will visit you. And you will not like what I have become."

Henderson fled.

The door closed behind him with a soft click, leaving Austerlitz and Kort alone in the laboratory full of preserved nightmares.

For a long moment, neither man spoke. Then Kort moved to the aquarium, watching the octopus pulse and shift in the water.

"Was necessary?" he asked.

"Yes. Henderson was going to force my hand anyway. This way, I control the narrative."

"But NATO position is real?"

"Very real. They've been courting me for eight months. This just accelerates the timeline." Austerlitz joined Kort by the aquarium, both men watching the cephalopod. "You know what's beautiful about this creature? It has no bones. No rigid structure. It can reshape itself to fit through any gap, survive in any environment. That's the future, Kort. Not strength through rigidity, but strength through adaptation."

"And humans? We are rigid. We have bones."

"For now." Austerlitz's reflection in the glass looked strange, distorted by the water. "But we don't have to stay that way. Life evolved from the sea, Kort. Everything we are—every adaptation, every survival mechanism—it all started in the ocean. And if we look carefully enough, if we understand the principles at work, we can reverse-engineer humanity itself."

"Using me as test subject."

"Using us both as test subjects." Austerlitz rolled up his sleeve again, showing the modified skin. "Soon, we will have other volunteers. This NATO contract, it is everything. Real funding, real support. I hope to find volunteers like you, Kort. Your body accepts modifications that would kill most people. Something in your genetic structure is perfectly suited for enhancement. Whatever fate or blind luck brought us together—you're the key to making this work on a broader scale. It would have taken a lifetime to find the genetic makeup for tolerating these adaptations. But with you, I have that makeup and will find others that match."

Kort's jaw tightened. "Sometimes I think about that day. In orphanage. When I stopped those boys from destroying your clocks. If I had walked away, if I had minded own business—"

"Then we wouldn't be here. Then you'd be another for-gotten soldier of a forgotten war, wandering the Ameri-can wasteland, empty and haunted by your lost comrades." Austerlitz turned to face his friend—his brother, by choice if not by blood. "You said it yourself. We are brothers. Brothers help each other. And I'm going to help you become some-thing the world has never seen."

"Or monster. Henderson's word."

"Henderson is afraid of change. Afraid of potential. Afraid of a future he can't control." Austerlitz walked to his desk, pulling out the NATO contract. "But we don't have to be afraid. We can shape that future. We can make sure that never again will good people die because their flesh is too weak to protect them."

Kort grinned wide, his eyes soft with fond memories.

Filibert noticed and asked, "What amuses you?"

"I was just remembering, back at the orphanage, when I first see how you repeat things."

"Things?" Filibert frowned.

"Like little actions, phrases, concepts," Kort explained. "I always admire it really."

"So you've said before, now you repeat!" Filibert said with as much of an eye roll that his stoic face could muster.

"Do you remember what I've taught you?"

"Yes," Kort said. "Never forget the important things and obsess the details and give it voice."

Filibert finished the sentence, "It is voice in the world that has power. Remember the Hebrew creation myth?"

Now Kort finished the sentence of a conversation the two men had had thousands of times and would have a million more times over in the future. "And God said, Let there be light: and there was light. God spoke, gave voice, and order came to the formless void."

Filibert and Kort nodded a period to the discussion.

Filibert spread the contract on the desk, and Kort moved to read it. The numbers were staggering. The scope of the project breathtaking. They would have access to facilities, equipment, test subjects—everything they needed to turn theory into reality.

"Algeria," Kort read. "French Foreign Legion. Why there?"

"Because the Legion takes men without countries. Men with no families, no ties, no one who will ask questions if they volunteer for experimental programs. And because Algeria is far from oversight. Far from ethics boards and university administrators and people like Henderson." Austerlitz's finger traced the contract's outline. "We'll have freedom there. Real freedom. To push boundaries. To cross lines. To discover what humans can truly become."

"And if it goes wrong?"

"Then we learn from the failure and try again. That's how science works. That's how evolution works. Through trial and error, through adaptation and refinement, through the willingness to risk everything for the possibility of something greater."

Kort studied the contract for a long time. Around them, the laboratory hummed with the quiet sounds of preservation—the gentle bubbling of aquarium filters, the tick of clocks on the walls (seven of them, all set to half past one), the drip of formaldehyde in specimen jars.

"You promise me something," Kort said finally.

"Anything."

"Promise me this is about saving lives. About making soldiers stronger so fewer die. Not about—" he searched for words in his imperfect English, "—not about making weapons for the sake of weapons. Not about power for power's sake."

Austerlitz met his eyes. "I promise. This is about protection. About giving good men the tools to survive evil men. About creating soldiers who can end conflicts quickly, decisively, with minimal casualties. That's all it's ever been about."

It was a lie, though Austerlitz would convince himself for many years that he believed it.

Kort nodded slowly. "Okay. Then I am with you. Like always. Brothers."

"Brothers," Austerlitz agreed.

They shook hands—a formal gesture that carried the weight of commitment. And in that moment, in that laboratory full of modified life and scientific ambition, the future was set in motion.

Neither man could have known then what that future would cost. Neither could have predicted how the promise made in earnest would twist into something dark and terrible. Neither understood that the road to hell is paved not with evil intentions, but with good intentions pushed past the point of reason.

All they knew was that they were together. That they had a purpose. That they were going to change the world.

And they would.

Just not in the way they imagined.

Three Hours Later

As the sun set over Manhattan, Austerlitz stood alone in his laboratory. Kort had gone to arrange their departure—giving notice at the dojo, settling affairs, preparing for the move overseas.

Austerlitz packed slowly, methodically, wrapping each specimen jar in newspaper before placing it in wooden crates. His entire life's work, carefully preserved. He would take it all to Algeria. Every sample. Every note. Every piece of evidence of what he'd accomplished and what he intended to accomplish.

As he worked, he passed by a small mirror hanging near the door—something the previous occupant had left behind. He paused, studying his reflection.

He looked the same as he always had. Pale. Controlled. Unremarkable, really, except for the intensity of his gaze.

But inside, he knew he was different. Had been different since that day in Berlin when the clocks stopped and the world ended and he learned that time itself could be controlled if you were strong enough, smart enough, ruthless enough.

His finger traced a small circle in the air, an old habit he'd never quite broken.

Half past one.

The moment before everything fell apart.

The moment he would spend his entire life trying to recreate, to control, to hold frozen in place so that nothing bad could ever happen again.

And if that required crossing boundaries? Breaking rules? Turning men into weapons?

So be it.

The world had taught him that only power mattered. Only control mattered. Only the willingness to do what others wouldn't mattered.

He would save humanity by remaking it.

Even if humanity didn't want to be saved.

Austerlitz returned to his packing, and the clocks on the wall—all seven of them—continued their eternal countdown.

Half past one.

Always half past one.

Forever.

Four

Recruitment

French Foreign Legion Recruitment Center, Sidi Bel Abbès, Algeria – 1962

The heat was a physical presence, a weight that pressed down on everything with the persistence of a bully who knew you couldn't fight back. It shimmered off the packed dirt of the parade ground, distorting the distant mountains into wavering mirages. The air smelled of dust, sweat, and diesel fuel from the trucks that rumbled past with metronomic regularity.

Kort Sokolov stood in a line of men who had come to the end of the world seeking a new beginning.

The recruitment center at Sidi Bel Abbès was not designed for comfort. It was a collection of low, whitewashed buildings arranged around a central square, their walls thick enough to provide some relief from the Algerian sun but never quite enough. Faded posters decorated the exterior walls—heroic legionnaires in kepis blancs, the iconic white caps, standing vigilant over desert landscapes or marching through jungle terrain. "Legio Patria Nostra," the motto proclaimed. The Legion is Our Fatherland.

For men without countries, it was the only fatherland they would ever have.

Kort counted thirty-seven men in various stages of the recruitment process. He'd counted them automatically, the same way he counted exits in any room, steps between cover points, seconds between heartbeats. Some habits from the jungles of Laos never left you. Twenty-one appeared to be European—German, French, Italian, Polish accents mixing in the desultory conversations. Eight looked Middle Eastern. Five were African. Two appeared Asian. One defied easy categorization, his features suggesting a ancestry that had mixed and traveled until origins became irrelevant.

All of them looked hungry in a way that had nothing to do with food.

The Legion specialized in hungry men. Men running from something. Men searching for something. Men who had exhausted every other option and found themselves here, at the edge of civilization, willing to trade five years of their life for a new identity and a rifle.

"Sokolov!" A sergeant bellowed the name like a curse. "Kort Sokolov!"

Kort stepped forward, separating himself from the line. The sergeant was a weathered man in his fifties, his face carved into permanent lines of disapproval by decades of dealing with the dregs of humanity. His uniform was immaculate despite the heat—pants bloused into paratrooper boots, shirt pressed with knife-edge creases, medals from conflicts nobody remembered anymore glinted on his chest.

"Follow me," the sergeant said in French, not waiting to see if Kort complied.

They walked across the parade ground, past groups of recruits being drilled by screaming corporals, past the obstacle course where men crawled through sand under barbed wire, past the armory where the scent of gun oil mixed with the omnipresent dust. The sergeant said nothing, and Kort asked nothing, content to observe and catalog.

The administration building was marginally cooler, its thick walls and high ceilings providing some relief. The sergeant led him down a corridor lined with photographs—generations of legionnaires staring out from black and white, then color, then back to black and white as the wars changed but the faces remained essentially the same. Young men with old eyes. Old men with young eyes. All of them wearing the same expression of having seen things they could never unsee.

They stopped at a door marked "Commandant Maurice Leroux, Chef de Poste." The sergeant knocked twice, waited for a gruff acknowledgment, then opened the door and gestured Kort inside.

The office was spartan but organized. A large desk dominated the center, its surface holding neat stacks of files, a French flag in a wooden stand, and an ashtray carved from what appeared to be an artillery shell casing. The walls displayed maps—Algeria, France, Indochina—and more photographs of legionnaires in various states of victory or defeat. A ceiling fan rotated lazily overhead, pushing hot air around without cooling anything.

Behind the desk sat Commandant Maurice Leroux, a man who looked like he'd been carved from the same stone as the mountains visible through the window behind him. Sixty years old, maybe more, with silver hair cropped military-short and a face that suggested he'd forgotten how to smile sometime around 1944. His uniform was identical to the sergeant's but carried more weight, more medals, more evidence of a life spent in service to an institution that demanded everything and promised only survival.

"Sit," Leroux said in French, not looking up from the file he was reading.

Kort sat in the wooden chair facing the desk. It was deliberately uncomfortable, designed to keep visitors ill at ease. He settled into it like it was a throne, his posture perfect, his hands resting lightly on his thighs.

Leroux read for another two minutes—a power play, establishing dominance through controlled indifference. Kort waited with the patience of a man who had spent weeks in foxholes waiting for enemies who might never come.

Finally, Leroux looked up. His eyes were gray, cold, analytical.

"Kort Sokolov," he said, reading from the file. "Russian. Born 1940, according to these papers, though I suspect that's approximate."

Kort risked a wry smile and slight shrug.

Leroux continued, "No surviving family. Emigrated to United States in 1946. Served Special Forces Green Berets from 1955 to 1959." He looked up. "You were fifteen - sixteen when you enlisted."

"Papers said eighteen," Kort replied in French. His accent was thick, his grammar imperfect, but comprehensible.

"Papers lie. Men lie. Bureaucrats are happy to believe lies when it suits them." Leroux flipped a page. "With a tour in Southwest Asia 1959. Where exactly? United States was mostly providing advisory and training missions then."

Kort looked at Leroux soldier to soldier and respectfully answered, "Tell that to my dead comrades." And added, "Sir."

Leroux leaned back with a small nod, allowing the momentary lapse in military etiquette to pass. "Loas I'm guessing. Project Hotfoot ring a bell?"

Nothing on Kort's face or in his body language acknowl-edged the question. He was well trained to hold classified information.

"Honorable discharge," Leroux read on with a hint of re-spect for Kort's demeanor. "Combat citations. Purple Heart. Silver Star. Either you were very brave or very lucky."

"Lucky to be brave," Kort said. "Brave men who are not lucky are dead."

A corner of Leroux's mouth twitched—not quite a smile, but an acknowledgment. "You were wounded twice. Shrap-nel in the leg, bullet in the shoulder. Both times you refused medical evacuation and returned to your unit within days. The medical reports note 'unusually rapid healing.' Care to explain?"

Kort shrugged. "I heal fast. Always have. Doctor in or-phanage said some people are like this. Good genes."

"Good genes." Leroux made a notation in the file. "Af-ter discharge, you returned to New York. Employment as trainer at some sort of combat gym? No criminal record. No political affiliations. No religious extremism." He closed the file and leaned back in his chair, fingers steepled. "So why are you here, Monsieur Sokolov? Why does a decorated American veteran want to join the French Foreign Legion?"

This was the question Kort had been preparing for since Filibert first suggested the idea six months ago. The answer needed to be believable but not too detailed. Plausible but not rehearsed.

"In America, I am always Russian," Kort said simply. "Russian who fought for America, but still Russian. People look at me, hear my accent, remember Cold War, remember fear. I am useful when they need someone to hit things, to teach young men how to fight. But I am not... American. Not really."

"And you think you'll be French?" Leroux's tone carried skepticism.

"No. I will be legionnaire. Legion does not care where I come from. Only where I go. This is what I need."

It was a good answer—emotional enough to be believable, practical enough to seem honest. Men joined the Legion for a thousand reasons, but they all boiled down to the same thing: running from a past or toward a future or simply away from the present.

Leroux studied him for a long moment. "Your French is terrible."

"I learn quickly."

"You'll need to. The Legion is a French institution. Commands are given in French. Traditions are French. You will sing French songs, march to French cadence, and if you die here, you'll die for France."

"I understand."

"Do you?" Leroux stood, walking to the window. Outside, another group of recruits was being put through close-order drill, their movements ragged but improving. "The Legion is not a place for men who want easy lives, Monsieur Sokolov. We take the abandoned, the desperate, the criminal, the lost—and we forge them into something useful. The process breaks many. Kills some. But those who survive become something they never were before."

He turned back to face Kort. "We're also not stupid. A man with your record—combat veteran, decorated, skilled—doesn't usually end up in the Legion unless he's running from something. Wife? Debts? The law?"

"Truth," Kort said.

"Excuse me?"

"I am running from truth." Kort chose his words carefully, aware that this moment would determine everything that followed. "In the service, I knew who I was. I was soldier. I had purpose. mission. Brothers who depended on me. Then my service ended, and I did not know who I was anymore. Just man who was good at fighting, at hurting people. This is not enough."

He met Leroux's eyes directly. "Legion gives new identity. New purpose. This is what I need. Not to run from something but to run toward something."

It was close enough to truth to be convincing. And it left out everything that mattered—Filibert's plans, Project 19.5, the experiments already conducted, the modifications already made to Kort's body that made him heal faster, react quicker, endure longer.

Leroux returned to his desk, pulling out a different file—much thicker, marked with NATO stamps and security classifications that Kort recognized but pretended not to.

"I received an interesting communication two weeks ago," Leroux said, his tone shifting to something more guarded. "From NATO Research and Development. They're interested in running an experimental program using Legion volunteers. Something about enhanced combat effectiveness, new equipment testing, advanced training protocols."

He opened the file, revealing documents that Kort had helped Filibert prepare. Diagrams. Specifications. Promises of funding and resources that would benefit the Legion enormously.

"The program would be voluntary," Leroux continued. "Extra pay, better equipment, specialized training. But also experimental. Unproven. Potentially dangerous." He looked up. "Your name appears in this file, Monsieur Sokolov. Listed as a potential candidate. Care to explain how NATO knows about you before you've even enlisted?"

Kort had prepared for this question too. "My... friend. He works for NATO now. Scientist. He knows my military record, knows I am enlisting. He suggested I might be good for special program."

"This friend. He have a name?"

"Dr. Filibert Austerlitz."

Recognition flickered in Leroux's eyes—he'd clearly read the NATO proposal, seen Austerlitz's credentials. "The German scientist. The one who wants to play God with Legion volunteers."

"He wants to make soldiers safer. Stronger. Better able to survive."

"And you trust him?"

"With my life. He is my brother."

"The file says he's German, you're Russian."

"Not by blood. By choice. This is stronger bond."

Leroux lit a cigarette, the smoke curling up toward the lazy fan. "I'm going to be honest with you, Sokolov. This NATO program makes me uncomfortable. Scientists experimenting on soldiers—it reminds me of things best forgotten. But the funding is substantial. The equipment they're offering would modernize our entire facility. And the proposal claims minimal risk with significant benefit."

He exhaled smoke. "The question is whether I believe that. Whether I trust that your 'brother' has the Legion's best interests at heart, or whether we're being used as guinea pigs for some mad scientist's fantasy."

Kort leaned forward slightly. "Commandant, may I speak freely?"

"You may."

"I have seen what modern war does to men. I have carried friends whose legs were blown off by mines. I have watched men die from wounds that should not be fatal—they bled out because help came too slow, or wasn't coming at all, and because their bodies were too fragile. If Filibert's work can prevent this, if it can save lives, then it is worth risk."

"Noble sentiment. But you're not the one making the decision. I am. And I'm responsible for every man under my command."

"Then test it on me first. Before you let Filibert work with anyone else. I volunteer. If I survive, if I am improved, then you will know it is safe for others."

Leroux studied him through a haze of cigarette smoke. "You're very eager to be a test subject."

"I am eager to be useful. To have purpose. This gives me both."

The commandant smoked in silence for a moment, then crushed the cigarette in the artillery shell ashtray. "The Legion has a saying: 'Marche ou crève.' March or die. It means you keep moving forward or you fall behind and perish. Simple. Brutal. Honest."

He stood, extending his hand. "If you're willing to march into the unknown, Sokolov, then the Legion will have you. And if this NATO program proves viable, then perhaps you'll help us forge a new kind of legionnaire. One who doesn't die quite so easily."

Kort shook his hand, feeling the calluses of decades of service. "I will not disappoint, Commandant."

"See that you don't. Report to Sergeant Dubois for processing. You'll begin basic training tomorrow morning at 0500 hours. Do you have any questions?"

"Just one. This program—when does it begin?"

"Dr. Austerlitz arrives in three weeks. Training cadre is being selected now. If you survive basic training and prove suitable, you'll be among the first volunteers." Leroux's expression hardened. "But understand this: the Legion comes first. Always. If this program compromises Legion effectiveness or endangers Legion personnel, I will terminate it immediately. NATO funding or not. Clear?"

"Clear, Commandant."

"Dismissed."

Kort left the office, walking back through the corridor of photographs. He felt the eyes of dead legionnaires watching him, judging him, wondering if he would join their ranks or become something else entirely.

Outside, the heat hit him like a physical blow. He crossed the parade ground, following Sergeant Dubois's shouted directions toward the barracks where new recruits were processed.

A group of men sat in the shade, waiting their turn. They looked up as Kort approached—assessing, calculating, determining whether he was threat or victim or ally.

One of them, a scar-faced German with prison tattoos crawling up his neck, spat into the dust. "Another one," he muttered in German. "How many desperate fools do they need?"

His companion, younger, French or Belgian by his features, laughed. "Legion takes everyone. The damned, the desperate, the insane. Welcome to hell, comrade."

Kort didn't respond. He found a patch of shade and settled into it, his back against the barracks wall, and began the waiting that defined military life.

But inside, he felt something he hadn't felt since Laos ended: purpose. Direction. The sense that he was part of something larger than himself.

And underneath that, deeper, was the knowledge of what was coming. The experiments. The enhancements. The transformation from mere soldier into something that the world had never seen.

Filibert had promised him this. Had promised that together they would change what it meant to be human, to be a warrior, to survive in a world designed to kill you.

Kort intended to keep that promise.

Even if it killed him.

Which it very well might.

Three Weeks Later

Filibert Austerlitz arrived at Sidi Bel Abbès in a cloud of dust and barely controlled chaos.

The military transport truck that brought him from Algiers had broken down twice during the six-hour journey. His equipment—crates upon crates of it—had been delayed at the port. And the liaison officer assigned to escort him, a nervous lieutenant named Beaumont, had spent the entire trip explaining in increasing detail why this posting was beneath his rank and abilities.

Filibert had ignored him completely, instead focusing on the landscape rolling past the truck's windows. Algeria was beautiful in a harsh, unforgiving way. Dry mountains. Sparse vegetation clinging to life in defiance of logic. The occasional village that looked like it had been there for a thousand years and would be there for a thousand more, outlasting empires and ideologies through sheer stubborn endurance.

It reminded him, oddly, of Kort. That same quality of surviving through adaptation, through refusal to accept defeat.

When the truck finally rumbled through the gates of Sidi Bel Abbès, Filibert felt something shift in his chest. This was it. This was where theory would become reality. Where his years of research, his decades of preparation, would finally be put to the test.

Commandant Leroux was waiting in front of the administration building, his posture suggesting he'd rather be anywhere else. Beside him stood Kort, now in Legion fatigues, his head shaved, his bearing military-perfect.

Filibert stepped out of the truck, blinking in the afternoon sun. He wore civilian clothes—khaki pants, white shirt, already soaked with sweat—and carried a leather satchel that contained his most important documents. The rest could follow when the equipment arrived.

"Dr. Austerlitz," Leroux said, his tone formal. "Welcome to Sidi Bel Abbès."

"Commandant Leroux. Thank you for hosting me." Filibert's French was flawless, his accent the educated Parisian kind that came from years of study rather than native birth. "I trust the facilities are adequate?"

"They will suffice. We've converted a section of the medical building for your use. It's isolated from the main barracks, which should provide the privacy your work requires."

"Excellent." Filibert's eyes found Kort's, and something unspoken passed between them. "And the volunteers?"

"Being selected. Per our agreement, all volunteers must pass standard Legion training first. Only then will they be eligible for your program."

"Of course. I wouldn't want untrained men regardless. The enhancements require baseline fitness and discipline."

Leroux's jaw tightened at the word "enhancements," but he let it pass. "Your equipment is scheduled to arrive tomorrow. Until then, you're welcome to inspect the facilities and meet with the medical staff. They've been briefed on your presence but not on the specific nature of your work."

"Discretion is essential," Filibert agreed. "The less the general personnel know, the better."

"I couldn't agree more." Leroux gestured toward the building. "If you'll follow me, I'll show you to your quarters. They're modest but—"

"Commandant," Filibert interrupted gently. "Before we proceed, I'd like a few moments with Recruit Sokolov. To ensure he's adjusting well to Legion life."

Leroux glanced between them, clearly suspicious of their relationship but unable to articulate why. "Five minutes. Then Sokolov returns to his training. He's not receiving special treatment simply because you're acquainted."

"I would expect nothing less."

Leroux walked away, leaving them standing in the dusty yard. Filibert waited until the commandant was out of earshot, then allowed himself a small smile.

"You look terrible," he said in Russian.

"Thank you," Kort replied in the same language. "You look like you've been dragged behind that truck."

"Accurate assessment." Filibert pulled out a handkerchief and wiped his forehead. "How has training been?"

"Brutal. As expected. They're trying to break us down, rebuild us as legionnaires. Standard military conditioning."

"And?"

"And I let them think they're succeeding. But the modifications you made—they're holding. My endurance is beyond what the instructors expect. Recovery time is a fraction of the other recruits. I have to deliberately perform worse to avoid drawing too much attention."

"Good. That's exactly what we need." Filibert's eyes scanned the compound, noting the layout, the positions of buildings, the sight lines. Always calculating. Always planning. "The real work begins soon. Within a month, we'll have approval to start the enhancement program. I've already identified the next four candidates from the files Leroux provided and blood samples from the unit physician—an old friend."

"Jean, Hans, D'Arcy, and Razo," Kort said. "I've been watching them during training. Good men. Solid soldiers. They'll be perfect."

"Perfect is a strong word. They'll be suitable. There's a difference." Filibert's voice dropped even lower. "What we're about to do, Kort... it's never been done before. Not on this scale. Not with this level of integration. There will be risks. Failures. Possibly deaths."

"I understand."

"Do you? Because once we start, there's no going back. These men will be changed permanently. If something goes wrong, if the enhancements reject or the modifications fail—"

"Then we will learn from the failure and try again," Kort said, echoing Filibert's own philosophy back at him. "This is how science works. How evolution works. You taught me this."

Filibert studied his friend's face, looking for doubt or fear or hesitation. He found only certainty.

"We're going to change the world," Filibert said quietly. "Create something that has never existed. Soldiers who can survive anything. Who can complete any mission. Who are limited only by human will rather than human biology."

"And if the world doesn't want to change?"

"Then we'll change it anyway. Because the world doesn't get to decide. We do. People like us—people willing to cross boundaries that others are too afraid to approach—we're the ones who write the future."

Kort nodded slowly. "Then let's write a good one."

"We will. Starting here. Starting now." Filibert extended his hand, and Kort shook it. "Brothers?"

"Brothers."

They stood like that for a moment, two men who had found each other in an orphanage sixteen years ago, who had survived when they shouldn't have, who had made promises to each other that most would call impossible.

Then Kort saluted—the crisp Legion salute, hand to forehead—and returned to his training.

Filibert watched him go, then turned to follow Leroux into the administration building.

The clocks on the wall—there were three in the compound, he'd counted them immediately—all showed different times. Sloppy. Disorganized. He would need to fix that.

But first, he had work to do.

Soldiers to transform.

Promises to keep.

And if those promises required sacrifices?

Well.

The clock struck half past one in his mind, as it always did.

And the future opened before him like a door he'd been waiting his entire life to walk through.

Five

Legionnaires

Somewhere Over the Algerian Sahara Desert – Dawn, 1963

The DHC-4 Caribou shuddered and bucked as it cut through the pre-dawn darkness, its twin engines screaming against the thin air. Inside the aircraft's metal belly, five men sat in silence, each wrapped in thoughts darker than the sky outside.

Kort Sokolov checked his equipment for the third time in as many minutes. Not because he needed to—everything was exactly where it should be—but because the ritual gave his hands something to do besides shake. Not from fear. He'd left fear behind in Laos, buried it with the friends who hadn't made it home. This was something else. Anticipation, maybe. Or the electric hum that ran through his body whenever the enhancements activated, the modifications Filibert had spent the last eight months perfecting.

Beside him, Jean-Baptiste Mercier—Jean to everyone who valued their teeth—hummed something tuneless under his breath. A nervous habit from a man who claimed to have no nerves. He was Parisian, or had been before whatever sent him running to the Legion. Thirty-two years old, built like a middleweight boxer, with the kind of face that women found interesting and men found threatening. His French was pure Parisian argot, the language of back alleys and criminal enterprise, but he could code-switch to educated speech when he needed to pass in better company.

"How much longer?" Jean asked in French, not looking up from his hands. He turned them over slowly, studying the palms, the fingers, as if they belonged to someone else. Which, in a way, they did now.

"Twenty minutes," replied the jumpmaster from his position near the rear ramp. He was a Legion veteran named Sergeant Pelletier, a man who'd done this same jump probably a hundred times before, who treated dropping men into hostile territory with the same casual indifference as ordering coffee.

Twenty minutes. Kort closed his eyes, feeling the modifications coursing through his system. The enhanced muscle tissue that Filibert had grafted at the cellular level. The reinforced skeletal structure—not replaced, but augmented with compounds that made bones nearly unbreakable. The neural enhancements that increased reaction time by factors that shouldn't be possible. And the armor.

The armor was the masterpiece.

It covered their forearms now, visible where their "tenue leopard" combat fatigues were rolled up—translucent panels that looked like they'd been carved from amber or horn, but were actually something far stranger. Bioengineered tissue, Filibert called it. Grown in his laboratory from a combination of spider silk proteins, marine organism cellular structures, and something he'd extracted from lamprey eels that he'd never fully explained. The panels were grafted directly onto their skin, integrated at the cellular level so completely that the body's immune system read them as self rather than foreign.

They were proof against small arms fire. Resistant to edged weapons. Adaptive to temperature extremes. And they were just the visible portion. Beneath their fatigues, each man wore a full body suit of the same material, form-fitting, flexible, and absolutely revolutionary.

Revolutionary and untested in actual combat.

"Did you hear what D'Arcy said?" Hans Krueger muttered from across the aircraft. He was German, from Frankfurt, with the kind of face that suggested multiple encounters with hard surfaces—broken nose, scar through his left eyebrow, teeth that were slightly too perfect to be original. His French carried a thick German accent that no amount of Legion training had been able to smooth out. "That this morning's injection made him sick as a dog."

"Everyone gets sick," Razo van der Berg replied. He was Dutch, the youngest of the group at twenty-four, with the lean build of a distance runner and a nervous energy that never seemed to settle. "It's part of the program. The doctor said it would pass."

"The doctor says many things," Hans grumbled. "Doesn't mean they're all true."

"The doctor is Kort's brother," Jean said quietly, his eyes finding Kort's in the dim red light of the aircraft interior. "Which means Kort vouches for him. And I trust Kort. So I trust the doctor."

It was a logical chain, but Kort heard the question underneath it: *Do you trust him? Really? With our lives?*

"Filibert knows what he's doing," Kort said, his voice carrying the authority that came from being the most combat experienced, the unofficial leader of this mad experiment. "Every modification has been tested. Every compound verified. What we're carrying into this mission—it works. I've seen it work."

"You've seen it work on lab rats and yourself," D'Arcy said from his position near the rear. Luc D'Arcy was the skeptic of the group, a French Canadian who'd been kicked out of the regular Canadian forces for reasons he'd never fully explained. He had the look of someone who expected betrayal as a matter of course. "Not quite the same as actual combat."

"Then today we find out," Kort said simply.

The Caribou pitched suddenly, and several men grabbed for handholds. The Jump Master didn't react, planted solid in his position like he was rooted to the deck.

"Receiving ground fire," the pilot's voice crackled over the intercom. "Nothing serious. Just the locals saying hello."

Nothing serious. Kort almost smiled at that. Small arms fire at a transport aircraft—nothing serious. Six months ago, before the enhancements, the prospect would have made his heart rate spike, his palms sweat, his mouth go dry. Now? He registered it as data. Information to be processed and filed away.

The enhancements had changed more than just their bodies. They'd changed how their minds processed threat. Filibert had explained it as an alteration to the limbic system's fear response, a dampening of the amygdala's alarm signals. Kort thought of it more simply: the modifications had removed the part of him that knew how to panic.

Which should have been terrifying, except he couldn't feel terrified anymore.

"Equipment check," Kort ordered, falling back on procedure. "Jean, you're on point when we hit ground. Hans, you're on my six. D'Arcy, you cover our left flank. Razo, right flank. We move as a unit. No heroics. No lone wolves. We are Legion. We are brothers. We survive together or not at all."

"*Legio Patria Nostra*," they responded in unison. The Legion is Our Fatherland. The motto had been drilled into them during basic training, but now it carried different weight. They weren't just legionnaires anymore. They were something else. Something new.

Something that would either revolutionize warfare or die screaming in the Algerian desert.

Kort thought there was roughly equal probability of either outcome.

The rear ramp began to lower, the hydraulics groaning. Dawn light spilled into the aircraft's interior—harsh, unforgiving, the color of old brass. The temperature dropped immediately as desert-cold air rushed in. They were at ten thousand feet, and at this altitude the Sahara was freezing despite the scorching heat that would come once the sun climbed higher.

"Five minutes!" The Jump Master shouted over the engine roar and wind howl. "Check your chutes! Check your weapons! Check your balls to make sure they're still attached!"

Nervous laughter rippled through the group. Even modified soldiers appreciated crude humor in the face of death.

Kort stood, the rest following his lead. They formed a line, each man checking the parachute of the man in front of him. It was sacred ritual, this checking. You trusted your life to the man behind you, and he trusted his to the man behind him, all the way down the line until everyone was linked in a chain of mutual dependence.

That was what made the Legion work. Not the training or the equipment or the traditions. The knowledge that you were never alone. Never abandoned. That the man beside you would die before leaving you behind.

Kort wondered if that would still be true once the shooting started. Once they discovered whether Filibert's enhancements turned them into supermen or monsters.

"Three minutes!"

They moved toward the ramp, shuffling forward in the awkward waddle that came from carrying seventy pounds of equipment plus parachute. Kort could feel the weight, but it didn't slow him the way it would have before. The enhanced musculature carried the load easily, his breathing steady, his heart rate barely elevated.

"You think we're doing the right thing?" D'Arcy asked suddenly, his voice low enough that only Kort could hear. "Letting the doctor turn us into lab experiments?"

Kort considered the question seriously. It deserved that much. "I think we're doing the necessary thing. How many men have you seen die from wounds that shouldn't be fatal? How many friends bled out because help came too slow? If these modifications give us even a ten percent better chance of survival, then they're worth it."

"And if they don't? If something goes wrong?"

"Then we die doing something no one has ever done before. There are worse deaths."

D'Arcy didn't look convinced, but he nodded. What else could he do? They'd all volunteered. They'd all signed the papers—reams of them, half in technical language that none of them fully understood, all of them essentially saying the same thing: *We consent to experimental procedures. We understand the risks. We will not hold anyone liable if this turns us into corpses or madmen.*

"One minute!"

The Caribou banked, and through the open ramp Kort could see the ground below. Desert, mostly. Tan and brown and gray, broken by the occasional wadi or rocky outcropping. And there—a cluster of buildings. Mud brick walls. Flat roofs. The village of Hassi Beida, a vital water hole, an oasis with a long history of being fought over, though it wasn't much of a village anymore.

Intelligence said maybe fifty fighters were using it as a staging area. Fifty men, Goumiers they were called. Tribal indigenous Moroccan soldiers with a reputation of committing atrocities back in Italy during the big war. That piece of intel was enough to ignite in Kort a serios disliking. Fifty men who'd killed three Legion patrols in the last month. Fifty men who'd declared this territory under Moroccan control in an ongoing border dispute, promising to kill anyone who disagreed.

Their mission was simple: go in, extract hostages, neutralize the fighters, and get out. The intel confirmed that a small group of Cuban medical aid workers, sent to Algeria to help support its rebuilding following the country's liberation from France, had failed to get out when warned. And now they were trapped and turned from healthcare professionals to political bargaining chips or martyrs for the cause. As operations go, it was a standard surgical strike, the kind the Legion had been conducting for decades.

Except this time, they were the experiment. The proof of concept. The demonstration that Filibert's vision of enhanced soldiers could work in actual combat conditions.

No pressure.

"Thirty seconds!"

Kort moved to the front of the line, feeling the modifications activate fully now. His vision sharpened, details snapping into hyperfocus. The pattern of sunlight on the desert floor. The shadow of the aircraft racing across the sand. The minute adjustments in air pressure as they approached the drop zone.

And something else. A sensation he'd never experienced before the enhancements. A kind of low-level awareness of his team, as if he could feel them in his peripheral consciousness. Filibert had mentioned something about this—neural synchronization, he'd called it. A side effect of the modifications that created a subtle electromagnetic signature that enhanced soldiers could sense in each other.

Kort had thought it was theoretical nonsense.

Now, standing at the ramp with his team arrayed behind him, he could feel them like pressure points in his awareness. Jean's nervous energy. Hans's solid reliability. D'Arcy's skeptical caution. Razo's barely-controlled excitement.

They were more than a team now. They were something closer to a single organism with five bodies.

"Go! Go! Go!"

Kort didn't think. Thinking was for people who had time. He launched himself out of the aircraft, arms and legs spread, feeling the prop wash try to tumble him before his body automatically adjusted, finding stability in the chaos.

The Algerian desert spread below him like a map drawn by a drunk cartographer. Beautiful and deadly and utterly indifferent to whether he lived or died.

Four more shapes blossomed from the aircraft behind him—his team, his brothers, following him into the unknown.

The wind screamed past, cold and violent. Kort counted down—five seconds, four, three, two, one—and pulled his ripcord.

The chute deployed with a violent jerk that could result in cervical hyperextension and severe spinal nerve damage in a normal man. Kort felt it as a mild discomfort, quickly forgotten as the canopy caught air and his descent slowed to something manageable.

Above and around him, four more chutes bloomed like strange flowers. They'd all deployed successfully. First hurdle cleared.

The ground rushed up—slower than free fall, but still fast enough to kill if you landed wrong. Kort pulled his toggles, steering toward the designated landing zone, a stretch of flat sand about half a kilometer from the target village.

Fifty meters.

Twenty-five.

Ten.

He hit and rolled, the enhanced bones in his legs absorbing impact that would have shattered normal femurs. He came up in a crouch, already scanning for threats, his MAT-49 submachine gun coming up to ready position.

The others landed around him in a loose perimeter—Jean to his left, Hans to his right, D'Arcy and Razo completing the circle. They'd drilled this a thousand times, but this was the first time it mattered. The first time failure meant death rather than extra training.

"Status," Kort barked in French.

"Clear," Jean replied.

"Clear," from Hans.

"Clear," D'Arcy and Razo echoed.

Kort allowed himself a moment of satisfaction. Good landing. No injuries. No compromises. They gathered their chutes quickly, stripping off the harnesses and burying them in shallow scrapes of sand. Regulations said to police your equipment and pack it out, but regulations were written by people who didn't have to hump gear through hostile territory.

"Five hundred meters to target," Kort said, checking the heading. The sun was fully up now, the temperature climbing rapidly. Within an hour it would be over a hundred degrees. But by then they'd either be extracted or dead. "Standard approach. Eyes open. Weapons tight until we make contact."

They moved out, transitioning seamlessly from parachute landing to ground patrol. The desert was deceptively flat—what looked like smooth sand from the air became a landscape of dips and rises, hidden wadis and rocky outcroppings that could conceal a hundred men.

Kort felt his enhancements working, processing information faster than conscious thought. The angle of shadows suggesting cover. The texture of sand indicating recent foot traffic. The faint scent on the wind that might be cooking fires or might be explosive compounds.

They moved silently, a patrol of ghosts. The Legion had taught them fieldcraft. The enhancements made them perfect.

Two hundred meters from the village, Jean raised his fist—stop signal.

Everyone froze.

Kort crawled forward to where Jean crouched behind a low rise, his eyes fixed on something ahead. Kort followed his gaze and saw it: a sentry post. Sandbags piled in a rough semicircle, two men visible, rifles slung casually. Probably bored. Definitely not expecting company.

"Your call," Jean whispered.

Kort considered. They could try to bypass, come at the village from a different angle. But that risked being spotted from a different sentry post they hadn't identified yet. Better to neutralize this threat and maintain the element of surprise.

"Hans, with me," Kort said. "Jean, you're overwalk. D'Arcy, Razo, maintain position and cover our withdrawal if this goes sideways."

He didn't wait for acknowledgment. They were Legion. They knew their jobs.

Kort and Hans moved forward in a crouch, using the terrain for cover, closing the distance to the sentry post. Fifty meters. Forty. Thirty. Close enough that Kort could see the sentries clearly now—young men, maybe twenty, wearing a mix of military surplus and civilian clothes. One was smoking. The other was staring off into the distance, his rifle across his knees.

Twenty meters.

The smoking sentry said something—Kort caught the word "tired" in Arabic—and his companion laughed.

Ten meters.

The enhancements made everything sharp, clear, slowed down. Kort could see the individual grains of sand displaced by his boots. Could hear the rasp of Hans's breathing beside him. Could feel the exact weight of his knife in his hand.

Five meters.

The smoking sentry turned, perhaps sensing something, and his eyes went wide as he saw them—two men who had crossed fifty meters of open ground in complete silence, who now stood close enough to touch.

He opened his mouth to shout.

Kort moved.

The enhancements made him fast—faster than human reaction time, faster than the sentry's brain could process threat and send signals to his vocal cords. Kort's hand clamped over the man's mouth as his knife found the soft spot beneath the jawbone, angling it up into the brainstem with a fatal twist. The sentry stiffened, twitched violently, then went limp, dead before he could make a sound.

Hans moved simultaneously, his own knife flashing in the morning sun. The second sentry died with a surprised gurgling sound, clutching at the wound in his throat, blood pumping between his fingers.

It was over in seconds.

Kort lowered the first sentry to the ground gently, almost reverently. He'd killed before—in Laos, up close and impersonal. But this was different. The enhancements had made it mechanical, emotionless. He'd processed the threat, calculated the solution, executed without hesitation or doubt.

He should have felt something. Remorse. Satisfaction. Horror. Something.

He felt nothing.

"Jesus," Hans whispered, staring at his hands. "Did you see how fast we moved? I barely thought about it and it was done."

"That's what they're for," Kort said, checking the sentry post for intelligence. He found nothing useful—some food, water, a radio that wasn't working. "The modifications remove hesitation. Make us faster. Better."

"Or make us killers who don't feel anything." Hans was still staring at his hands, at the blood that stained them.

"We were already killers. That's what soldiers are." Kort signaled for the rest of the team to move up. "The question was never whether we could kill. It was whether we could survive. Come on. Mission's not over."

They moved past the sentry post, leaving two bodies cooling in the desert sun. Behind them, Jean crossed himself quickly—a vestigial Catholic gesture from a childhood he claimed to have forgotten.

The village was close now. Kort could see the walls, the buildings beyond, could hear voices and the sound of activity. Morning routine in a terrorist stronghold. Men waking up, preparing for another day of planning violence.

He signaled the team into position—a standard entry formation that the Legion had perfected over decades of colonial warfare. Jean on point. Hans and Kort on flanks. D'Arcy and Razo providing rear security.

And then, just as they were about to move in, something went catastrophically wrong.

The explosion came from behind them—a massive detonation that threw sand and smoke and shrapnel in a deadly radius. The sentry post they'd just cleared erupted in a fireball.

Secondary explosion. Booby trap. Something they'd missed in their haste to move forward.

The blast wave hit them like a physical fist, throwing Jean forward, catching D'Arcy and spinning him like a top. Kort felt shrapnel impact his back—dozens of pieces, traveling at lethal velocities, any one of which should have been fatal.

Should have been.

The armor absorbed most of it. Kort felt impacts, felt the suit distribute kinetic energy across its surface, felt individual panels flex and harden in response to threat. But nothing penetrated. Nothing reached his actual body.

He rolled to his feet, already bringing his weapon up, as the village erupted in gunfire.

They'd been compromised. The mission was blown. And now they were in a fight for their lives.

"Contact!" Jean shouted, unnecessary but automatic. "Contact rear and flanks!"

Kort's mind processed the tactical situation in fractions of a second: they were in the open, taking fire from multiple directions, cut off from their egress route. Standard doctrine said withdraw to cover, call for support, wait for extraction.

Screw standard doctrine.

"Into the village!" Kort shouted. "We push through! Jean, on me!"

They charged—five men running toward superior numbers in prepared positions, running toward certain death, running because the modifications in their bodies told them they could survive what normal men couldn't.

Jean reached the village wall first and instead of seeking cover, he simply...jumped. Launched himself at the three-meter wall with a strength that shouldn't have been possible, caught the top edge with one hand, and pulled himself up and over in a single fluid motion.

Gunfire erupted from inside the wall. Jean's silhouette disappeared.

"Jean!" Hans shouted, but Kort was already moving, following his friend over the wall.

He hit the ground inside and rolled, coming up to see Jean surrounded by four fighters, all of them firing at point-blank range. Bullets impacted Jean's armor—Kort saw the translucent panels flash and absorb impacts, saw Jean stagger but not fall, saw him bring his MAT-49 up and return fire in one continuous motion.

Three fighters went down. The fourth tried to run.

Hans came over the wall, then D'Arcy, then Razo. They were all inside now, all committed, and there was no going back.

The village became chaos.

Kort moved through it like a scythe through wheat, his enhanced reflexes allowing him to process threats faster than they could develop. A fighter appeared from a doorway—Kort's knife was in the man's throat before he could shoulder his rifle. Another tried to take cover behind a cart—Kort's submachine gun stitched a line across the cart's side, and the fighter went down.

Everywhere he looked, his team was performing miracles. D'Arcy took multiple hits to his chest armor and barely slowed, pressing forward to clear a building with clinical precision. Razo moved like water, flowing around obstacles, his weapons always exactly where they needed to be. Hans fought with methodical efficiency, each shot placed, each movement economical.

And Jean—Jean was beautiful in his violence, moving with a grace that shouldn't have been possible, engaging multiple targets, never stopping, never hesitating.

They carved through the village like wolves through sheep.

But there were so many sheep.

Kort felt rounds impact his armor—chest, shoulder, thigh. Felt the panels absorb and distribute, felt bruising underneath but nothing serious. He returned fire, dropped two more fighters, pushed forward toward the largest building where intelligence said hostages were being held.

The door was barricaded. Kort didn't slow, didn't stop, just lowered his shoulder and hit it at full speed. The enhanced bone structure and musculature did the rest—the door exploded inward, hinges tearing free, and Kort tumbled into the room beyond.

Five fighters. All armed. All turning toward the threat.

Time slowed.

Kort's enhanced nervous system kicked into what Filibert called "combat state"—a mode where perception of time dilated, where fractions of seconds stretched into usable decision-making moments. He saw the fighters' weapons coming up, saw fingers tightening on triggers, saw muzzle flashes beginning to bloom.

He moved between the bullets.

His mind calculated trajectories, his body responded faster than conscious thought, weaving through a storm of gunfire that should have cut him apart. His own weapon tracked and fired, tracked and fired, and fighters fell.

All five. Dead in less than three seconds.

Time snapped back to normal speed, and Kort stumbled, nearly fell. The combat state drained him, left him dizzy and nauseous. Filibert had warned about this—the enhancements allowed superhuman performance, but the toll on the system was severe. You could push beyond human limits, but only briefly, and the cost was high.

"Clear," Kort gasped into his radio. "Building secure. Search for hostages."

The rest of the team flowed in around him, spreading out, weapons up, moving with the kind of coordination that would have taken normal soldiers years to develop. They'd had it in months, thanks to the neural synchronization.

They found the hostages in a back room—five Cuban medical workers and one girl, seventeen maybe, who looked out of place in the group. She wasn't Cuban, she was local.

The hostages sat huddled together on the floor bound and terrified, except for the girl, she stood against the wall and she wasn't terrified. She looked at Kort with eyes that had seen too much. She didn't flinch when he approached, didn't cry out in fear.

"You save us?" she asked in Arabic-accented French.

"Yes—we're French Foreign Legion," Kort replied, cutting her bonds. "You're safe now."

"Safe." She said the word like it was foreign.

"What are you doing here with this group?" Kort asked as the other team members cut the bonds of the hostages.

"I am translator—guide. This is a dangerous region."

Kort smiled at the understatement. "You are young for such work."

The girl squared her shoulders and looked him in the eye. "Monsieur, everyone must help make the world better."

Kort nodded. The statement hit deeply, underscored his own beliefs, which this mission solidified.

"Can you walk?" he asked.

"Yes."

"Then stay close. We're getting you out."

The extraction was supposed to be the easy part. They'd secured the hostages, neutralized the threats, accomplished the mission objectives. All that remained was to move to the extraction point and wait for the helicopter.

Except the helicopter wasn't coming.

"Negative on exfil," the radio crackled. "Heavy ground fire in the area. Unable to approach. Hold position and await further instructions."

Hold position. In the middle of hostile territory. With wounded hostages and depleted ammunition. With modifications that were beginning to fail as the stress took its toll.

D'Arcy vomited suddenly, doubling over, a stream of blood and bile. The others looked at him in shock.

"Side effects," he gasped. "Doctor said... said there might be side effects."

His nose was bleeding. So was Kort's. So was Jean's. The enhancements were breaking down, the foreign materials in their bodies triggering immune responses that Filibert's suppressants couldn't fully control.

They were running out of time.

"We move now," Kort decided. "We can't wait for extraction. We head for the secondary LZ on foot. Ten kilometers. We can make it if we move fast."

"What about the hostages?" Razo asked. "They can't move that fast."

Kort looked at the girl. "Can you run?"

"I can try."

"Then try hard. And help them to understand."

The girl nodded.

He addressed the medical team now in French while the girl translated his words into Spanish so there would be no misunderstanding. "The men who held you are dead. But more will come. Many more. We need to move, and we need to move fast. If you fall behind, we cannot wait. Understand?"

They understood. Even without a translator they would have understood. Terror was a universal language.

The team formed up around the hostages, creating a protective box. Kort took point, Jean rear guard, the others on flanks. And they ran.

Through the village. Past the bodies they'd created. Over the wall and into the desert beyond. Running toward a secondary extraction point that was ten kilometers away across hostile terrain, running while their enhanced bodies slowly broke down, running because the alternative was death.

The sun climbed higher. The temperature soared. The desert became a furnace.

One of the hostages—a young doctor who clearly got more than he bargained for—collapsed after three kilometers. Hans picked him up, threw him over his shoulder, kept running without breaking stride. Enhanced musculature made it possible, but Kort could see the strain on Hans's face, could see the blood running from his nose increasing.

At five kilometers, Jean stumbled. Caught himself. Kept moving.

At seven kilometers, D'Arcy's eyes were bleeding. Not just nose now, but actual blood tears running down his face. He looked like something from a nightmare, but he didn't stop, didn't slow.

The enhancements, eating them alive from the inside.

But they kept moving.

Because they were Legion. Because they'd made promises to each other. Because stopping meant dying, and they'd all decided long ago that dying would have to wait until after the mission was complete.

At nine kilometers, they heard the helicopter.

At nine and a half kilometers, they saw it—a H-21 "Flying Banana," its twin rotors beating the air, coming in low and fast.

At ten kilometers exactly, they collapsed in the landing zone, five enhanced soldiers and six rescued hostages, all of them spent, all of them damaged in ways that wouldn't be fully understood for years.

The helicopter landed. Medics ran out. Kort felt hands on him, felt himself being loaded onto a stretcher, felt the cool interior of the aircraft as they lifted off.

He turned his head, looking at his team. Jean was unconscious. Hans was conscious but not responsive. D'Arcy's eyes had stopped bleeding, but he looked like a corpse. Razo was trying to sit up, trying to tell the medics he was fine, trying to maintain the fiction that they weren't all falling apart.

"We did it," Kort whispered to no one in particular. "Mission complete."

And then the world went dark.

Sidi Bel Abbès - Three Days Later

Kort woke up in a hospital bed, his body wrapped in bandages, tubes running in and out of him like he was some kind of science experiment.

Which, he supposed, he was.

Filibert sat in a chair beside the bed, reading through a thick file of medical reports. He looked up when Kort stirred, and something like relief crossed his face.

"You're awake. Good. The doctors were concerned."

"The others?" Kort's voice was ragged.

"Alive. All of them. Recovering." Filibert set the file aside. "The mission was a success, by the way. Six hostages rescued. Forty-three enemy combatants neutralized. Zero friendly casualties. Command is calling it flawless."

"Doesn't feel flawless."

"No. I imagine it doesn't." Filibert leaned forward. "The enhancements saved your lives. Multiple times. But they also almost killed you. The stress on your systems was far greater than I'd calculated. The immune responses, the cellular breakdown—"

"Was it worth it?" Kort interrupted.

"Worth it?"

"The modifications. Turning us into... whatever we are now. Was it worth it?"

Filibert was quiet for a long moment. "You completed a mission that should have been impossible. You survived injuries that would have killed normal soldiers. You rescued innocent lives. So yes. It was worth it."

"And if we'd died?"

"Then we would have learned from the failure and tried again." Filibert's voice was matter-of-fact. "That's how progress works, Kort. Through trial and error. Through risk and reward."

Kort closed his eyes, feeling the modifications still humming in his body, quieter now, healing rather than enhancing. "I killed men today without thinking. Without feeling. The enhancements made it easy. Too easy."

"Soldiers are supposed to kill efficiently."

"Soldiers are supposed to be human."

"Then perhaps," Filibert said quietly, "humans need to be something more than human. The world is getting more dangerous, Kort. The weapons more destructive. If we don't evolve, we'll be extinct."

Kort didn't answer. He thought about the girl in the village, so young, so willing to live her ideals no matter the cost. What had she said? *Everyone must help make the world better.*"

He thought about the ease with which he'd killed. Thought about the future Filibert was building, one enhanced soldier at a time.

And he wondered, not for the first time, if they were saving humanity or destroying it.

The clock on the wall read half past one.

But that was wrong. It was three in the afternoon.

Kort closed his eyes and tried not to think about what that might mean.

Six

Operation Oranie

Somewhere Over Algeria – Dawn, 1964

The pre-dawn darkness pressed against the windows of the DHC-4 Caribou like something alive and malevolent. Inside the aircraft's cramped fuselage, the five men of Operational Detachment Alpha—though they'd never call themselves that, preferring simply "the team"—sat in the red-lit dimness, each lost in his own thoughts.

Six months had passed since their first mission. Six months of operations, modifications, adjustments, and an ever-growing body count that Command was simultaneously celebrating and refusing to officially acknowledge. The enhancements worked—that much was undeniable. But they worked in ways that made the bureaucrats nervous and the traditionalists apoplectic.

Kort Sokolov checked his equipment with the automatic precision of someone who'd done it a thousand times. His MAT-49 submachine gun—cleaned, loaded, safety on. His web gear—full magazines, grenades, knife, first aid kit. His parachute—properly packed, reserve accessible. And the modifications—always the modifications, humming beneath his skin like a second heartbeat, foreign and familiar all at once.

The enhancements had been refined since that first disastrous breakdown. Filibert had adjusted the cellular integration, modified the immune suppressants, recalibrated the neural interfaces. The team no longer bled from their eyes after combat. No longer vomited blood when they pushed too hard. The modifications had become more stable, more reliable.

More permanent.

Kort flexed his forearm, watching the translucent armor panels shift and adjust beneath his rolled-up sleeve. They were beautiful in their own terrible way—organic technology that blurred the line between man and machine, between human and something else entirely.

"Thinking too much again," Jean-Baptiste Mercier said from across the fuselage. He'd noticed Kort's thousand-yard stare, the way he got when the philosophical questions threatened to overwhelm the practical necessities. "Bad habit for a soldier."

"Better than not thinking at all," Kort replied in French, his accent still thick despite years of practice.

"Is it?" Jean grinned, but there was an edge to it. There was always an edge to everything now. "Sometimes I miss being stupid. Back when all I had to worry about was who I was going to rob and whether the gendarmes would catch me."

"You were never stupid, Jean. Just impatient."

"Same thing in Paris."

Hans Krueger shifted in his seat, the motion drawing everyone's attention. He was the biggest of them, built like a brick wall, and when he moved it was an event. "How long?" he asked in his German-accented French.

"Thirty minutes to jump," replied Sergeant Pelletier, the jumpmaster. He was the same career legionnaire who'd supervised their first combat jump, a man who treated the experimental supersoldiers with the same casual indifference he showed to regular recruits. Kort appreciated that. It was refreshing to be treated like a normal human, even when you weren't.

"Thirty minutes," Hans repeated, settling back. "Time for a nap then."

"How can you sleep?" Luc D'Arcy demanded. The French-Canadian was wound tight today, tighter than usual. His leg bounced with nervous energy, and his fingers drummed against his thigh in a staccato rhythm that was driving everyone crazy. "We're about to jump into a hot LZ, rescue hostages from terrorist insurgents who've already killed three Legion patrols, and you want to nap?"

"What else should I do? Worry?" Hans closed his eyes. "Worrying won't change anything. The mission happens whether I'm anxious or rested. I choose rested."

"German pragmatism," Razo van der Berg muttered. The young Dutchman was cleaning his weapon for the third time, breaking it down and reassembling it with the kind of obsessive focus that spoke of deeper anxieties. "Must be nice to have such simple philosophy."

"Nothing simple about it," Hans said without opening his eyes. "Simple would be staying in Frankfurt, working in my father's shop, never seeing combat. This—" he gestured vaguely at the aircraft, the team, himself, "—this is complicated. So I simplify where I can. Sleep when possible. Kill when necessary. Try not to think too hard about what we've become."

Silence settled over the group, broken only by the steady drone of the engines and the occasional creak of the aircraft's frame. It was the kind of silence that came before action, heavy with unspoken thoughts and suppressed fears.

Kort understood the fear, even if the modifications made it harder to feel. They'd done seventeen operations in the last three months. Seventeen times they'd jumped into hostile territory with orders to neutralize threats and extract assets. Seventeen times they'd succeeded when normal soldiers would have failed.

But the cost was adding up.

Not in casualties—they'd taken no KIA, no serious WIA. The enhancements saw to that. Wounds that should have been fatal became minor inconveniences. Injuries that should have ended careers healed in days instead of months.

No, the cost was measured in different currency. In the way Jean sometimes forgot to reload his weapon because the combat state made everything feel like a dream. In the way Hans had stopped writing letters home because he couldn't explain what he'd become. In the way D'Arcy flinched at loud noises when he was off-duty, his enhanced nervous system interpreting every stimulus as potential threat. In the way Razo had started talking to himself during missions, carrying on conversations with people who weren't there.

And in the way Kort could no longer remember what it felt like to be fully human.

"This one's different," D'Arcy said suddenly, breaking the silence. "This operation. It feels different."

"How so?" Kort asked, though he'd felt it too. Something in the briefing had been off, some detail that didn't quite align.

"The hostages." D'Arcy pulled out a small photograph from his breast pocket—one of the mission briefing materials. "University students. French and Algerian. Doing marine biology research off the coast when *Front des Forces Socialistes* fighters grabbed them. Why would insurgents take marine biology students? What's the tactical value?"

"Propaganda," Jean suggested. "Show they can strike anywhere, take anyone. Create fear in the civilian population."

"Maybe." D'Arcy didn't sound convinced. "Or maybe someone wanted these students for a specific reason."

"You're paranoid," Razo said.

"I'm enhanced. There's a difference." D'Arcy tapped his temple. "Ever since Filibert did his neural modifications, I notice patterns I never saw before. Connections. Anomalies. And this whole operation has anomaly written all over it."

Kort leaned in, interested despite himself. "Explain."

"Okay. First: the timing. These students were taken three days ago, but we're only getting the mission now. Why the delay? Second: the location. Saida is way south, almost in the deep desert. Why would FFS move hostages that far from the coast? Third: the intel. It's too good. We know exactly which building, which room, how many guards. When has intel ever been that precise?"

"You think it's a trap," Hans said, eyes still closed.

"I think it might be a test," D'Arcy corrected. "Someone wanted to see what we could do. So they created a scenario—grab some hostages, put them in a specific location, wait to see if the Legion's experimental supersoldiers can pull off a rescue."

"That's insane," Razo said.

"Is it?" D'Arcy looked around the fuselage. "We're modified humans being used as weapons. Insane is our job description."

Kort considered the theory. It had the ring of paranoia to it, but D'Arcy was right about the patterns. The operation did feel staged, too neat, too convenient. And if it was a test...

"Who would be testing us?" Kort asked. "FFS doesn't know we exist. Command treats us like a classified experiment. So who—"

"Filibert," Jean said quietly. "Your brother would know. If anyone's running experiments within experiments, it would be him. Think of the series of untested new modifications we just underwent." Jean nodded his head rhythmically, beckoning the others to come along with his reasoning.

The accusation hung in the air like smoke. Kort wanted to defend Filibert, to explain that his brother was trying to save lives, to create soldiers who could survive the unsurvivable. But another part of him—the part that had started asking uncomfortable questions about consent and ethics and the price of progress—wondered if Jean was right.

"We'll find out when we get there," Kort said finally. "Until then, we focus on the mission. Six hostages. Unknown number of hostiles. Standard extraction protocol. In and out before the sun gets high enough to cook us."

"Standard extraction," Hans repeated with dark humor. "Nothing about us is standard anymore."

"Then we improvise. We adapt. We overcome." Kort fell back on the old Legion maxims, the institutional memory that predated the enhancements. "We are Legion. That hasn't changed."

"Hasn't it?" D'Arcy asked softly.

Before Kort could answer, Sergeant Pelletier stood up, grabbing a handhold. "Twenty minutes! Final equipment check! Prepare for combat jump!"

Kort let out a sharp whistle and caught Razo's attention. Kort pointed at Razo's half disassembled weapon. "Time to secure that shit, son," he said, flashing a broad smile.

Razo rolled his eyes at the good-natured ribbing and had the weapon assembled in an instance—like an illusionist.

The conversation ended as training took over. They went through the ritual—checking parachutes, weapons, securing equipment, each man verifying the readiness of the man beside him. It was automatic, instinctive, the kind of muscle memory that survived even when the muscles themselves had been fundamentally altered.

Kort ran through his own checklist, but his mind kept circling back to D'Arcy's question: *Hasn't it changed?*

The Legion was built on traditions that stretched back over a century. *Legio Patria Nostra*—The Legion is Our Fatherland. A motto for men without countries, without families, without pasts they wanted to remember. The Legion gave them identity, purpose, brothers who would die for them.

But what happened when those brothers became something other than men? When biology itself became just another piece of equipment to be upgraded and modified? When the thing that made you brothers wasn't shared humanity but shared modifications?

Were they still Legion? Or were they something new, something that had no traditions, no history, no identity beyond what Filibert created for them?

"Ten minutes!"

The rear ramp began to lower, hydraulics groaning. Cold air rushed in—the desert at altitude was freezing despite the inferno it would become once the sun climbed higher. Dawn light painted the horizon in shades of brass and copper, beautiful and deadly.

Kort stood, the team rising with him in synchronized motion. They'd developed that—a kind of unconscious coordination that came from the neural enhancements. Filibert called it "low-level telepathy," though it wasn't reading minds so much as sensing intent, anticipating movement, operating as a single organism in five bodies.

It was useful in combat.

It was also deeply unsettling when Kort thought about it too much.

They moved to the ramp in single file, each man carrying seventy pounds of equipment like it weighed nothing. The enhancements made them strong, fast, resilient. Made them into weapons that thought and bled and sometimes, in quiet moments, questioned what they'd become.

"Five minutes!"

Below, Kort could see the target area. Saida was a small town, really—a collection of mud-brick buildings clustered around a French colonial administrative center that had been abandoned years ago. Intel said the FFS was using it as a staging area. Intel said the hostages were being held in a specific building on the eastern edge of town. Intel said there were maybe twenty fighters, poorly trained, lightly armed.

Intel said a lot of things.

Kort had learned to trust intel about as far as he could throw the person who'd compiled it.

"Three minutes!"

"Hey Kort," Jean called over the engine noise. "When we get back, drinks are on you, yes?"

"Why me?"

"Because you're solid, man," he said in a mock jazzy tone. Then with a grin he counted off on his fingers, "And because Hans will drink the cheap stuff and D'Arcy will try to start a philosophical debate about the nature of consciousness, and Razo will try to pick up the bartender's daughter. Someone needs to be responsible."

"I hate being responsible."

"Too bad. You're naturally good at it. It's annoying."

Despite everything—the fear, the uncertainty, the questions about what they'd become—Kort smiled. This was why the Legion worked. This banter, this brotherhood, this stubborn insistence on treating each other like human beings even when you were becoming something else.

"One minute!"

Kort moved to the front of the line, his team arrayed behind him in order of exit: Jean, Hans, D'Arcy, Razo. They'd done this dozens of times now, but his heart still raced in the seconds before the jump. The modifications had dampened his fear response but couldn't eliminate it entirely. He was still human enough to know that jumping out of an aircraft into hostile territory was objectively insane.

"Thirty seconds!"

The team shifted, tightened up, prepared. Kort could feel them in his peripheral awareness—Jean's nervous energy, Hans's calm readiness, D'Arcy's analytical focus, Razo's barely-controlled excitement. Five men about to become a weapon system.

"Go! Go! Go!"

Kort launched himself into the void.

The aircraft disappeared above him, the prop wash trying to tumble him before his enhanced reflexes found stability. The Algerian desert spread below—tan and brown and gray, beautiful in its desolation, deadly in its indifference.

Four more shapes blossomed from the aircraft behind him. His team. His brothers. Modified humans following him into battle because they trusted him, because the Legion demanded it, because they didn't know how to do anything else anymore.

The ground rushed up. Kort pulled his ripcord, felt the parachute deploy with a violent jerk that his reinforced skeleton absorbed without damage. The canopy caught air, slowed his descent to something survivable.

He steered toward the LZ—a flat stretch of sand two kilometers from the target. Close enough for rapid approach. Far enough to avoid immediate detection.

The landing was textbook. Roll, disengage, weapon up, scan for threats. The others landed around him in a loose perimeter, their training and enhancements making them efficient even in the chaos of combat insertion.

"Status," Kort ordered.

"Good," from Jean.

"Good," from Hans.

"Good," from D'Arcy and Razo.

They gathered up their chutes quickly, burying them in shallow scrapes. Then they formed up for movement—Kort on point, Jean and Hans on flanks, D'Arcy and Razo providing rear security. Standard patrol formation, executed with superhuman precision.

The sun was just beginning to clear the horizon as they set out toward Saida, painting their shadows long across the sand. In an hour it would be unbearably hot. By afternoon, the desert would be a furnace.

But they'd be gone by then. One way or another.

The approach was textbook. They moved in bounds—one element moving while another provided overwatch, leapfrogging forward across terrain that offered minimal cover. The enhancements made them fast, but Kort forced discipline, forced them to move tactically rather than relying purely on their modifications.

Because eventually, the enhancements would fail. Or they'd face an enemy who'd figured out how to counter them. And on that day, the only thing that would save them was training, discipline, and the brotherhood that tied them together.

One kilometer from the target, they found the bodies.

Three men, French by their features and equipment, wearing Legion uniforms. They'd been dead maybe twelve hours, killed with professional efficiency—single shots to the head, no unnecessary brutality, just clinical elimination.

"Legion patrol," Hans said quietly, examining the bodies. "The third one that went missing last week."

Kort studied the scene with enhanced vision that could pick out details normal humans would miss. Shell casings —7.62mm, Soviet manufacture. Boot prints in the sand—at least eight different patterns. And something else, something that made his modified nervous system ping with warning.

"They were executed," D'Arcy said, coming to the same conclusion. "Not killed in combat. Captured, then shot."

"Why?" Razo asked. "FFS usually takes prisoners for ransom or propaganda."

"Unless they were sending a message," Jean said. "Or eliminating witnesses."

"Witnesses to what?" But even as Kort asked the question, he knew the answer. Witnesses to the hostage operation. Proof that the hostages existed, that they'd been moved through this area.

Which meant D'Arcy had been right. This whole thing was staged. The question was: staged by whom, and for what purpose?

"We continue," Kort decided. "But weapons hot. Trust nothing. If this smells like a trap, we abort and extract."

They moved past the bodies, leaving them for the recovery team that would come later. In the Legion, you never left your dead behind. But you also never let sentiment compromise a mission.

The town appeared ahead—low buildings, narrow streets, defensive walls that spoke of colonial paranoia. Intel had indicated light activity, minimal guards, a soft target.

Kort's enhanced hearing picked up voices, movement, the sounds of a town waking up. More activity than intel had suggested. Much more.

He raised his fist—stop signal.

The team froze, becoming invisible in the desert dawn. Kort crawled forward to a low rise that gave him a vantage point on the town.

What he saw made his blood run cold.

The town wasn't lightly defended. It was a fortress. Sandbag positions at every corner. Sentries walking patrols with professional spacing. Technical vehicles—trucks with mounted weapons—positioned at key intersections. And everywhere, fighters. Not twenty poorly-trained insurgents, but easily fifty or sixty organized soldiers.

"This is wrong," Jean whispered, crawling up beside Kort. "This is very wrong."

"It's an ambush," D'Arcy said from Kort's other side. "They knew we were coming. They've been preparing."

"How?" Hans demanded. "How could they know about us? We're classified. Our existence is compartmentalized. Even most of the Legion doesn't know what we are."

"Someone told them," Kort said quietly. "Someone with access to our operations, our capabilities, our mission parameters."

"Filibert," Jean said. It wasn't a question.

Kort wanted to deny it, wanted to defend his brother, wanted to believe that the man who'd saved him from an orphanage and life as a drifter wouldn't use him as an experimental test subject in a live-fire exercise. But the evidence was overwhelming. The timing too perfect. The scenario too controlled.

This wasn't a rescue mission.

This was a field test.

"We abort," Kort said. "This is beyond our operational parameters. We call for extraction and—"

A scream cut through the morning air. High-pitched, terrified, unmistakably human. Coming from the center of town.

The hostages.

"Damn it," Kort hissed.

Another scream, followed by shouting in Arabic. The guards were agitated, moving with purpose toward the sound.

"They're killing them," Razo said, his voice tight. "They're executing the hostages."

Standard doctrine said abort. Intelligence compromise plus overwhelming enemy force equals extraction and reassessment. No argument, no debate. You didn't throw good soldiers after bad intel.

But Legion doctrine said something different. *Legio Patria Nostra.* The Legion is our Fatherland. And you didn't abandon your countrymen. You didn't leave civilians to die when you had the power to save them.

Even if the whole thing was a setup. Even if they were being used. Even if the hostages were bait in a trap designed to test modified supersoldiers' combat effectiveness.

"We go in," Kort decided.

"Kort—" D'Arcy started.

"We go in. But we don't follow the plan. We don't hit the building intel specified. We improvise, we adapt, we find the hostages wherever they actually are, and we get them out. Then we have a very serious conversation with Filibert about operational ethics."

"Assuming we survive," Hans said.

"Assuming that," Kort agreed.

They moved forward, abandoning stealth for speed. The enhancements made them fast—faster than human reaction time, faster than the sentries could process. They covered the two hundred meters to the town perimeter in under thirty seconds, a sprint that would have left normal soldiers gasping but barely winded the modified team.

The first sentry never knew what hit him. Kort's knife found his throat before his brain could send the signal to shout. The second sentry managed half a scream before Jean silenced him permanently.

Then they were inside, stealth became impossible.

"Contact!" Someone shouted in Kabyle. There was enough Arabic and French in that language for the team to understand they had been compromised. "Intruders!"

Gunfire erupted from multiple directions. Kort felt rounds impact his armor—chest, shoulder, thigh—felt the modified material absorb and distribute kinetic energy, felt bruising but nothing serious.

He returned fire, dropping two fighters, then three, moving forward in a crouch. The combat state kicked in—time dilation, enhanced perception, his nervous system processing information faster than conscious thought.

The world became slow motion violence.

Jean moved like a dancer, weaving through gunfire that seemed to crawl through the air, his submachine gun tracking and firing with mechanical precision. Hans was a battering ram, smashing through obstacles, his enhanced strength turning doors into splinters and walls into rubble. D'Arcy and Razo worked in tandem, covering each other's movements, operating with the kind of coordination that looked more choreographed then the spooky neural action at a distance that bound them together.

Kort's enhanced hearing tracked multiple contacts—behind, flanking, overhead. Fighters on rooftops, in doorways, around corners. Too many to fight directly. They needed to move, to stay mobile, to use their speed and modifications as force multipliers.

"Keep moving!" he shouted. "Don't stop! Don't get pinned down!"

They flowed through the town like water, following the sounds of distress. Another scream—closer now. A woman's voice, young, terrified but defiant. Not begging for mercy but demanding it, which suggested education, confidence, the kind of person who refused to be a victim even when circumstances made victimhood inevitable.

The sound came from a building at the town's center—a two-story structure that had probably been the French administrator's residence back when Algeria was a colony. Stone walls, narrow windows, defensible position.

And absolutely crawling with fighters.

"That's where they are," Jean said, unnecessarily.

"That's where they want us to go," D'Arcy corrected. "It's a kill box."

He was right. The building was perfectly positioned—open ground on all approaches, elevated firing positions, multiple avenues for reinforcement. Anyone trying to assault it would be cut to pieces.

Anyone normal, anyway.

"Ideas?" Kort asked, because good leaders listened to their team even when time was critical.

"I have one," Hans said. "It's stupid."

"Most of our best ideas are stupid," Jean pointed out.

"Fair. Okay: we don't assault the building. We assault through it."

"Explain," Kort said.

"Look at the structure. Stone walls, yes. But old stone. Colonial construction, which means they used local materials. Soft limestone, mostly. Good for keeping heat out, bad for structural integrity under stress."

"You want to knock it down," D'Arcy said flatly.

"I want to *modify* the building. Create our own entrance. Bypass their kill zones entirely." Hans pointed to the western wall. "That section there—I can see the stress patterns, the way the stones are fitted. Hit it hard enough in the right spot, the whole wall comes down."

"And collapses on the hostages," Razo objected.

"Not if we're fast. We breach, we enter, we extract before the structure fails completely."

It was insane. Reckless. Exactly the kind of plan that would get normal soldiers killed.

Kort grinned. "Let's do it."

They repositioned, using the town's narrow streets for cover as they approached the western wall. Gunfire tracked them—the defenders had spotted their movement—but the enhancements made them fast enough to stay ahead of aimed fire.

Hans reached the wall first, placing his hands against the stone. Kort saw him shift his weight, saw the armor panels on his arms ripple and harden, saw him take a breath and then—

He punched the wall.

Not a casual punch. Not even a hard punch. A punch that drew on every enhancement Filibert had given him, that channeled modified musculature and reinforced bone structure and the kind of force that shouldn't be possible from a human frame.

The wall cracked. A spider web of fractures radiating from the impact point.

Hans punched again. And again. And again.

The stone began to crumble.

"Contact rear!" D'Arcy shouted, laying down suppressing fire as fighters tried to close on their position.

Hans kept punching, mechanical and relentless. The wall buckled. Started to fail.

One more hit.

The stone collapsed inward, tons of limestone crashing down, dust billowing out in a choking cloud. And before the dust could settle, before the defenders could react, Kort led his team through the breach.

Into chaos.

The interior of the building was a maze of rooms connected by narrow corridors. Fighters everywhere, some still reacting to the wall's collapse, others already bringing weapons to bear. Kort engaged the nearest threats on pure instinct, his submachine gun tracking and firing, dropping men before they could return fire.

Jean went left, clearing rooms with brutal efficiency. Hans went right, his enhanced strength turning furniture into weapons as he threw tables and chairs at defenders. D'Arcy and Razo pushed forward, following the sounds of distress toward wherever the hostages were being held.

Kort found himself in a long corridor, three fighters at the far end raising their rifles. Time dilated—the combat state taking full hold—and he saw their fingers tightening on triggers, saw muzzle flashes beginning to bloom.

He moved between the bullets.

His enhanced nervous system calculated trajectories, his body responded faster than thought, weaving through a storm of gunfire. His own weapon tracked and fired, tracked and fired.

All three fighters went down.

The combat state released him, and Kort stumbled, fighting nausea. Using the enhancements at full capacity always cost him, left him dizzy and disoriented for precious seconds.

Seconds that could be fatal.

Movement behind him. Kort spun, weapon up, finger on trigger—

And froze.

A young woman stood in a doorway, her left hand limp and swaying beside her body, her right hand fisted, knuckles grinding into her thigh, her face dirty and bruised but her eyes... her eyes were extraordinary. Green, piercing, intelligent. Looking at him not with fear but with scientific curiosity. He had no doubt she belonged to the defiant voice demanding mercy they had heard.

She was maybe nineteen, dark-complexioned, possibly Moroccan or Algerian. Her clothes—practical field gear, researcher's clothing—were torn and stained. But her bearing was unbroken. Unbowed.

"You're French?" she asked in French, her accent marking her as educated, cosmopolitan. She crossed her arms in front of her like a self-hug.

"French Foreign Legion," Kort replied automatically, unable to look away from those eyes.

"You move wrong," she said, tilting her head. "Too fast. Too precise. What are you?"

Before Kort could answer—before he could even process the question—gunfire erupted from the room behind her. She ducked instinctively, and Kort was moving, pulling her behind him, his body becoming a shield as rounds impacted his armor.

He returned fire blind, spraying the doorway with suppressing fire, then grabbed the woman's arm and pulled her down the corridor. "How many hostages?"

"Five plus me. Four are in the back room. The guards took Farah upstairs—I heard her screaming—"

"Jean!" Kort shouted into his radio. "Hostage on second floor! Female, being held separately!"

"On it!" Jean's voice came back, strained with combat.

Kort pushed the woman toward where D'Arcy and Razo were emerging with four of the six hostages—college students, terrified, stumbling in shock. "Get them out. Western breach point. Move!"

"What about you?" D'Arcy demanded.

"I'm going for the last one."

"Kort—"

"Move! That's an order!"

He didn't wait to see if D'Arcy obeyed. He was already heading for the stairs, taking them three at a time with enhanced leg strength. Behind him, the building groaned—Hans's breach had compromised structural integrity, and the whole edifice was starting to fail.

They had minutes. Maybe less.

The second floor was smoke and chaos. Hans had found the remaining defenders and was systematically dismantling them, his enhanced strength and armor making him effectively invincible at close range. Bodies littered the floor—fighters who'd made the mistake of trying to stop him.

"Where's Jean?" Kort shouted.

Hans pointed to a closed door at the end of the hallway. "In there. With at least three hostiles."

Kort reached the door just as it exploded outward, Jean tumbling through followed by gunfire. Kort grabbed his teammate, pulled him to cover, returned fire into the room.

"I'm fine," Jean gasped. "But the girl—they've got her at knifepoint—won't let me close—"

Damn it.

Kort moved to the doorway, assessing. The room beyond was large, probably the master bedroom when this had been an administrator's residence. Three fighters inside, one holding a young woman—the sixth hostage—from behind with one arm across her chest and the other hand hoovering a knife in front of her throat.

Standard hostage situation. Standard tactics said negotiate, wait for an opening, don't escalate.

Kort didn't have time for standard tactics.

He stepped into the room, hands empty, weapon slung. "Let her go."

The fighter with the knife laughed, said something in Kabyle that was probably profane. The other two raised their rifles, fingers on triggers.

Kort's enhanced hearing picked up the minute sounds boots shifting on the floor to ready positions, breathing patterns changing as the fighters prepared to fire.

The combat state activated, the imminent threat providing a fresh boost of adrenaline, forcing action whether Kort wanted it to or not.

Time dilated. The world became slow motion. Kort could see the exact moment when the fighters decided to shoot—could see muscles tensing, triggers being squeezed, firing pins beginning their descent.

He moved.

Fast. Faster than the human eye could track. His knife was in his hand though he couldn't remember drawing it, was across the room though he couldn't remember crossing the distance, was inside the reach of the man holding the hostage.

The knife slid up and exploited the space between the girl's throat and the inside of the fighter's wrist. Twist. Blade edge to inside wrist. Downward slash to the bone. Tendons severed. Radial arterial spray. The man's grip released involuntarily, and Kort grabbed the hostage, spun her behind him, his armor panels hardening as the other two fighters opened fire.

Bullets impacted. Kort felt them like punches, felt the armor absorb kinetic energy, felt one panel crack under repeated impacts. But nothing penetrated. Nothing reached his actual body.

He threw his knife. One fighter went down, the blade buried in his throat.

He closed with the second fighter before the man could adjust his aim, drove his palm into the fighter's face with enough force to snap his neck.

The man with the spaghetti wrist laceration was crawling away, screaming. Kort let him go. He'd bleed out in minutes.

The combat state released him, and Kort fell to one knee, fighting nausea and disorientation. Using the full capacity of the enhancements always cost him. The price was getting higher each time.

Jean appeared in the doorway. "Building's failing! We need to go now!"

Kort looked at the hostage—she was maybe twenty, local features, terrified but trying to be brave. "Can you run?"

She nodded, unable to speak.

"Then run."

They fled.

Through the collapsing building, past bodies and rubble, through smoke and dust. Hans had already extracted, was waiting at the breach point with the other hostages. D'Arcy and Razo provided covering fire as Kort, Jean, and the last hostage emerged into the morning sunlight.

Behind them, the building collapsed with a groan of tortured stone. A century of colonial architecture reduced to rubble in seconds.

"All hostages accounted for?" Kort asked, doing a quick count. Six students, all alive, all mobile if traumatized.

"Confirmed," D'Arcy said. "Now we just need to get out of a town full of fighters who want to kill us."

"Details," Jean muttered.

They moved, forming a protective box around the hostages. Kort took point, Hans rear guard, the others on flanks. Standard extraction formation, executed with super-human precision.

The fighters tried to stop them. Tried to cut them off, to pin them down, to overwhelm them with numbers. But the enhancements made the team too fast, too strong, too re-silient. They moved through opposition like ghosts, leaving a trail of bodies in their wake.

Two hundred meters from the town.

Four hundred meters.

Six hundred meters.

They were going to make it.

Then D'Arcy went down.

Not hit—something else. His legs just... failed. He col-lapsed mid-stride, convulsing, blood streaming from his nose and eyes. The enhancements breaking down under stress, the foreign materials in his body triggering immune responses that Filibert's suppressants couldn't fully control.

"D'Arcy!" Razo grabbed his teammate, trying to pull him up.

"Leave me," D'Arcy gasped. "Get the hostages out."

"Screw that." Razo threw D'Arcy over his shoulder in a fireman's carry, kept moving. The enhanced strength made it possible, but Kort could see the strain, could see Razo's own modifications starting to fail under the added stress.

One kilometer.

One and a half.

Hans started bleeding from his eyes. Jean's nose hemorrhaged. Kort felt his own systems beginning to shut down, the enhancements that had made them superhuman now turning against them as their bodies finally rebelled.

But they kept moving. Because they were Legion. Because they'd promised to get the hostages out. Because stopping meant dying, and none of them were ready to die yet.

At two kilometers from the town, they heard chopping.

At two point two kilometers, they saw it—the H-21 "Flying Banana" coming in fast and low.

At two point five kilometers, they collapsed.

All of them. Enhanced soldiers and rescued hostages, falling to the sand in a tangle of bodies and equipment and modifications that had finally, catastrophically failed.

Kort looked up at the blue Algerian sky, feeling his consciousness slipping away, and saw one face with perfect clarity.

Green eyes. Curious. Unafraid.

The young woman from the doorway, looking at him like he was something fascinating rather than monstrous.

"What are you?" she'd asked.

Kort didn't know anymore.

Then the medics were there, and the world went dark.

Sidi Bel Abbès - Four Days Later

Kort woke to find the green eyed woman sitting beside his hospital bed.

She'd cleaned up—the dirt gone and the bruises transitioning from bluish purple to greenish-yellow, her clothes replaced with a simple dress that suggested she'd been provided quarters somewhere on the base. But the eyes were the same. Intelligent. Curious. Looking at him with that same scientific fascination.

"Hello," she said in French when she saw him wake. "I'm Zahra. I wanted to thank you for saving my life."

"Just doing my job," Kort replied, his voice rough from disuse.

"No. You did more than that. You risked your life—risked your team's lives—to save strangers. That's not just a job. That's character."

Kort didn't know what to say to that. He'd been called many things in his life, but never characterized as having character.

"What are you?" Zahra asked, repeating the question from the battlefield. "What did they do to you?"

"What makes you think they did anything?"

"Because I'm studying marine biology. I study adaptation. And what you displayed wasn't human adaptation. It was something else. Something engineered."

Kort studied her, trying to decide how much to say. Operational security demanded silence. But something about those green eyes made him want to be honest.

"They made me better," he said finally. "Stronger. Faster. More resilient. Modified me at the cellular level to survive things that would kill normal soldiers."

"And the cost?"

"I'm not sure yet. The modifications work, but they're unstable. Every time we push too hard, our bodies try to reject them. Eventually..." He shrugged. "Eventually they'll probably kill us. But until then, we can save lives. So it's worth it."

Zahra was quiet for a long moment. "Who did this to you?"

"My brother. Dr. Filibert Austerlitz. He's a scientist. A genius. He believes humanity needs to evolve or we'll destroy ourselves."

"And you believe that?"

"I believe my brother is trying to do good. I believe the enhancements save lives. But I also believe there are costs we don't fully understand yet."

Zahra reached out, touched his arm where the translucent armor panels were visible beneath his hospital gown. Her fingers traced the material with scientific precision.

"It's beautiful," she said softly. "And terrible. And fascinating. Who designed the biointegration?"

"Mostly Filibert. But he's looking for help. For someone who understands marine biology, cellular adaptation, the way organisms evolve to survive hostile environments."

Their eyes met, and something passed between them. Understanding, maybe. Or recognition.

"Tell your brother," Zahra said, "that I'd like to meet him. I have some ideas about how to stabilize the integration. Make the modifications less likely to reject. You see, my bachelor's thesis is on the application of entrainment theory to marine adaptation."

"Hey, I'm just a simple military grunt; you'll have to break that down." Kort gave a wide grin. It hurt—his face was still healing from the mission—but he grinned anyway.

Zahra laughed a hypnotic laugh, tossing her hair lightly. She pointed to his eyes and corrected him. "I don't think so. I see you in there, *Monsieur*." She rolled her shoulders, still sore from the ordeal. "Entrainment theory is the phenomenon of how interacting physical, biological, or social systems synchronize their rhythms or cycles, leading to a shared, stable pattern.

The synchronization facilitates organisms to time their physiological and behavioral activities—very key to survival in marine life."

"I believe you," Kort nodded impressed. "You want to help?"

"You want to help?"

"I want to understand. And yes, if understanding can help save lives—can help save people like you—then I want to help."

Kort smiled. "I'll tell him."

Zahra stood to leave, then paused at the door. "By the way—what's your name? You saved my life, seems like I should at least know what to call you."

"Kort. Kort Sokolov."

"Russian," she observed. "In the French Foreign Legion. That must be a story."

"It is. Maybe I'll tell you sometime."

"I'd like that."

She left, and Kort lay back in his hospital bed, feeling something he hadn't felt in a long time.

Hope.

Not for himself—he'd accepted long ago that the enhancements would probably kill him eventually. But hope that maybe, just maybe, they could perfect the modifications. Make them safe. Create a future where soldiers didn't have to choose between being human and being able to survive.

Outside his room, he could hear voices. Filibert's, arguing with someone. Probably Command, trying to decide whether the mission had been a success or a catastrophic failure.

Kort closed his eyes and let the argument fade into background noise.

They'd saved six lives. That was success enough.

Everything else was just details.

The clock on the wall read half past one.

But that couldn't be right.

It was never half past one.

Kort closed his eyes and tried not to think about what that might mean.

Seven

The Weapon's Source

Filibert's Laboratory, Sidi Bel Abbès, Algeria – 1963

The desert night pressed against the laboratory windows like something living, patient, waiting for mistakes. Inside, fluorescent lights cast everything in stark whites and deep shadows—no gray areas, just binary distinctions between illumination and darkness.

Filibert Austerlitz stood before a makeshift workbench covered with equipment that would have looked more at home in a university physics department than a military medical facility. Copper coils wound around ceramic cores. Vacuum tubes glowing faintly orange. A modified Tesla transformer that hummed with building voltage, the sound rising and falling like mechanical breathing.

And beside all of it, connected by a tangle of wires and monitoring electrodes: Kort Sokolov's exposed forearm.

"The readings are stable," Iniko said from her position at the monitoring station. She was twenty-three, brilliant, already Filibert's most trusted research assistant despite her youth. Her English carried a Nigerian accent that she'd never bothered to soften. "Heart rate elevated but within parameters. Tissue response is minimal."

"Increase the field strength," Filibert instructed. "Point-five tesla increments."

"Filibert—"

"Do it."

The hum deepened. The air itself seemed to vibrate, charged particles aligning with invisible force lines. Kort's forearm twitched, muscles contracting involuntarily as induced currents flowed through his enhanced tissue.

"That's... uncomfortable," Kort said through clenched teeth.

"Pain?" Filibert didn't look up from his instruments.

"No. Like my arm is asleep but also on fire. Hard to explain."

"Your nervous system is adapting to the electromagnetic field. The bioelectric modifications I made six months ago—they're responding exactly as predicted." Filibert adjusted a dial, watching the oscilloscope trace change patterns. "The enhancement tissue generates significantly higher baseline electrical potential than normal muscle. When exposed to external fields, it amplifies the effect rather than dampening it."

"In Russian, brother."

"Your modified cells are like living capacitors. They store energy. Release it on demand." Filibert finally looked up, his eyes bright with the fever of discovery. "Do you understand what this means? The enhancements don't just make you stronger or faster. They make you a biological battery."

Kort flexed his fingers experimentally. Static discharge sparked between his fingertips—tiny lightning arcs that shouldn't be possible from human contact alone.

"How much energy are we talking about?"

"Right now? Enough to power a radio for several hours. Enough to disrupt nearby electronics." Filibert moved to a different instrument panel. "But that's baseline. With proper augmentation, with integrated storage and release mec hanisms..." He trailed off, doing calculations in his head.

"Enough for what?"

Filibert met his eyes. "Enough to kill."

The laboratory fell silent except for the transformer's hum and the quiet beeping of monitoring equipment.

Iniko spoke carefully. "Are you suggesting weaponizing the bioelectric field?"

"I'm suggesting that NATO is funding this research for military applications. Enhanced soldiers who can move faster, heal quicker, survive longer—yes, valuable. But enhanced soldiers who can project electromagnetic pulses? Who can disable enemy electronics? Who can deliver lethal voltage on contact?" Filibert returned to his workbench, hands moving with practiced precision. "That becomes a weapon system. That becomes something NATO will fight to keep."

"Or fight to terminate," Kort said quietly.

"Only if they understand what we're building." Filibert disconnected the electrodes from Kort's arm. "Which is why we keep the electromagnetic research separate. Why we document only the biological enhancements in the official reports. Why what I'm building here"—he gestured to the Tesla equipment—"never appears in any NATO file."

"Insurance," Iniko understood.

"Leverage." Filibert began winding copper wire around a new core, his movements mechanical, practiced. "If they try to shut us down, if they try to steal the research, I have something they can't replicate. Something they don't even know exists."

Kort rolled down his sleeve, covering the translucent bio-armor that now looked like ordinary skin in the low light. "You're planning for betrayal before it happens."

"I'm learning from history. Berlin taught me that good intentions don't matter when power is involved. That people will take everything from you and call it necessary." His fingers traced a small circle in the air—unconscious gesture, childhood habit. "I won't let that happen again."

The transformer's hum rose in pitch, then dropped. In the oscilloscope's green glow, electromagnetic waves danced in complex patterns that only Filibert could fully understand.

Part II: Escalation
Classified Test Site, 80km South of Sidi Bel Abbès - 1963

The rock face exploded.

Not from conventional explosives—from directed electromagnetic energy that superheated the stone's mineral content until structural cohesion failed catastrophically. One moment: solid granite. The next: a crater twenty meters across, edges glowing red-hot, air shimmering with waste heat.

Filibert lowered the targeting apparatus, his expression showing both satisfaction and concern. The weapon was crude—essentially a scaled-up version of his laboratory Tesla coil, mounted on a truck bed, requiring a diesel generator to power. But it worked.

"Energy output exceeded projections by thirty-two percent," Iniko reported from the instrumentation panel. "Beam coherence maintained for full 2.3-second duration.

Temperature at impact point reached approximately 1,400 degrees Celsius."

"Casualties would be catastrophic," Commandant Leroux said from his position behind the test line. He'd insisted on observing personally, despite—or perhaps because of—his deep misgivings about Filibert's work. "That kind of heat, that kind of energy release... it would liquify flesh. Boil blood. Turn a human being into vapor."

"Yes," Filibert agreed simply. He made notes in his journal, hands steady despite the implications of what he'd just demonstrated. "Though the range is currently limited. Atmospheric interference causes beam dispersal beyond 500 meters. And the power requirements are prohibitive—this unit consumed enough electricity to run a small village."

"Then what's the point?" Leroux lit a cigarette with hands that shook slightly. "You've built something that can't be deployed. Too large, too power-hungry, too limited in range."

"I've built proof of concept." Filibert closed his journal. "The physics work. The energy can be directed and focused. What remains is miniaturization and power source optimization."

"Which could take decades."

"Or months, with proper funding and resources." Filibert watched the smoke rising from the crater. "The biological enhancements—those are progressing faster than expected. Kort and the others are demonstrating capabilities that exceed even my optimistic projections. Jean completed a 40-kilometer forced march yesterday in full gear without showing fatigue. Hans's strength has increased forty percent. D'Arcy's reaction time is now below human cognitive processing limits."

"I've read your reports."

"Then you know that the real breakthrough isn't just making better soldiers. It's the integration of biological and technological systems." Filibert turned to face Leroux directly. "The enhanced tissue generates bioelectric energy far beyond normal human levels. With proper modification, with integrated capacitors and release mechanisms, each soldier could become his own power source. Could carry directed energy weapons powered by his own metabolism."

Leroux's cigarette stopped halfway to his mouth. "You want to turn my legionnaires into walking death rays."

"I want to keep them alive." Filibert's voice hardened. "You've seen the casualty reports from Indochina. From Korea. From every colonial conflict where superior numbers overwhelm superior training. Conventional soldiers die, Commandant. They die because human bodies are fragile and human weapons have limited ammunition and human endurance fails at exactly the moment when endurance matters most."

"And your solution is to make them less human?"

"My solution is to make them *survivable*." Filibert gestured to the smoking crater. "That weapon there—impressive but impractical. But imagine a handheld version. Imagine soldiers who can project electromagnetic pulses to disable enemy vehicles, who can defend themselves without reloading, who carry power sources that never run dry because they're fueled by the same enhanced metabolism that makes them stronger and faster."

"You're describing science fiction."

"I'm describing our research timeline for the next five years." Filibert picked up his equipment case. "The biological modifications are Phase One. Already functional, already successful. The electromagnetic augmentation is Phase Two. Currently in early testing. And Phase Three"—he paused—"Phase Three integrates everything. Creates soldiers who are self-sufficient weapon platforms."

Leroux dropped his cigarette, ground it out with his boot. "And if NATO decides they don't want Phase Three? If they terminate the program after Phase One?"

Filibert's smile was cold. "Then Phase Two and Three never appear in any official documentation. They remain my work. My leverage. My insurance policy against betrayal."

"You don't trust NATO."

"I don't trust anyone who holds power over my research." Filibert started walking back toward the transport vehicles. "Berlin taught me that. The Reich fell, the Allies came, and everyone who had power used it to take what they wanted. To control what they couldn't understand. To destroy what they couldn't control."

He stopped, looked back at the crater. "I won't be controlled again. I won't let anyone destroy what I'm building."

Leroux watched him go, then turned to Iniko. "Your assessment? Professional opinion, off the record."

She considered carefully. "Dr. Austerlitz is brilliant. Perhaps the most gifted theoretical physicist and biologist alive today. His integration of electromagnetic theory and cellular biology is genuinely revolutionary."

"But?"

"But he's also traumatized. Obsessive. Paranoid." She glanced toward Filibert's retreating figure. "He sees betrayal everywhere because he's experienced it. And he's preparing for war with people who haven't decided yet if they're his enemies."

"Self-fulfilling prophecy."

"Potentially." Iniko began shutting down the test equipment. "Or potentially justified paranoia. NATO has a history of terminating programs they consider too dangerous or too expensive. If they shut down the biological research, they'd never know about the electromagnetic work. Dr. Austerlitz would disappear with knowledge that could change warfare forever."

"And you think he'd do that? Just vanish with classified research?"

"I think he'd do whatever necessary to continue his work." Iniko secured the instruments. "Including things most people would consider unethical or illegal."

"Then we're all in danger."

"Yes, Commandant. I believe we are."

The crater continued smoking as the sun climbed higher, heat and light transforming the destroyed rock into a warning no one was quite ready to heed.

Part III: Convergence
Filibert's Private Workshop, Sidi Bel Abbès - 1963
Two in the morning. The hour when secrets felt safest, when the rest of the base slept and the only witnesses were shadows and the creatures in Filibert's aquarium tanks.

Kort sat shirtless on the examination table, his chest marked with surgical ink—precise lines mapping where Filibert intended to make incisions. The room smelled of antiseptic and ozone, that particular electric scent that came from high-voltage equipment running for extended periods.

"This is different from the other modifications," Kort observed.

"Yes." Filibert prepared the surgical instruments with ritualistic care. Each tool cleaned, aligned, positioned exactly where needed. "Previous enhancements were biological—modified muscle tissue, reinforced bone structure, enhanced nervous system. This is hybrid. Bio-technological integration at the cellular level."

"Meaning?"

"Meaning I'm going to embed micro-scale electromagnetic projectors directly into your modified tissue. Specifically, the palms of your hands." Filibert held up what looked like a small seed—metallic, barely five millimeters long. "These contain miniaturized Tesla coils, capacitors, and focusing arrays. Once integrated with your enhanced cells, they'll be powered by your own bioelectric field."

Kort examined the device. "What do they do?"

"They kill." Filibert's voice was clinical, detached. "When activated, they project focused electromagnetic pulses. Lethal range: approximately one meter. Effects: cardiac arrest, neural disruption, electromagnetic hemorrhaging. Death in under three seconds."

"And you want to put these inside me."

"I want to give you a weapon that can never be taken away. That requires no ammunition. That leaves no forensic evidence except catastrophic organ failure that appears natural." Filibert set down the device. "Your body generates enough bioelectric energy to power these implants continuously. You'll feel a slight warmth in your palms when they're active, nothing more."

"How do I control them?"

"Neural interface. I'll be modifying the nerve clusters in your hands—similar to the other enhancements, but more precise. You'll think about activating them, and they'll respond. Like flexing a muscle."

Kort was quiet for a long moment. "This is permanent."

"Yes."

"And you're not documenting this in the NATO reports."

"Correct."

"Why?"

Filibert moved to his aquarium, watched the lamprey eels circle in their tank—ancient predators whose basic design hadn't needed to change in millions of years. "Because NATO will eventually betray us. I don't know when. I don't know how. But they will. Someone with power will decide our research is too dangerous, too expensive, too controversial. They'll shut us down, steal the data, disappear the evidence."

"And when they do?"

"When they do, you'll have capabilities they don't know about. Weapons they can't detect or defend against." Filibert turned back to Kort. "I'm doing this for both of us. Giving you power that can't be stripped away. Giving myself insurance against those who would steal everything I've built."

"You're preparing for war."

"I'm preparing for survival." Filibert picked up the first implant. "Your enhancements make you strong, fast, resilient. But these"—he held up the device—"these make you *untouchable*. A weapon that walks like a man. A soldier who can complete missions impossible for normal humans."

Kort looked at the surgical marks on his chest, then at Filibert. "If I agree to this, there's no going back."

"There hasn't been 'going back' since you first volunteered. We crossed that line back at Columbia." Filibert's expression softened slightly. "But I need your consent. This changes you in ways that can't be undone. Makes you something that NATO, that humanity, isn't ready for. And Kort,"

Filibert added, changing his tone—serious and direct, "You mustn't use this on any of your missions. Not currently."

"Why not?"

"First, it may take some time for it to integrate safely without fully draining you. And secondly. it is too soon to expose this to the world. We can't risk inquiries."

Kort frowned. "A little late for that don't you think? I mean Leroux has seen the demos."

"Leroux?" Filibert chuckled. "Don't worry about Leroux. He hates NATO and other false global powers as much as I do. He is from the old times. He knows. He's felt the Boot. He will be there for us."

Kort nodded. He understood. "How many of these implants?"

"Four total. Two in each palm, positioned to provide optimal coverage. They'll integrate with your existing bio-armor, become part of your tissue structure within three weeks."

"And the others? Jean, Hans, D'Arcy, Razo?"

"They're not ready. Their enhancement integration is still unstable. Razo shows signs of early rejection. D'Arcy's nervous system hasn't fully adapted. Hans is strong but lacks fine motor control." Filibert shook his head. "You're the only one whose body has accepted the modifications completely. You're the template. The proof that this works."

"The guinea pig."

"The pioneer." Filibert prepared the anesthetic injection. "Every advancement requires someone willing to be first. Someone willing to risk everything for a future that doesn't yet exist."

Kort lay back on the table. "Do it."

"You're certain?"

"I've never been more certain of anything in my life." Kort closed his eyes. "We're building something that will save lives, Filibert. Something that will make soldiers like us strong enough that we don't have to watch our brothers die. If that requires becoming something more than human—fine. I've already crossed that line."

The surgery took four hours.

Filibert worked with the precision that came from years of study and the obsessive focus that came from childhood trauma. Each implant placed exactly where planned. Each connection to enhanced nerve tissue verified and secured. Each integration point monitored for complications.

Iniko assisted, though her expression showed concern that went beyond professional caution.

"These won't appear on any scans," she said quietly while Filibert worked. "Not X-ray, not MRI, not any conventional imaging."

"By design." Filibert connected the final neural interface. "The implants are bio-compatible at the atomic level. To medical equipment, they'll look like slightly denser bone tissue. To physical examination, they're undetectable."

"You're creating invisible weapons."

"I'm creating survival mechanisms." Filibert closed the final incision with surgical adhesive that would dissolve as the enhanced tissue healed. "Kort will carry these for the rest of his life. They'll be as much a part of him as his own bones."

"And he'll be able to kill with a touch."

"Yes." Filibert cleaned his instruments. "But more importantly, he'll be able to defend himself when conventional weapons fail. To complete missions others can't. To survive situations that would kill normal soldiers."

"You're playing God."

"I'm playing chess." Filibert covered Kort's unconscious form with a thermal blanket. "And I'm preparing for an opponent who doesn't yet know we're in the game."

The surgery was successful. The implants integrated. And Kort Sokolov became something that had never existed before—a human weapon system, carrying death in his hands, powered by his own enhanced biology. Though it would be several years to fully integrate and be functional—it would, in time, be functional and deadly.

NATO never knew.

And thirty years later, when Filibert needed him for dark deeds that the current Kort would never have agreed to, those implants would still be there. Still functional. Still lethal.

Still secret.

Part IV: Testament

Filibert's Laboratory - 1964

The test was simple.

A steel plate, ten millimeters thick, suspended between two stands. Kort positioned himself one meter away, his right hand raised, palm facing the target.

"Remember," Filibert instructed from behind his instruments, "the activation is purely neural. Think about heat, about energy projecting from your palm. Your enhanced nervous system will do the rest."

Kort concentrated. For a moment, nothing happened.

Then his palm grew warm. Not painfully—just a pleasant heat, like holding a mug of hot coffee. And the steel plate began to glow.

Red. Orange. Yellow. White.

The metal sagged, edges curling as molecular cohesion failed. Then suddenly—catastrophic structural failure. The plate collapsed into itself, edges liquifying, center section dropping to the floor in molten droplets.

Kort lowered his hand. The warmth faded.

"Impact temperature approximately 2,200 degrees Celsius," Iniko reported, her voice carefully neutral. "Duration: 1.8 seconds. Energy output... Jesus, Filibert. He just projected enough energy to vaporize a human skull."

"And he'll get more efficient with practice." Filibert made notes with the mechanical precision that meant he was deeply excited but refusing to show it. "The implants are drawing less than fifteen percent of his total bioelectric capacity. With training, he could maintain that projection for extended periods. Could target multiple threats in sequence without depleting his reserves."

"You've created an assassination weapon."

"I've created an enhancement." Filibert looked up from his notes. "This is no different than giving a soldier a rifle. It's a tool. How it's used determines morality, not the tool itself."

"A rifle can be taken away. This can't."

"Exactly." Filibert stood, approached Kort. "How do you feel?"

"Normal." Kort flexed his fingers. "Maybe slightly fatigued, like I'd been exercising. But nothing dramatic."

"Good. That confirms the power draw is sustainable." Filibert examined Kort's palm—perfectly normal in appearance, no visible scarring or modification. "The integration is complete. For all practical purposes, you're now carrying a directed energy weapon that will function for as long as your enhanced biology remains viable."

"Which is how long?"

"Unknown. Outside of you, the other enhancement subjects are only a couple of years into the program. But theoretically—if the modifications remain stable, if your immune system continues accepting the hybrid tissue—decades. Possibly indefinitely."

Kort stared at his hand. "I can kill with a touch."

"Yes. And at some distance to be determined."

"Without a weapon. Without ammunition. Without leaving evidence."

"The electromagnetic pulses would be detectable with specialized equipment immediately after use. But within minutes, no trace remains. To autopsy, it would appear as massive organ failure—heart attack, stroke, neural trauma. All technically accurate but without obvious external cause."

"The perfect murder."

Filibert was quiet for a moment. "That's not the intended application. This is for mission completion when conventional weapons aren't viable. For self-defense when you're disarmed. For scenarios where enhanced physical capabilities aren't enough."

"But it could be used for assassination."

"Any weapon can be used for assassination. A knife. A garrote. A pillow over someone's face." Filibert returned to his workbench. "I'm not creating murderers. I'm creating soldiers with enhanced survivability."

"You're creating something the world isn't ready for."

Filibert closed his eyes methodically, his hands curled into loose fists, thumbs rubbing the index fingers in slow circles. He exhaled through teeth set for stability. "Kort. You are my brother—my partner in this monumental endeavor."

His eyelids rose and he set his measured gaze on Kort. "And yet, you increasingly have been questioning and, dare I say, cross-examining me, putting me and my work, our work, Kort, on trial. Even Iniko is adapting this stance!"

Kort stood stoic, calculating how to navigate this development.

Filibert softened and managed a smile with eyes sad. "I have indulged, but now I need to know your intentions, your commitment."

Kort soften has well and nodded his head, the tension of the moment draining and the years of camaraderie welling up. Kort said, "Forgive me, brother. I am with you, fully, as fully as when we first started. Please don't mistake my skepticism as suspicion or uncertainty about you or this important work. I admit, I cannot grasp the full vision. But, you taught me to be skeptical and have scientific curiosity, if you remember?"

Filibert smiled now with his eyes and said, "Indeed, indeed I did."

Kort continued, "There's something more you should know. These changes, whatever I am becoming, are difficult for my mind. I feel less human and that frightens me. Funny, eh? I easily run into a hail of gunfire, but I fear the weakening of my humanity most of all. What happens when Kort is gone?"

The smile left Filibert's eyes and the sadness returned. "It is not my intention for you to disappear into the modifications. If you will keep me informed of these mental alterations, I promise I, and the whole team, will work to keep you—you."

Kort nodded.

Filibert added, "Please, brother, continue your healthy skepticism. I see now its importance for you and for the work."

The two men stood silently. After all the years between them, they did not know how to end the moment and move to safer ground.

Filibert found the way out by acting like the moment hadn't just occurred. "The world is never ready for advancement. But it comes anyway." Filibert began preparing equipment for the next test. "In 1945, humanity wasn't ready for atomic weapons. We created them anyway. In 1960, we weren't ready for biological enhancement. We began research anyway. You and I. Progress doesn't wait for philosophical comfort, Kort. It waits only for people willing to push boundaries."

"And the consequences?"

"Are manageable." Filibert met his eyes. "As long as we control the research. As long as NATO doesn't steal it and deploy it without ethical oversight. As long as we maintain leverage."

"This is your insurance policy."

"Yes. When they inevitably try to shut us down—when Mathias Sørensen or someone like him decides this research is too dangerous—I'll have something they can't take. Knowledge they can't replicate. Capabilities that exist only in you."

"And if they torture it out of me?"

"Then you use these." Filibert gestured to Kort's hands. "You defend yourself. You escape. You come find me, and we continue the work elsewhere."

"You really think NATO will betray us?"

"I *know* they will." Filibert's voice carried absolute certainty. "Because that's what institutions do when they're afraid. They destroy what they can't control. They steal what they can. They protect themselves at the cost of everything else."

He picked up another steel plate, positioned it for the next test. "Berlin taught me that. When the Russians came, they took everything. When the Americans came, they took what the Russians missed. Then the British and the French joined in the plunder and divided my Germany between all four allied occupying powers, they took control itself. Everyone with power used it to strip away what others had built."

"And you won't let that happen again."

"Never." The word came out like a vow. "I'll burn every laboratory, destroy every file, disappear completely before I let NATO steal my research. Before I let them turn my work into weapons without conscience or oversight."

"Then we're conspirators."

"We're brothers." Filibert smiled slightly. "And brothers protect each other. Even from institutions that claim to act in their best interests."

The next test went smoothly. And the one after that. By the end of the session, Kort could activate and control the implants with thought alone—precision that would make him deadly at close range, surgical in application, impossible to defend against without specialized equipment.

And NATO would never know these implants existed.

Not now in 1964. Not in 1990 when Filibert broke his promise to Kort. Not even in 2005 when Filibert finally lost his own humanity in madness and betrayed the core foundations of his vision.

Filibert had planned for betrayal before it happened.

Had created insurance before he needed it.

Had turned his only successful test subject into a walking weapon system that could complete missions decades in the future.

And when those missions came—when Filibert finally decided to take revenge on the people who'd stolen everything from him—Kort would be ready.

Would be armed.

Would be exactly what Filibert had always intended him to be.

A soldier who could never be disarmed.

A weapon that could never be taken away.

A promise of vengeance that would wait years fulfill.

The clock on the wall showed half past one.

It was actually three in the afternoon.

But in Filibert's mind, time had stopped that day in Berlin.

And everything since—every experiment, every enhancement, every calculation toward inevitable revenge—was just the long, patient march back to that frozen moment when he'd learned that power was the only thing that mattered.

When he'd decided to become powerful enough that no one could ever take anything from him again.

Even if it took a lifetime.

Even if it cost him everything.

Even if it meant creating monsters.

Eight

Casualties of Science

Sidi Bel Abbès – Five Years Later, 1969

The letter arrived on a Tuesday morning, delivered by a nervous corporal who clearly didn't want to be the bearer of bad news. He knew from the return address and state of the envelope that it continued unpleasantries. Kort sat in his small quarters—barely more than a cell, really, but private in a way barracks could never be—and stared at the envelope without opening it.

He knew what it would say. He'd known for months, watching his brothers-in-arms deteriorate one by one. The modifications that had made them superhuman were killing them. Slowly. Inexorably. Like a promise that had curdled into a curse.

The letter was from a hospital in Paris. The handwriting on the envelope was shaky, barely legible. Razo's handwriting.

Kort finally opened it, though his hands—enhanced hands, modified hands, hands that could punch through walls and crush rifles like tin cans—trembled.

Mon frère,

The doctors say I have maybe two months. The cancer is everywhere now—lungs, liver, bone marrow. They're surprised I lasted this long. I'm not. We were always too stubborn to die on schedule.

D'Arcy passed three years ago, as you know. Peaceful, they said, though I don't know how peaceful it can be when your own body turns against you. Hans is in the bed next to mine. We joke that we're having one last mission together, except the enemy is inside us and we can't shoot it.

Jean refuses treatment. Says he'd rather die on his feet than waste away in a hospital. Stupid bastard. Brave, but stupid. I tried to talk sense into him, but you know Jean—once he makes up his mind, a tank couldn't change it.

I'm writing to say goodbye, Kort. And to tell you what the doctors told me. You're different. Your genetic structure accepts the modifications in ways ours never did. While we're rotting from the inside, you're still strong. Still whole. Still the superman Filibert promised we'd all become.

I don't know if that's a blessing or a curse. Maybe both.

Tell Filibert I don't blame him. We volunteered. We knew the risks, even if we didn't fully understand them. We saved lives. That counts for something.

Tell Zahra to keep working. Maybe she can perfect what Filibert started. Maybe the next generation of enhanced soldiers won't die like rats in a laboratory.

And tell yourself—tell yourself every day—that we were brothers. Not by blood, but by choice. And that means something. That will always mean something.

Au revoir, mon ami. March or die, right? We're still marching. Just in a different direction now.

Razo

Kort read the letter three times, each word cutting deeper than any blade ever had. Then he folded it carefully, placed it in the small wooden box where he kept the few things that mattered—a photograph from the orphanage, his Legion Képi Blanc brass pin presented upon basic graduation, a pressed flower that Zahra had given him on their wedding day.

The box of a life reduced to fragments.

He sat on the edge of his narrow bed and allowed himself something he rarely permitted: memory.

Six years ago, when they executed that first mission, they'd been invincible. Five enhanced soldiers who could do the impossible, who'd completed nineteen missions with zero casualties, who'd rescued hostages and eliminated threats and proven that Filibert's vision wasn't madness but genius.

Then the symptoms started.

D'Arcy first. He'd complained of headaches, of seeing things that weren't there. The neural enhancements that had made him brilliant in combat were misfiring, creating hallucinations, phantom threats. He'd started sleeping with his rifle, convinced enemies were everywhere. Eventually, they'd had to sedate him, send him back to France for treatment.

The diagnosis came back like a death sentence: glioblastoma. Brain cancer, aggressive and inoperable. The neural modifications had triggered cellular mutations that replicated out of control.

Six months later, he was dead.

Then Hans started showing symptoms and functional problems. The big German who'd been able to punch through walls started losing weight, his enhanced musculature wasting away despite eating twice what a normal man required. The doctors diagnosed it as a form of aggressive muscular dystrophy—the modified muscle tissue was breaking down faster than his body could repair it.

Naturally robust, from good stock, Hans held on until the process accelerated. He grew weaker each day, until he couldn't stand without assistance. The man who'd carried wounded soldiers across miles of desert now laying in a hospital bed barely able to lift his own arms.

Jean's cancer was in his bones. The reinforced skeletal structure that had made him nearly unbreakable was riddled with tumors, his marrow producing malignant cells at an exponential rate. He'd refused treatment, as Razo said, choosing to spend his final months in Paris rather than a hospital bed.

The last Kort heard, Jean was still walking the streets of his childhood, visiting old haunts, saying goodbye to a city that had never really been his home but was the closest thing he had.

And Razo—young, optimistic Razo who'd believed Filibert's promises about a better future—was dying in a hospital bed in Paris, his organs systematically failing as the enhancements that had saved his life a dozen times over finally extracted their price.

Four men dead or dying.

One man inexplicably surviving.

Kort stood, walked to the small mirror hanging on the wall, and studied his reflection. Thirty years old, but he looked younger than his peers as if the last six years hadn't touched him. The modifications had slowed his aging, kept him strong and vital while his brothers withered.

Why?

That was the question that haunted him. Why was he different? Why did his body accept what theirs rejected? What genetic quirk or cosmic accident had made him the one who survived? The technology wasn't advanced enough for a blood test to unlock all the variables and allow a perfect candidate selection. He was still one in three billion—a freak at the tail end of the curve.

Filibert had theories. Always theories. Something about Kort's Russian ancestry, about genetic markers that predisposed him to accepting cellular modifications. Something about his childhood trauma creating psychological resilience that translated to physiological adaptation.

Theories. Hypotheses. Scientific speculation that couldn't change the fundamental truth: his brothers were dying, and he was watching it happen, powerless to stop it.

A knock at the door interrupted his spiral of guilt and grief.

"Come in," Kort said, his voice flat.

The door opened, revealing Zahra. She was twenty-four now, no longer the frightened hostage he'd rescued five years ago but a brilliant marine biologist who'd become Filibert's research partner—and Kort's wife. Her green eyes, which had fascinated him from that first moment, were filled with concern.

"You got Razo's letter," she said. Not a question.

"Yes."

"I'm sorry, Kort."

"Are you?" The words came out harsher than he'd intended. "Sorry that the experiment failed? Sorry that the modifications you and Filibert have been perfecting killed four of my brothers?"

Zahra flinched but didn't look away. "I'm sorry that men I care about are dying. I'm sorry that the work we're doing came too late to save them. And I'm sorry that you're hurting. Don't conflate those things."

Kort turned away from her, from the compassion in her eyes that he didn't deserve. "I should have said no. When Filibert first proposed the modifications, I should have refused. Should have told him to find other test subjects. Should have—"

"Should have what? Let terrorists continue killing Legion patrols? Let hostages die in the desert? Let Filibert's research remain theoretical forever?" Zahra moved to stand beside him, her reflection joining his in the mirror. "You made a choice, Kort. They all made choices. Informed consent, signed documents, full disclosure of risks."

"Full disclosure?" Kort laughed bitterly. "We were soldiers, Zahra. We signed papers we barely understood, written in technical language about cellular integration and neural enhancement and adaptive armor. We knew there were risks, but we didn't know the risks meant slow, agonizing death."

"No one knew that. Not Filibert, not me, not the NATO oversight committee. The modifications should have been stable. By every model, every simulation, every test—they should have integrated without rejection."

"But they didn't. And now one man is dead and three are dying."

Zahra was quiet for a moment, then: "Five years ago, you saved my life. You and your team. You pulled six hostages out of certain death, risked everything to save strangers. Do you regret that?"

"Of course not."

"Then don't regret the modifications that made that rescue possible. Don't dishonor your brothers by treating their sacrifice like a mistake." Her hand found his, squeezed.

"They were soldiers. Soldiers die. The only question that matters is what their deaths meant. And they meant everything. Every hostage you saved, every mission you completed, every life you protected—those mean something."

Kort wanted to believe her. Wanted to accept that there was purpose in the tragedy, meaning in the loss. But all he could see were the faces of his brothers, young and vital in his memory, contrasted with the wasting bodies they'd become.

"I need to see them," he said suddenly. "Razo, Hans, and Jean. I need to go to Paris."

"I'll arrange it. We can leave tomorrow."

"Not we. Me. I need to do this alone."

Zahra studied him for a long moment, then nodded. "Okay. But Kort? When you get back, we need to talk. About the future. About what comes next."

"What do you mean?"

"I mean Filibert is planning something. Something big. He won't tell me the details, but he's been working obsessively on new modifications. Better integration, stronger enhancements, removal of the cancer risk." She paused. "He wants to start again. Create a new team. And I think he wants you to lead it."

Kort felt something cold settle in his chest. "No."

"You don't even know what he's proposing."

"I don't need to know. I watched four of my brothers die from Filibert's genius. I'm not going to lead more men to the same fate."

"The new modifications are different. We've isolated the genetic markers that made you compatible. We can screen potential candidates, eliminate anyone whose biology would reject the enhancements. The success rate should be—"

"*Should be*," Kort interrupted. "That's what he said last time. 'Should be stable. Should integrate cleanly. Should revolutionize warfare.' And now four men are paying—have paid the price."

"And how many people are alive because of those four men? How many hostages rescued? How many terrorists neutralized? How many Legion soldiers saved because your team could do what they couldn't?" Zahra's voice was rising, passion overriding her usual scientific detachment. "I'm not saying their deaths don't matter. I'm saying their deaths had purpose. And throwing away everything they achieved—everything we learned—would make their sacrifice meaningless."

Kort pulled his hand from hers, needing distance. "I need to think. And I need to see my brothers before—" His voice caught. "Before it's too late."

Zahra nodded, understanding. "I'll make the arrangements."

She left, closing the door softly behind her. Kort stood alone in his small room, surrounded by the accumulated detritus of a life spent in service to something he'd once believed in completely.

Now he wasn't sure what he believed.

He picked up Razo's letter, read it again. *Tell yourself—tell yourself every day—that we were brothers. Not by blood, but by choice.*

Brothers by choice.

That had meant something once. Maybe it still did.

Kort placed the letter in his wooden box, closed the lid, and began to pack for Paris.

Paris - Three Days Later

The Hôpital de la Pitié-Salpêtrière was one of the oldest hospitals in Europe, its origins stretching back to the 17th century. Kort found it grimly appropriate that men dying from the most advanced biomedical modifications ever created were doing so in a building that had witnessed centuries of human suffering.

The oncology ward was on the fourth floor, a long corridor of private rooms where the wealthy and connected came to die with dignity. Razo and Hans had been placed in adjacent rooms—whether by coincidence or by someone understanding they'd want to be close, Kort didn't know.

He stopped outside Razo's room, suddenly unsure. What did you say to a brother who was dying? What comfort could you offer when you were the one who'd survive, the one who'd walk away whole while they rotted in the ground?

The door opened before he could decide. A nurse—middle-aged, efficient, her eyes kind but clinical—stepped out.

"You're Kort Sokolov?" she asked in French.

"Yes."

"He's been asking for you. Every day. 'Is Kort coming? When will Kort come?'" She touched his arm gently. "Be prepared. He doesn't look like you remember."

That was an understatement.

The man in the hospital bed was barely recognizable as the young Dutchman who'd jumped out of airplanes and cleared buildings—a soldier's solider. Razo had always been lean, built like a runner, but now he was skeletal. His skin was gray, stretched too tight over bones that seemed to press outward as if trying to escape. Medical equipment surrounded him—monitors tracking failing systems, IV lines delivering morphine and fluids, oxygen tubes feeding lungs that couldn't properly extract oxygen from air anymore.

But his eyes—those were still Razo's eyes. Young. Bright. Refusing to accept what his body was telling him.

"Kort," Razo said, his voice barely above a whisper. "You came. I wasn't sure you would."

Kort crossed to the bed, pulled up a chair. "Of course I came. We're brothers."

"Brothers." Razo smiled, and it was like watching a skull grin. "By choice, not by blood. I wrote that, didn't I? In my letter?"

"You did."

"Good. Good. I was worried I'd forgotten. The morphine makes everything... fuzzy sometimes. But I wanted you to know. Wanted you to remember." He coughed, a wet, rattling sound that spoke of lungs filling with fluid. "Hans is next door. He's worse than me, if you can believe it. At least I can still talk. He can barely whisper."

"I'll see him after."

"Good. He'd like that. He doesn't say it—you know Hans, stubborn German pride—but he's scared. We all are, I think. Scared of what comes next. If there's anything next."

Kort didn't know what to say to that. He'd never been particularly religious. The orphanage had tried to instill faith in them, but Kort had seen too much suffering to believe in a benevolent God. And the modifications had made him feel even further from human spirituality—if you could modify the body so completely, what did that say about the soul?

"Do you blame him?" Razo asked suddenly. "Filibert? For this?"

"I don't know," Kort answered honestly. "Part of me does. Part of me thinks he used us, turned us into experimental subjects without fully understanding the consequences. But another part..."

"Another part knows we volunteered. Knew the risks. Signed the papers." Razo nodded weakly. "I've been thinking about that. Lying here with nothing to do but think. And I've decided—" He coughed again, harder, and Kort reached for the water cup on the bedside table, helped him drink. "I've decided I'd do it again. Even knowing how it ends. We saved people, Kort. We did things no one else could do. That matters. That has to matter."

"It does matter. You mattered. You all mattered."

"Past tense already?" Razo's smile was sad. "I'm not dead yet, brother. Though I suppose it's close enough. The doctors say maybe a week. Maybe two if I'm unlucky. The pain medication keeps me comfortable, but eventually my organs will just... stop. One by one, like lights going out in a building."

The image was vivid, terrible. Kort felt his throat tighten.

"I'm sorry," he said, inadequate but all he had.

"Don't be. We were Legion. *Legio Patria Nostra.* We knew what we signed up for." Razo's eyes drifted closed, his breathing shallow. "Will you do something for me?"

"Anything."

"When Filibert starts the new program—and he will start a new program, I know him—will you make sure the next team knows what they're getting into? Really knows? Not just papers to sign but the truth. That the modifications might kill them. That the enhancements come with a price."

"I will."

"Good. Good." Razo's hand found Kort's, squeezed with what little strength remained. "And Kort? Don't blame yourself. You survived because your body accepted what ours rejected. That's not your fault. That's just... biology. Genetics. The random lottery of existence."

"It doesn't feel random. It feels like I'm being punished."

"For what? For living?" Razo opened his eyes again, and they were sharp, focused. "Listen to me, brother. Guilt is a useless emotion. It doesn't change anything. It doesn't bring us back. It just makes you suffer for no reason. So don't do it. Don't waste your survival on guilt. Use it. Live enough for all of us. Love your wife. Help Filibert perfect the modifications. Make sure our deaths meant something by making sure the next generation doesn't die the same way."

Kort nodded, not trusting his voice.

They sat in silence for a while, Razo drifting in and out of consciousness, Kort simply being present. Eventually, a nurse came to check vitals, and Kort took that as his cue to leave.

"I'll visit again tomorrow," he said.

"I'd like that." Razo's eyes were already closing. "And Kort? Tell Hans I'm still beating him. I'm going to last longer. Tell him... tell him I said he's soft."

Despite everything, Kort smiled. "I'll tell him."

Hans's room was identical to Razo's—same equipment, same clinical smell, same sense of impending finality. But Hans's deterioration was different. Where Razo had wasted away, Hans looked bloated, swollen, his body retaining fluid as his kidneys failed. His face was puffy, almost unrecogniz-able, his breathing labored even with the oxygen.

A priest sat beside the bed, reading from a Bible in German. Hans's eyes were closed, but Kort could tell he wasn't asleep—his jaw was tight, his hands clenched, fighting pain that medication could only barely touch.

The priest looked up as Kort entered, marked his place, stood, and continuing in German said, "You're Kort? He's been waiting for you." He switched to French. "I'll give you privacy. But I'll be in the chapel if he needs me."

After the priest left, Kort pulled up the chair, studied his friend's ravaged face. "Hans?"

"Kort." Hans's voice was barely audible, each word an effort. "Took... long enough."

"Had to arrange leave. You know how Command is."

"Bastards." Hans tried to smile, failed. "Razo... next door. Bet he told you... he's going to outlast me."

"He did."

"Bastard. Always... competitive." Hans's breathing was becoming more labored. "Doctor says... maybe days. Kidneys... shutting down. Liver. Everything... turning off."

"I'm sorry, brother."

"Don't be. We were... Legion. We knew... what we signed up for." He paused, gathering strength. "That's... a lie. We didn't know. Not really. But we... should have guessed. Nothing good... comes free."

Kort leaned forward. "Hans, if you could go back—knowing what you know now—would you still volunteer?"

Hans was quiet for so long that Kort thought he'd lost consciousness. Then: "Yes. Because of... what we accomplished. And because... of the alternative."

"Alternative?"

"Being nothing. Being nobody. Just another... legionnaire. Just another... soldier. Instead... we were something. Something new. Something that... changed the world. Even if the world... doesn't know it yet." He coughed, a horrible wet sound. "You survived. Why?"

"I don't know."

"Genetics. Has to be. Something in your... Russian blood. Something that made you... compatible." Hans's eyes opened, found Kort's. "Filibert will want... to study you. Figure out why. Use it to... make better modifications."

"I know."

"Let him. Don't refuse... out of guilt. Out of anger. Let him learn... from our failures. Make sure... the next team... doesn't die like us."

"That's what Razo said."

"Smart man. Always was." Hans tried to shift position, grimaced in pain. "There's something... I need to tell you. About the missions."

"What about them?"

"They were... tests. All of them. Filibert knew. He was... experimenting. Pushing us... to see how far... the modifications could go. How much stress... we could handle. He needed... the data."

Kort felt something cold settle in his chest. "You knew? You knew and you didn't tell me?"

"We all knew. Jean figured it out... after the third mission. D'Arcy confirmed it... did a midnight recon and broke into Filibert's files. We discussed it. Decided... to continue anyway."

"Why?"

"Because we trusted you. And you trusted... Filibert. And because... the missions were real. The hostages... were real. Even if Filibert... was using us... we were still... saving lives." Hans's breathing was becoming more irregular. "Don't hate him. He's doing... what scientists do. Pushing boundaries. Seeking knowledge. The problem isn't... his methods. The problem is... our biology. We weren't... compatible enough."

"But I am."

"Yes. Which means... you carry the torch. You lead... the next team. You make sure... what we started... continues. Promise me."

Kort wanted to refuse. Wanted to tell Hans that he was done with Filibert's experiments, done with being a modified soldier, done with watching brothers die for the advancement of science.

But looking at Hans—dying Hans, who'd punched through walls and stormed into the thick of any fight and believed that their sacrifice meant something—he couldn't.

"I promise."

"Good." Hans's eyes closed. "Now get out. I need... to sleep. And you need... to visit Jean. He's in... some café in Montmartre. Being dramatic. Tell him... we're waiting for him. Tell him... not to take too long."

Kort stood, started toward the door.

"Kort?"

He turned back.

"Thank you. For being... our brother. For leading us. For surviving." Hans's voice was fading. "Make it... worth it. Make our deaths... worth something."

"I will."

He left Hans to his priest and his prayers and his slow descent into darkness.

Kort found Jean in a café on the Rue Lepic, sitting at an outdoor table despite the chill autumn air, a glass of wine in front of him and a cigarette burning between his fingers. He looked almost healthy compared to Razo and Hans—still thin, still obviously ill, but mobile, alert, defiant.

"Kort." Jean gestured to the empty chair across from him. "I wondered when you'd track me down."

"Not hard. You always said if you came back to Paris, you'd be on this street."

"Did I? I don't remember. But it sounds like something I'd say." Jean took a drag on his cigarette, winced at the pain it caused. "The doctors are very upset with me. They say I should be in hospital, accepting treatment, making myself comfortable for the end. But comfort is overrated. I'd rather spend my last days here, watching life happen, than in a sterile room watching monitors measure my decline."

"How long do you have?"

"Weeks. Maybe a month if I'm unlucky. The tumors are in my spine now, pressing on nerves, causing all sorts of interesting pain. But morphine is wonderful, and wine is better, and watching pretty women walk by is better still. So I'm managing."

Kort signaled the waiter, ordered wine for himself. They sat in silence for a moment, two enhanced soldiers—one dying, one thriving—watching Paris go about its evening.

"I saw Razo and Hans," Kort said finally.

"How bad?"

"Bad. Days, maybe. A week at most."

Jean nodded, unsurprised. "I should visit. Say goodbye properly. But I'm a coward, it turns out. I don't want to see what I'm going to become. I'd rather remember them as they were. Strong. Capable. Alive."

"They asked about you. Said you should hurry up and die so they're not waiting around."

Jean laughed, then coughed, then laughed again. "Bastards. Always competitive. Fine. I'll try to die faster. For them."

The wine arrived. They toasted silently, drank.

"Do you blame Filibert?" Kort asked.

"For killing us?" Jean considered. "No. We volunteered. We knew there were risks. Maybe we didn't understand the specific risks, but we understood the general principle: experimental modifications might have side effects, and those side effects might be fatal. So no, I don't blame him." He paused. "But I do think he should have been more honest. Should have told us he was pushing us deliberately, testing our limits, using our missions as opportunities to gather data. We deserved that honesty."

"Hans said you all knew."

"Suspected. But never had proof. Well, D'Arcy did break into Filibert's files, but was that proof of anything? You know Filibert thinks on a whole different level—different universe. D'Arcy could only guess at what he was reading. But, still, by the third or fourth mission, it became obvious. The scenarios were too perfect, too controlled. We were being tested." Jean shrugged. "But like Hans probably told you, the missions were still real. The lives we saved were still real. So we made peace with being experimental subjects."

"I didn't know."

"We didn't tell you because you'd have confronted Filibert. Demanded explanations. Maybe refused to continue. And we needed you to continue, Kort. You were our leader. Our anchor. If you'd lost faith in the program, we all would have. And then what? All those hostages we saved would be dead. All those terrorists we eliminated would still be operating. All that good we did would be undone."

Kort felt anger rising—anger at being deceived, at being managed, at being kept in the dark while his brothers made decisions about their own deaths.

"You should have told me."

"Maybe. Probably. But we didn't, and now here we are. Me dying in a café, you living with guilt you don't deserve, and Filibert somewhere planning his next generation of modifications." Jean stubbed out his cigarette, immediately lit another. "The question isn't whether we made the right choice then. The question is what you're going to do now."

"I don't know."

"Well, figure it out. Because Razo and Hans and D'Arcy and I—we're the prototype. We're the failures that teach Filibert what doesn't work. But you? You're the success. You're the proof that the concept is valid, that humans can be enhanced and survive the enhancement. You're the future, Kort. Whether you want to be or not."

"I don't want to be."

"Too bad. History doesn't care what you want. It only cares what you do." Jean finished his wine, poured another glass from the bottle. "Here's what I think you should do: help Filibert perfect the modifications. Make sure the next generation doesn't die like us. Lead the new team, teach them what we learned, give them the benefit of our experience and our failures. And when it's all done, when the enhancements are stable and safe and everything Filibert promised they'd be—then you can rest. Then you can grieve. Then you can let go of the guilt."

"And if I can't? If I can't watch another team go through what we went through?"

"Then our deaths mean nothing. Then we died for a failed experiment that gets buried in classified files and forgotten. Is that what you want?"

"No."

"Then you know what you have to do."

They sat in silence as the sun set over Paris, painting the sky in shades of orange and purple. Around them, life continued—people laughing, arguing, falling in love, planning futures. Oblivious to the fact that two modified humans sat among them, one dying, one surviving, both carrying the weight of choices made in the service of science.

Eventually, Jean stood—slowly, carefully, his body betraying him even as his spirit remained unbroken. "I need to go. There's a woman I knew once, back before the Legion. I want to see if she's still here, still alive, still remembers me. Probably foolish, but I'm dying. I'm entitled to foolishness."

"Jean—"

"Don't." Jean held up a hand. "Don't say goodbye. Don't make it maudlin. We're brothers. Brothers don't need goodbyes." He put money on the table for the wine. "Just promise me you'll do what needs to be done. Promise me you'll make our deaths matter."

"I promise."

"Good enough."

Jean walked away, disappearing into the Parisian evening. Kort watched him go, knowing he'd never see his brother alive again.

He sat alone at the café table as night fell, thinking about promises made and promises kept, about brothers who'd died for science and the one brother who'd survived.

Somewhere in Algeria, Filibert was working in his laboratory, perfecting modifications, planning the next generation of enhanced soldiers.

Somewhere in that same compound, Zahra was conducting her own research, trying to understand why Kort's biology accepted what others rejected.

And here in Paris, three men were dying because they'd believed in a vision of superhuman soldiers who could save lives and end conflicts and make the world safer.

Maybe that vision was worth dying for.

Maybe Kort owed it to his brothers to make sure their deaths advanced that vision rather than ending it.

Or maybe he was just rationalizing, trying to find meaning in senseless tragedy, trying to convince himself that watching his brothers die had some purpose beyond advancing scientific knowledge.

The waiter approached. "Another glass, Monsieur?"

Kort looked at his empty glass, thought about his dying brothers, about his wife waiting in Algeria, about Filibert and his promises of a better tomorrow built on today's corpses.

"No," he said finally. "I'm done here."

He left money on the table and walked into the Parisian night, carrying the weight of promises he wasn't sure he could keep, haunted by ghosts who weren't quite dead yet but soon would be.

Behind him, the clock on the church tower struck half past one. But that couldn't be right. It was never half past one.

Kort walked faster, trying to outrun the sound of bells that shouldn't be chiming, that never chimed at that hour, that existed only in his mind and in Filibert's obsession with a moment frozen in time.

The moment before everything fell apart. The moment they were all trying, in their different ways, to return to or to prevent. The moment that defined everything that came after.

Half past one.

Nine

The Betrayal

Filibert's Laboratory, Sidi Bel Abbès, Algeria – 1970

The laboratory was dying.

Not suddenly—nothing in bureaucracy ever happened suddenly. But piece by piece, day by day, Filibert could feel it slipping away. The equipment requisitions that went unanswered. The supply deliveries that arrived incomplete. The budget reviews that stretched from days to weeks to months without resolution.

And now this. The telegram sat on Filibert's desk, its words precisely typed in the emotionless language of institutional termination:

> PROJECT 19.5 DISCONTINUED EFFECTIVE IMMEDIATELY. RESEARCH DIRECTOR DR. F. AUSTERLITZ REASSIGNMENT PENDING. ALL DOCUMENTATION AND MATERIALS TO BE INVENTORIED AND TRANSFERRED TO NATO CENTRAL COMMAND. REPRESENTATIVE ARRIVING 14 APRIL FOR OVERSIGHT. MATHIAS SØRENSEN, DIRECTOR, NATO RESEARCH AND DEVELOPMENT DIVISION.

Filibert had read it seventeen times. The words didn't change.

He stood at the window of his laboratory, watching the Algerian dusk turn the sky blood-red. The compound was quieter than usual—news of the project's termination had spread quickly. Soldiers avoided looking at him. Officers gave him wide berth. Even Commandant Leroux had been notably absent for the past forty-eight hours.

Behind him, the laboratory hummed with life that would soon be silenced. Aquarium pumps circulated water through tanks of lamprey eels, octopi, electric rays—the specimens that had provided biological templates for the enhancement protocols. Monitor screens displayed vital signs from subjects in various stages of recovery. And in the corner, covered with a white sheet, the preserved tissue samples of D'Arcy, Hans, Razo, and Jean. A painful reminder of his greatest failures.

The door opened without warning—Iniko rushed in breathless. "Doctor, I couldn't stop..."

Filibert looked past her as a man strode into the lab, his face beamed arrogance. Filibert reached out and touched Iniko's elbow. "It is okay, Iniko. I have been expecting him. Please tend to the matters I assigned."

Iniko nodded with understanding and obedience and left, but not before giving the intruder a burning glare.

"Dr. Austerlitz." The voice was calm, professional, utterly devoid of warmth. "I'm Mathias Sørensen."

Filibert finally turned.

The man in the doorway was thirty-two, Norwegian, wearing a perfectly tailored suit that looked absurd in the dusty, equipment-crowded laboratory. Sandy hair. Blue eyes that assessed everything with the clinical detachment of someone trained to evaluate value and liability. He carried a leather briefcase and wore an expression of polite neutrality that somehow felt more threatening than open hostility.

"You're early," Filibert said. His German accent had thickened—it always did when he was stressed. "Telegram said fourteenth."

"I arrived ahead of schedule. I find that efficiency in these matters minimizes... complications." Mathias stepped further into the lab, his eyes scanning the equipment with interest that bordered on hunger. "You've accomplished quite a lot with limited resources."

"Limited resources that are now being withdrawn."

"Yes. Regrettable, but necessary." Mathias set his briefcase on the nearest workbench, opened it with practiced precision. Inside: forms, inventories, official documentation bearing NATO's highest security classifications. "The mortality rate for your enhancement program is unacceptable. Four subjects deceased. Cause of death: systemic rejection of modification protocols, aggressive cancers, organ failure. The remaining subject—" He consulted his papers. "—Sokolov, Kort. Russian-born, naturalized American citizen. His long-term viability remains unconfirmed."

"His enhancements are stable. Fully integrated. He represents proof that the technology works."

"He represents an unacceptable risk." Mathias pulled out a pen, began making notations on the inventory forms. "One success out of five attempts is an eighty percent failure rate. That's not research, Dr. Austerlitz. That's carnage with a theoretical justification."

"Those men volunteered. They understood the risks."

"And yet they still died." Mathias's tone remained carefully neutral. "NATO cannot continue funding research with such catastrophic human costs. The program is being terminated, as you know. Your documentation and materials will be transferred to our central archives. You will be reassigned to a position more suited to your... particular expertise."

Something in the way he said it—the slight pause, the careful emphasis—made Filibert's stomach tighten.

"What position?"

"That hasn't been determined yet. But your work here is finished." Mathias moved to the aquarium tanks, observed the lamprey eels with what looked like genuine fascination. "Remarkable creatures. I was briefed on your research notes on their regenerative capabilities. I'm told the neurochemistry work is particularly impressive."

"Then you understand why terminating the program is premature. We're on the verge of significant breakthroughs. Another year, perhaps two, and we could solve the rejection problem entirely."

"Perhaps. Or perhaps another year would produce four more bodies and continued failure." Mathias turned from the tanks. "NATO has reviewed your work comprehensively, Dr. Austerlitz. The biological science is sound. The theoretical framework is brilliant. But the practical applications are too dangerous, too unpredictable. Too likely to produce weapons we can't control."

"Weapons?" Filibert's voice hardened. "I'm creating enhanced soldiers. Men who can survive injuries that would kill normal troops. Who can complete missions impossible for conventional forces. How is that weaponization?"

"Because you're transforming human beings into something post-human. Something that exists outside normal military command structures, normal legal frameworks, normal ethical boundaries." Mathias's expression didn't change, but his voice carried a note of finality. "Project 19.5 is over. Your cooperation in the transition would be appreciated. Your resistance would be... noted."

The threat was unspoken but clear.

Filibert looked at his laboratory—eight years of work. Eight years of research, modification, failure, and painful incremental progress. Eight years of trying to prove that human enhancement wasn't just possible but necessary. That the future of warfare required soldiers who were more than merely human.

And now this bureaucrat—this Norwegian administrator who'd never spent a day in combat, never watched men die because human bodies were too fragile for the demands placed on them—was terminating everything.

"I need to brief my team," Filibert said finally. "The remaining enhanced subject requires ongoing monitoring. The deactivation protocols are complex—"

"Already handled." Mathias returned to his briefcase, pulled out another document. "Subject Sokolov will be transferred to NATO medical oversight. We have specialists who can manage his care."

"Specialists who don't understand the enhancement integration. Who weren't there when—"

"Dr. Austerlitz." Mathias's voice remained calm but carried steel underneath. "Your authority over this program ended the moment I arrived. You can cooperate in the transition and maintain some dignity. Or you can resist and be removed from the premises by military security. Your choice."

The room felt suddenly smaller, the walls closing in.

"When?"

"The transfer team arrives tomorrow morning. By noon, all materials will be crated and ready for transport. You'll have tonight to organize your personal effects." Mathias began packing his briefcase. "I'd recommend you use the time wisely. Nostalgia serves no one."

He walked to the door, then paused. "One more thing. Your electromagnetic research—the Tesla coil experiments you've been conducting separately from the biological work. Those are also being discontinued. All equipment and documentation will be included in the transfer."

Filibert felt ice spread through his chest. The electromagnetic work wasn't in any official reports. Wasn't in any documentation Mathias should have access to. Which meant—

"You've been monitoring me."

"We monitor all NATO research programs, Dr. Austerlitz. Especially ones that show potential for... expansion beyond their stated parameters." Mathias's expression revealed nothing. "Your work on directed energy projection has impressed our physicists. Theoretical, of course. Not practical. But impressive nonetheless. NATO appreciates thoroughness."

"You're stealing everything."

"We're securing NATO assets. There's a difference." Mathias opened the door. "Enjoy your last evening in the laboratory, Doctor. Tomorrow it becomes part of history."

He left without waiting for a response.

Filibert stood alone in the laboratory he'd built, surrounded by eight years of research that would be gone in twelve hours. Around him, the aquarium pumps hummed. The monitors beeped. The tissue samples waited under their white sheet.

And in the distance, through the window, Filibert could see Mathias walking across the compound toward the administration building. His posture confident. His stride purposeful.

The walk of a man who'd just acquired something valuable.

Part II: The Last Night
Filibert's Laboratory – 1970, 2:47 AM

Kort found Filibert exactly where he knew he'd be—sitting on the floor beside the deceased subjects' tissue samples, surrounded by scattered papers, a bottle of whiskey two-thirds empty beside him.

"The guards let you through," Filibert said without looking up. His voice was thick, slurred slightly. Not drunk exactly, but definitely not sober.

"The guards think I'm on authorized patrol." Kort lowered himself to the floor beside his friend—his brother in everything but blood. "I heard about the termination."

"Of course you did. Everyone's heard. The great experiment ends. The mad German scientist gets shut down. Very tidy. Very bureaucratic." Filibert took another drink directly from the bottle. "They're taking everything, Kort. Every specimen. Every note. Every piece of equipment. The tissue samples. Your medical files. Eight years of work, gone by noon."

"Your work. Not gone. They can take the equipment, but they can't take what you know. What we've learned."

"Can't they?" Filibert finally looked at Kort, and his eyes were red-rimmed, haunted. "That man—Mathias—he knows about the electromagnetic research. The Tesla experiments. Work I've kept completely off the books. Which means NATO's been watching me. Reading my private notes. Monitoring everything."

"Then we assumed correctly. You prepared for this."

"I prepared for the possibility of betrayal. I didn't prepare for how it would feel." Filibert gestured to the laboratory around them. "This is my life, Kort. This is what I built from nothing. From the rubble of Berlin and the nightmares of watching my mother die and the certainty that I could prevent it from happening to anyone else. And tomorrow a bureaucrat is going to box it up and ship it away like it's surplus equipment."

Kort was quiet for a moment. Then: "The guys would have understood."

"Would they have?" Filibert looked at the white sheet covering the preserved tissues. "I killed them, Kort. My first team of test subjects. Those brave men. The modifications failed and I watched them deteriorate, begging me to stop the pain, but I couldn't save them. I was too much of a coward to actually be there when they died."

"You tried—"

"I failed. And now they're taking even that. Even their remains. Even the proof that they existed, that they volunteered, that they believed in what we were doing." Filibert's hands clenched. "Mathias is stealing our dead comrades!"

The words hung in the air, stark and terrible.

"Then we don't let him."

Filibert looked up sharply. "What?"

"You said you prepared for betrayal. You have contingencies. Backups. Hidden research." Kort's voice was steady, certain. "We don't let NATO take everything. We give them enough to satisfy the inventory. But the important things—the breakthrough research, the enhancement protocols that actually work, the electromagnetic integration data—those we keep."

"They'll know. Mathias will notice—"

"Mathias will get exactly what his forms say he should get. Standard documentation. Basic research files. Equipment inventories that match his lists perfectly." Kort stood, offered his hand to pull Filibert up.

"What he won't get is eight years of actual understanding. The failures we learned from. The modifications that worked. The integration sequences that made me"—he gestured to himself—"possible."

"You're talking about doctoring the files. Hiding research from NATO oversight."

"I'm talking about keeping promises." Kort pulled Filibert to his feet. "You promised them you'd make their deaths matter. That you'd continue the work until you got it right. That promise doesn't end because some bureaucrat files termination papers."

Filibert swayed slightly, then steadied himself. "They're transferring you to NATO medical oversight. Taking you away from here."

"I belong to the Legion. They have no love for NATO. Remember you told me? Leroux hates NATO. He will be there for us. He will deny NATO access to me and if that becomes a problem—he will aid in my disappearance if needed." Kort met his eyes. "I meant what I said before. I won't abandon you. We'll show them. We'll prove the work has value."

"You'd throw away your military career—"

"My military career ended the moment you injected me with enhancement protocols. I stopped being a normal soldier then. I became something else. Something that only you understand." Kort moved to the storage cabinets, began pulling out Filibert's personal research journals—the ones never meant for official reports. "Besides, I'm Russian. Germans and Russians understand betrayal. We've been doing it to each other for centuries. Now it's NATO's turn to learn what happens when they steal from people who have nothing left to lose."

The heaviness of the conversation, of the shared history of betrayals, and of the struggle to evolve nature, pushed down on them. And the loss, the unbearable weight of loss—so much death.

Filibert attempted to steer the moment from the crushing darkness. He asked, "How's Zahra—did she get out all right?"

"What?" Kort responded, not prepared for the shift, but welcoming it.

"Zahar—you know, your wife? Supposed to have been on that 0600 flight to the States yesterday?"

"Was it only yesterday?" Kort sighed. "Seems like a lifetime ago."

Filibert shook his head. "I don't know how you two will keep it together across such vast amounts of time and distance. Don't you have two years left on your enlistment?"

Kort nodded. "Roger that."

"Never understood the need for that type of companionship anyways."

Kort chuckled. "You did look perplexed at the wedding, such as it was."

"Yeah," Filibert said.

Kort said, "She'll do great—Columbia snatched her up as soon as she applied for a position."

"Columbia," Filibert snorted, recalling his expulsion. "Second-rate diploma mill."

Shaking his head with a smile, Kort added, "And don't worry about us—R-H-I-P don't you know? Rank-has-its-privileges. I'll get plenty of authorized and *unauthorized* RR there or I'll sneak her here. We'll be fine."

Filibert smiled. "That's good, that's good."

They worked through the night.

By dawn, they'd created two sets of documentation. One set—official, complete, exactly matching NATO's inventory requirements—would be handed over to Mathias. The other set—containing the real breakthroughs, the actual enhancement protocols, the electromagnetic integration data, the team's complete genetic sequencing—was carefully packed into three waterproof containers that Kort would smuggle out before the transfer team arrived.

Filibert watched the sunrise through the laboratory window, feeling something shift in his chest. Hurt. Anger. A burning need for vindication that felt like touching an exposed electrical wire.

"I'm going to continue the work," he said quietly. "Somewhere they can't reach. Somewhere I can finish what we started."

"I know."

"And when I've perfected it—when I've created enhancement protocols that work reliably, sustainably, without killing the subjects—I'm going to make Mathias regret what he did today."

"I know that too." Kort placed a hand on his shoulder. "Just tell me when and where. I'll be there."

"You're certain?"

"I swore to you I wouldn't abandon you. That still stands." Kort's grip tightened. "Brothers. Until the end."

"Until the end."

At 8:47 AM, the NATO transfer team arrived.

Part III: The Theft
Filibert's Laboratory – 1970, 9:15 AM

Mathias Sørensen arrived with military precision and bureaucratic efficiency.

Six NATO security personnel. Four technical specialists. Two physicians who would oversee Kort's transfer. All carrying clipboards, inventory sheets, transport authorization forms.

All moving through Filibert's laboratory like locusts, methodically stripping it of eight years of accumulated research.

Filibert stood to the side, watching. Saying nothing. His face carefully neutral, showing none of the rage burning in his chest.

"Dr. Austerlitz." Mathias approached with his clipboard, making check marks as his team worked. "Your cooperation is appreciated. This is proceeding smoothly."

"You have what you came for."

"Indeed." Mathias gestured to a NATO security officer, who began carefully packing the tissue samples into a specialized transport container. "Everything is being preserved properly. Your research will be archived with full security protocols."

"Archived. Locked away. Forgotten."

"Protected." Mathias made another notation. "From those who might misuse it. You should consider yourself fortunate, Doctor. Many researchers in your position face criminal charges. NATO is being generous."

"Generous." Filibert's voice was flat. "You're stealing eight years of work and calling it generosity."

"We're securing dangerous research that produced an eighty percent mortality rate. That's called responsible oversight." Mathias moved to the aquarium tanks, where technicians were already draining water, preparing the specimens for transport. "These will continue to be studied. Your protocols will be reviewed by appropriate specialists. The work doesn't end—it simply moves to more suitable venues."

"Venues you control."

"Yes." Mathias didn't pretend otherwise. "NATO research programs require NATO oversight. Surely you understand this."

Filibert watched a technician carefully net one of his lamprey eels, transfer it to a transport tank. Seven months he'd spent studying that particular specimen. Mapping its neural pathways. Understanding how its regenerative capabilities could be adapted to human tissue. And now some NATO technician who didn't know a lamprey from a leech was handling it like it was cargo.

"My personal effects," Filibert said. "I was told I could remove those."

"Of course. Nothing classified, naturally." Mathias gestured to a small stack of boxes near the door.

"Your team already packed them. Two boxes of personal items, pre-cleared by security. You're welcome to inspect them before transport."

Filibert moved to the boxes, made a show of checking their contents. Civilian clothes. A few books. Personal journals—the declassified ones, carefully sanitized of anything truly valuable. The real research was already gone, smuggled out by Kort at 0400 hours, hidden in three locations across Algeria that only the two of them knew about.

"Everything in order?" Mathias asked.

"Yes."

"Excellent." Mathias consulted his forms again. "Subject Sokolov will be prepared for medical transfer and transported to our facility in Oslo for ongoing monitoring. You won't need to concern yourself with his care any longer."

"He requires specific protocols. The enhancement integration is stable but sensitive—"

"Our physicians have reviewed your files. They're quite competent, I assure you." Mathias's tone suggested the conversation was over. "Your concern for your test subject is noted, but ultimately unnecessary."

"He's not a test subject. He's—"

"He's NATO property now. Like everything else in this laboratory." Mathias closed his inventory clipboard with a decisive snap. "Including the research that created him."

The words were carefully chosen. Deliberately provocative. Mathias was testing him, seeing if Filibert would react, would reveal something that might indicate hidden materials or undocumented research.

Filibert forced his expression to remain neutral. Showed nothing.

"If you're quite finished," he said coldly, "I'd like to be gone before noon."

"Of course. Just one final matter." Mathias gestured to his security team, who'd been working their way methodically through the laboratory. "We're doing a comprehensive inventory. Standard procedure. It will take another hour, perhaps two."

"I've given you everything."

"I'm sure you have. But thoroughness is essential in these matters." Mathias smiled—polite, professional, utterly without warmth. "You understand, I'm certain. After all, you strike me as someone who appreciates attention to detail."

The senior NATO physician entered the room looking unsettled. "*Herr Sørensen*," he said speaking in Norwegian under the false belief Filibert wouldn't understand.

Mathias spoke in Norwegian as well, making the same error. "*Ja, hva er det, doktor?*"

The doctor looked about the room and said, "We could not find the Sokolov subject. We talked to Commandant Leroux and he told us Sokolov had been deployed to a classified location—a 'hot spot' of communism, he said."

Mathias glared, jaw clenched so tight his grinding molars were audible. He looked at Filibert.

Filbert maintained a visage of not understanding.

Mathias returned his attention to the physician. He managed a tight, steady tone. "Then return to Commandant Leroux and use your NATO authority and get Sokolov back."

"I did," the physician replied, the anxiety mounting in his demeanor. "I asserted my NATO authority, and he just chuckled and now—"

"And now?" Mathias's impatience had peaked. "And now—what?"

The physician steadied himself, and said, "And now there is a phone call for you from... *Monsieur Pompidou*. The President of France."

How Mathias managed to neither explode nor implode was a tribute to his breeding and experience. "I know who he is."

Filibert piped up as if only understating one term, "*Monsieur Pompidou*?"

Mathias ignored him, addressing the team in French. "Finish up—I'll return." Then to the NATO physician, "Come with me." And left.

The team finished the inventory by noon.

Filibert stood outside the laboratory he'd built—now stripped bare, reduced to empty benches and disconnected equipment—and watched NATO personnel load the last transport truck. The tissue samples. His aquarium specimens. Eight years of documented research that represented perhaps thirty percent of what he'd actually discovered.

The other seventy percent was gone. Hidden. Waiting for him to reclaim it.

Mathias approached for the final time, carrying his completed inventory forms. His composure regained. Everything neat. Everything accounted for. Everything perfectly documented.

"Your reassignment orders will arrive within thirty days," Mathias said. "You'll be contacted with details. In the meantime, you're on administrative leave. Full pay, naturally. NATO values your contributions, Doctor."

"My contributions that you're stealing."

"Securing." Mathias extended his hand for a formal good-bye. "There is a difference, Dr. Austerlitz. I wish you would recognize it."

Filibert didn't take the offered hand. "You said yesterday that your scientists read my research notes. That they found my work impressive."

"They did. Your biological integration protocols are groundbreaking. The electromagnetic research shows remarkable theoretical insight."

"Then you understand what you're destroying."

"I understand what I'm protecting." Mathias lowered his hand. "From well-meaning but reckless researchers who don't appreciate the implications of what they're creating. Who don't consider what happens when enhanced soldiers become enhanced weapons. When the line between human and post-human is erased."

"The line is already erasing. War is becoming more deadly. More technological. Soldiers need to evolve or they'll become obsolete."

"Perhaps. But that evolution needs proper oversight. Ethical boundaries. Control mechanisms." Mathias turned to leave, then paused. "One more thing. Your friend—Sokolov—won't be coming with us. Commandant Leroux assures me there is a deactivation protocol that will be followed?" Mathias lowered his brow—the warning made clear.

"There is. And it will," Filibert lied.

Mathias nodded. We will still study him from the record and samples. We've already found some... irregularities in his medical files. Discrepancies between reported enhancement protocols and his actual capabilities."

Filibert's chest tightened. "What kind of discrepancies?"

"The details aren't important. What matters is that you've been less than forthcoming about the full extent of his modifications." Mathias's eyes were sharp, assessing. "We'll discover what you've hidden eventually. We have his tissue samples. His genetic profile. Given enough time and analysis, we'll understand exactly what you did to him. And even you must know he can't hide in the Legion forever."

"He volunteered for everything. Every modification, every protocol—"

"I'm sure he did. That doesn't change the fact that you've created something outside documented parameters. Something you deliberately concealed from oversight." Mathias's expression hardened slightly. "Did you really think NATO wouldn't notice?"

"I think NATO is more concerned with control than with science. More interested in power than in progress."

"And you, Dr. Austerlitz? What are you interested in?"

"Keeping promises. To my brother. To the men who volunteered for my research. To everyone who believed that human enhancement could save lives rather than just end them."

"Noble sentiments from a man whose research has an eighty percent mortality rate." Mathias started walking toward his vehicle, then stopped one final time. Turned back. And smiled.

Not polite. Not professional. A genuine smile that showed teeth and triumph and the absolute certainty that he'd won. That he had something up his sleeve and closing in on checkmate.

"Enjoy your administrative leave, Doctor. We'll be in touch."

He drove away in a NATO sedan, leaving Filibert standing alone in the North African sun, watching the dust settle on an empty laboratory and a terminated career and eight years of work that had just been boxed up and stolen by a bureaucrat who'd smiled at him like he was a problem finally solved.

Filibert stood there for five minutes.

Then ten.

Then he walked back into the building, into his stripped laboratory, and stood in the center of the empty room where he'd tried to change the world.

On the wall, a clock showed 12:32 PM.

But in his mind, in the place where trauma lived forever, it was always half past one. The moment before everything fell apart. The moment before the soldiers came and his mother died and his world ended.

He'd spent his entire adult life trying to prevent that moment from happening to anyone else. Trying to create soldiers strong enough, resilient enough, enhanced enough to survive anything.

And NATO had just stolen it all. Had smiled while doing it. Had made it clear they considered him a reckless fool who needed to be contained. And had the audacity to think he was their asset. Reassigned? A delusion of truly psychotic portion!

And then Mathias Sørensen had smiled.

That smile would haunt Filibert for twenty years. Would fuel decades of obsession, of hidden research, of careful planning toward a revenge that would make Mathias understand what he'd taken. What he'd destroyed.

What he'd stolen with his bureaucratic efficiency and his ethical concerns and that smile that said "I've won and there's nothing you can do about it."

But Mathias was wrong.

Because Filibert still had the real research. Still had Kort, enhanced and stable and loyal. Still had the team's genetic data, carefully copied before NATO took the physical samples. Still had twenty years ahead of him to perfect the work. To prove that enhancement wasn't just possible but necessary.

And when he was ready—when he'd built a weapon system that would terrify even NATO—he would come for Mathias Sørensen.

Would make him watch as everything he'd built with Filibert's stolen research came crumbling down.

Would make him understand that betrayal had consequences.

That theft had a price.

That some people, when pushed far enough, would spend decades plotting revenge.

The clock on the wall ticked forward. 12:33 PM.

But in Filibert's mind, frozen in the trauma of a six-year-old boy watching his world end, it would always be half past one.

Always.

Forever.

Until he could make the clock move again by resetting someone else's world to zero.

By destroying Mathias Sørensen the way Mathias had destroyed him.

The betrayal was complete.

The war had begun.

It would take twenty years to reach its conclusion.

But Filibert was patient.

And Mathias would learn that some people never forgave.

Never forgot.

Never stopped plotting revenge.

Ten

A Dormant State

The Hidden Years 1970–1990

Filibert Austerlitz arrived in New York with three water-proof containers, a false identity, and enough money to disappear for exactly six months.

The containers held everything NATO hadn't stolen: The team's complete genetic sequencing, the real enhancement protocols, the electromagnetic integration data that explained how Kort's body could power weapons from his own bioelectric field. Research that would have terrified Mathias Sørensen if he'd known it existed.

But Mathias didn't know. And that was the point.

Filibert rented a basement apartment in the Bronx under the name "Dr. Friedrich Dreyfus," paid six months in advance, and began the work of resurrection. Not his own—he had excommunicated himself and would never fall under bureaucratic oversight again. Rather, the work of resurrecting the project from the ashes, from the lessons taught to him by Jean, Hans, D'Arcy, and Razo. The men whose modifications had failed, whose deaths NATO had dismissed as acceptable losses.

Their deaths would matter. Filibert would make them matter.

By day, he worked as a visiting researcher at Stony Brook University in Long Island in the marine biology department—legitimate credentials under a false name, connections arranged through underground academic networks, questions no one asked because genius was always in demand. This also allowed him to avoid Columbia where he had been expelled and where he knew Zahra now worked. He tolerated the three-hour subway ride each way to lower his profile. By night, he refined the enhancement protocols, correcting the errors that had killed four men, perfecting the integration sequences that had saved one.

Kort was still in Algeria. Still officially a Legionnaire. Still pretending the modifications had been deactivated as ordered. They communicated through coded letters, through dead drops arranged across three continents, through a network of trust built in war and sealed with the blood of D'Arcy, Razo, Hans, and Jean.

Hold position, Filibert's letters said. *Maintain cover. Wait.*

And Kort waited. Because brothers kept promises. Because the mission wasn't over. Because somewhere in the Algerian desert, four men had died believing their deaths would advance something important.

Filibert would prove them right.

Part II: Foundation (1971-1975)

Abandoned Steel Mill, Rural Pennsylvania - 1971

The facility cost $47,000—money Filibert had earned through three years of careful fraud, embezzlement disguised as research grants, patents sold under false names.

Money that built a laboratory in the ruins of American industry.

The steel mill had closed in 1962, a victim of foreign competition and economic collapse. Local authorities were happy to sell it to "De Novo Industrial Properties"—a shell company with clean paperwork and no questions asked. The building was structurally sound despite its appearance. The power infrastructure was intact. The isolation was perfect.

Filibert spent six months converting it. Legitimate construction crews for the obvious work—roof repairs, electrical upgrades, basic maintenance. Then he did the rest himself, working through nights and weekends, building laboratories behind locked doors, installing equipment purchased through academic channels, creating a facility that didn't officially exist.

By December 1971, it was operational. State-of-the-art research capabilities hidden in industrial decay. A place where work that couldn't happen legally could happen secretly.

And it was there, in that converted steel mill, that Filibert began perfecting what NATO had stolen.

And in his Pennsylvania laboratory, Filibert studied the tissue samples of the deceased soldiers, analyzed the progression of their cancers, searched desperately for the variable that separated Kort's survival from their failure.

He found it in Razo's final blood sample. He had woken from a feverous dream after 36 hours of exhausting work. Waking with a start, all the pieces that had formed in his unconscious during a deep slumber, fell neatly into place.

It was the pace of modification. They'd all been enhanced simultaneously, their modifications administered over the same six-month period in 1962. Their bodies had accepted the changes initially—but over time, the enhancements had destabilized. Accumulated mutations. Corrupted cellular replication until cancer became inevitable.

Kort was different. His first modifications had come earlier in Filibert's work at Columbia, before the NATO Project 19.5. His body had adapted gradually; achieved cellular equilibrium before the next enhancement layer was added. The difference was measured in months. But those months had meant survival versus death.

Filibert stared at the data until dawn with new eyes, a liberated mind, understanding finally crystallizing. The modifications worked. They just needed time. Patience. Gradual integration rather than rapid enhancement.

He could save people. Could create stable enhancements. Could perfect the protocols.

He just needed test subjects.

And time—precious time to get it right.

Algeria - November 1972

Kort's enlistment ended at midnight.

Ten years in the French Foreign Legion.

Ten years of service that officially never involved experimental modifications or enhanced capabilities.

He walked out of the compound at 0100 hours with a discharge certificate, a handshake from Commandant Leroux, and modifications that were supposed to be deactivated but weren't.

He felt relief, though not surprised, that NATO forces weren't there to whisk him away. Then—a little disappointed. In just two years, he apparently had transitioned from a top priority to inconsequential. He remembered Filibert's instructions to not let his guard down—*they will hide in plain sight; they will be watching*—he had said. And Kort would counter by *living* in plain sight.

The dusty bus to the airport squealed to a bumpy stop. The door hissed open and Zahra stepped off the bus cool and confident, but the grin on her face betrayed her unbearable excitement. Kort's eyes lit up at the sight of her and that was all it took for her restraint to vanish, and she ran headlong into his arms.

By 0330 hours, they were on a plane to New York. And after agonizing hours in public view, they finally landed, pushed through customs, and made their way to the apartment Zahra had been renting. They scrambled to the bed and collapsed exhausted from jet lag.

"Welcome home," Zahra whispered in his ear with a nibble on his neck.

And in her arms, Kort—for the first time in years—felt like he was home.

A week later, he was standing in Filibert's laboratory, looking at what one year of hidden research had yielded, understanding for the first time what his brother had built while the world thought him harmless.

Part III: Building (1980-1990)
West Nyack, New York - 1980

Kort and Zahra bought a house in West Nyack, trading in eight years of city life for a normal suburban life for a couple who were anything but normal. The house on Hillside Avenue was everything Kort had promised Zahra it would be. Colonial style, three bedrooms, a yard large enough for the garden she'd always wanted, close enough to Columbia that her commute was manageable, but far enough that they felt like they'd escaped the city.

They would build a life here for ten years. Never imagining what tragedy lay ahead—or just not wanting to acknowledge the signs piling up in those ten years.

The home took shape to reflect their unique personalities in those years. The bathroom had been Zahra's design—spacious, modern, with a large walk-in shower and a stained-glass window Kort had commissioned as an anniversary gift. The window was shaped like a clock face, the colored glass depicting stylized ocean waves. Zahra laughed when she first saw it, understanding the private joke: Kort's acquired obsession with time merged with her lifelong passion for marine biology.

She'd never asked why all the clocks in their house were set to different times, never questioned why Kort sometimes seemed fixated on 1:30. She knew Filibert, after all, and the influence he had on Kort. An influence she felt weary about. She knew Kort had assimilated Filibert's fixation on time—especially historical time and undoing historical atrocities. She'd also never pushed when he grew distant talking about his Legion days or Project 19.5. Some questions she'd learned were better left unasked. This was *their* time and the past had no place in it.

Kort flew down to Virginia several times a month to teach tactical training at Quantico, consulted for private military contractors, and ran weekend warrior courses that kept him physically sharp and financially stable. Zahra continued her research and teaching as a tenured faculty at Columbia, publishing papers on octopus regeneration and other marine anomalies that put her top of her field.

To their neighbors, they were the perfect couple. Young, successful, mysterious in that appealing way that suggested interesting pasts rather than dangerous secrets.

Filibert knew the truth. That Kort spent three days a week at the Pennsylvania facility, testing new enhancement protocols, allowing Filibert and Iniko to refine the modifications that kept him alive. That Zahra's octopus research was secretly funded by money Filibert embezzled from NATO through the creative accounting of Filibert's professional enabler Felix—a contact deep in NATO. That their marriage was built on a foundation of science that grew more dangerous every year.

But they were happy. For a while. In the way people can be happy when they've decided which truths to acknowledge and which to ignore.

NATO Joint Warfare Centre, Norway - 1980

Felix established first contact on a Tuesday.

The memo was simple: Research funding irregularities in Project 19.5. Minor discrepancies. Nothing that warranted investigation. Just wanted Director Sørensen aware.

Mathias read it, filed it, forgot about it.

He didn't know Felix had been embezzling for fifteen years. Didn't know the "irregularities" were actually millions of dollars siphoned into offshore accounts. Didn't know that somewhere in rural Pennsylvania, Filibert Austerlitz was using NATO money to perfect the research NATO thought they'd terminated.

Felix knew. And Felix kept excellent records. Video recordings of meetings. Audio transcripts of conversations. Documentary evidence of Mathias's illegal continuation of Project 19.5 under different names.

Insurance. Leverage. Protection.

The same thing Filibert had built with his hidden electromagnetic research—but Felix's version was bureaucratic rather than technological.

And when the time came, when Filibert needed NATO resources without NATO knowing, Felix would provide them. For a price. For a percentage. For the guarantee that when everything collapsed, Felix wouldn't go down alone.

NATO Joint Warfare Centre - 1990

Mathias reviewed the security footage for the third time, still not quite believing what he was seeing.

A break-in at the Paris research annex. Nothing stolen.

Just surveillance cameras triggered, showing a figure moving through restricted areas with impossible speed and precision.

A figure that looked like it was wearing armor. Or skin that moved like armor.

And then—two days later—Felix called. Nervous. Twitchy. Said he had something important to discuss. Something about Dr. Austerlitz. Something about Project 19.5 never really ending.

Mathias arranged a meeting. Brought Rune as backup. Prepared to hear whatever confession Felix was working toward.

He didn't know it yet, but the hidden years were ending. Twenty years of secret research. Twenty years of perfecting what NATO had stolen. Twenty years of preparation for revenge.

Filibert was ready.

The war was about to begin.

Eleven

The Turning Point

West Nyack, New York – 1990

Zahra sat not at the dining room table, but at the more intimate breakfast nook table. What had to be said needed this level of gravitas. She waited for Kort. Her fingers played mindlessly on the stem of the half-finished wine glass, wine not for courage but for restraint lest her temper flared.

She'd known for months that something was changing. Subtle things at first—Filibert calling more frequently, coded conversations that ended when she entered the room, Kort disappearing for days at a time with vague explanations about "consulting work."

But the blood had been the final straw.

Two weeks ago, she'd found Kort's shirt in the laundry, the collar stained with what could only be blood. When she'd confronted him, he'd claimed a nosebleed. But the stain pattern was wrong—not the spatter of someone tilting their head back but the seepage of someone who'd been bleeding and hadn't noticed.

That's when she'd started really looking and piecing together years of unacknowledged clues she hadn't trusted herself to believe. And what she'd seen terrified her.

Kort was healing too fast. A cut from working in the garden—deep enough to need stitches—was barely visible three days later. A bruise from bumping into the car door faded in hours instead of days. His stamina was increasing; she'd found him running at 2 AM, returning drenched in sweat but not winded. The modifications, dormant for decades, were reactivating.

Or evolving.

Or something else she didn't have the scientific data to understand.

Zahra turned to look out the window that viewed her garden. The sun had set low enough on the other side of the house that she could see her reflection in the window and stared at it. Forty-five years old, still beautiful in her own eyes, but marked by time in ways Kort increasingly wasn't. He looked maybe late thirties, his hair barely touched by gray, his skin unwrinkled, his body maintained at a level of fitness not typical of a fifty-one-year-old man.

How long until people notice?

That was the question that kept her awake at night. How long until their neighbors started wondering why Kort aged so slowly? How long until someone connected the dots, started asking questions, brought attention to things that had been buried in classified files for thirty years?

How long until Filibert's past caught up with them?

Kort arrived, haggard and drained as was the case when he returned from a Pennsylvania trip.

"Zahra?" he called out in the darkened house.

"In here," she replied.

Kort made his way to the kitchen, the only lit room in the house.

"Hi," he greeted, mustering a smile on his tired face.

Zahra's pulse jumped. Kort stood before her. Still handsome, still vital, still the man she'd fallen in love with in an Algerian desert nearly three decades ago. But there was something in his eyes now—something ancient and tired and afraid.

"Will you sit?" she asked.

Kort sat, attempted another smile and asked, "What's up, my love?"

"Your love?"

Kort squirmed, his mind catching up to the tone of the room. "Yes? My love, my wonderful wife".

"Twenty-six years, Kort. Don't you think I know you? I've held my tongue hoping I was just having silly notions, but the evidence kept piling up and piece by piece falling into place."

Kort lowered his eyes. "I just wanted to protect you."

"You don't protect your life partner from truth; you pair up and journey together."

"Yes, my love."

"Do you think I'm stupid?" Zahra felt anger rising, hot and righteous. The wine not doing its duty. "Did you forget that I am a prominent marine biologist, a scientist?"

"No, my love, I don't think you're stupid and I did not forget. The stakes were just so high."

"The evolution of female bodies includes a heightened sense of smell for their particular survival needs; a sense of smell beyond the comprehension of male bodies. I've been smelling the change in you, your biochemical scent isn't you, not the you of five years ago—maybe more. I sit by you, I sleep with you, I shower with you, I hold you tight in our passion. And then a hundred other pieces, none of consequence alone, but together—I know. I know you and Filibert have started the alterations again. Behind my back. A betrayal."

Kort looked up at her, looked into those piercing green eyes, his own eyes welling, "No, Zahra, not a betrayal. Please, I only wanted your protection. I love you above all else."

"Again, life partners... "

"I know, they don't protect from the truth. I still didn't want to worry you."

"Too late. I'm worried. I'm fucking terrified, actually." This time Zahra shifted in her seat, readied herself. Perhaps the wine was for a little courage after all. She said, "Tell me everything. No more avoiding, no more protecting me from the truth. Everything."

Kort nodded slowly. "It started with the healing. I cut myself working in the garage, bad enough that I was going to ask you to look at it. But by the time I came inside, it was already closing. At first, I thought I'd imagined how bad it was, but then it happened again. And again. Small injuries healing in hours instead of days."

"What else?"

"Strength. Not dramatically different, but noticeable. Things that used to require effort became easier. I can lift the lawn mower with one hand now. I accidentally crushed a door handle last week—just grabbed it normally and the metal crumpled."

"Enhanced reflexes?"

"Yes. I can track movements that used to be too fast. Birds in flight, cars on the highway. Everything seems... slower sometimes. Not all the time, but enough."

Zahra processed this clinically, falling back on scientific training to manage her fear. "The modifications were de-signed to be permanent but dormant. They needed regular chemical triggers to remain fully active—the injections Filibert gave you before missions. Without those triggers, they should have stabilized at baseline human normal. Are you taking something? Has Filibert been giving you anything?"

"No. Nothing. I'm not even taking vitamins. Whatever's happening is spontaneous."

Zahra considered this carefully, searching the years of stored knowledge. She stopped with a small gasp. She said, "Horizontal gene transfer."

"What's that?"

"It occurs often in marine life when there is an exchange of large DNA segments including genes directly. It enables rapid acquisition of new traits without waiting for reproduction. Frederick Griffith first observed it in 1928. Marine life has also demonstrated the reactivation of ancient genes and spontaneous mutations." She stopped and took in a sharp breath. Tears welled up in her eyes.

"Zahra?" He reached his hands out to hers across the table.

Zahra withdrew her hands to herself. "Goddamn you, Kort, what have you done to yourself? These processes won't just stop on their own. How is Filibert involved?"

"What makes you think he's involved?"

She shook the tears away and refocused her eyes on him. "Because he calls three times a week now when he used to call a couple of times a month. Because you have secret conversations in Russian that stop when I enter the room. Because you've been teaching and consulting in Virginia less and traveling to Pennsylvania more, coming home in a depleted state—like tonight. Don't lie to me, Kort. Say the words into this void between us! How is he involved?"

Kort reached for Zahra's wine glass and finished it off. His shoulders sagged, the last of his resistance crumbling.

Her command pulled in a string of memories of late-night conversations with Filibert that now, with this reality growing in him, shook him to the core. "He's been monitoring me. Taking blood samples, running tests. He says the modifications are evolving, that my body is integrating the bioengineered components more fully than he'd designed them to. He's trying to understand why—why after being dormant all these years."

"And?"

"And he doesn't know. The modifications were supposed to be stable at a fixed level of enhancement. Instead, they're becoming more sophisticated, more efficient. It's like my body is refining them, optimizing them, making them better."

"Better how?"

"Faster healing. Greater strength. Enhanced cognitive processing—I can remember things I shouldn't be able to remember, process information more quickly, make connections that should take longer." He paused. "And the aging has stopped. Or slowed to the point that it's barely noticeable."

Zahra nodded with new understanding and muttered, "Like some species of jelly fish." She fixed her green eyes on Kort with a newfound horror and whispered, "Some that can reverse the aging process."

And there it was. The truth she'd suspected but hadn't wanted to confront. Kort wasn't just enhanced—he was becoming something post-human. Something that wouldn't age at the same rate as her, might even reverse, wouldn't deteriorate, wouldn't die on schedule.

Something that would watch her grow old while he remained vital.

"How long?" Zahra asked, her voice small. "How long will you live?"

"Filibert doesn't know. Decades longer than normal, certainly. Maybe a century. Maybe... indefinitely. The cellular regeneration is too efficient. Telomeres aren't shortening the way they should. DNA damage is being repaired faster than it accumulates."

"Biological immortality," said, her voice fading with her anger, replaced by defeat and resignation.

Kort felt the weight of the mood that came over her. "I mean, maybe. Or maybe I'll hit some critical threshold and my body will reject the modifications the way Hans and Razo and the others did. Filibert says there's no way to predict. I'm the only long-term survivor of the enhancement program. I'm the only data point. A true N-of-one."

Zahra reached out and pulled the empty wine glass back to her. Her fingers played mindlessly on the stem of the glass. Twenty-six years of marriage, and now she was learning that her husband might outlive her by centuries. That the man she'd grown old with wouldn't grow old himself.

She pulled her hands in and crossed her arms over her chest. "You should have told me, Kort, you should have fucking told me."

"I was afraid, my love."

"Of what?"

"Of this. Of seeing that look in your eyes—the one you have right now. The look that says I'm not really your husband anymore. That I'm a scientific specimen. An experiment. Something to be studied rather than loved."

"That's not fair."

"Isn't it?" Kort straightened up and met her eyes. "You're a scientist, Zahra. When you look at me now, do you see your husband? Or do you see a biological anomaly that defies everything you know about human physiology?"

She wanted to protest, to insist that she still saw the man she'd married, the soldier who'd rescued her, the partner who'd built a life with her. But he was right. Part of her—the scientist part, the part that had spent decades studying cellular biology and genetic modification—was already cataloging his symptoms, theorizing about mechanisms, wondering what data Filibert had collected and what it might reveal.

"Both," she said finally. "I see both. My husband and the anomaly. And I'm trying to figure out how to be wife to one while studying the other."

"That's honest, at least."

Zahra stood up in slow motion from her seat. "I have to move around," she said, heading out of the kitchen.

Kort stood up as well and followed her out of the kitchen and to their bedroom. When he got to the bedroom Zahra was curled up on the bed and he sat on the edge.

They sat in silence, years of unspoken truths now filling the space between them. Outside, the neighborhood was settling into evening routine—families having dinner, children doing homework, lives proceeding normally while two people grappled with the implications of biological immortality.

"I need to see Filibert's data," Zahra said eventually. She uncurled and sat up next to Kort. "Everything he's collected. All his test results, all his theories. If we're going to understand what's happening to you, I need access to his research."

"He won't share it. You know how he is about his work."

"Then we'll make him share it. I'm not some graduate student he can dismiss anymore, Kort. I'm one of the leading marine biologists in the country. I have resources, contacts, research facilities. If Filibert wants to understand what's happening to you, he needs my expertise."

"And if we understand it? What then?"

"Then we figure out if it can be reversed. If you can be returned to normal human physiology."

Kort was quiet for a moment, then: "What if I don't want it reversed?"

The question hung between them, loaded with implications Zahra wasn't ready to confront.

"What do you mean?"

"I mean for my whole life, I've been consumed with survivor's guilt. Starting with surviving that war and sent to America when my family was left to starve or be murdered. Watched my brothers die while I thrived. Wondered why I deserved to live when they didn't. And now—now I'm being given a gift. Extended life. Enhanced capabilities. The ability to do more, help more, matter more. What if I don't want to give that up?"

"Even if it means watching me die? Watching everyone you know die while you continue?"

"I don't know. Maybe. Is that selfish?"

"Yes. But it's also human." Zahra took his hand, felt the strength in it, the barely contained power. "Kort, I need you to be honest with me about something else. Does Filibert want you to do something? Is that why he's been calling? Why you've been meeting with him so much?"

Kort didn't answer immediately, and in that hesitation, Zahra found her answer.

"He does. He wants you to do something for him. Something involving the modifications."

"He wants me to help him restart the program," he finally confessed. "Create a new generation of enhanced soldiers. Use what we've learned from my survival to perfect the process."

"And you told him no."

"I told him I'd think about it."

Zahra pulled her hand back, anger flaring again. "Think about it? Kort, four men died from these modifications. Four of your brothers in arms. And you're considering helping Filibert make more modified soldiers?"

"They died because the technology wasn't ready. Because Filibert was working with primitive understanding of cellular integration and genetic compatibility. But we know so much more now. With your marine biology research, with my survival as a template, with modern biotechnology—we could create stable modifications. Safe enhancements. Soldiers who could save lives without sacrificing their own."

"Or you could create a new generation of men who die slowly and horribly like Hans and Razo and the others. Or worse—become non-human. Isn't that's what's happening to you? You're willing to risk that?"

"I'm willing to consider it. There's a difference."

"Not much of one."

They were arguing now, really arguing, in a way they rarely did. Twenty-six years of marriage had taught them how to navigate disagreements, how to compromise, how to respect boundaries. But this was different. This cut to fundamental questions about who they were and what they believed.

"I watched my brothers die," Kort said, his voice low and intense. "I held Razo's hand while his organs shut down. I sat with Hans while he drowned in his own fluid retention. I drank wine with Jean a week before he was found dead in his apartment. And do you know what they all said to me? Every single one of them?"

Zahra shook her head, not trusting her voice.

"They said 'make it worth it.' Make our deaths mean something. Don't let this be the end of the research. Perfect the modifications. Create the next generation. Ensure that our sacrifice advanced something larger than ourselves."

Kort stood, paced to the window, looked out at their suburban paradise. "I promised them. All of them. That I'd make their deaths matter."

"And you think creating more enhanced soldiers honors that promise?"

"I think refusing to continue the research because I'm afraid dishonors it. Yes, there are risks. Yes, the next generation might fail the way they did. But they might not. They might survive. They might become what Filibert always envisioned—soldiers who can end conflicts quickly, save civilian lives, protect the innocent without becoming monsters themselves."

"Or they might become monsters. Enhanced humans with no moral constraints, no empathy, no connection to regular humanity. Weapons that think for themselves."

"That's why I'd lead them. Train them. Ensure they maintain their humanity even as their bodies transcend it."

Zahra felt cold settling into her bones. "You've already decided, haven't you? You're going to say yes to Filibert."

Kort turned from the window, and she saw it in his eyes—the determination, the conviction, the certainty that he was doing the right thing even if it destroyed everything they'd built.

"I'm going to consider it seriously. That's all I can promise right now."

"And what about us? What about our marriage? Our life here?"

"That doesn't have to change."

"Of course it has to change!" Zahra was standing now, her voice rising. "If you restart the enhancement program, you become a classified asset again. You disappear into black ops and secret facilities and lies about where you are and what you're doing. We've built a normal life here, Kort. A real life. With friends and neighbors and community. You want to throw that away to become Filibert's experiment again?"

"I want to honor my brothers' sacrifice. I want to perfect something that could save countless lives. I want to stop feeling guilty for surviving when they didn't."

"So this is about guilt. About your need to atone for being the one who lived."

"Maybe it is. Is that so wrong?"

"Yes! Because you're using guilt to justify putting yourself in danger. To justify abandoning our life together. To justify—" She stopped, a realization hitting her. "To justify leaving me. That's what this is really about, isn't it? You're aging slower than me. In ten years, I'll be sixty and look it. You'll still look forty. In twenty years, I'll be old and you'll still be vital. You're looking for an excuse to leave before that gap becomes unbearable."

"That's not—"

"Isn't it? Be honest with yourself, Kort. You're facing the prospect of biological immortality, and I'm facing the normal human lifespan. That gap is only going to widen. So maybe helping Filibert isn't about honoring your dead brothers. Maybe it's about finding an honorable way to leave your dying wife."

The words hung between them, brutal in their honesty.

Kort's face went white. "How can you say that? How can you think that?"

"Because I'm watching you choose Filibert over me. Choose the enhancement program over our marriage. Choose immortality over growing old with me. What else am I supposed to think?"

"I love you, Zahra. I've loved you from the moment I first saw you. That hasn't changed."

"But you love the promise of transcending humanity more. You love the idea of being superhuman more than you love being human with me."

Kort opened his mouth to respond, then closed it. Because she was right. On some level he couldn't quite articulate but knew instinctively, she was right. He did love the promise of enhancement more than he loved their ordinary life. He did want to transcend the limitations that bound him.

He did want to leave her behind.

Maybe not consciously. Maybe not deliberately. But the truth was there, undeniable and terrible.

"I need to shower," Zahra said, her voice hollow. "I need to think. Please be gone when I come out."

"Zahra—"

"Please. Just... please."

She walked into the bathroom, closed the door, locked it. Leaned against it and listened to Kort's footsteps retreat down the hallway, down the stairs, out of their bedroom and maybe out of their marriage.

The clock-shaped stained-glass window caught the evening light, casting colored shadows across the white tile. Zahra stared at it, remembering when Kort had commissioned it, how proud he'd been to merge their two passions into one piece of art. That was the man she'd married. The one who thought of her, who honored her work, who wanted to build something beautiful together. But his passion was tainted by Filibert's madness—a madness that now tainted their marriage—their love.

And that man was disappearing, replaced by something enhanced and immortal and increasingly alien.

She turned on the shower, let the steam fill the room, stepped under the hot water. Let it beat against her skin, let the sound of it drown out her thoughts, let the heat provide comfort her husband couldn't.

How did we get here?

The question had no answer. Or too many answers. A cascade of choices starting decades ago in an Algerian desert, when a young biology undergrad student had been rescued by an enhanced soldier and fallen in love with the man underneath the modifications.

She should have known then. Should have understood that loving someone who'd transcended normal humanity meant accepting that the transcendence would never stop. That enhancement was a process, not a destination. That Kort would always be evolving, always changing, always moving further from the human baseline she represented.

She should have chosen differently.

But she hadn't. She'd chosen love. And love, it turned out, wasn't enough when one partner was human and the other was becoming post-human.

Zahra stayed in the shower until the water ran cold. Then she stood in the bathroom, wrapped in a towel, looking at her reflection in the mirror and trying to recognize the woman looking back.

Forty-five years old. Still beautiful, by some measures. But marked by time in ways Kort increasingly wasn't. Crow's feet at her eyes, softness at her jawline, gray threading through her dark hair. The normal markers of a life lived in normal time.

But her husband was leaving normal time behind.

And she couldn't follow.

She opened the bathroom door, half-hoping, half-fearing that Kort would still be there. But the bedroom was empty. Just the lingering scent of his cologne and the depression in the bedspread where he'd sat.

She walked to the window, looked out at their neighborhood. Saw Kort in the driveway, loading a bag into his car. Watched him pause, look back at the house, up at the bedroom window where she stood silhouetted by the bedroom glow behind her.

Their eyes met across the distance.

He raised a hand—not quite a wave, not quite a goodbye. A gesture that meant *I'm sorry* or *I love you* or *I don't know what else to do.*

She didn't raise hers back.

Kort got in his car, started the engine. Sat there for a long moment, probably hoping she'd run downstairs, stop him, tell him to stay.

She didn't.

He pulled out of the driveway, drove down their quiet suburban street, turned at the corner, and disappeared.

Zahra stood at the window for a long time after, watching the empty street, replaying twenty-six years of marriage in her mind, trying to find the moment when they'd lost each other. Trying to understand how love could be so strong and still not strong enough.

Finally, she turned away from the window. The bedroom suddenly felt too large, too empty, too filled with the absence of the person who should be there.

She walked downstairs, poured herself some more wine, sat at the breakfast nook with the phone within reach. Part of her wanted to call Kort, tell him to come back, tell him they'd figure it out together. But the larger part knew that wouldn't solve anything. The gap between them had opened, and it would only widen. Better to acknowledge it now than watch it slowly destroy them.

The phone rang.

She stared at it, willing it to be Kort. But knowing it wouldn't be.

On the fifth ring, she answered.

"Zahra?" Filibert's voice, German accent still strong after spending most of his years in America. "Is Kort there? We had an appointment tonight."

"He's gone."

"Gone where?"

"I don't know. We had a fight. About you. About the enhancement program. About everything."

Silence on the other end. Then: "I see. Did he tell you about the reactivation?"

"Yes. And about your proposal to restart the program."

"And?"

"And you're a monster, Filibert. You've been experimenting on my husband for decades. You killed four men with your enhancements. And now you want to create more victims. How do you live with yourself?"

"The same way you will." Filibert's voice was calm, almost gentle. "By understanding that progress requires sacrifice. That the advancement of human potential is worth the cost in individual lives. That we're working toward something larger than ourselves."

"Spare me the philosophy. You're using Kort. You've always been using him. He's just a test subject to you."

"He's my brother. And yes, he's also my most successful subject. Those two facts aren't mutually exclusive." Filibert paused. "Zahra, I understand you're angry. You have every right to be. But before you dismiss everything I've done, consider this: in thirty years, Kort will still be vital while you grow old. In fifty years, he'll be unchanged while you're in a grave. That gap will destroy your marriage far more effectively than any enhancement program. At least if he's working with me, he has purpose. Direction. Something to occupy him while he watches everyone he loves die."

The words were cruel, but they were also true. Zahra felt them hit like physical blows.

"You're a bastard," she whispered.

"Yes. But I'm an honest bastard. And I'm offering you a choice."

"What choice?"

"Join the program. Use your marine biology expertise to help perfect the enhancements. Work alongside Kort instead of watching from the sidelines. Be part of the solution instead of part of the problem."

"You want me to help you create more enhanced soldiers?"

"I want you to help me create stable enhancements that don't kill their hosts. I want you to ensure the next generation survives where the first generation died. I want you to be the scientist who solves biological immortality." He paused. "And yes, I want you to save your marriage by making yourself invaluable to the work that will define Kort's future."

Zahra's hand tightened on the phone. "I need to think."

"Of course. But don't think too long. Kort must already be on his way here. By morning, he'll have committed to the program. And once he's committed, he'll be gone—not physically, but psychologically. He'll be focused on the work, on training the new team, on perfecting what we started. If you want to be part of his life, you need to be part of his work."

"And if I refuse?"

"Then you lose him. Not today, not tomorrow, but eventually. The gap between enhanced and unenhanced will become unbridgeable. He'll outlive you by centuries. He'll move beyond you in ways you can't follow. Your marriage will end—painfully, tragically, but inevitably." Filibert's voice softened. "Or you can join us. Use your skills. Help us succeed. And maybe—just maybe—we can develop enhancements that work for you too. Maybe we can bridge that gap. Maybe we can make you immortal too."

The offer hung there, tempting and terrible.

"I need time," Zahra said again.

"You have until morning. Then Kort makes his decision. And you make yours."

Filibert hung up.

Zahra sat at the table, wine forgotten, mind racing. Everything she'd built—her career, her marriage, her normal suburban life—was crumbling. And she had to decide: watch it collapse, or become part of the force destroying it.

Outside, the neighborhood settled into darkness. Inside, Zahra sat alone, trying to understand how a rescue in an Algerian desert thirty years ago had led to this moment of impossible choices.

The kitchen clock struck half past one.

But that couldn't be right. It was barely nine.

Zahra looked at the clock, saw it was indeed showing 1:30. Had been showing 1:30 since they'd bought it at a yard sale years ago. Kort had insisted on keeping it despite the broken mechanism, said the time was "perfect." She'd never understood why it still randomly chimed or what "perfect" meant. Now, sitting alone in her kitchen contemplating the death of her marriage, she thought maybe she did.

Half past one.

The moment before everything changed. The moment before the Russians burst through the door. The moment before innocence ended and violence began.

The moment Filibert had been trying to return to for his entire life. The moment when things were still fixable, still hopeful, still safe.

The moment that no amount of enhancement or modification or biological immortality could ever truly restore.

Zahra poured more wine, stared at the malfunctioning clock, and waited for morning to decide what kind of monster she was willing to become. The night stretched on, endless and terrible. And somewhere in Pennsylvania, Kort and Filibert began planning the future.

A future Zahra was no longer certain she wanted to be part of.

But couldn't imagine existing without.

Twelve

The Price of Perfection

Abandoned Steel Mill, Rural Pennsylvania
– Three Days Later

The exterior of the facility retained the dilapidated appearance of being abandoned. It attracted little attention, taxes were paid, no trespassing signs with "under surveillance" helped, save some curious teens looking for a place to drink and make out from time to time. But inside its rusted shell, Filibert had built something extraordinary.

State-of-the-art laboratory equipment hidden behind corroded facades. Medical bays disguised as storage rooms. Vast aquariums teeming with marine life, some common, some rarely seen, and some that had never before existed. And then there was the tightly secured arachnid lair populated by large genetically altered spiders who spun steel-strength fibers for experiments in body armor. A research facility that would make Columbia or MIT jealous, all concealed within a building that looked ready to collapse.

It was perfect for work that couldn't exist officially.

Kort had arrived two days ago, driving through the night after his fight with Zahra. He'd stood at the entrance, looking at the decrepit building, and felt something like coming home. This was where he belonged—not in a suburban house with a garden and neighbors who asked about lawn care. Here, where the boundaries of human potential were being rewritten.

Filibert had greeted him warmly, while noting the heavy loss coming here this time had etched in his face. Coming here for good. Iniko had been more reserved, her Nigerian accent soft as she explained the modifications they'd been creating in the past 3 months and were now ready to show him.

"We've perfected the neural interface," she'd said, gesturing to a bank of monitors displaying complex brainwave patterns.

"The combat state can now be triggered consciously rather than through adrenaline response. Full control over the enhancement cascade. You enter when you choose, exit when you choose. No more uncontrolled activation."

"Is it safe?" Kort had asked.

Filibert's response had been characteristically confident. "We've tested it extensively on simulations. The mathematics are perfect. The biological models confirm safety. All we need is a human trial to verify the theory."

That should have been the first warning.

After a couple of days rest, it was time to go to work. The training room occupied what had once been the main smelting floor. Filibert had converted it into a tactical testing environment—modular walls that could be reconfigured, threat simulation systems, biometric monitoring stations. It looked like something from a military research facility, which was exactly what it was.

Kort stood in the center of the space, wearing a bodysuit covered in sensors. Electrode patches dotted his temples, throat, chest, monitoring every biological system. Around him, Filibert and Iniko worked at control stations, preparing the test.

"The neural interface is active," Iniko reported, her fingers flying across a keyboard. "Baseline readings are stable. Kort, can you hear me?"

"Clearly." Kort's voice echoed in the empty space.

"Good. We're going to start with a simple test. I want you to enter combat state for thirty seconds. Just thirty seconds. Focus on the sensation, on the enhancement cascade, then exit cleanly. Don't push beyond that time frame."

"Understood."

Filibert moved beside Iniko, studying the monitors with intense focus. "The new neural interface should give you complete control. You'll feel the enhancement activating—increased strength, enhanced reflexes, time dilation. But unlike before, you control when it stops. Your conscious will overrides the biological imperative."

"What happens if I can't exit the state?"

"You will. The fail-safes are absolute. If your conscious control fails, the neural interface will force disengagement after forty-five seconds." Filibert's smile was reassuring, confident. "We've thought of everything, brother. Trust me."

That should have been the second warning.

Kort took a breath, centered himself. He'd entered combat state hundreds of times over the decades—in Algeria, during Legion operations, in training exercises. It was as familiar as breathing. The surge of adrenaline, the sharpening of senses, the feeling of time slowing around him while his body sped up.

But this was different. This was controlled, conscious, deliberate.

"Beginning test in three... two... one... now."

Kort closed his eyes and reached for the combat state.

It answered immediately.

The sensation was familiar but amplified. His heart rate spiked, his muscles tensed, his perceptions sharpened. But there was something new—a feeling of control, of directing the enhancement rather than being carried by it. He could feel the modifications activating in sequence: neural acceleration first, then muscular enhancement, then the sensory amplification.

Time slowed. The ambient hum of the facility's electrical systems became individual oscillations. He could hear Filibert's heartbeat from thirty feet away, count Iniko's breaths, track the movement of air currents through the room.

Perfect.

"Fifteen seconds," Iniko's voice, stretched and distorted by his time-dilated perception. "Readings are nominal. Neural interface stable. Kort, how do you feel?"

"Good. Strong. Controlled." His own voice sounded strange to him, echoes within echoes.

"Excellent. Twenty seconds now. Prepare to disengage at thirty."

Kort felt the power coursing through him. This was what the modifications were meant to be—not a curse that killed his brothers, but a gift that elevated humanity. Controlled enhancement. Directed evolution. The future Filibert had always promised.

"Twenty-five seconds."

Something shifted.

It was subtle at first—a sensation like pressure building behind his eyes. The combat state deepening slightly, the enhancements pushing just a fraction harder. Not alarming, just... noticeable.

"Thirty seconds. Kort, disengage now."

He tried. Reached for the off-switch in his mind, the conscious override that should terminate the combat state. But the switch wasn't where it should be. The neural interface that had felt so responsive moments ago was suddenly distant, unreachable.

The enhancements pushed harder.

"Kort? We're not seeing disengagement. Kort, can you hear me?"

He could hear her perfectly. Could hear the concern in her voice, the quickening of her heartbeat, the subtle intake of breath that preceded alarm. But he couldn't respond. His vocal cords were locked, his jaw clenched, his body following protocols that his conscious mind couldn't override.

"Thirty-five seconds. Filibert, something's wrong."

"The fail-safe should be triggering. Why isn't the fail-safe triggering?"

The pressure behind Kort's eyes intensified. His perception continued to accelerate—time stretching thinner and thinner until each second felt like minutes. He could see dust motes hanging suspended in air currents. Could track the electrical signals flowing through monitoring cables. Could count individual pixels on the display screens.

Too much information. Too much clarity. His brain processing data faster than neurology should allow.

"Forty seconds. Neural activity is spiking. Kort, if you can hear me, you need to fight this. You need to force disengagement."

He was trying. God, he was trying. But the combat state had momentum now, a cascade reaction feeding on itself. Each enhancement triggered the next, which amplified the first, creating a positive feedback loop that his consciousness couldn't interrupt.

"Forty-five seconds. Fail-safe should be active. Filibert, the fail-safe isn't working!"

"I can see that! Override it manually!"

"I'm trying! The neural interface isn't responding!"

Kort felt his body temperature rising. The muscular enhancements were pushing beyond safe parameters, forcing his muscles to perform at levels that generated dangerous heat. His skin felt like it was burning from the inside.

"Fifty seconds. Core temperature rising. One hundred three degrees. One hundred four."

The modifications in his throat activated.

That wasn't supposed to happen. The lamprey-eel enhancements were supposed to be vestigial, dormant, locked behind biological safeguards. But the combat state was stripping away safeguards, activating every enhancement system simultaneously.

Kort felt the flesh of his throat rippling, changing. The modified tissue that had remained stable for decades suddenly became active, malleable, dangerous. He tried to scream, but the sound that emerged was inhuman—a shriek that belonged to something from the deep ocean, not a human throat.

"Fifty-five seconds. He's losing control. We need to sedate him!"

"No! Sedation could kill him while the enhancements are active. We need to force disengagement from the interface!"

"The interface isn't responding! It's locked in a feedback loop!"

Kort's vision was fragmenting now—overlapping images, too much visual data, his brain trying to process information from spectrums humans shouldn't perceive. He could see the infrared signatures of Filibert and Iniko, the electromagnetic fields around the equipment, the molecular bonds in the air itself.

Madness dressed as enlightenment.

"Sixty seconds. Temperature one hundred six. Neural activity at dangerous levels. Filibert, we're going to lose him!"

His jaw clenched harder, muscles contracting with enough force to crack teeth. Kort felt one of his molars shatter, felt the fragments cutting his gums, felt blood pooling in his mouth. But the pain was distant, processed through a brain that was running too fast to properly interpret damage signals.

"Sixty-five seconds. His skeletal structure is showing stress fractures. The muscular enhancement is exceeding bone tolerance."

The modifications had always been carefully balanced—enhanced muscles paired with reinforced bones, increased strength calibrated to structural limitations. But now that balance was breaking down. His muscles were pulling against bones that couldn't handle the force.

Something in Kort's jaw cracked. Not a tooth this time, but bone itself—the mandible fracturing under the pressure of his own muscular contraction.

"Seventy seconds. Jaw fracture detected. Multiple stress fractures in the cervical vertebrae. We need to shut this down NOW!"

"I'm trying! The neural interface has full control. It's not accepting override commands!"

Kort tried to open his mouth, to relieve the pressure, but his jaw wouldn't respond. The muscles were locked, contracting harder and harder, and he felt more bone giving way. The right side of his mandible collapsed inward, fragments pressing against his tongue, cutting tissue, filling his mouth with blood.

"Seventy-five seconds. Catastrophic failure imminent. Filibert, what do we do?"

"Cut the power to the neural interface!"

"That could cause brain damage!"

"He's going to die if we don't! Cut it!"

Through his fragmenting perception, Kort saw Iniko reaching for an emergency switch. Saw her hand moving in slow motion, saw the electrical current flowing toward the control panel, saw the mechanical components preparing to interrupt the neural interface's power supply.

Too slow.

The enhancements in his throat activated fully.

The lamprey-eel modifications—biological weapons that Filibert had incorporated decades ago—were designed to be controllable. A secondary attack method, activated only when needed. But control required conscious direction, and Kort's consciousness was drowning in a combat state he couldn't escape.

The modified tissue of his throat tore open.

It happened from the inside out. The specialized muscles, designed to allow the lamprey mouth to extend and retract, contracted with catastrophic force. Kort felt his throat rupturing, felt the modified tissue shredding itself, felt blood flooding his airways.

But the worst part—the truly horrifying part—was that he could track every detail of the injury with his enhanced perception. Could see the cellular level damage. Could watch his own trachea collapsing. Could observe the arterial bleeding with clinical precision.

He was dying, and his enhanced brain was cataloging every stage of his death in excruciating detail.

"Eighty seconds. Massive tissue damage to the throat. He's hemorrhaging. Filibert!"

"Cutting power now!"

The world went white.

The neural interface's power interruption was like being struck by lightning. Kort felt the combat state collapse instantly—all the enhancements shutting down simultaneously, all the sensory amplification cutting off, all the processing speed vanishing.

He dropped to his knees, blood pouring from his mouth and throat. His vision, so crystalline moments before, became a blur. His hearing, which had tracked individual heartbeats, now barely registered the sounds of people rushing toward him.

Time returned to normal speed.

And with it came pain.

Real pain. Unfiltered by combat state. His jaw was shattered, fragments of bone moving wrong inside his face. His throat was torn open, every breath pulling blood into his lungs. The stress fractures in his neck screamed with each movement.

He tried to speak, to tell them he was okay, that he could handle the pain. But his jaw wouldn't move right, and his throat couldn't form sounds, and all that emerged was a gurgling wheeze.

Kort pitched forward, catching himself on his hands. Blood pooled beneath him, spreading across the concrete floor in a pattern his fading consciousness tried to analyze, tried to understand, tried to categorize with the last remnants of enhanced cognition.

"Get the med-cart! We need to stabilize him!"

"The damage is too severe. We can't treat this here. He needs a hospital."

"We can't take him to a hospital! They'd ask questions. They'd discover the modifications."

"Then what do we do? Let him bleed out?"

Kort's arms gave out. He collapsed face-first into his own blood, the impact sending fresh agony through his shattered jaw. He tried to roll over, to keep breathing, but his body wouldn't respond. The combat state's collapse had taken all his strength, left him weaker than a normal human.

Footsteps running. Hands on his shoulders, rolling him onto his back. Iniko's face above him, tears streaming down her cheeks, her hands pressing something against his throat trying to stop the bleeding.

"Stay with us, Kort. Don't you dare die. Don't you dare."

He wanted to tell her it was okay. That he'd survived worse. That the modifications would heal him like they always did. But even as he thought it, he knew it wasn't true. The enhancements had damaged him, not external enemies. His own biology was killing him.

Filibert's face appeared beside Iniko's, older and more terrified than Kort had ever seen it.

"Brother," Filibert whispered. "I'm sorry. I'm so sorry. This shouldn't have happened. The calculations were perfect. The safeguards were absolute. I don't understand what went wrong."

Kort tried to respond, but his throat was too damaged. Blood bubbled up instead of words.

"We need to do something," Iniko said, her voice breaking. "He's dying, Filibert. Look at him. He's dying."

"I know. I know." Filibert's hands were shaking as he pulled back the makeshift bandage to examine the damage. "The throat is destroyed. The jaw is fractured in multiple places. The trachea is collapsed. Even with the enhancements, healing this would take weeks. He doesn't have weeks."

"Then what? There has to be something!"

Filibert was quiet, his brilliant mind racing through possibilities, discarding options, calculating probabilities. Then his eyes widened—realization and horror in equal measure.

"The regeneration protocols," he said softly.

"What?"

"The protocols we developed off of Zahra's research projects at Colombia. The octopus regeneration research. Complete cellular restructuring. It's experimental, untested on humans, but—"

"But it might save him."

"It might. It might kill him." Filibert looked at Kort's face, at the ruin of what had once been his brother's jaw and throat. "If we do this, he won't be the same. The level of biological reconstruction required—it goes beyond enhancement. Beyond human. He'll be something else entirely."

Iniko's hands pressed harder against the bleeding. "Will he be alive?"

"Yes. Probably. Maybe. I don't know." Filibert's voice cracked. "The mathematics say yes. The biology says yes. But I said the same thing about the neural interface, and look what happened."

"We have to try. We can't just let him die."

"No. No, we can't." Filibert stood, decision made. "Get him to the reconstruction bay. Prep the cellular tanks. And call Zahra."

"Zahra? Filibert, she told you she needed time to—"

"Time just ran out. If we're going to save Kort's life, we need her expertise. Call her. Tell her there's been an accident. Tell her to get here as fast as she can."

"And if she refuses?"

"She won't." Filibert looked down at Kort's broken body, at the man who'd been his brother since they first met as boys at the orphanage all those years ago. "Whatever else is between us, she loves him. She'll come."

Iniko nodded and ran toward the communications room.

Filibert grabbed more handfuls of wound packing gauze supplies from the med-cart, which was a 1920s industrial hospital gurney, and knelt beside Kort, packing the most severe wounds. "Stay with me, brother. I know it hurts. I know you're scared. But I'm going to fix this. I'm going to make you whole again. I promise."

Kort's vision was fading now, darkness creeping in from the edges. He could feel his heart struggling, blood pressure dropping, systems starting to fail. The enhanced healing that had saved him dozens of times was overwhelmed, unable to cope with the catastrophic internal damage.

"I'm going to move you now. It's going to hurt. I'm sorry, but I need you to help and push up with your feet."

Filibert armed-swiped the medical supplies off the gurney tabletop and, approaching from the side to minimize wheel movement, lifted him best he could with Kort straining to give his own body a boost on failing legs. Together they managed after two failed attempts to get Kort slumped over on the gurney. Filibert hurried to swing Kort's legs half onto and half hanging off the gurney table.

Then Filibert grabbed table edge and wheeled the gurney with all he had deeper into the facility, his own breathing heaving, heart pounding from the unaccustomed exertion.

Each bump and buckle of the rickety gurney sent fresh agony through Kort's body. Each breath pulled blood deeper into his lungs. Each heartbeat was weaker than the last.

They passed through the main laboratory, through the aquarium room where Filibert's marine specimens lived in their tanks, past the spider room where genetically modified arachnids created the ultra-strong webbing used in body armor. Finally, they reached the double-acting doors marked with biohazard symbols. Filibert plowed the gurney through them, swinging the doors violently open as he pushed Kort inside.

The room was dominated by a massive cylindrical tank, empty now but obviously designed for human occupancy. Around it, medical equipment that looked more like torture devices—surgical tools designed for alien biology, monitoring systems displaying data Kort's fading consciousness couldn't interpret.

Filibert wheeled him over next to a padded table beside the tank.

"The cellular restructuring will take days. Maybe weeks. You'll be unconscious for most of it—medically induced coma to prevent shock. When you wake up..." Filibert's voice broke. "When you wake up, you'll be different. Your face will be reconstructed. Your throat will be rebuilt. But the modifications required—the level of intervention—you won't look the same. Won't sound the same. Won't be the same."

Kort tried to signal understanding, but couldn't move his hands.

"I need you to know that I never meant for this. The neural interface should have been safe. The calculations were perfect. But somewhere—somehow—I missed something. And now you're paying the price for my mistake." Filibert leaned close, his old face streaked with tears. "I'm sorry, brother. I'm so sorry. But I'm going to save you. Whatever it takes. Whatever you become. I'm going to save you."

The door burst open. Iniko rushed in, breathless.

"Zahra's on her way. She'll be here in four hours."

"Four hours. He might not have four hours."

"Then we start the prep work now. Get him stable enough to survive until she arrives."

"Right. Yes. Good. Help me transfer him."

Iniko took Kort's shoulders, wedging her foot under a wheel, and Filibert took Kort's legs; they managed to slide him onto the padded table.

Filibert was moving now, gathering equipment, preparing solutions, his hands steadying as the scientist in him took over from the frightened brother. "Start an IV line. Maximum dose of morphine—we need to stop that pain and keep him unconscious or the pain could kill him."

Iniko worked quickly, finding a vein, inserting the needle, starting the flow of drugs. Kort felt the morphine hit his system—warm and heavy and pulling him down into darkness. As consciousness faded, he had a final moment of clarity.

This is what the others felt. Hans, Razo, D'Arcy, Jean. Dying because of enhancements they'd trusted. Because of modifications that promised power but delivered destruction. I'm sorry, brothers. I understand now. I finally understand.

The darkness took him.

Four Hours Later

Zahra drove like a woman possessed, breaking every speed limit, her mind racing faster than the car. Iniko's call had been brief, cryptic, terrifying: "There's been an accident. Training exercise went wrong. Kort is critical. We need you here. Now."

She'd thrown clothes into a bag, grabbed her briefcase crammed full of research notes she blindly hoped would contain lifesaving clues, and left West Nyack without locking the door. Nothing mattered except getting to Pennsylvania. Getting to Kort.

The facility looked even more decrepit than she remembered from a previous visit years ago. But she knew the exterior was deception—inside was some of the most advanced biomedical research in the world. Legal or not.

Iniko met her at the entrance, and Zahra's breath caught. The woman looked destroyed—eyes red from crying, clothes stained with blood, hands trembling.

"How bad?" Zahra asked.

"Bad. Come. Filibert will explain."

They moved quickly through the facility, past laboratories Zahra vaguely recognized, into sections she'd never seen before. The deeper they went, the more the environment changed—less like a research facility, more like something from a nightmare. Aquarium tanks full of creatures that shouldn't exist. Spiders the size of dinner plates. Equipment that looked medical but felt wrong.

Finally, they reached the reconstruction bay.

Filibert stood beside the cylindrical tank, now filled with a luminous gray liquid that pulsed with its own light. Beside it, a table where something lay covered by a sheet.

Something that was trying to breathe.

"Zahra. Thank you for coming." Filibert's voice was hollow, aged decades in hours. "I need to show you something. It's going to be difficult. But I need you to see what we're dealing with before you commit to helping."

"Just show me."

Filibert pulled back the sheet.

Zahra's stomach lurched.

The thing on the table was recognizable as Kort only because she knew it was him. His body was intact, still showing the muscular enhancement of the modifications. But from the cheekbones down, his face was gone.

Not gone like in an explosion or acid attack. Gone in a way that suggested his own biology had consumed it. The jaw was shattered beyond recognition, fragments of bone visible through torn flesh. His throat was opened in a way that exposed the trachea, the esophagus, the major blood vessels—all damaged, all leaking fluids despite the medical foam packed into the wounds.

But the worst part was his mouth. Or what should have been his mouth. Instead, there was a circular opening lined with what looked like teeth—small, backward-pointing, arranged in concentric rings like a lamprey eel's mouth. The modified tissue was still partially active, still trying to fulfill its biological purpose.

Zahra covered her mouth, fighting the urge to vomit.

"What happened to him?"

"A training accident. We were testing a new neural interface—controlled access to the combat state. But something went wrong. The interface malfunctioned. Instead of thirty seconds, he was locked in full enhancement for over a minute. His body pushed beyond safety parameters."

"Beyond safety parameters? Filibert, his face is—"

"The jaw shattered from his own muscle contractions. The throat modifications activated uncontrollably and tore themselves apart from the inside. The lamprey enhancements—" Filibert gestured to the circular mouth. "Those were supposed to be dormant. Vestigial. But the combat state activated them fully."

Zahra forced herself to look at the damage clinically. To see it as a medical problem rather than her husband's destroyed face. "Can he heal naturally?"

"No. The damage is too severe. The enhancements are trying to heal him, but they're fighting against each other. Some systems are trying to regenerate human tissue. Others are trying to complete the lamprey modifications. Still others are attempting to seal the wounds with scar tissue. The result is chaos at the cellular level."

"So he needs intervention."

"He needs complete reconstruction. Not healing—rebuilding. Taking what remains and restructuring it into something, somethiing that will allow him to survive."

Zahra looked at the tank, at the gray liquid pulsing with light. "The regeneration protocols. You want to use my research."

"It's the only chance. Octopus regeneration allows complete cellular restructuring. Damaged tissue can be broken down and rebuilt from genetic templates. Combined with the modifications already in his system, we can reconstruct his face and throat from scratch."

"That's never been tested on humans. We don't even know if human cells can undergo that level of restructuring without rejection."

"I know. But it's this or watch him die." Filibert moved closer, his eyes intense. "Zahra, I know you're angry with me. You have every right to be. I did this to him. My arrogance, my certainty that I'd solved the problems that killed the others—it almost killed Kort too. But right now, anger doesn't matter. Blame doesn't matter. The only thing that matters is saving his life."

Zahra looked at the man on the table—the man she'd married, the man she'd fought with three days ago, the man whose face was now a ruin of modified flesh and shattered bone.

She thought about walking away. Letting Kort die and ending this nightmare. Returning to her normal life, her legitimate research, her comfortable suburban existence.

But even as she thought it, she knew it was fantasy. She couldn't walk away. Not from Kort. Not after twenty-six years of marriage. Not after everything they'd built together.

Even if saving him meant becoming a monster herself.

"What do you need from me?" she asked quietly.

"The octopus regeneration triggers. The enzymes that allow cellular restructuring. The genetic templates that guide tissue reconstruction. I only got so far with what you published. But I am in the dark now with this new development. I need what you haven't published."

"That research is classified. Columbia doesn't know half of what I've discovered. If I use it here, if it becomes public—"

"It won't become public. This facility doesn't exist. This research doesn't exist. And when we're done, Kort won't exist in any official capacity. He'll be a ghost. A classified asset. A weapon that no government will acknowledge."

"And me? What do I become?"

"My research partner. The civilian consultant who helps perfect biological enhancement. The marine biologist whose discoveries revolutionized human modification." Filibert paused. "And the woman who saved her husband's life when no one else could."

Zahra stared at the tank, at the gray liquid that could rebuild a human being from the cellular level up. At the equipment designed to restructure tissue. At the monitoring systems that would track every stage of a transformation that would change Kort from human to something else.

"If we do this—if I help you—I need access to everything. All your research, all your data, all the modifications you've made to Kort over the years. No more secrets. No more classified information I'm not allowed to see. Complete transparency."

"Agreed."

"And I make decisions about the reconstruction. Not you. Me. I control the cellular templates, the regeneration parameters, the final result. You're the biomechanical engineer, but I'm the cellular biologist. This is my field. My rules."

"Agreed."

"And after this—after we save him—we figure out how to reverse the modifications. How to make Kort human again. That's the end goal. Not perfecting enhancement. Not creating more modified soldiers. Making Kort human. Agreed?"

Filibert hesitated, and in that hesitation, Zahra saw the truth. He had no intention of making Kort human again. This was about perfecting the modifications, about learning from failure, about creating the stable enhancement he'd always envisioned.

But she'd deal with that later. Right now, the only thing that mattered was saving Kort's life.

"Agreed," Filibert said, the lie smooth and practiced.

"Then let's begin. I'll need my research materials from Columbia. And we'll need to start tissue sampling immediately—I need to see how his cells respond to the regeneration triggers before we commit to full reconstruction."

"Iniko can retrieve whatever you need from Columbia. She has access to university facilities."

"Good. Then we have work to do." Zahra moved to the table, forced herself to touch Kort's ruined face, to feel the damaged tissue. "How long has he been unconscious?"

"Four hours. We had him on maximum morphine to stomp on the pain and then IV pentobarbital to medically induce a coma. If he wakes up in this condition, the shock could kill him."

"Then we keep him under until the reconstruction is complete," Zahra directed with the air of authority she earned from years in her profession.

Filibert nodded in agreement and asked, "How long do guess that will take?"

Zahra cocked her head, "Days. Maybe weeks. The cellular restructuring is slow. Rushing it could cause rejection."

Filibert pulled out a tablet, showing her diagrams and formulas. "This is what I have so far, the proposed protocol built from your available research. We break down the damaged tissue using enzymatic dissolution. Then we use the regeneration triggers to rebuild from genetic templates. Layer by layer, cell by cell, until we have functional structures again."

Zahra studied the diagrams, her scientific mind analyzing the approach. It was brilliant. Terrifying, but brilliant. And it might actually work. And then, without moving an incriminating facial muscle, she spied the defect in the protocol. She held that to her chest, not wanting to play that hand and empower Filibert to not need her, not yet.

"His DNA will be the template? Or are you using modified genetic sequences?" she asked, voice flat and clinical.

"Both. We use his original DNA for the basic structures—bone, muscle, nerve. But the modified sequences for the enhanced tissues. The result will be stronger than human normal but more stable than the current modifications."

"You're rebuilding him as an enhanced human from the ground up."

"I'm saving his life using the tools available. What he becomes is a consequence of survival, not a goal."

Another lie. But Zahra let it pass.

"We'll need to monitor him constantly during reconstruction. Any sign of rejection, any indication that the regeneration is failing, we stop immediately and try a different approach."

"Of course."

"And Filibert?" Zahra looked at him directly, her eyes hard. "If he dies during this—if the reconstruction fails and we lose him—I will make sure the world knows what you've done. Every experiment, every modification, every death. I'll expose all of it. Are we clear?"

"Crystal clear." Filibert didn't look threatened. If anything, he looked relieved. "But he won't die. I won't let him. He's my brother. The only family I have left. I've already lost everyone else. I won't lose him too."

For a moment, Zahra saw past the brilliant scientist to the damaged child underneath. The six-year-old boy who'd watched his mother die. Who'd obsessed over clocks frozen at 1:30. Who'd spent his entire life trying to go back to that moment before everything fell apart.

She almost felt sorry for him.

Almost.

"Let's get started," she said. "The longer we wait, the worse his chances."

They worked through the night—Zahra analyzing Kort's cellular structure, Filibert preparing the reconstruction tank, Iniko coordinating the acquisition of materials from Columbia. By dawn, they were ready to begin the process that would save Kort's life or end it.

They transferred him to the tank, suspended him in the gray liquid—a mixture of Zahra's octopus-derived enzymes and Filibert's cellular scaffolding. Attached monitors to track every system. Initiated the dissolution protocol that would break down the damaged tissue.

And watched as Kort's ruined face began to dissolve, cell by cell, into the gray liquid.

Zahra stood beside the tank, her hand pressed against the glass, watching her husband transform into something that was no longer quite human.

"I'm sorry," she whispered. "I'm so sorry this happened to you. But I promise—I promise I'll bring you back. Maybe not as you were, but as something that can survive. Something that can live."

The gray liquid pulsed with light, responding to the cellular activity. Inside the tank, Kort's body floated, unconscious, unaware that his wife was crossing every ethical line she'd ever drawn to save him.

Outside the reconstruction bay, Filibert stood with Iniko, watching through the observation window.

"She'll never forgive us for this," Iniko said quietly.

"No. But she'll help us anyway. Love makes us do terrible things." Filibert pulled out a pocket watch, checked the time. "One-thirty. Always one-thirty. The moment before everything changes."

"Or the moment when everything is finally set right."

"Perhaps. Or perhaps we're just making new mistakes to replace the old ones." Filibert closed the watch, tucked it away. "Either way, there's no going back now. Kort will survive. But what he becomes—what we all become because of this—remains to be seen."

In the tank, gray liquid swirled around Kort's dissolving face, beginning the slow process of cellular reconstruction.

The resurrection had begun.

Thirteen

Resurrection

Abandoned Steel Mill, Rural Pennsylvania – Sixteen Days Later

The laboratory had become Zahra's entire world. She took an emergency leave of absence from Columbia and arranged for one of her interns to watch the house.

Sixteen days since Kort's catastrophic training accident. Sixteen days of watching her husband dissolve and rebuild, cell by cell, in a tank of luminous gray liquid that pulsed with its own alien heartbeat. Sixteen days of balancing on the knife's edge between scientific breakthrough and complete biological collapse.

She hadn't left the facility. Couldn't leave. Every four hours required new measurements, new adjustments to the enzymatic balance, new decisions about which tissue structures to prioritize in the reconstruction. Sleep came in ninety-minute increments snatched on a cot beside the observation window. Food was whatever Iniko brought her—usually forgotten until it grew cold.

Nothing mattered except the body in the tank.

The reconstruction bay had become her domain. Filibert had ceded control after the first forty-eight hours, when it became clear that Zahra's understanding of cellular regeneration exceeded his own.

He still contributed—his expertise in biomechanical enhancement was crucial—but the fundamental decisions about what Kort would become rested with her.

It was a responsibility that weighed like lead in her chest.

The tank itself was a marvel of bioengineering. Seven feet tall, four feet in diameter, constructed from a transparent polymer that could withstand both pressure and chemical exposure. The gray liquid inside—officially designated "Regenerative Suspension Medium" but which everyone called "the soup"—was a complex mixture of Zahra's octopus-derived enzymes, Filibert's cellular scaffolding compounds, and a dozen other components that existed nowhere outside this facility. It looked like something from science fiction. It smelled like the ocean mixed with formaldehyde and something else—something organic and alive and vaguely disturbing.

It also contained Zahra's formulaic corrections to Filibert's calculations—additions she administered without his knowledge. If he betrayed her, it would take him years to figure out his errors and course correct—years she would dedicate to exposing him and shutting this insanity down for good.

And suspended in the center, connected to life support systems by a web of tubes and monitoring cables, was what remained of Kort Sokolov.

Calling it "Kort" felt like a lie. What floated in the tank bore only superficial resemblance to the man Zahra had married. The body was his—still showing the enhanced musculature, still recognizably male, still possessing his general proportions. But from the cheekbones down, his face was gone entirely.

Where his jaw and throat should be, there was only raw tissue in various stages of reconstruction—bone scaffolding being laid down by the cellular regeneration, muscle fibers weaving themselves into functional structures, nerve bundles seeking connections they'd never had before.

His eyes remained intact, mercifully. Closed now, but structurally sound. Zahra clung to that detail like a lifeline. If his eyes survived, if he could still see when he woke up, then some part of the Kort she knew would remain.

But she knew that was fantasy. The man who eventually emerged from this tank would be fundamentally different from the one who'd entered it.

If he emerged at all.

Zahra stood at her primary monitoring station, reviewing the overnight data. Iniko had taken the 2 AM to 6 AM shift, monitoring vital signs and adjusting the soup's chemical balance. Now it was Zahra's turn again—6 AM to noon, the shift where the most critical decisions got made.

The monitors displayed information in layers of complexity. Basic vitals—heart rate, blood pressure, oxygen saturation—ran across the top. Below that, cellular activity metrics tracked the regeneration process at the microscopic level. Deeper still, genetic sequencing data showed which DNA templates were being activated and how successfully.

And at the bottom, in red text that made Zahra's stomach clench every time she looked at it: **REJECTION RISK: 67%**

Too high. Still too high. For sixteen days, they'd been fighting a war at the cellular level—Kort's enhanced biology trying to accept the octopus regeneration protocols while his human DNA fought to maintain baseline structure. The result was a constant battle, his immune system attacking newly formed tissue, the regeneration process trying to overcome that attack, a cycle that consumed energy and threatened to spiral into catastrophic failure.

They'd managed to keep the rejection risk below 70%—the threshold where collapse became inevitable—but barely. Every day was a gamble. Every adjustment could tip the balance toward survival or death.

Zahra pulled up the tissue development scans, examining the progress with clinical detachment she didn't feel.

The jawbone was maybe 60% complete. The cellular scaffolding had established the basic structure—mandibular arch, temporomandibular joints, bone density appropriate for enhanced musculature. But the final layers weren't forming correctly. Too porous in some areas, too dense in others. The regeneration protocol was fighting against Kort's existing enhancement modifications, trying to integrate two incompatible biological systems.

She made notes for adjustment—decrease calcium deposition rate, increase collagen synthesis, modify the genetic template to account for enhanced muscle attachment points.

The throat was worse. The trachea had been completely destroyed in the accident, the esophagus torn apart, the major blood vessels shredded. Reconstructing functional anatomy from that level of damage required essentially building new organs from scratch.

The regeneration protocol was attempting it—creating new tissue layer by layer, guided by DNA templates that told cells how to organize themselves. But the lamprey modifications were complicating everything.

The specialized tissue that had torn itself apart during the accident was trying to regenerate too, following its own genetic instructions, creating structures that belonged in deep-sea creatures rather than human throats.

Zahra had made the decision on day three to let some of that tissue develop. It was too integrated with Kort's biology to safely remove, and attempting to suppress it completely had pushed the rejection risk above 80%. Better to control the lamprey modifications than fight them.

But it meant Kort's throat wouldn't be fully human when the reconstruction finished. The tissue would be hybrid—part human, part something else. Functional, hopefully. But alien.

She pulled up the 3D reconstruction model, rotating it to examine from different angles. The computer had generated a projection of what Kort's face would look like when the process completed, based on current trajectories.

It was... not terrible. Not quite human either.

The jaw would be strong—probably stronger than his original, the bone density increased to handle the enhanced musculature. The skin would be smooth, unmarred, new tissue that had never known sun damage or scarring. But the proportions were slightly wrong. The jaw too wide, the cheekbones too pronounced, the angles of his face more aggressive than they'd been.

And his mouth. God, his mouth.

The computer projection showed normal lips, normal teeth. But Zahra knew what lay beneath—the ring of lamprey teeth, the specialized musculature, the modified tissue that could extend and retract like a biological weapon. They'd covered it, hidden it behind reconstructed human tissue. But it was there. Waiting.

She closed the projection, couldn't look at it anymore. Turned her attention to the metabolic data instead.

Kort's energy consumption was increasing. The cellular regeneration required enormous resources—protein synthesis, bone formation, nerve development all demanded constant fuel. They were feeding him intravenously, a nutrient solution that flowed through the tubes connecting him to the support systems. But it wasn't enough. His body was beginning to catabolize its own muscle tissue to fuel the reconstruction.

They needed to increase the feeding rate. But that carried its own risks—too much too fast could overwhelm his digestive system, cause metabolic acidosis, trigger organ failure.

Another impossible balance. Another decision that could kill him.

Zahra made the adjustment—increased nutrient flow by 15%, added supplemental amino acids, included additional calcium and phosphorus for bone development. Watched the monitors to see how his body responded.

Heart rate increased slightly. Metabolic activity spiked. The rejection risk climbed to 69%.

She held her breath.

Then slowly, gradually, the numbers stabilized. Heart rate settled. Metabolic activity found equilibrium. Rejection risk dropped back to 67%.

Crisis averted. For now.

The door opened behind her. Zahra didn't turn, knew from the footsteps it was Filibert.

"How is he?" he asked, moving to stand beside her at the monitoring station.

"Alive. Stable. Progressing." Zahra kept her eyes on the screens. "The jawbone is developing faster than projected. Should be structurally complete in another three days. The throat tissue is... complicated."

"Complicated how?"

"The lamprey modifications are integrating more extensively than I'd hoped. I've tried to suppress them, but his biology keeps defaulting to the modified structures. It's like his DNA has been rewritten at a fundamental level—the enhanced tissues aren't additions anymore, they're part of his base genetic code."

Filibert nodded slowly, unsurprised. "Thirty years of enhancement. The modifications have had time to become permanent. To rewrite his genome from the ground up. He's not human with enhancements anymore. He's post-human. A new species."

"Don't." Zahra's voice was sharp. "Don't turn my husband into one of your evolutionary theories. He's a man who got hurt. We're fixing him. That's all this is."

"Is it? Look at him, Zahra. Really look at him. That's not a man being healed. That's a new form of life being born. We're not reconstructing Kort—we're creating something that's never existed before."

Zahra finally turned to face him, saw the excitement in his eyes. The scientific fascination overwhelming any human concern.

"You're enjoying this," she said, disgust thick in her voice. "Your brother is dying in that tank, and you're excited about the data you're collecting."

"My brother is surviving in that tank because of the data we're collecting. Because we're pushing the boundaries of what's biologically possible. Because we're proving that human enhancement isn't just feasible—it's inevitable." Filibert gestured to the monitors, to the projections, to all the evidence of successful regeneration. "Yes, I'm excited. This is my life's work now manifested. The proof that humans can transcend their limitations. That we can direct our own evolution. That death itself can be overcome with sufficient knowledge and courage."

"Courage? You call experimenting on your own brother courage?"

"He volunteered. Thirty years ago, he volunteered. And every day since, he's accepted the consequences of that choice. The enhancements, the risks, the transformation into something more than human—he wanted this."

"He wanted to help people. To be a better soldier. He didn't want to become a monster floating in a tank while his own biology tries to kill him."

"Monster?" Filibert's voice hardened. "You think he's a monster? Look at what he can do, Zahra. Look at what he's survived. He's taken injuries that would kill any human and recovered. He's aged slower than anyone else alive. His body is adapting, evolving, becoming more efficient with each passing year. That's not monstrous—that's beautiful. That's the future of our species."

"Our species is human. What's in that tank isn't human anymore."

"Then what is it?"

Zahra didn't have an answer. Because Filibert was right, even if she hated admitting it. What was developing in the tank wasn't quite human. The regeneration protocols, the enhancement modifications, the hybrid tissue structures—they were creating something new. Something that existed in the liminal space between human and post-human.

Something that would be her husband when it finally emerged.

If it emerged.

She turned back to the monitors, ending the conversation. After a moment, Filibert left, his footsteps fading down the corridor.

Zahra stood alone in the reconstruction bay, surrounded by the hum of equipment and the pulse of the gray liquid and the slow metamorphosis of the man she loved.

Day Nineteen

The jawbone was complete.

Zahra watched the final calcification phase on the cellular scanners, seeing the last gaps fill in, the bone density reach appropriate levels, the structure stabilize into functional anatomy. It had taken longer than projected—three extra days of careful adjustment, fighting rejection responses, managing the integration of enhanced bone tissue with re-generated structures.

But it was done. Kort had a jaw again.

She allowed herself a moment of satisfaction. Then moved on to the next crisis.

The throat tissue was rejecting.

It had started twelve hours ago—subtle at first, easy to miss if you weren't watching closely. Increased inflamma-tion markers. Elevated white blood cell counts. The begin-nings of an immune response that could cascade into full rejection if left unchecked.

Zahra had caught it early, immediately began immune suppression therapy. But the situation was deteriorating faster than she could control it. The hybrid tissue—part human esophagus, part lamprey-modified structure—was triggering immune responses that the suppressants couldn't fully block.

The rejection risk had climbed to 71%.

Past the safe threshold. Into the danger zone where collapse became likely.

"We need to make a decision." Iniko stood beside her, reviewing the same data. "If the rejection continues, we could lose all the throat tissue. He'd be back to where he started."

"Or worse. If the immune response spreads to other systems, if it triggers a cascade—" Zahra didn't finish the thought. They both knew what full systemic rejection would mean. Organ failure. Death within hours.

"So what do we do?"

Zahra pulled up the tissue development scans, examined the problem structures. The hybrid tissue that was causing the rejection was concentrated in a specific area—where the human esophagus transitioned to the lamprey-modified tissue. The boundary zone between human and post-human.

She could try to remove it. Cut away the hybrid tissue, force a complete separation between human and enhanced structures. But that would require invasive surgery while Kort was still in the regeneration tank, and the risk of complications was enormous.

Or she could lean into it. Stop trying to maintain the separation between human and enhanced tissue. Let the regeneration protocol complete the transformation, create a fully integrated hybrid throat that wouldn't trigger rejection because there'd be no boundary zones to react against.

But that would mean Kort's throat wouldn't be human at all when he woke up. Would be entirely composed of modified tissue. Functional, yes. But fundamentally alien.

"Zahra?" Iniko prompted. "We need to decide. The rejection is accelerating."

Zahra closed her eyes, tried to think past her exhaustion, past her fear, past the weight of responsibility that threatened to crush her. She was making a decision that would define what her husband would become. Human or post-human. Familiar or alien.

And she had maybe an hour before the choice was made for her by biological collapse.

What would Kort want?

That was the question she couldn't answer. Because Kort wasn't here to ask. Was unconscious in a tank, unaware that his wife was deciding his future. His nature. His very species.

But she knew what he'd chosen thirty years ago. When Filibert had offered enhancement, Kort had said yes. When the modifications had made him different from regular humans, he'd accepted it. When his brothers had died and he'd survived, he'd viewed it as obligation rather than curse.

Kort had always chosen to be more than human. Even when it cost him everything.

"We integrate the tissue," Zahra said finally. "Full hybrid structure. Let the regeneration protocol complete the transformation without trying to maintain human baseline."

"Are you sure? Once we do this, there's no reversing it. His throat will be permanently modified."

"I know. Do it."

Iniko moved to the chemical control station, began adjusting the soup's composition. Decreasing the immune suppressants. Increasing the regeneration catalysts. Removing the genetic constraints that had been trying to maintain human tissue parameters.

Essentially, they were telling Kort's body to stop fighting the enhancements. To accept them fully. To complete the transformation into whatever he was becoming.

The monitors showed immediate response. The rejection markers began to drop. The immune system, no longer fighting against hybrid tissue, settled into equilibrium. The inflammation decreased.

And the throat tissue began to transform.

Zahra watched on the cellular scanners as the hybrid structures propagated. Human tissue cells receiving the enhancement modifications, restructuring themselves according to new genetic instructions, becoming something that was neither fully human nor fully lamprey but an integration of both.

The esophagus remained functional—could still transport food, still perform the basic biological functions required. But now it was lined with modified tissue that was stronger, more resilient, capable of regeneration that human tissue couldn't achieve.

And deeper in the throat, where the lamprey mouth had torn itself apart, new structures were forming. The circular ring of teeth, small and backward-pointing. The specialized musculature that could extend and retract. The modified tissue that could function as both human throat and biological weapon.

Zahra had covered it with reconstructed human tissue—lips, normal-looking mouth, the appearance of humanity. But underneath, Kort would carry capabilities that no human possessed.

She watched the transformation complete over the next six hours.

Watched the rejection risk drop steadily—71%... 65%... 58%... 52%... finally settling at 45%. Still elevated, but manageable. No longer critical.

Crisis averted. Again.

But at what cost?

Zahra pulled up the 3D reconstruction model, updated it with the new tissue parameters. The computer generated a projection of what Kort would look like now.

Still recognizably him. The enhanced jaw, the reconstructed face, the features that were almost human. But his throat showed different proportions now—thicker, more muscular, the modified tissue creating visible changes even through the skin.

And if he opened his mouth wide enough, the lamprey ring would be visible. Hidden normally, but there. Always there.

"He's going to hate this," Zahra whispered.

"He's going to be alive," Iniko countered. "That's what matters."

"Is it? Is being alive worth becoming something you don't recognize?"

"That's not for us to decide. We kept him alive. He can decide what that means when he wakes up."

If he wakes up, Zahra thought but didn't say.

Because there was still the final phase. The emergence. Bringing Kort out of the regeneration tank, transitioning him from the soup's support to independent biological function. It was the most dangerous part of the whole process—the moment when all the reconstructed tissue would be tested, when his body would have to function without chemical assistance.

The moment when everything could still fail.

Day Twenty-Four

The regeneration was complete.

All major tissue structures had been reconstructed. The jaw was functional, the throat was integrated, the skin had regenerated over the raw tissue. Cellular scans showed stable development across all systems. Rejection risk had dropped to 38%—still elevated, but within acceptable parameters.

Kort was ready to wake up.

Or as ready as he'd ever be.

Zahra stood at the control station, her hand hovering over the emergence protocol initiation button. Around her, Filibert and Iniko monitored their respective systems—Filibert tracking the biomechanical responses, Iniko managing the life support transition.

"Whenever you're ready," Filibert said quietly.

Zahra wasn't ready. Didn't think she'd ever be ready. But waiting wouldn't help. The longer Kort remained in the tank, the greater the risk of complications. They needed to bring him out. Now.

She pressed the button.

The emergence protocol began.

First, the chemical composition of the soup changed. The regeneration catalysts were gradually replaced with standard saline solution. The cellular scaffolding compounds were diluted and removed. Over the course of two hours, the gray liquid that had supported Kort's reconstruction was slowly replaced with clear fluid.

Zahra watched the transformation—the luminous gray fading to murky blue-gray, then to cloudy white, finally to clear. Like watching fog lift. Like watching the world come into focus.

Suspended in the clear fluid, no longer obscured by the soup, was the result of twenty-four days of reconstruction.

Kort looked... wrong.

Not monstrous. Not inhuman. But not quite himself either. His face was recognizably his—same basic structure, same features, same general proportions. But everything was slightly off. The jaw too strong, the cheekbones too pronounced, the angles of his face more aggressive. His skin was too perfect—no scars, no age marks, no weathering from decades of life. Like a statue of Kort rather than the man himself.

And his throat. Even relaxed, even covered by the reconstructed skin, she could see the difference. The musculature was too developed, the structure too thick. Modified tissue that couldn't quite pass for human.

"He's beautiful," Filibert breathed, scientific wonder overwhelming any other emotion. "Look at him. Perfect integration. The enhancement modifications fully expressed. This is what I always envisioned—humanity transcended. Biology optimized. The next stage of human evolution made flesh."

Zahra wanted to argue. Wanted to insist that Kort wasn't an evolutionary achievement, wasn't a scientific triumph, was just a man who'd been hurt and reconstructed. But looking at him suspended in the clear fluid, she couldn't deny that Filibert was right.

Kort had transcended humanity. Become something new. Something that existed in the space between human and post-human.

Something that was still her husband but also not her husband.

The emergence protocol continued. The fluid level in the tank began to drop, slowly draining away. Kort's body, supported by the liquid for twenty-four days, gradually took its own weight. His enhanced musculature adjusted automatically, responding to the changing environment even while unconscious.

When the tank was empty, they opened it. The transparent polymer front panel swung open with a hiss of escaping pressure. The sweet stench that rushed out filled the room and gave all pause. Kort's body remained suspended by the monitoring cables and support tubes—held upright but not yet independent.

"Disconnecting life support," Iniko reported. "Transitioning to autonomous function in three... two... one..."

The tubes disconnected. The monitoring cables released. Kort's body sagged forward, and Filibert and Iniko caught him, supporting his weight as they lowered him to a prepared medical bed beside the tank.

His skin was cool to the touch. Too cool. The soup had maintained his body temperature artificially; now his metabolism had to do it alone.

"Temperature dropping," Iniko warned. "We need to get him warm."

They covered him with thermal blankets, placed heating elements around the bed, adjusted the room temperature higher. Slowly, gradually, Kort's body began generating its own heat. His metabolism, dormant during the reconstruction, started to reactivate.

Heart rate increased. Blood pressure rose. Respiratory rate picked up. All the autonomous functions that had been suppressed by the medically induced coma began to return.

"He's stabilizing," Filibert reported, watching the monitors. "All vitals approaching normal ranges. The reconstruction is holding. He's going to make it."

Zahra stood beside the bed, looking down at her husband's reconstructed face. His eyes were still closed, the eyelids flickering slightly as his brain began to wake from weeks of forced sleep.

She took his hand—enhanced hand, modified hand, hand that was cool and strange and familiar all at once.

"Kort? Can you hear me? It's Zahra. You're safe. The reconstruction was successful. You're going to be okay."

No response. But his hand twitched in hers, fingers flexing slightly. Unconscious movement, or the beginning of awareness?

"We're going to bring you out of the coma now," she continued, not sure if he could hear but needing to say it anyway. "When you wake up, you're going to feel different. Your jaw and throat were reconstructed. You won't look exactly the same. But you're alive, Kort. You survived. That's what matters."

The weaning protocol, safely tapering the infusion of pentobarbital, had been in place for the last three days. Iniko intravenously administered the methylethylglutarimide to counter the remaining pentobarbital and bring Kort back to consciousness without shocking his system. She said, "Could be 30 minutes—for normal person."

They waited.

Minutes passed. Ten. Fifteen. Twenty.

Kort's brain activity increased on the monitors. Moving from deep unconsciousness to light sleep to the edge of waking.

Then his eyes opened.

The eyes that looked up at Zahra were Kort's—same dark brown, same intensity, same fundamental awareness. But there was something else there too. Confusion. Fear. And underneath that, something alien and predatory that hadn't existed before.

His mouth opened. Tried to speak. No sound emerged.

"Don't try to talk yet," Zahra said quickly. "Your throat was reconstructed. The tissue needs time to learn how to function. Just breathe. Just focus on breathing."

Kort's eyes moved—taking in the medical bay, the equipment, the tank that had held him. Taking in Filibert and Iniko standing nearby. Taking in Zahra holding his hand.

Then his free hand moved to his face. Touched his jaw, his cheeks, his throat. Exploring the reconstructed tissue, feeling the differences, understanding without words that something fundamental had changed.

His eyes found Zahra's again. And she saw the question there: *What have you done to me?*

"You were hurt," she said, her voice breaking. "Training accident. Your jaw was shattered, your throat destroyed. We had to reconstruct everything. I'm sorry. I'm so sorry. But we saved your life."

Kort's hand moved from his throat to his mouth. Touched his lips. Then—tentatively, fearfully—he opened his mouth wider.

Zahra heard Iniko gasp. Saw Filibert lean forward with scientific interest.

Inside Kort's mouth, beneath the reconstructed human tissue, the lamprey ring was visible. Circular rows of small, backward-pointing teeth. Modified tissue that pulsed with its own blood supply. A biological weapon hidden behind human lips.

Kort's eyes widened. He made a sound—not words, but a keening noise of distress that came from somewhere deep in his reconstructed throat. He tried to close his mouth, but the lamprey tissue was partially extended, and closing it meant feeling those alien teeth against his tongue.

He convulsed, rolling onto his side, gagging and choking on his own modified anatomy.

"Get him stabilized!" Filibert commanded.

Iniko administered sedatives. Kort fought against them, his enhanced strength making it difficult to restrain him even in his weakened state. He was panicking, horrified by what he'd felt in his own mouth, traumatized by the realization of how extensively he'd been modified.

"Kort, please," Zahra begged. "Calm down. Let the sedatives work. We'll explain everything. Just please calm down."

But Kort wasn't calming down. His panic was triggering the combat state—she could see it in his eyes, in the way his muscles were tensing, in the speed of his movements. The enhancements were activating, responding to his fear and distress by preparing him for battle.

"His vitals are spiking," Iniko warned. "Heart rate over 160. Blood pressure 180 over 120. Temperature rising. If he goes into full combat state now, with the reconstructed tissue still adapting—"

"More sedatives. Maximum dose."

"That could suppress his respiratory drive!"

"Do it!"

Iniko injected the maximum dose of sedatives directly into Kort's IV line. For a terrible moment, nothing happened. Kort continued to thrash, his panic overwhelming the drugs, his enhanced metabolism burning through the sedatives faster than they could take effect.

Then finally, gradually, his movements slowed.

His eyes remained open but began to glaze. His body went slack as the sedatives finally overwhelmed even his enhanced system.

He looked up at Zahra one last time. And she saw the accusation in his eyes: *You did this to me. You made me a monster.*

Then his eyes closed, and he was unconscious again.

Zahra stood beside the bed, still holding his hand, tears streaming down her face.

"He hates me," she whispered. "He woke up for thirty seconds, and now he hates me."

"He was confused," Filibert said, attempting comfort. "Disoriented. Don't read into his reaction—it was just shock."

"Was it? Will he understand that his wife turned him into something that has teeth in its throat? That I made the decision to complete his transformation into post-human because it was easier than fighting to keep him human?" She looked at Filibert, anger and grief warring in her expression. "You were right. I didn't reconstruct my husband. I created something new. Something that looks at me like I'm the monster."

"You saved his life."

"Did I? Or did I just create a living being that wishes it was dead?"

Filibert had no answer to that. All he could do was mutter and repeat, "It was just shock."

They stood in silence beside Kort's unconscious body, surrounded by the evidence of their success and the weight of what they'd done to achieve it.

"He needs to go back into the tank to repair again and until we can figure this out," Zahra said, her voice distant, a shell of her prior strength. To Iniko she instructed, "Light sedation this time, we can't risk another medically induced coma—he was already in that one way too long."

"Agreed," was all Filibert could muster in response.

Outside the reconstruction bay, in the main laboratory, the clocks all showed different times. Disorganized. Chaotic. The normal flow of temporal existence.

But in Filibert's office, hidden away where no one else would see, a single clock remained stopped at half past one.

The moment before everything changed.

The moment that could never be returned to, no matter how much reconstruction or enhancement or biological modification they achieved.

The moment that haunted them all.

And now Kort would carry that moment in his own body. In the modified tissue that marked him as post-human. In the alien structures hidden beneath human skin. In the teeth that filled his throat and the horror he'd felt in his own mouth.

The resurrection was complete.

But what had been resurrected wasn't what had died.

And Zahra wasn't sure any of them could live with what they'd created.

Fourteen

The Cascade

Abandoned Steel Mill, Rural Pennsylvania – Day 8 of Reconstruction

The cellular scanner showed something impossible.

Zahra had been reviewing the hourly tissue development data when she noticed the anomaly. A pattern in Kort's DNA that shouldn't exist. At first, she'd dismissed it as imaging artifact, equipment malfunction, something explainable by technology rather than biology.

But it persisted. Hour after hour. Scan after scan. Always the same impossible pattern.

She ran it again. Then again. Then pulled up archival samples—Kort's baseline DNA from before any enhancements, an analysis ran five years ago from a blood sample taken by Filibert in 1960 after Kort returned home from the Army—before the preliminary experiments at Columbia. She loaded them into the comparison algorithm and waited for the results.

The differences made her stomach clench.

"Iniko," she called out, voice carefully controlled. "I need you to look at something."

Iniko appeared from the equipment room, still wearing gloves from handling the regeneration medium cultures. "Problem?"

"I don't know. Maybe. Look at this." Zahra pulled up the comparison screens side by side. "Left: Kort's DNA from 1960. Right: current tissue scan from the regeneration."

Iniko studied the displays, her expression shifting from curiosity to confusion to something approaching alarm.

"That's... that can't be right. The chromosome structure is completely different."

"I ran it six more times. Same result every time." Zahra highlighted a specific sequence. "Look at chromosome seven. In his baseline DNA, there's a regulatory gene complex that should be dormant. Non-coding sequences that don't express in normal human development."

"And now?"

"Now it's active. Expressing. Producing proteins that shouldn't exist in human biology." She switched to a different view. "And it's not just chromosome seven. Chromosome twelve. Fourteen. Nineteen. All showing activation of sequences that were completely silent in his original DNA."

Iniko leaned closer, her scientific training warring with growing unease. "Junk DNA activation?"

"That's the hypothesis. But these aren't random sequences. They're coordinated. They're *organized*." Zahra pulled up a protein synthesis model. "And look what they're producing."

The screen showed complex molecular structures—proteins that integrated marine organism traits with mammalian biology. Structures that facilitated enhanced tissue regeneration. Mechanisms that allowed rapid adaptation to environmental stress.

"These proteins," Iniko said slowly, "they're the same ones we've been introducing externally. The octopus regeneration factors. The lamprey neural interface compounds."

"Exactly. We've been injecting proteins to facilitate the reconstruction. But Kort's DNA is now producing them independently. His own genetic code has been rewritten to generate the very modifications we've been adding artificially."

"That's impossible. DNA doesn't just rewrite itself—"

"Doesn't it?" Zahra pulled up another dataset. "I went back through the Project 19.5 enhancement protocols from 1962. Filibert's original work. Look at what he was actually doing."

The documents spread across the screens—dense technical notes in German, enhancement sequences, genetic modification protocols. Buried in the middle: references to "dormant sequence activation" and "evolutionary potential unlocking."

"He wasn't just adding new capabilities," Zahra said quietly. "He was activating genetic sequences that were already present. Sequences from our evolutionary past. From when our ancestors lived in the ocean. From proto-mammalian stages of development."

"You're saying the enhancements aren't artificial. They're... archaeological?"

"I'm saying human DNA carries genetic memory from millions of years of evolution. Most of it is turned off, dormant, non-coding. But it's still there. Still waiting." Zahra's hands trembled slightly as she brought up the next dataset. "And Filibert's modifications didn't add new DNA. They activated what was already present. Unlocked sequences that evolution had silenced."

Iniko stared at the screens, processing the implications. "Then the lamprey tissue in Kort's throat—"

"Isn't alien biology grafted onto human tissue. It's human biology expressing ancient genetic programs. Programs from when our ancestors had different survival strategies. Different anatomical structures." Zahra felt sick. "We're not creating post-human soldiers. We're creating retro-humans. We're rewinding evolution."

"Or fast-forwarding it." Iniko pointed to a specific sequence. "Look at this regulatory cascade. It's not just activating old genes. It's creating new combinations. New structures that never existed in evolutionary history."

Zahra examined the sequence, felt her scientific understanding collide with horror. "The modifications are *mutating*. The activated sequences are recombining. Creating genetic variations that—" She stopped, unable to finish.

"That could spread," Iniko completed. "If these activated sequences got into someone else's genome—"

"—the cascade could trigger in them. The dormant DNA would wake up. Start expressing. Start changing them." Zahra sat down heavily. "That's why Filibert kept the enhancement program so secretive. That's why only five men were ever modified. He wasn't just worried about technology being stolen. He was worried about creating a genetic pandemic."

The implications settled over them like radioactive fallout. In the reconstruction bay, Kort floated peacefully in the gray liquid, unaware that his DNA was rewriting itself. Unaware that he was becoming something humanity had never seen. Unaware that the modifications making him stronger might also make him contagious.

Part II: Progression

Day 12 of Second Reconstruction

The cascade was accelerating.

Zahra had been monitoring the genetic changes hourly, watching with growing alarm as more dormant sequences activated. What had started on day eight as isolated chromosome modifications was now spreading through Kort's entire genome.

Chromosome by chromosome. Gene by gene. Ancient instructions waking up and demanding expression.

She'd created a visual map—a holographic display showing Kort's DNA with active sequences highlighted in green, dormant sequences in blue. On day one, the display had been mostly blue with scattered green highlights showing Filibert's original enhancement protocols.

Now it was half green. And spreading.

"It's like watching an infection," Zahra said to the empty reconstruction bay. She'd sent Iniko to rest four hours ago, needed time alone with the data. And Filibert had been holed up in his office space surrounded by computer monitors and whiteboards. Working? Or repenting? The son-of-a-bitch. She was alone now though—alone with the implications of what she was witnessing.

The scanner showed new protein synthesis every hour. New cellular structures emerging. New capabilities developing that hadn't been in Filibert's original design.

Kort's nervous system was rewiring itself. Neural pathways optimizing for faster signal transmission. Synaptic connections multiplying. His brain literally restructuring to process information more quickly.

His cardiovascular system was adapting too. Heart muscle cells showing enhanced efficiency. Blood vessels developing new elasticity. Red blood cell production increasing, oxygen-carrying capacity exceeding normal human limits.

And his immune system—that was the most terrifying part.

The rejection risk should be climbing. Should be through the roof with this much genetic change. But instead it was dropping. Because Kort's immune system was *accepting* the changes. Was recognizing the activated ancient DNA as "self" rather than "foreign."

His body was treating the cascade as normal development rather than modification.

Zahra pulled up the tissue integration scans, examined the reconstruction progress. The jaw was complete now, fully formed, stronger than his original. The throat tissue was nearly finished—only the final surface layers remained. But the structures underneath were nothing like what she'd planned.

The lamprey modifications had integrated far more extensively than intended. The circular ring of teeth was fully developed. The specialized musculature was in place. But now there were additional structures—developing primordia posterior salivary glands like octopuses use to produce tetrodotoxin to paralyze prey. The presence of modified salivary tissue that could sense chemical signatures in the air, specialized nerve endings that detected electromagnetic fields.

None of that was in Filibert's protocols. None of that was in her reconstruction design.

Kort's DNA was making it anyway. Drawing from genetic memory. Creating capabilities that made evolutionary sense even if they'd never been part of the plan.

She ran predictive models, trying to project where the cascade would end. The computer took twenty minutes to process—longer than usual, indicating the complexity of the calculation.

The results made her blood run cold.

PREDICTED GENETIC STABILITY: DAY 18-22 PREDICTED DEVIATION FROM HUMAN BASELINE: 35-40% PREDICTED SPECIES CLASSIFICATION: UNDEFINED

Thirty-five percent genetic deviation. That was the line. Beyond that point, Kort wouldn't be *Homo sapiens* with modifications. He'd be something else. A new species. Something that shared human ancestry but had diverged too far to breed with unmodified humans. Something that would be taxonomically distinct.

And there was nothing she could do to stop it.

The cascade had its own momentum now. Kort's DNA wasn't following her protocols anymore. It was following ancient instructions, optimizing itself, becoming something that evolution had prepared for millions of years ago and was only now being allowed to express.

"I'm sorry," she whispered to the figure in the tank. "I tried to save you. I tried to keep you human. But I don't think that's possible anymore."

The gray liquid pulsed with light. Inside, Kort's body continued its transformation. Cell by cell. Gene by gene. Becoming less like the man she'd married and more like something from the deep evolutionary past. Or the distant evolutionary future.

Or both.

Part III: Ethical Crisis
Day 16 of Second Reconstruction

Filibert found Zahra sitting on the floor outside the reconstruction bay at 3 AM, staring at her hands like they belonged to someone else.

"You should be sleeping," he said, lowering himself beside her with the careful movements of someone whose body had finally caught up with the high stress of looming catastrophic failure.

"Can't sleep. Keep seeing the scans. The genetic maps. The cascade spreading." She didn't look at him. "Do you know what we've done?"

"I know what I've always known. We're creating the next stage of human evolution."

"No." Her voice was flat, exhausted. "We're unlocking genetic programs that evolution silenced. Programs that didn't lead to successful species. Dead ends. Evolutionary experiments that failed."

"Or experiments that were interrupted before they could succeed." Filibert pulled out his pocket watch—always the watch, always checking the time against the frozen moment in his memory.

"Evolution doesn't optimize for individual success. It optimizes for species survival. Sometimes that requires capabilities that seem extreme. Dangerous. Monstrous."

"You're wrong," she challenged. "Natural selection acts at the individual level, not the species level. That's what accounts for cooperation, altruism, free will, and..." She paused for maximum effect. "Love."

Filibert bristled at the word. "Sentimental sophistry. Is that how low Columbia's degenerative decline has gone? Free will... love... indeed."

Zahra quickly parried the conversation, satisfied with the scored hit that put him off balance. "Kort has venom glands now. Did you know that? Paralytic venom glands. Well, they are deformed, possibly inert, but not part of the engineering is the point. His DNA spontaneously activated unintended sequences from the octopus genetic material, created structures that are rare in mammals outside of shrews, platypuses, and some bats." She finally looked at him. "Do you understand? The process is evolving outside our control and protocols. Where does it stop? What other genetic nightmares are waiting to be expressed?"

"I don't know," he admitted, still regaining his mental footing. Then that unsettling smile spread on his face. "That's what makes this exciting."

"*Exciting?*" Zahra's voice rose. "Filibert, we're not doing science. We're playing genetic Russian roulette. Activating random sequences and hoping they don't kill him. Or worse—hoping they don't spread to other people."

"The cascade isn't random. It's directed. The activated sequences work together. They're coordinated."

"By who? By what? Ancient evolutionary pressures that no longer exist? Environmental challenges that were solved millions of years ago?" She stood, started pacing. "Human DNA carries genetic memory from aquatic ancestors, from tree-dwelling primates, from savannah hunters. All of it dormant. All of it waiting. And we just unlocked it all at once."

"In one subject. Under controlled conditions."

"*Controlled?*" Zahra laughed bitterly. "I've lost control. Kort's DNA is rewriting itself faster than I can track it. He's becoming something I don't have genetic templates for. Something that's never existed in evolutionary history."

"Then you're creating something new. Something unprecedented." Filibert's eyes glowed with the fever that had driven him for forty-five years. "This is what I've worked for, Zahra. Not just enhancing humans. Not just making better soldiers. But unlocking our full genetic potential. Letting humanity become what it was always meant to be."

"And what if what we're meant to be is *dangerous*?" She stopped pacing, faced him directly. "What if these dormant sequences are dormant for a reason? What if evolution silenced them because they were maladaptive? Because they created organisms that couldn't integrate into ecosystems? Because they were too aggressive, too predatory, too—"

"Too powerful?" Filibert finished. "Yes. Probably. Evolution silences extremes. Moderates populations toward average. But we don't need average anymore. We need exceptional. We need humans who can survive anything, adapt to anything, overcome anything."

"We need *humans*, Filibert. Not post-humans. Not evolutionary throwbacks. Not genetic chimeras created from activated junk DNA." Her voice dropped. "Kort started this reconstruction at maybe five percent genetic deviation from baseline. He's at thirty-two percent now. And climbing. At what point does he stop being my husband and become something else?"

"He's still Kort. Still has his memories, his personality, his—"

"His memories are encoded in neurons that are currently restructuring. His personality is expressed through brain chemistry that's being rewritten by new genetic instructions. When he wakes up—*if* he wakes up—he might not be the man I married. He might be someone who just has Kort's memories."

Filibert was quiet for a moment. Then: "Would that be so terrible? If he retained his identity but gained capabilities that make him stronger? Faster? More resilient?"

"It would be terrible if he lost what made him human. If the cascade stripped away empathy, or moral reasoning, or the ability to form emotional bonds." Zahra's voice cracked. "You talk about unlocking genetic potential. But what if potential includes predatory instincts? Territorial aggression? Breeding competition? All the things that evolution had to suppress for humans to form societies?"

"Then we'll deal with those challenges when they arise."

"We're creating them, Filibert. Deliberately activating genetic programs that could destroy civilization. And you talk about it like it's an engineering problem."

"It *is* an engineering problem. With proper controls, proper oversight—"

"There are no proper controls for rewriting someone's genome from the ground up. There's no oversight for creating new species." Zahra sat back down, suddenly exhausted. "I thought I was reconstructing Kort's face and throat. But I'm not. I'm midwifing the birth of something humanity has never seen. And I'm terrified of what it's going to be."

They sat in silence. In front of them, behind the double-acting doors, the reconstruction bay hummed with machinery and pulsed with the blue-gray light of the tank. Inside that tank, a man was dissolving and reforming. Dying and being reborn. Transforming from human into post-human into something that defied classification.

"The cascade will stabilize," Filibert said finally. "Around day eighteen, maybe twenty. The genetic activation will reach equilibrium. Stop spreading. Lock in."

"How do you know?"

"Because that's what happened to Jean. And Hans. And D'Arcy. And Razo." His voice went quiet. "They all showed cascade effects. All had dormant DNA activating. It always stopped between thirty and forty percent deviation. Always locked in."

"And they all died."

"Yes. Because I didn't have your regeneration protocols. Didn't have a way to manage the rejection response. But the cascade itself—that was stable. Reproducible. Always reached the same endpoint."

Zahra felt ice in her chest. "You've known about this. The whole time. You knew Kort's DNA would rewrite itself and you didn't tell me."

"I told you enough. I said the modifications were self-optimizing. The enhancements would adapt to his biology."

"That's not the same as saying his *genome would mutate.* That he'd activate thousands of dormant sequences. That he'd become a different species." She stood again, moved toward the reconstruction bay doors. "I'm done. When Kort wakes up—if he survives emergence—I'm taking him and leaving. We're going back to our life. And you can find someone else to help you play God."

"You can't leave. Not now. Not when we're so close to—"

"Close to what? Creating an army of post-humans? Triggering genetic cascades in more subjects? Seeing how far we can deviate from human baseline before we create something that can't survive?" She looked back at him. "I'm a marine biologist, Filibert. I study adaptation. And I know that extreme adaptations usually lead to extinction. Species that become too specialized, too removed from their base population—they die out when conditions change."

"Or they replace their base population entirely. Become dominant. Survive when others fail." Filibert pulled himself to his feet. "That's what we're creating. Not a deviation from humanity. The *future* of humanity."

"Then humanity's future is going to happen without me." Zahra put her hand on one of the double-acting door panels, rubbed her palm against it, soothed herself. "I'll finish the emergence protocols. Make sure Kort survives the transition from tank to independent function. But after that, I'm gone. We're gone. And I'm taking every note, every protocol, every piece of data about the cascade with me."

"You can't. This research belongs to—"

"This research belongs to no one. Because it should never have happened." She pushed on the door panel. It swung inward in quiet response to her applied pressure. She desperately needed to see Kort, watch him float, and fantasize it was all a dream and she would wake up at home in his arms. "And when I leave, I'm destroying everything. Burning my notes. Wiping the genetic sequences. Making sure no one can ever replicate what we've done."

"Zahra—"

"No. I'm done arguing. Done justifying. Done pretending that what we're doing is science rather than playing with forces we don't understand." She stepped into the reconstruction bay. "Kort survives. Then we disappear. That's my price for finishing this."

Filbert's sleep deprivation got the best of his judgment and he muttered mindlessly, "So disappointed in you, Zahra. You don't want a world with clean, surgical strike capabilities. You don't want to reduce war suffering."

Zahra froze in mid-step. She experienced a glimpse of the combat state Kort had described. It gushed through her worn out mind, body, and soul. The situation had hit a critical mass, a point of no return, in which composure collapsed into chaos.

She wrenched around, the door swung back against her. And for the first time in a long time, Filibert felt fear as she stared him down with fire in her green eyes.

"You goddamn sociopath!" Her body shook, unable to contain the rage cascade searing through her. Tears burst out along with a guttural yowl. Her right fist punched into her thigh in rapid succession. Her chest heaved, her body desperate for oxygen, and she stabbed the air with one finger towards Filibert to the rhythm of her diatribe. "War and violence are not supposed to be surgical or clean! It has to be in-your-face, grotesque and tragic and appalling, so we think twice before hurting and killing each other!"

Filibert stood, immobilized by her swift fury, feeling six years old, emerging from behind the sofa to see pieces of his mother splatter over the apartment. Trapped in time, in memory. He barely had an awareness of the double doors swinging rapidly back and forth in Zahra's wake. Alone in the corridor, absently rubbing his pocket watch in his hand, he lost track of time. But he felt time.

Half past one. Always half past one.

The moment before everything changed. The moment he'd spent forty-five years trying to recreate, trying to control, trying to master.

And Zahra wanted to walk away. Wanted to take the most important discovery in human history and bury it. Wanted to save one man while damning all of humanity to remain weak, fragile, limited.

He couldn't allow that.

But he couldn't stop her either. Not without losing Kort. Not without losing the only successful subject of the enhancement program.

So he would lie. Promise her she could leave. Promise her she could destroy the data. And then, when Kort woke up, when he was stable, when Zahra finally let her guard down—

Filibert would take everything. The genetic sequences. The cascade protocols. The proof that human DNA could be rewritten. The evidence that evolution could be accelerated, directed, controlled.

And he'd use it. Would continue the work. Would create more enhanced subjects. Would build the army of post-humans that NATO should have embraced twenty years ago.

Because some promises needed to be broken.

Some ethics needed to be violated.

Some prices were worth paying.

Even if it cost him the one person who'd come closest to understanding his work.

Even if it cost him any remaining claim to humanity.

The clock struck half past one in his mind.

And time, as always, moved forward. Inexorable. Unstoppable.

Carrying them all toward futures they couldn't control.

Part IV: Stabilization
Day 18 of Second Reconstruction

The cascade stopped.

Zahra noticed it first in the hourly genetic scans. The activation rate had been climbing steadily since day eight—new sequences expressing every hour, the percentage of active DNA growing relentlessly toward some unknown threshold.

Then at 0347 hours on day eighteen, it flatlined.

No new activations. No new sequences waking up. The percentage locked at 38.7% deviation from human baseline and stayed there.

She ran the scan again. Same result. Again. Same result. Six more times through the morning. Every scan showed the same thing.

The cascade had reached equilibrium and stopped.

Kort's DNA had finished rewriting itself.

"It's over," she said to Iniko during the morning observation shift. "The genetic activation. It stabilized."

"At what percentage?" Iniko asked.

"Thirty-eight point seven. Just below the forty percent threshold for species classification." Zahra pulled up the comparison charts. "His genome is fundamentally different from baseline human. But not different *enough* to be taxonomically distinct. He's right at the edge. The boundary between human and post-human."

"Can he breed with unmodified humans?"

The question hung in the air like smoke.

"I don't know. The reproductive compatibility tests would require..." Zahra trailed off, not wanting to complete the thought.

"Theoretically, yes. His reproductive cells should be compatible. But any offspring would carry the activated sequences. Would show cascade effects themselves."

"So it could spread. Through reproduction."

"Maybe. If the activated DNA is heritable. If it expresses in second-generation offspring." Zahra closed the comparison charts. "Or maybe the cascade only happens under specific conditions. When someone with dormant potential is exposed to the right triggers, the right environmental factors."

"The right modifications," Iniko said quietly.

"Yes. The enhancements might be the trigger. Might be what tells dormant DNA it's safe to wake up. That the organism is strong enough to handle the activation."

They watched Kort float in the tank, his reconstruction nearly complete. The jaw fully formed. The throat tissue integrated. The surface layers regenerating. In another six days, he'd be ready for emergence.

"What are you going to tell him?" Iniko asked. "When he wakes up. When he realizes what he's become."

"The truth." Zahra's voice was steady, resigned. "That we tried to save his life. That the reconstruction activated genetic sequences we didn't know existed. That he's no longer quite human but not quite post-human either. That he's something in between. Something new."

"And if he hates what he's become?"

"Then he hates it. But he'll be alive to hate it." She turned away from the observation window. "That's all I could give him. Life. Not the life he had before. Not the life he would have chosen. But life nonetheless."

"Filibert thinks you're going to leave. Disappear with Kort."

Zahra was quiet for a long moment. "I am. When he's stable. When I'm certain he can survive without constant monitoring. We're going to vanish. Live quietly somewhere Filibert can't find us. And I'm going to spend the rest of my career making sure no one can replicate what we've done here."

"By destroying the data."

"Every file. Every note. Every genetic sequence. The only record of the cascade will be what's locked in Kort's DNA. And that dies with him." She met Iniko's eyes. "Will you help me?"

Iniko considered. "Filibert saved my life. Brought me out of Nigeria when the war came. Gave me purpose, education, a career. I owe him everything."

"But?"

"But this research is too dangerous. Too unpredictable. Too likely to end badly for everyone involved." She nodded slowly. "Yes. I'll help you. When the time comes. When Kort is ready to leave."

Without betraying her thoughts, Zahra smiled and said, "Thank you." She marveled at how easily and smoothly Iniko could lie. Or maybe it was the truth at this moment. But she knew. She knew when the critical time came, Iniko would struggle to betray Filibert. She would still try and enlist Iniko. It would be better if Iniko kept her promise, but she couldn't go all in on that plan. Zahra would have to create an alternate way.

They returned to watching the tank. Inside, Kort's body pulsed with the light of the regeneration medium, his DNA stabilized at the edge of human classification, his future uncertain but at least possible.

The cascade had stopped. The genetic activation had reached its natural endpoint. And Zahra had approximately six days to finish the reconstruction, prepare Kort for emergence, and plan their escape from the facility that had transformed her husband into something unprecedented.

Six days to save what remained of his humanity.

Six days to prevent Filibert from using what they'd learned.

Six days to close Pandora's box before more horrors escaped.

The clock read 8:30 AM.

But in Zahra's mind—in the place where trauma now lived alongside hope—it felt like half past one. She began to understand the seductive quality of the obsession. Fought against it. But, oh, it was so beautiful, so inviting.

Half past one. The moment before everything changed. The moment when you could still go back, could still choose differently, could still save yourself from the future you were creating.

But you never could go back. You could only move forward. Into whatever came next. Into whatever future you'd earned through your choices.

Even if that future was something you'd never wanted. Something you'd never imagined. Something that would haunt you for the rest of your life. The tank hummed. The monitors beeped. And deep in Kort's DNA, ancient instructions slept again, their work finished, waiting for conditions that would never quite repeat. Waiting for another chance to wake up. To spread. To cascade through populations and remake humanity from the genetic level up.

Waiting.

Always waiting.

Fifteen

Awakening

Abandoned Steel Mill, Rural Pennsylvania
– Day Twenty-Eight

The second awakening was more controlled.

Zahra had insisted on it—no rushing, no immediate consciousness, no shocking Kort into panic again. They would bring him out of sedation even more gradually, in stages, allowing his reconstructed nervous system time to adjust to sensory input before demanding higher cognitive function. In Kort's favor, they had not put him into a deep medically induced coma this time. But managed his unconscious sedation with propofol. With reduction in dosage over time and Iniko's patient administration of aminophylline to facilitate the wakening, it would be quicker than the first awakening from the pentobarbital coma would allow. Still.

It took eighteen hours.

Eighteen hours of carefully titrated drug adjustments, of monitoring brain activity as it climbed from deep unconsciousness through various sleep stages toward awareness. Eighteen hours of Zahra sitting beside the medical bed, holding Kort's hand, rehearsing what she would say when his eyes opened.

I'm sorry. I had no choice. You were dying. I saved your life. Please forgive me. Please don't hate me. Please still be you underneath all the modifications.

She'd tried a hundred different combinations of words, and none of them felt adequate. None of them could bridge the gap between what she'd done and what he'd become.

Filibert and Iniko had given her privacy for this awakening. They monitored from the observation room, watching through the glass partition, ready to intervene if medical complications arose. But the actual moment of consciousness—that belonged to Zahra and Kort alone.

The morning sun filtered through the high windows of the reconstruction bay, casting long shadows across industrial architecture that had been converted into something between medical facility and biological laboratory. The tank that had held Kort for twenty-four days stood empty now, drained and cleaned, its transparent surface reflecting the morning light in fractured patterns.

A monument to transformation. Or a warning about hubris. Zahra wasn't sure which.

She watched the monitors, tracking the slow climb toward consciousness. Brain activity moving from theta waves to alpha waves. Muscle tone gradually returning. Autonomic functions stabilizing at waking parameters.

And finally—finally—his eyes began to move beneath closed lids. REM sleep. The last stage before consciousness.

Zahra squeezed his hand gently. "Kort? I'm here. It's Zahra. You're safe. Take your time waking up. Everything is okay."

It wasn't okay. Nothing was okay. But she needed to believe the lie, and she needed him to believe it too.

Kort's eyelids fluttered. Once. Twice. Then slowly opened.

The eyes that looked at her were clearer than they'd been after the first wakening. Still confused, still processing, but without the immediate panic. He studied her face silently, and Zahra couldn't read his expression. Was he angry? Grateful? Horrified? All of the above?

"Hi," she said softly. "Welcome back."

Kort tried to speak. His mouth opened—carefully, slowly, aware now of what lay beneath the human exterior—and his reconstructed throat attempted to form words.

What emerged was a rasp. Barely audible. Not human.

His eyes widened slightly. He tried again, adjusting something in the mechanics of his new throat, engaging different muscles.

"Zahra." The word was rough, distorted, but recognizable. His voice, but changed. Deeper than it had been. With an edge that suggested gravel grinding against metal.

"Yes. I'm here." She blinked back tears. "How do you feel?"

Kort was silent for a long moment, clearly taking inventory of his body. Testing systems. Feeling the differences. His free hand moved to his throat again, touched the reconstructed tissue, traced the too-thick musculature.

"Different," he finally said. Each word seemed to require effort, as if he was learning language from scratch. "Every thing... different."

"I know. I'm so sorry. But you're alive."

"Alive." He repeated the word like it was a foreign concept. Then: "Show me."

"Show you what?"

"Mirror. Need to see."

Zahra hesitated. She'd prepared for this request, had a hand mirror ready on the nearby equipment table. But she wasn't sure he was ready. The face that would look back at him wouldn't be the one he remembered.

"Maybe we should wait. Give yourself time to—"

"Show. Me." The command was clear despite the damaged voice. Despite the strangeness of his new vocal apparatus. This was still Kort, still the man who'd led soldiers and made hard decisions and faced difficult truths head-on.

Zahra retrieved the mirror, handed it to him.

Kort held it up, angled it to catch his face in the morning light.

What he saw made him go completely still.

Zahra watched his eyes move across his reflection, cataloging every change. The stronger jaw. The sharper cheekbones. The too-perfect skin. The subtle asymmetries that marked reconstructed tissue. The throat that was clearly modified even through the skin.

He touched his face with his free hand, fingers tracing the contours, confirming that the reflection matched the tactile reality. He looked younger than he should—the new tissue unmarked by age, by sun damage, by the accumulated weathering of fifty-one years of a hard-lived life.

He looked like himself viewed through a distorted lens. Recognizable but wrong. Familiar but alien.

"Jaw was shattered," Zahra said quietly, needing to fill the silence. "We had to reconstruct from cellular level up. Used your DNA as template, but the enhancement modifications influenced the development. The result is... stronger. More durable. But not identical to what you had before."

Kort tilted his head, examining the angle of his jaw. Then slowly—with visible trepidation—he opened his mouth.

The lamprey ring was hidden behind reconstructed human tissue. Normal lips. Normal tongue. Normal-looking mouth. But Zahra could see him testing it. Feeling the weight of the modified tissue. The presence of structures that shouldn't exist in a human throat.

He opened wider.

There—just visible if you knew to look for it—the beginning of the circular tooth pattern. Small protrusions barely breaking the surface of the soft tissue. Ready to extend if needed. Always present, even when hidden.

Kort closed his mouth quickly. Set the mirror down with hands that trembled slightly.

"Training accident," Zahra continued. "Neural interface malfunction. You were locked in combat state. The enhancements activated uncontrollably. Your own modifications destroyed your jaw and throat from the inside."

"How long?"

"Twenty-eight days since the accident. Twenty-four days in the regeneration tank. Four days recovering from the initial awakening."

"Don't remember. First awakening."

"You panicked. Felt the modifications in your throat. Went into combat state. We had to sedate you heavily." She paused. "I'm sorry. I should have prepared you better. Should have explained before letting you discover it on your own."

Kort was quiet, processing. His hand remained on his throat, feeling the modified tissue, adjusting to the reality of what he'd become.

"Pain?" he asked.

"No. The nerve reconstruction included enhanced pain management. You should feel pressure, temperature, touch—but pain signals are dampened unless the damage is severe enough to threaten structural integrity."

"Convenient."

The word was bitter. Sarcastic. The first indication of emotion breaking through the shock.

"Kort—"

"How much?" he interrupted.

"How much is still... human?"

Zahra had known this question was coming. Had prepared for it. But actually answering felt like betrayal.

"Your skeletal structure is human-based," she said carefully. "Enhanced, but recognizably derived from your original anatomy. Musculature is hybrid—some human, some modified tissue. Nervous system is heavily modified but maintains human organization patterns. Organs are enhanced but functional. Cardiovascular system is—"

"Numbers, Zahra. Percentages."

She took a breath. "Genetically, you're approximately 73% baseline human. The rest is modified DNA expressing non-human characteristics. Cellular composition is roughly 60% human tissue, 40% enhanced or hybrid. Structurally—"

"Enough." He closed his eyes. "Understood."

The room fell silent. Zahra wanted to touch him, to comfort him, but wasn't sure if contact would help or hurt. Wasn't sure if she had the right to comfort him when she'd made the decisions that had transformed him so completely.

"The alternative was death," she said quietly. "The damage was catastrophic. Healing naturally wasn't possible. We could let you die, or we could reconstruct. Those were the only options."

"Could have let me die."

"I couldn't. I'm sorry, but I couldn't."

Kort opened his eyes again, looked at her directly. "Why?"

"Because I love you. Because twenty-six years of marriage meant something. Because—" Her voice broke. "Because I'm selfish. I wasn't ready to lose you."

"Even if saving me meant creating... this?" He gestured to his face, his throat, his transformed body.

"Yes. Even then. I know that's not fair to you. I know you didn't consent to the extent of the modifications. But you were dying, and I couldn't let that happen."

Kort studied her face for a long moment. Zahra couldn't read his expression—the reconstructed features didn't move quite right yet, the micro-expressions that had been so familiar were different now, harder to interpret.

"Not your fault," he finally said. "Filibert's experiment. His neural interface. His failure."

"I made the decision about the reconstruction protocols. About how much modification to allow. About—" She stopped, then forced herself to continue. "About the lamprey tissue. I could have tried to remove it, suppress it, keep you more human. But the rejection risk was too high. So I let it integrate. Let it become part of your permanent biology. That was my choice, not Filibert's."

"Did you make the right choice?"

"I kept you alive. That was right."

"That wasn't the question."

Zahra didn't have an answer for that. Because she didn't know if she'd made the right choice. She'd made the choice that resulted in Kort's survival. But survival at the cost of humanity—was that right? Or just the lesser of two terrible options?

"I don't know," she admitted. "Ask me again in a year."

Kort almost smiled. The expression was strange on his reconstructed face—the muscles not quite coordinated yet, the proportions slightly off. But it was recognizably an attempt at humor.

"Fair enough."

He tried to sit up, moving carefully, testing his body's response. The enhanced musculature engaged smoothly, supporting his weight despite weeks of inactivity. He swung his legs over the side of the bed, feet touching the cold concrete floor.

"Dizzy?" Zahra asked.

"No. Everything feels... precise. Clear. Like my body is responding faster than it should."

"The enhancements are fully integrated now. The regeneration process didn't just reconstruct your tissue—it optimized the modifications. Made them more efficient. You're probably stronger and faster than you were before the accident."

Kort flexed his hands, watching the play of muscles under perfect skin. "Stronger. Faster. More modified. More post-human." He looked at her. "Less me."

"You're still you. The modifications don't change who you are."

"Don't they? I have teeth in my throat, Zahra. Biological weapons growing inside my mouth. I can feel them. Always there. Always ready to activate. Tell me that doesn't change who I am."

Zahra had no counter-argument. Because he was right. The modifications did change him. Not just physically but psychologically. Knowing what he carried in his throat, what he could do with those lamprey teeth—that knowledge would shape every interaction, every conversation, every moment of self-perception.

You couldn't be human while carrying the tools of a deep-sea predator in your throat.

"I'm sorry," she said again, the words inadequate but all she had.

Kort stood—slowly, testing his balance, adjusting to the enhanced musculature and changed body proportions. He walked to the empty tank, placed his hand against the transparent surface, looked at his reflection in the curved polymer.

"Twenty-four days in there," he said. "Dissolving. Rebuilding. Becoming something new." He turned back to Zahra. "What did Filibert call it? Post-human? New species?"

"Something like that."

"He's right. I can feel it. This isn't enhancement anymore. This is transformation. I'm not a modified human. I'm something else that remembers being human."

"Kort—"

"It's okay." He cut her off gently. "Not blaming you. Not angry. Just... processing. Understanding what I've become." He walked back to the bed, sat down beside her. "Tell me everything. The accident. The decision to reconstruct. The protocols you used. All of it. I need to understand what happened to me."

So Zahra told him. Everything. The neural interface malfunction. The catastrophic enhancement cascade. The jaw fracturing from his own muscle contractions. The lamprey tissue tearing itself apart. The eighteen hours he'd spent dying while they tried to stabilize him.

The desperate call that had brought her to Pennsylvania. The decision to use her octopus regeneration protocols. The twenty-four days of cellular reconstruction, fighting rejection, balancing human and post-human biology.

The choice—her choice—to let the lamprey modifications integrate rather than suppress them. To allow his throat to become fully hybrid rather than maintain human baseline.

Kort listened without interruption, his face unreadable, his new voice silent as she explained how she'd transformed him.

When she finished, he was quiet for a long time.

"The other option," he finally said. "Suppressing the lamprey tissue. How high was the rejection risk?"

"Over eighty percent. Collapse would have been almost certain."

"So you chose guaranteed survival over probable death."

"Yes."

"And the cost of that survival was completing my transformation into post-human."

"Yes."

Kort nodded slowly. "Okay."

"Okay?" Zahra couldn't keep the surprise from her voice. "That's all? Just okay?"

"What else should it be? You made a decision under impossible circumstances. You chose life over death. I can't fault you for that, even if the life you chose isn't the one I would have picked."

"But the modifications—"

"Were already part of me. You didn't make me post-human, Zahra. Filibert started that process over thirty years ago. You just finished what he started. Completed the transformation instead of letting me die caught between human and enhanced." He took her hand. "I'm not happy about what I've become. But I'm grateful I'm alive to be unhappy about it."

Zahra felt tears fighting to spill out and stream down her cheeks. She held them in check. "I was so afraid you'd hate me."

"I don't hate you. I'm..." He paused, searching for words with his new voice. "I'm adjusting. Processing. Trying to understand what it means to be this thing I've become. But none of that is your fault. You saved my life. However transformed that life is now, it's still life. That's worth something."

"Is it? Is life worth living if you're not human anymore?"

"I don't know. But I'm going to find out." He squeezed her hand gently. "We both are." A tenderness somehow came through his eyes now and he said, "Zahra, thank you for coming to the lab, for getting involved, for being my life partner, my wife."

Zahra trembled. She couldn't have held back her tears any longer if her life depended on it.

Over the next three hours, Kort tested his new body systematically. Walking first—the enhanced musculature responded smoothly, balance and coordination better than they'd been before the accident. Then simple manipulations—picking up objects, adjusting grip strength, testing fine motor control.

All functional. All enhanced. All slightly alien.

Zahra monitored from the observation station, tracking his vitals, watching for signs of rejection or instability. But everything remained stable.

The reconstruction had succeeded. Kort's new biology was accepting itself, functioning as intended.

He was whole. Just not human anymore.

Filibert entered the reconstruction bay as Kort was testing his vocal range, experimenting with the reconstructed throat's capabilities.

"Brother," he said, his voice thick with relief and scientific satisfaction. "You survived."

Kort turned to face him. For a moment, Zahra thought he might attack—saw the tension in his enhanced musculature, the predatory focus in his eyes. But then Kort relaxed slightly, consciously choosing to not engage the combat state.

"I survived," Kort agreed. "Your experiment didn't kill me."

"It wasn't an experiment. The neural interface should have been safe. The calculations were perfect."

"Calculations are never perfect when applied to biology. You should know that by now. How many test subjects do you need to lose before learning that lesson?"

Filibert flinched. "The others were different. Their biology rejected the modifications. You accepted them. You've always accepted them."

"Until they nearly killed me."

"Yes. Until then." Filibert moved closer, studying Kort's reconstructed face with undisguised fascination. "But look at you now. The reconstruction is remarkable. The integration of enhanced and regenerated tissue. The optimization of the modifications. You're more advanced than you were before the accident."

"More post-human, you mean."

"Yes. More evolved. More capable. More—"

"Monstrous," Kort interrupted. "The word you're avoiding is monstrous."

"You're not a monster. You're the future. The proof that humans can transcend their biological limitations. That we can direct our own evolution toward something greater."

Kort laughed—a harsh sound that scraped through his reconstructed throat. "Something greater? Filibert, I have a lamprey mouth growing in my throat. I'm fifty-one years old but look thirty. My DNA is 27% non-human. I'm not greater. I'm just different. Other. Alien."

"Alien to what? To baseline humanity? Yes. But baseline humanity is limited. Weak. Prone to disease and aging and death. You've transcended those limitations. That's not monstrous—that's miraculous."

"It's both." Kort's hand went to his throat again, a gesture Zahra realized was becoming habitual. Touching the physical manifestation of his transformation. "The modifications give me capabilities beyond human norm. But they also mark me as non-human. Separate me from the species I was born into. That's both miraculous and monstrous. Both gift and curse."

Filibert seemed to deflate slightly. "You're right. I'm sorry. I get caught up in the science and forget the personal cost. Forget that you're not just a test subject but my brother." He paused. "Are we still brothers? Despite everything?"

Kort studied Filibert. They were the same age, but the man before him appeared old—ancient. The scientist who'd modified him, who'd nearly killed him, who'd spent thirty years transforming him from human to post-human. The brother by choice, not by blood. The architect of everything Kort had become.

"Yes," he said finally. "We're still brothers. But Filibert—no more experiments. No more untested interfaces. No more pushing the modifications to see what breaks. I'm done being your test subject."

"Then what will you be?"

"I don't know yet. But I need to figure that out without you making decisions about my biology."

Filibert nodded, accepting the boundary. "Understood. No more modifications without your explicit consent."

"Thank you."

Iniko appeared in the doorway, tablet in hand. "Kort, if you're feeling up to it, we should run some functional tests. Make sure all systems are responding properly. Baseline performance metrics for comparison with pre-accident data."

Kort looked to Zahra, silently asking permission. She nodded.

"Let's get it over with," he said.

The functional testing took hours. Strength measurements. Reflex tests. Cognitive assessments. Sensory evaluation. Every system checked and rechecked, compared against pre-accident baselines, measured against theoretical optima.

The results were undeniable: Kort was better.

Stronger—an increase in muscular force generation. Faster—reaction times improved by 40%. More durable—tissue resistance to damage significantly enhanced. Better healing—cellular regeneration rates doubled.

And his cognitive function was sharper. Information processing faster. Memory recall more precise. Pattern recognition more acute.

The accident that had nearly killed him had made him more capable in almost every measurable way.

"It's the optimization," Filibert explained, reviewing the data with barely contained excitement. "The regeneration process didn't just rebuild your tissue—it refined the modifications. Removed inefficiencies. Integrated systems that were previously separate. You're not just restored. You're upgraded."

Kort looked at the numbers on the screen, seeing the proof of his own post-humanity quantified in percentages and measurements. "And the cost of this upgrade? Besides the obvious physical transformation?"

"Unknown. We'll need to monitor long-term. But based on these results, the modifications appear stable. The rejection risk is minimal. Barring trauma or deliberate interference, you should remain at this enhancement level indefinitely."

"Indefinitely. Meaning I'll stay post-human forever."

"Meaning you'll stay alive forever. Or as close to it as we can currently achieve." Filibert pulled up cellular analysis data. "Look at this. Your telomeres aren't shortening at normal rates. DNA damage is being repaired faster than it accumulates. By every metric we can measure, your biological aging has slowed to near-zero."

Kort studied the data, understanding the implications. "So I'm not just post-human. I'm potentially immortal."

"Biologically, yes. You can still be killed by sufficient trauma. But barring that, your enhanced biology should maintain itself indefinitely."

"While everyone around me ages and dies."

"Yes."

Kort closed his eyes. "Including Zahra."

The room fell silent.

Zahra had known this was coming. Had understood the implications of Kort's enhanced longevity since before the accident. But hearing it stated so baldly—hearing the future quantified in years and decades she wouldn't live to see—made it real in a way it hadn't been before.

"We could modify you too," Filibert suggested quietly. "Use what we learned from Kort's reconstruction. Apply the regeneration protocols to your biology. Grant you the same extended lifespan."

"No." Zahra's response was immediate. "Absolutely not."

"But think about it. You could stay with him. Share his longevity. Continue your research for decades instead of years. Make contributions to science that would be impossible in a normal human lifespan."

"At the cost of my humanity? At the cost of becoming post-human myself? No. I've seen what that transformation requires. I've watched it happen to Kort. I won't do that to myself."

"Even if it means losing him? Even if it means watching him live on while you age and die?"

"Yes. Even then." She looked at Kort. "We'll have whatever time we have. And when my time ends, he'll continue without me. That's how it should be."

Kort opened his eyes, looked at her with an expression she couldn't quite read. Gratitude? Sadness? Relief that she wasn't asking him to watch her transform into something post-human?

"Thank you," he said quietly.

"For what?"

"For choosing to stay human. For not asking me to watch you go through what I went through. For accepting that we have different futures now, and that's okay."

Zahra felt tears threatening again. "It's not okay. None of this is okay. But it's what we have. So we'll make it enough."

They stood together in the reconstruction bay, surrounded by the evidence of successful biological transformation. The empty tank. The monitoring equipment. The data showing Kort's optimized post-human biology.

Behind them, Filibert reviewed the functional test results with scientific satisfaction. This was his life's work validated. Proof that human enhancement was not just possible but sustainable. That post-human biology could be stable, functional, superior to baseline humanity in every measurable way.

But looking at Kort—at his too-perfect face and modified throat and the weight of immortality settling on his shoulders—Zahra wondered if superior was the right word.

Different, certainly. Enhanced, measurably. But superior? That implied value judgment she wasn't sure she could make.

Kort was post-human now. But was he better for it? Or just other?

Time would tell. Decades of time. Centuries, possibly.

Time Zahra wouldn't live to see.

The morning sun continued its climb toward noon. Outside, the world proceeded normally—people aging at regular rates, dying on schedule, living their limited human lives with the certainty of finite time.

Inside the steel mill, a new form of life had awakened. Not quite human. Not quite other. Something in between.

Something that would have to learn how to exist in a world not designed for its longevity.

Something that still remembered being human.

And that memory—that ghost of humanity haunting post-human biology—might be the greatest burden of all.

The resurrection was complete.

The awakening had begun.

And now came the hardest part: learning to live with what they'd created.

And then that terrible night of betrayal; Kort secretly sedated and sequestered; Zahra fleeing for her life, vanishing; her job, their home abandoned.

The start of the full transformation of Kort into an ultimate weaponized being.

Years of Filibert struggling to unlock the critical formulas Zahra had applied and kept secret from him.

Fifteen dark years.

Sixteen

First Strike

Bismarck, North Dakota – Fall of 2005

The rooftop of the Belle Mehus City Auditorium was easy to access undetected in the waning daylight—for a skilled operative—by way of the World War Memorial Building. It afforded an unusual strategic and reconnaissance advantage. For thousands of years of military doctrine, securing the high ground was foundational to gather intel, to defend, and to strike. Professional security units, in their security assessment of a location before the principle arrived, always gave special attention to surrounding high ground.

That was their mistake today.

Foundational military doctrine did not constrain Kort. He counter-planned against it. Exploited known standard operations to his advantage.

The auditorium's rooftop provided a low-level vantage point to the nine-story Radisson Hotel—82.9056 meters across East Broadway Avenue from the auditorium. The Bismarck Civic Center located only blocks away, south of the hotel, completed the set-up for the mission.

Kort sat cross-legged on the auditorium's rooftop, his body absolutely still, a statue carved from living tissue and bioengineered modifications. The black electrified suit that encased him—texture like amphibian skin, leaking gray goo from joint-stress points—made him nearly invisible against the sky as nightfall set in.

Where his face should be, only an opaque faceplate. No features. No humanity. Just smooth surface that reflected the emerging city lights in fractured patterns. No external optic device was needed. The modifications Filibert had perfected over the past fifteen years allowed him to see through concrete walls, track heat signatures, identify targets with precision that made special equipment obsolete.

Across the street, the Radisson Hotel entrance glowed with warm exterior and lobby lighting, random room windows dotted the building with a golden-orange light pattern. Inside, Senator Jon Toresen prepared to address his supporters. A movement to secede from the Union. To create the Middle States of America. To challenge the federal government's authority.

Kort's faceplate display tracked the senator's heat signature. Seventh floor. Corner suite. Currently in the bathroom with his wife, arguing about whether to evacuate or stay and face the bomb threat that had delayed his arrival to his rally at the Civic center.

The bomb threat Kort had orchestrated. A diversion. Tactical misdirection. Classic military strategy applied to political assassination.

Inside his helmet, data scrolled across the display in Russian. Mission parameters. Power levels. Time remaining. Everything quantified, measured, controlled.

ELIMINATE TARGET. NO COLLATERAL.

Simple. Surgical. Precise.

This was what he'd been rebuilt for. Not family dinners and suburban normalcy. Not pretending to be human while carrying post-human biology. This—hunting, targeting, eliminating threats—this was where the modifications made sense. Where the monster Zahra had created found purpose.

Kort's breathing was steady, controlled, barely disturbing the suit's surface. The modifications that had terrified him fifteen years ago had become familiar. Comfortable, even. The lamprey teeth in his throat, the enhanced musculature, the bioengineered armor panels—all of it had integrated into his sense of self.

He wasn't Kort Sokolov the man anymore. He was Kort Sokolov the weapon. And weapons didn't agonize over their nature. They simply functioned.

The faceplate display shifted, tracking movement in the hotel. Senator Toresen's wife left the bathroom, checked on their two children with hugs and face strokes to reassure. She returned to the bathroom and shut the door.

Kort's hand moved to the pen-like device beside him. A detonator. Remote trigger for the car bombs he'd planted around the Civic Center. The diversion was ready for execution. His thumb hovered over the red button.

The senator's security detail actively worked the room. Quick checks from the side of the window; hallway checks through a cracked door. Standard high alert protocol underway. The security detail maintaining vigilance in a space that seemed to shrink as the tension mounted. As they waited for Jon's decision.

But his decision would come too late.

Inside the Radisson Hotel - Senator Toresen's Suite

Kari Toresen watched her husband with growing frustration. Jon stood at the bathroom sink, hands braced against the marble countertop, staring at his reflection like he could find answers in his own face. They had retreated to the bathroom to have their confrontation. Even though the hotel categorized the room as an "executive suite" it was too close-quartered for privacy.

Jon had hand-picked the historic downtown Bismarck area to kick off his campaign. In a city known for favoring messages of traditional family values and states' rights—the capital city of a state with the highest percentage of Norwegian ancestry in the U.S. And now, the result of his strategic brand management?—Trapped.

"We need to leave," she said, not for the first time. "Jon, please. The children are terrified."

"I can't abandon the people. Not now. Not when they need leadership."

"They need you alive. What good is a dead martyr to the Middle States movement?"

Jon turned from the mirror, his jaw set with stubborn determination. "This is exactly what Washington wants—to scare us into submission. To make us run like cowards. I won't give them that satisfaction."

In the main area, their two young children—Erik and Lisa—sat on the sofa with wide, frightened eyes. Hal and David, the executive protection agents, stood by the door with professional alertness that barely masked concern.

The TV showed news coverage of the Civic Center evacuation. A mixture of state, county, and city law enforcement officers directing crowds. No sign of the bomb that had supposedly been reported.

Jon and Kari emerged from the bathroom. Viewed the news report. Viewed the security detail on high alert. Viewed their scared children trying to look brave.

"It could be a false alarm," Jon said, gesturing to the screen. "Some crank caller trying to disrupt the rally. We can't let fear dictate—"

The television flickered. Static. The picture degraded for just a moment before returning.

Hal's hand went to his earpiece. "Sir, we're experiencing electronic interference. Communications are spotty."

David checked his radio. Dead. "Mine's not working either."

Outside, the street lights began to flicker. On and off. On and off. A pattern that suggested power fluctuation or something deliberately disrupting the electrical systems.

Kari felt cold dread settling in her stomach. "Jon—"

Massive, heavy thuds resonated through the room followed by loud, shaking: *BOOM, BOOM, BOOM, BOOM, BOOM, BOOM!*

"Down!" Hal shouted, drawing his weapon.

But before anyone could move, the lights in the suite died. Complete darkness except for the ambient glow from the city outside.

Rooftop of Belle Mehus City Auditorium - Moments Earlier

Kort's thumb pressed the detonator.

Two blocks south, six cars dispersed in the Civic Center's parking lots exploded in sequence. Massive fireballs that lit the night sky. Screams erupted from the evacuated crowd. Emergency vehicles scrambled. Every law enforcement officer on scene suddenly had a catastrophic crisis to manage.

Exactly as planned.

The chaos at the Civic Center meant no one was paying attention to the rooftop across from the Radisson. No one was monitoring the street lights flickering from electromagnetic interference. No one was tracking the heat signature of an enhanced soldier preparing to eliminate a political target.

Kort's display updated:

DIVERSION COMPLETE. ELIMINATE.

He stood slowly, his movements fluid despite the bulky suit. The adaptive camouflage began shifting with his change in posture, matching the surrounding environment and the night sky. His body shimmered, became nearly invisible, a predator using nature's own stealth technology enhanced by human engineering.

Kort moved to the edge of the rooftop, his enhanced vision penetrating the Radisson's concrete walls. Thermal imaging showed heat signatures moving in the seventh-floor suite. The senator's protection agents positioning themselves defensively. The wife gathering the children. The senator himself standing frozen, processing the explosion across the city.

Too many people, too small a space—he needed the senator isolated. Away from the children. Away from the family. The mission parameters were explicit: **NO COLLATERAL.**

Kort reached out with his enhanced senses, tracking electromagnetic patterns in the building. Found the suite's electrical system. And with a focused pulse of energy from his suit—a modification that Filibert had perfected over decades—he shut down the power.

Inside the Suite

"Tac lights!" David commanded, fumbling to toggle on the tactical light mounted on his weapon.

Hal was already moving toward the senator. "Sir, we need to evacuate now. Whatever's happening—"

"The explosion," Jon said pointing at the TV that had gone dark, his voice surprisingly steady. "At the Civic Center. That was real. This isn't a drill."

"Which is exactly why we need to get you to ."

Kari was already moving, gathering Erik and Lisa, speaking to them in low, calming tones. "It's okay, babies. We're going somewhere safe. Just like a game, remember? Like hide and seek."

Jon looked torn. Everything in him screamed to stay, to show leadership in crisis, to refuse to be intimidated. But looking at the fear in his family's faces, he knew there was only one choice.

"All right. We go. But carefully. Hal, my family is the priority now, understood?"

"Affirmative," Hal nodded.

Jon moved to the corner desk to retrieve his briefcase as Hal and David ushered Kari and the children towards the door at the opposite end of the room.

Hal called out as he reached for the door handle, "Sir, we need to go now, right—"

The room window exploded inward.

Not from a bullet. Just a crack—sudden, sharp—radiating outward from a single point. Like something had struck the glass with enough force to compromise its integrity. Glass shards sprayed into the room, but seemed to transform into a fine dust before hitting the floor. A wind rushed into the room, billowing the drapes, followed by the chaotic street noise of first responder sirens.

And in that moment of blindness, his eyes shielded against the explosion by his arm, Jon Toresen felt something he couldn't name. It gripped his heart, choked his breath. A presence. Like being watched by something that saw more than visible light could reveal.

Jon unshielded his eyes as Kari screamed. There, framed by the flapping drapes, backlit by ambient city light filtering through the broken window, something stood.

At first, Jon's mind refused to process it. The shape was wrong. Too tall. Too bulky. The surface seemed to shimmer, adapting to the available light, making it nearly invisible except for the outline.

Then it stepped forward, moving with liquid grace that contradicted its size. Hal and David's tactical flashlight beams caught it fully.

Black suit that looked grown rather than manufactured. No visible face, just a smooth plate where features should be. And leaking from joint points—some kind of gray fluid that looked organic and technological simultaneously.

"Jesus Christ," Hal breathed. He stepped forward in front of David and the family, unable to cover Jon, weapon raised with intent.

The creature's head tilted. Processing. Analyzing. The faceplate reflected the flashlight beams in patterns that suggested internal displays, data processing, targeting systems.

It shifted its weight towards Jon—and Hal's weapon discharged. Three shots. Close range. Can't miss.

All three rounds hit the creature center mass with audible impact. *CRACK! CRACK! CRACK!*

But instead of blood, instead of the creature going down, there was just a crackling sound. Like electricity arcing through damaged circuits. The bullets had struck something hard beneath the black suit—armor plating that absorbed kinetic energy and dispersed it.

The creature didn't even stagger.

"RUN!" David screamed, pushing Kari towards the door with a backward sweep of his left arm, stepping clear of the children.

Kort attacked.

He moved across the suite in three strides, his enhanced speed making him blur in the flashlight beams. He reached Hal before the agent could get off another burst, grabbed him by the throat with one hand, and simply squeezed.

The crunch of vertebrae was audible even over Kari's screams.

Hal dropped, dead before he hit the floor.

David was shooting now, advancing into the room, emptying his magazine into Kort's back. The rounds impacted with that same crackling sound, each bullet absorbed by the bioengineered armor. Kort turned, almost leisurely, and backhanded David across the room.

The agent crashed into the wall with enough force to leave a depression in the drywall. He slumped, unconscious or dead—Kort didn't care which.

That left the senator and his family.

Kari had gotten the door open, was pushing the children through into the hallway. "Run!" she screamed at them. "Run and don't look back!"

Erik and Lisa fled, their small feet pounding down the hotel corridor.

Jon Toresen stepped between Kort and his wife. No weapon. No training. Just a middle-aged politician in a suit, facing something that had killed two trained protection agents in seconds.

"Please," Jon said, his voice shaking but steady. "Let them go. If you want me, take me. But let my family go."

Kari backed slowly, reluctantly, into the hallway to Jon's subtle, flicking hand gesture for her to go.

Kort's faceplate display updated:

TARGET ACQUIRED. ELIMINATE.

But something held him. Some ghost of humanity that the modifications hadn't fully erased. Looking at the senator—unarmed, terrified, but standing between a monster and his family—Kort saw himself. Saw the soldier he'd been before Filibert's modifications. The man who'd believed in protecting the innocent. He directed his palm toward the door—a burst of energy slammed it shut—destabilizing its structure.

The mission parameters were clear:

ONE SHOT. NO COLLATERAL.

The children running. The wife shut out in the hallway. Only the senator in the room.

Parameters satisfied.

Kort's hand shot out, grabbed Jon by the throat, lifted him off his feet. The senator struggled, gasped, his hands clawing uselessly at Kort's bioengineered arm.

"You're Norwegian," Kort said, his voice filtered through the faceplate, distorted and mechanical. "Descendant of Vikings. You believe in your heritage? Your blood?"

Jon nodded, unable to speak.

"This is a message," Kort continued. "For someone who also believes in Norwegian heritage. In blood. In power." He leaned closer, his faceless plate reflecting Jon's terrified expression. "This is to tell him Filibert Austerlitz sends his regards. To tell him the clocks are being reset."

Jon's eyes widened. "I don't—I don't understand—"

"You don't have to."

Kort dropped the senator hard to the floor and dragged him by the collar to the bathroom. He roughly jerked Jon up in front of the bathroom mirror. Made him look at his own reflection. Then—with mechanical precision—Kort raised his free hand. His palm opened, revealing something in the center of the bioengineered suit. A focused emitter. A weapon that Filibert had developed from Tesla's research. Directed energy that could penetrate tissue with surgical accuracy.

"Not personal," Kort said. "A message."

"To who?" Jon gasped.

"To the man who ended my brother's work. Who stole his research. Who destroyed everything Filibert built." Kort paused. "Your death proves we still exist. That the project continued. That Mathias Sørensen's attempt to bury us failed."

Jon's eyes went wide with recognition. "Mathias—you mean the NATO—"

The emitter fired.

The focused energy beam punched through Jon's skull with precision that left no damage to surrounding tissue.

Just a perfect hole. The senator's eyes rolled back. His body went slack.

Kort lowered him to the bathroom floor, positioned him carefully. Made sure the message would be clear: this was an execution, not random violence. This was surgical. Professional. Impossible.

The kind of kill that would make people ask questions.

The kind of kill that would force Mathias Sørensen to respond.

Kort stepped back, looked at what he'd done. Felt nothing. The modifications that had horrified him years ago had done their work too well. He was a weapon now. Weapons didn't feel remorse.

But somewhere deep in the post-human biology, in the ghost of consciousness that still remembered being human, Kort Sokolov felt something break.

Another piece of humanity lost.

Another step toward becoming the monster Zahra had always feared he'd become.

Outside the Radisson Hotel

George, the elderly hotel security guard, stood in the middle of East Broadway Avenue staring up at the seventh floor. He'd heard the commotion, had come outside to investigate, and now he watched with growing horror as the street lights flickered wildly.

His pacemaker—thirty years old, analog technology—began to malfunction. The electromagnetic interference from Kort's suit wreaked havoc on the simple electronics. George clutched his chest, feeling his heart rhythm go erratic.

Then he saw it.

A shape on a seventh floor poured out over a window ledge. It climbed—or slid?—down the exterior wall, walking on feet, leaning back with one-handed contact to the wall, like gravity was optional. Moving with impossible grace. The black suit shifting colors as it descended, adapting to the building's surface, making the figure nearly invisible.

George pointed, tried to shout a warning. But his pacemaker was failing. His heart was fibrillating. He dropped to his knees, one hand clutching his chest, the other pointing at the impossible figure on the side of the building.

David stumbled out of the hotel entrance, one hand pressed to his bleeding head, his weapon drawn. He looked where George was pointing. Saw Kort for just a moment—a shimmer against the building surface—then the figure dropped to ground level and sprinted away.

David fired. Three rounds. Maybe hit, maybe didn't—impossible to tell with something that moved that fast.

Kort felt one bullet impact his shoulder blade with a *CRACKLE* of dispersed kinetic energy. The bioengineered armor absorbed most of it, but some damage got through. The shoulder panel would need replacement.

But he was alive. Mobile. Mission complete.

He ran down East Broadway Avenue, his enhanced speed carrying him past stopped traffic and shocked pedestrians. The street lights continued their manic flickering, tracking his passage, marking his electromagnetic signature.

Behind him, sirens. Screams. Chaos.

The Liberty Memorial Bridge loomed ahead. Kort vaulted the railing in a single leap, looked back at the burning chaos he'd created—the Civic Center parking lots still smoldering, emergency vehicles converging, a city in crisis—and allowed himself one moment of satisfaction.

The message had been sent.

Filibert's revenge had begun.

Mathias Sørensen would have no choice but to respond.

Kort fell from the bridge, plummeting into the dark waters of the Missouri River below. The impact into the cold 14°C river would have killed a human. Shattered bones, ruptured organs, catastrophic trauma—the rapid cold shock alone killing within seconds.

But Kort wasn't human anymore.

He hit the water and let the river carry him downstream, toward the extraction point where Filibert and Iniko waited. His faceplate display showed critical warnings:

POWER CORE LOW. TIME TO FAILURE: 2 HOURS.

The enhanced biology required constant energy. Without regular recharging, the modifications would begin to cannibalize themselves. System collapse within hours.

But two hours was enough. Enough to reach extraction. Enough to complete the mission. Enough to survive.

Always surviving. That's what the modifications had given him. Not humanity. Not peace. Not purpose. Just the ability to survive when death should have claimed him.

Kort floated in the dark water, looking up at the night sky, and wondered if survival was worth the price he'd paid for it. But weapons don't wonder. Weapons don't question. Weapons just function.

And he was a weapon now. Had been since that day in the regeneration tank. Since Zahra had made the choice to save him by transforming him. Since he'd awakened with teeth in his throat and immortality in his cells and humanity as just a memory.

The river carried him away from the burning city, away from the political target he'd eliminated—the message sent, away from the life he might have had if Filibert's modifications had never existed.

Carried him toward whatever came next in this post-human existence.

The clock struck half past one.

But that couldn't be right.

It was never half past one.

Except in Filibert's obsession. Except in the moment before everything changed. Except in the space between human and post-human where Kort now existed permanently.

Always half past one.

Forever.

The first strike was complete.

The war had begun.

Seventeen

Response

Homeland Security Headquarters, Washington D.C. – 36 Hours After Bismarck

Director Marcus Graven had been in crisis management for twenty-five years. One of the original FBI agents assigned to the first Joint Terrorism Task Force in New York City. And then when the towers fell, he was top pick for the newly formed Department of Homeland Security. The years of law enforcement weighed on his face; he had long ago neglected his body but could still leap into action when needed. His eyes were still sharp though, missing nothing—a tool of intimidation. He'd coordinated responses to terrorist attacks, natural disasters, assassination attempts, and infrastructure failures. He'd seen carnage that would break most people. He'd made decisions that cost lives to save more lives.

But nothing in his experience had prepared him for this.

The conference room reeked of stale coffee and desperation. Officials who should have been home sleeping sat hunched over laptops, reviewing footage for the hundredth time, looking for explanations that made sense. Looking for an enemy they could understand.

What they had instead was something from a nightmare.

Graven stood at the head of the table, watching the wall monitor cycle through surveillance footage. The images were grainy, corrupted by electromagnetic interference, but clear enough to be deeply disturbing.

Parking lot security camera: A pedestrian grabbing his ear in pain moments before the first car bomb detonated. Then static. Then nothing but burning vehicles.

Bridge camera sequence: Six different angles, each showing a pulse of interference traveling down the Liberty Memorial Bridge like an invisible wave. And in the moment between static bursts—if you knew where to look—a dark shape moving impossibly fast.

Hotel exterior camera: Street lights flickering wildly. An elderly man clutching his chest—pacemaker failure, the autopsy would later confirm. And in the background, barely visible, something descending the building's exterior wall.

"Run it again," Graven said. "Frame by frame on the bridge sequence."

The technician manipulated the controls. The video advanced one frame at a time. Static. Clear. Static. Clear. And in the clear frames—

There.

A figure. Dark. Humanoid but wrong somehow. The proportions slightly off. Moving between frames in ways that suggested speed beyond human capability.

"Freeze that. Enhance."

The image zoomed, pixelated, clarified as much as the technology allowed. The figure was wearing some kind of suit—black, seamless, conforming to the body like a second skin. No visible seams or fasteners. And where the face should be, just a smooth surface that reflected light wrong.

"Thirty-two feet," Agent Winstead reported, consulting trajectory analysis. The young man exemplified the valued agent traits: motivated, disciplined, and determined.

"He covered thirty-two feet between camera frames. That's point-two seconds at standard frame rate. That's—"

"A hundred and sixty feet per second," Graven finished. "Over a hundred miles per hour. On foot."

The room fell silent.

"Olympic sprinters top out around forty-four feet per second," Agent Freeh, a balding man in his fifties, said quietly. "This thing is moving more than three times faster than the fastest human alive."

"It's not human." The voice came from the corner of the room where Rune, the agency's newly assigned historian, sat chewing on his unlit pipe. A generally non-descript middle-aged man, he looked every bit the part of an academic. "We need to stop pretending this is a normal threat. Stop trying to fit it into categories we understand."

"Then what is it?" Winstead demanded. "Some kind of robot? Powered armor? Explain to me how a man moves that fast without mechanical assistance."

"Not mechanical." Rune stood, moved to the wall monitor, pointed at the interference patterns. "See this? The electromagnetic disruption? It travels with him. Emanates from him. That's not technology in the traditional sense—that's biological. Or bio-technological. Something that blurs the line between organism and machine."

Graven had been expecting this. Had known since the first reports came in that his department historian would connect the dots. That's why he'd been brought on board, after all,—his specialty in Cold War experimental weapons programs.

"Project 19.5," Graven said. Not a question.

"Yes." Rune pulled out a folder, spread documents across the conference table. Heavily redacted pages. Black bars covering most of the text. But enough visible to paint a disturbing picture. "NATO funded it in 1961. Goal: create enhanced soldiers. Genetic modification, biological augmentation, integration of organic and synthetic systems. The program was officially terminated in 1970."

"Officially," Freeh repeated. "But unofficially?"

"Unofficially, someone kept working. Took the research underground. And thirty-five years later, that someone has perfected what NATO abandoned as impossible."

Graven moved to the table, scanned the documents. Names jumped out at him: Dr. Filibert Austerlitz, primary researcher. Kort Sokolov, test subject. Project terminated due to "unacceptable mortality rates" among subjects.

"Four men died," Rune continued. "All enhanced soldiers. Their modifications caused aggressive cancers, organ failures, systemic rejections. The program was shut down because the technology killed everyone it was supposed to help."

"Everyone except one," Graven said, reading further. "Sokolov survived. Subject demonstrated 'unprecedented integration of enhancement protocols.' Where is he now?"

"Unknown. Disappeared in 1990. Vanished without a trace like Dr. Austerlitz did over 30 years ago." Rune paused. "Until thirty-six hours ago, when something impossible killed Senator Toresen in a way that suggests technology that shouldn't exist."

Winstead pulled up autopsy photos on the monitor. Jon Toresen's body, focusing on the head wound. A perfect circular hole through the skull. No burning, no spalling, no exit wound. Just precise tissue destruction that suggested directed energy weapon technology decades ahead of current capability.

"The wound pattern matches theoretical models for particle beam weapons," Winstead explained. "But those are laboratory curiosities. They require massive power sources, cooling systems, targeting computers. You can't miniaturize that technology down to man-portable size."

"Unless," Rune said quietly, "your power source is biological. Unless the weapon is integrated into living tissue. Unless you've been perfecting the technology for thirty years without oversight or ethical constraints."

The implications settled over the room like a suffocating blanket.

"So, we're hunting a sixty-six-year-old man who moves at superhuman speeds, generates electromagnetic pulses, carries directed energy weapons in his body, and has been modified to the point where he's barely human anymore." Graven said it flatly, forcing himself to acknowledge the reality. "And this man is working with—or for—a scientist who disappeared thirty years ago with classified research."

"That's, yeah that's the assessment," Rune confirmed.

"Then we need to find them. Fast. Before whoever they're working for decides to kill someone else." Graven turned to his team. "What do we have on Dr. Austerlitz? Where would he hide? What resources would he need?"

Freeh pulled up a new file. "Austerlitz was brilliant but paranoid. Published papers suggest he didn't trust institutional oversight. Multiple complaints about him conducting unauthorized experiments at Columbia and MIT before his NATO involvement."

"Hmm... he'd want somewhere isolated," Graven reasoned. "Somewhere he could work without scrutiny. Probably near industrial infrastructure for power and equipment. Probably near water for cooling and disposal."

"There's something else," Freeh said, pulling up financial records. "In the years before he disappeared, Austerlitz liquidated significant assets. Sold properties, cashed out investments. Approximately twelve million dollars moved through various offshore accounts and shell corporations. That's enough to establish a significant research facility."

"Trace the money. Find out where it went."

"Already on it. But the trail goes cold around 1972 after he reportedly had returned to the States. Whoever helped him hide it knew what they were doing."

Graven's phone rang—his private line. Only a handful of people had the number. He answered. "Graven."

"Director Graven, this is Deputy Secretary Morrison at State. We have a situation."

Graven's jaw tightened. In his experience, calls from State never brought good news. "Go ahead."

"NATO's Joint Warfare Centre in Norway has requested our assistance. They believe the Bismarck incident is connected to classified research that originated in their facilities. They're setting up a secure emergency video call for a representative to brief you."

"Who?"

"Mathias Sørensen. He heads their Research and Development division. I'll meet you in the Pennsylvania Boardroom at the Ronald Regan Building in one hour."

After Morrison hung up, Graven stood staring at his phone. NATO involvement meant this was bigger than a single assassination. Meant international implications. Meant someone at a very high level was very worried.

"Rune," he said. "This Mathias Sørensen—that name mean anything to you?"

Rune's face went carefully neutral. Too neutral. "He was the NATO bureaucrat who terminated Project 19.5 in 1970. He's been with NATO ever since. Currently heads all classified research programs."

"So the man who shut down the original program is conferencing in to discuss the fact that someone is using that program's technology to commit political assassinations." Graven felt pieces clicking together. "Why do I get the feeling this is less about helping us and more about protecting NATO's interests?"

"Because you're not stupid," Rune said quietly. "Mathias didn't just shut down Project 19.5—he seized all the research. Classified it beyond black. If Austerlitz is using that technology now, it means either Mathias failed to secure it properly, or—"

"Or he's been running his own program," Graven finished. "And now someone is using his work without permission."

The implications were staggering. If NATO had been secretly continuing Project 19.5, creating enhanced soldiers in violation of international law, the diplomatic fallout would be catastrophic. And if Austerlitz had stolen that research—or worse, if he'd been working with NATO's blessing before going rogue—then this wasn't a terrorism investigation anymore.

This was institutional cover-up at the highest levels.

Stavanger, Norway - NATO Joint Warfare Centre

Mathias Sørensen stood in his office, looking out at the Norwegian coastline. Sixty-seven years old. Distinguished gray hair. Perfectly tailored suit. The picture of European bureaucratic competence.

And absolutely terrified.

The call from Bismarck had come at 3 AM local time. He'd been awake anyway—insomnia had plagued him for years, ever since the nightmares started. Ever since he'd begun to suspect that terminating Project 19.5 hadn't been the end, just a pause.

Now his worst fears were confirmed.

The television on his office wall showed American news coverage. Senator Toresen's assassination. The impossible technological capabilities displayed. The electromagnetic interference that suggested modification technology decades ahead of public knowledge.

And the calling card—the precision, the surgical nature of the kill—that screamed Filibert Austerlitz.

His phone rang. Private line. Encrypted.

"*Hallo,*" Mathias answered.

"It's happening." The voice on the other end was tense. "Just like you predicted. Filibert is coming out of hiding."

"I know. I'm watching the coverage." Mathias spoke in English—his caller preferred it. "Has Rune made contact with the Americans?"

"Yes. He's with Homeland Security, providing historical context on Project 19.5. Carefully edited historical context, of course."

"Good. We need the Americans looking in the right direction but not asking the wrong questions." Mathias paused. "What about Felix?"

"Terrified. He knows Filibert will come for him eventually. All the NATO personnel who were involved in the original project—we're all potential targets now."

"Then we need to find Filibert before he finds us. And we need to do it quietly, without drawing attention to what we've been doing for the past thirty-five years."

"Mathias, if this becomes public—if people learn that NATO has been secretly funding enhancement research, that we never really terminated Project 19.5—"

"Then careers end and governments fall. I'm aware of the stakes." Mathias's voice hardened. "That's why Filibert can't be allowed to continue. That's why we need to eliminate him and everyone associated with him before this becomes a scandal we can't contain."

"And if the Americans discover the truth?"

"They won't. Rune will manage them. He's been doing this for years—feeding government officials just enough truth to satisfy curiosity while hiding the deeper realities." Mathias turned from the window. "But I need to brief Washington personally. Need to assess how much they know and steer the investigation away from areas we can't afford to have exposed."

"When do you leave?"

"Not leaving—going to conference in. I'll brief the Americans, express NATO's concern, offer carefully limited cooperation. Standard diplomatic theater." He paused. "And then I'll do what should have been done thirty-five years ago—find Filibert Austerlitz and end this permanently."

After hanging up, Mathias stood alone in his office. Around him, the trappings of a successful career in international defense bureaucracy. Awards on the walls. Photos with various heads of state. The appearance of legitimacy and respectability.

But underneath, the rot of secrets that couldn't be exposed. Especially Project 19.5.

And now the original architect of it all—the brilliant, damaged, obsessive Filibert Austerlitz—had apparently survived decades in hiding and decided to announce his existence by killing a Norwegian-American politician in a way that screamed advanced modification technology.

It was a message. A very personal message. And Mathias understood exactly what it meant:

I'm still here. I remember what you stole. And I'm coming for you.

He opened his desk drawer, pulled out a file marked with the highest classification level. Inside, surveillance photos taken by NATO intelligence over the years. Grainy images of a figure that might be Filibert, spotted in various locations. Pennsylvania. New York. Always near industrial areas. Always near water.

They'd never been able to confirm. Never been able to pin down his exact location. Filibert was too careful, too paranoid, too skilled at staying invisible.

But now he'd revealed himself. Shown his hand. Demonstrated capabilities that could only come from continued research and development.

Which meant he had a facility. Resources. Test subjects.

And most importantly—he had Kort Sokolov. The only successful subject from the original program. The only enhanced soldier who'd survived the modifications.

Kort's whereabouts after he discharged from the Legion had not been a mystery, almost making sure he wasn't hidden, which, as Mathias considered this now, in the context of the recent events, was a way of hiding in plain sight—a smoke screen for Filibert. Kort had provided services at Quantico, his wife was a prominent research scientist and professor at Colombia, and as his periodic updates provided, they had lived an almost mundane suburban life. Damn! How had he missed this clever rouse? But that ended in 1990 when Kort's trail went cold and Mathias's one reliable source, who had come to him in shattered spirits, swore to have lost track. A proclamation he doubted at the time but let it go. And now it became clear it was a lie. He would deal with that later if needed. But was Kort still alive now? And why now this appearance and demonstration of destruction? Was it because Filibert had solved the stability problem? Had perfected what NATO's researchers had been struggling with for decades?

That knowledge was worth killing for. Worth dying for. Worth starting a war for.

Mathias closed the file, locked it back in his desk. Then he made another encrypted call, this one to a different number. A facility in central-western Norway that didn't appear on any NATO assets register, inventory, or funding stream.

The clock ticked toward 1:30.

Abandoned Steel Mill, Rural Pennsylvania

The van neared the facility just as dawn broke over the Pennsylvania hills. Filibert sat in the back, monitoring Kort's vital signs on portable equipment. Iniko drove with grim focus, her usual warmth replaced by tactical efficiency.

They'd been running non-stop since extraction. Forty miles downstream from Bismarck to the Missouri River extraction point. Private plane from a rural airstrip. Three layover points to scramble any tracking. Finally arriving at the steel mill as the sun rose on what would be a very complicated day.

"How is he?" Iniko asked without taking her eyes off the road.

"Power core at 8%. He needs the tank immediately or system collapse becomes inevitable." Filibert's hands moved across the monitors, adjusting chemical balances remotely. "But he completed the mission perfectly. Exactly as designed, precise elimination, clear message delivered. And no witnesses who could identify him."

Iniko risked a glance back to Filibert and corrected, "Not perfectly!" She whipped her eyes back to the road and gave a rundown of facts counter to Filibert's glowing review of the mission. "He violated the mission parameter of 'No Collateral.' He killed an unauthorized person directly and unknown collaterals. And I heard some of the news report interviews—he was seen by the family and the surviving agent. Something went wrong; he went off mission. Are you blind to that?"

"Iniko!" Filibert snapped a stern rebuke. "Even after Algeria, have you not learned that no operation is free of unforeseen circumstances that require immediate action? The confusion of the battle, the inherent chaos and uncertainty of combat. What Carl von Clausewitz coined as the fog of war. He was made to adapt—and he did!"

"Yes, Doctor," Iniko said, switching to a submissive tone. Underneath her breath she muttered, "Something went wrong." Then to Filibert, in an effort to smooth over the rift, she said, "The suit functioned perfectly—adaptive camouflage exceeded projections. Electromagnetic interference disrupted all electronic surveillance." Iniko paused.

"But the Americans will still figure it out. They have the surveillance footage, corrupted as it is. They'll see the interference pattern, track it to NATO's historical programs, connect to you."

"Let them. That's the point. I want Mathias to know I'm still here. Want him to understand that stealing my research didn't end Project 19.5—it just changed ownership." Filibert's voice carried satisfaction and bitterness in equal measure. "For thirty years I've rebuilt in secret. Perfected what he abandoned. And now I'm going to use it to destroy everything he's built on the foundation of my work."

The van passed through the facility's perimeter—rusted chain-link fence that looked abandoned but was actually monitored by sensors Filibert had installed. The steel mill loomed ahead, industrial Gothic against the morning sky.

Inside, they moved quickly. Iniko backed the van to the loading dock. Filibert opened the rear doors, began disconnecting Kort's portable life support.

"Come on, brother. Let's get you to the vat before the power core fails."

They lifted him out and onto a gurney—still in the black suit, still leaking gray goo from stress points, still faceless and inhuman. Wheeled him through the facility's corridors, past laboratories and research stations, into the vat room where Kort could recharge and recover.

The vat was already prepared—filled with the luminous gray liquid that served as both nutrient bath and power supply. Filibert and Iniko strapped Kort into the chair, positioned his abdomen against the feeding port, connected the tubes that would cycle the lithium gel through his system.

As the connection sealed, Kort's faceplate flickered. Internal displays coming back online as power began flowing.

His body, pushed beyond safe limits during the mission, started to relax as the vat's support systems took over.

"There," Filibert said softly, touching his brother's shoulder. "Rest now. You did well. You did exactly what needed to be done."

He pulled the lever. Kort lowered into the gray liquid, submerging face-first, his body supported by the vat's chemical suspension. The monitors showed vital signs stabilizing, power core beginning to recharge, damage to the shoulder panel being repaired by the suit's self-healing protocols.

Filibert stood watching for a long moment. Pride and guilt warring in his chest. Pride at what he'd created—proof that human enhancement was not just possible but perfectible. Guilt at what it had cost—his brother's humanity sacrificed on the altar of scientific achievement.

"You're thinking about Zahra again," Iniko said, reading his expression.

"She's out there. Still researching. Still brilliant. Still refusing to acknowledge that what we're doing is necessary." His jaw went slack; his gaze lost in the hypnotic swirl of the vat's liquid. "There aren't many places she can go and hide and still work. Another asset stolen from me." Filibert shook off the spell and turned from the vat. "If she knew what Kort had become, what he'd done in Bismarck—she'd be horrified. Would probably try to stop us."

"Would she? Or would she understand that this is the natural evolution of the work she helped create?" Iniko moved to the control station, began adjusting the vat's parameters. "She saved Kort's life by transforming him. Made him post-human. Maybe she'd see this as the logical continuation of that choice."

"Don't forget she tried to take him out of the lab and hide him away. If it wasn't for your warning to me, she might have done it under the cover of night."

Distracted by his own musings, Filibert missed seeing the flash of shame that rippled over Iniko's face and vanished.

Filibert continued, "Even then she recognized the betrayal—my using her husband as a weapon to fight battles he didn't choose."

"He chose. Forty years ago in Algeria, he chose. Every mission since, he's chosen. Stop pretending Kort is your prisoner. He's your partner. Your willing accomplice in all of this."

Filibert wanted to argue but couldn't. Because Iniko was right. Kort had volunteered for the enhancements back when Filibert was at Columbia even before the NATO project. Had accepted every modification since. Had agreed to the enhancements, without hesitation, that took over a decade and was demonstrated in the Bismarck operation.

The man in the vat—if he could still be called a man—was there by choice. Was a weapon by choice. Had traded humanity for power and purpose.

Just like Filibert had.

"The Americans will be looking for us now," Filibert said, changing the subject. "And Mathias will be looking even harder. We need to accelerate the timeline."

"How accelerated?"

"The next strike happens in a week. No more waiting. No more preparation. We move while they're still reacting, before they can organize an effective response."

"Target?"

"Felix." Filibert's voice hardened. "He's been Mathias's lieutenant for decades—thinks I'm ignorant of that—

schmieriger kleiner Dreckskerl!" Greasy little bastard. "Helped hide the research. Helped cover up what they did to the original program. He knows where all the bodies are buried—literally and figuratively."

"Meaning he would know about Zahra if anybody does," Iniko added.

Filibert stiffened but did not respond to the statement. "We eliminate him, we send another message and gather intelligence on Mathias's current operations."

"Felix will be protected. After Bismarck, everyone connected to the original program will be on high alert."

"Good. Let them be alert. Let them understand that their protections are inadequate. That enhanced soldiers can go anywhere, kill anyone, and disappear like ghosts." Filbert sighed and paused, lost for a moment in a cascade of memories of wrongs, losses, and revenge. He shook that off as well and said, "And pack up. I've already downloaded the relevant data into a secure site. We won't be coming back here. They will find this soon. They will have a surprise waiting for them."

Filibert moved to the communications station. "I need to contact our asset at NATO. Get confirmation on Felix's location and security arrangements."

As Filibert worked, Iniko remained by the vat, watching Kort float in the gray liquid. She thought about the man he'd been thirty even forty years ago—strong but human, enhanced but still fundamentally himself. And she thought about what he'd become—a living weapon, barely recognizable as human, existing in that liminal space between man and monster.

"He's still conscious in there," she said quietly. "Even submerged, even recharging. The modifications don't let him fully sleep. He's aware. Processing. Remembering."

"I know."

"He remembers killing Toresen. Remembers the fear in the man's eyes. The feel of crushing vertebrae when he killed that bodyguard. The sound of his own voice threatening a politician who didn't understand what was happening to him."

"That's what weapons do, Iniko. They kill. Efficiently and without remorse. That's what Kort has become."

"And that's what you made him become."

"Yes." Filibert didn't flinch from the accusation. "I made him a weapon because the world needs weapons. Because men like Mathias will always seek power, and they need to understand that their power isn't absolute. That there are consequences for theft, for betrayal, for destroying the work of people who trusted them."

"This isn't about justice, Filibert. This is about revenge."

"Can't it be both?"

Iniko had no answer for that.

They worked in silence—Filibert coordinating with his NATO asset, Iniko monitoring Kort's recovery. Around them, the steel mill hummed with the sounds of hidden technology. Laboratories where genetic and technical research had given rise to revolutionary shifts in established paradigms. Aquarium rooms where marine organisms provided biological templates. Spider colonies producing ultra-strong webbing for armor.

A facility that shouldn't exist, conducting research that violated every international law, creating capabilities that would terrify anyone who understood their implications.

And at the center of it all, floating in his vat of gray liquid, the proof that it all worked.

Kort Sokolov. Enhanced soldier. Post-human weapon. Living testament to what science could achieve when freed from ethical constraints.

The clock in Filibert's office showed 1:30. Always 1:30. The moment frozen in time. The moment everything changed. The moment he could never return to, no matter how much he tried to reset the world around him.

But maybe—if he destroyed enough of what Mathias had built, if he reclaimed enough of what had been stolen, if he proved sufficiently that his work had value—maybe then the clock could finally move forward.

Maybe then he could forgive himself for what he'd done to his brother.

Or maybe not.

Maybe some sins were too great for forgiveness. Too fundamental to be erased by revenge or justice or any combination of the two.

Maybe he'd damned them both—himself and Kort—when he'd first injected those enhancement protocols over forty years ago in Algeria.

And maybe this war he was starting, this campaign of assassination and terror against NATO's hidden programs, was just the death spiral of two damaged men trying to justify what they'd become.

The vat bubbled softly. Kort floated, healing. The modified tissue knitting back together. The power core recharging. The weapon preparing for its next deployment.

Homeland Security Headquarters, Washington D.C. - 72 Hours After Bismarck

Graven shifted through files at his office, grumbling at the sip of coffee gone cold. Still ruffled by yesterday's video conference with NATO. The truckload of bureaucratic double-speak Mathias spewed had required an extra helping of aspirin with a whiskey chaser afterward.

The fluorescent lights hummed overhead, casting that particular shade of institutional gray that made everything look washed out and lifeless. Case files sprawled across his desk in organized chaos—reports from Bismarck, intercepted communications, surveillance photos of known associates. Three days of chasing ghosts, and they were no closer to finding Filibert Austerlitz than they'd been the day after the act of terror in North Dakota. It was no myth that after the first forty-eight hours the chance of success in an investigation dropped dramatically. And they were a day past the golden window of opportunity.

The office smelled like burnt coffee, old paper, and the particular staleness that came from late nights and not enough windows that actually opened. Graven hadn't gone home since the crisis began, running on short naps on a worn office couch and pure stubbornness.

Agent Winstead popped up from his seat across the bullpen like a jack-in-the-box, waving the phone toward Graven, snapping his fingers hard. The sharp crack of it cut through the monotonous hum of the office. "Boss, boss!"

Graven didn't look up, still scanning a report about unusual power fluctuations in the Midwest.

"What is it, Winstead?"

Winstead hung the phone up and headed toward Graven with quick, excited steps that made his cheap shoes squeak on the linoleum. He was young, eager, still believed that every lead was the one that would crack the case wide open. Graven had been that young once before he'd learned that most leads went nowhere and the ones that did usually ended badly. "Hot tip, boss. We have a fix on Dr. Austerlitz and his hideout in Pennsylvania."

That got Graven's attention. He set down his coffee mug—NASA logo faded almost to illegibility—and leaned back in his chair, which protested with a metallic groan. "I take it the tip came from the anonymous type?"

"Yeah, but what else we got?" Winstead's enthusiasm was barely contained, his hands moving as he talked. "It's an abandoned steel mill in eastern-central Pennsylvania with a high electricity use rate. Sounds right, doesn't it?"

Graven frowned, his gut already sending up warning flares. Anonymous tips were like loaded dice—sometimes they worked in your favor, but usually somebody else was controlling the game. "High use rate, huh? This source has some detailed information." He rubbed his jawline, feeling the stubble there. He'd forgotten to shave again. "Too detailed, maybe."

"Boss, we've been spinning our wheels for days. This is the best lead we've had—"

"Or a red herring." Graven cut him off, but his tone wasn't harsh. The kid meant well. They all did. And he was right—what else did they have? "Okay, go with the gut. Get hold of our tactical assets in Pennsylvania and have them wait for me. Tell them full tactical gear, expect hostiles, but preserve the area—this is a possible crime scene."

"On it, boss." Winstead was already moving.

"Freeh!" Graven called across the office.

Freeh looked up from his computer terminal, reading glasses perched on his nose. "Yeah, boss?"

"Check with the power company in that location and update me if the mill indeed is eating power. Slap them with the Patriot Act right away, so there's no bullshit delays. I want confirmation before we roll in there."

"On it, boss," Freeh said, already dialing, his fingers dancing across the phone with practiced efficiency.

Graven stood, grabbed his jacket from the back of his chair. "Winstead—get a chopper ready for me." Then, half to himself as he shrugged into the jacket, "I don't like this anonymous call shit."

But he was going anyway. Because what else could he do? Filibert Austerlitz was out there somewhere, and if there was even a chance this tip was legitimate, he had to take it. The bodies in Bismarck demanded nothing less.

Pennsylvania Steel Mill - Two Hours Later

The mill rose out of the Pennsylvania landscape like a rusted tombstone, a monument to American industrial slow death. Broken windows gaped like empty eye sockets. Graffiti covered the lower walls—territorial markings from local kids, declarations of love, crude drawings that would have been funny if the whole place didn't feel so oppressive.

Four black tactical utility vans sped down the access road, kicking up dust and gravel. They'd come in fast and quiet, no sirens, no advance warning. The vans slid to a hard stop in a practiced maneuver, forming a semi-circle in front of the steel mill's main entrance. Dust kicked up in clouds and then settled as engines idled, creating an eerie quiet punctuated only by the tick of cooling engines and the distant caw of crows.

The tactical team emerged smoothly, weapons ready, moving with the coordinated precision of men who'd done this a hundred times before. Lieutenant Morrison was a twenty-year veteran, his tactical vest decorated heavily with patches worn with pride. His team spread out without needing orders, covering angles, checking sight lines, establishing a perimeter.

From the horizon, a helicopter began to loom large as it approached, the deep thump of its rotors growing louder. It circled the area once, twice, the pilot getting a visual on the entire complex before settling into a hover position about fifty yards out.

From inside the chopper, Graven had a bird's-eye view of the operation. The mill looked even worse from up here—roof partially collapsed, sections of wall fallen away, decades of decay and neglect. Perfect place to hide. Perfect place for a trap.

He pressed the mic button on his headset. "All right, Lieutenant, breach and clear! Assume hostile presence, but capture and contain subjects at all costs. Anyone sees anything weird, you call it out immediately. Understood?"

"Copy that," Morrison's voice came back, calm and professional. Then to his team, "Stack up on me."

Tactical team members hustled toward the building in a tactical column, weapons up, each man covering a sector. They moved like a single organism, flowing around obstacles, maintaining spacing and angles. Morrison took point, Sergeant Horn at his six, the rest of the team falling in behind.

They breached the main entrance—a rusted metal door that gave way with minimal resistance, the lock long since corroded past usefulness.

The hinges screamed as they pushed through, announcing their presence to anything inside.

"If anyone worked out of here, they didn't use this entrance," Morrison reported to Graven. "Looks like a false front."

The interior was darker than expected. Flashlight beams cut through the darkness, illuminating dust motes that hung in the air like snow in a shaken globe.

"Structure appears compromised," Morrison's voice updated. "Multiple structural hazards. Proceeding."

The team split up to clear the hallways and rooms, each fire team taking a sector. Standard operating procedure. Nothing unusual yet. Just darkness and rust and the smell of decay. As the team penetrated deeper into the mill, the interior revealed high-tech renovations compared to the entrance areas.

"Now we got something. There's definitely been some goings on in this place," Morrison half said to himself and half to all listening on the comm.

Graven watched from above, impatient, blind to the action inside, his jaw tight. Something felt wrong. That feeling when he first heard about the tip, the tip too specific, the timing too—

A team member's boot crossed over a doorway; Morrison grabbed his shoulder and pulled him back. The member looked at Morrisson puzzled and then followed Morrison's gaze to the floor. A thin tripwire ran across the bottom of the doorway.

The lieutenant touched his vest-mounted comm button, "Keep sharp—we've got tripwires." He patted his troop on the back and said, "Step high, son."

They both stepped carefully over the wire, never suspecting that when they crossed the threshold, they broke an invisible infrared beam.

Deep in the mill's interior, in an open industrial area that the team hadn't yet reached, a rusty metal monolith with a bulbous top activated with a soft reverb. The sound was almost musical, almost pleasant. A low hum began building slowly, like the world's largest tuning fork beginning to vibrate.

Graven had felt his stomach drop at the report of tripwires. "Lieutenant? Report!"

Inside the mill, Lieutenant Morrison clicked his comm and responded, his voice echoing slightly in the empty spaces, "Someone's been working out of here and looks like they left in a hurry." His flashlight beam swept across a makeshift laboratory—beakers and tubes, a centrifuge, stacks of notebooks covered in equations. "Lot of equipment. Looks scientific." Then to his team members he directed, "Clear the other rooms. And watch tripwires."

The team members fanned out, their footsteps echoing on concrete floors. Some of the rooms they entered produced confusion and pained looks on their faces—cages with strange scratch marks on the inside, stains that might have been blood or something worse, equipment whose purpose was unclear and deeply unsettling.

Sergeant Horn approached what he mentally designated "the spider room" based on the webbing visible even from the hallway. He stepped with the caution of a man who'd survived "The Suck" in Iraq by trusting his instincts, and his instincts were screaming at him that something was very, very wrong.

He peered through the wide-open door without entering, letting his flashlight beam dance around the darkness. The room was larger than the others, some kind of former storage area with high ceilings and exposed rafters. Webbing covered everything—not spider webs exactly, but something similar, something that glistened wetly in the flashlight beam and seemed to pulse with an organic rhythm.

Sergeant Horn's nose wrinkled from an acidic odor that burned his sinuses and made his eyes water. It smelled like ammonia mixed with rotting meat, with an underlying chemical tang that suggested this was no natural spider infestation. He called out over his shoulder, his voice tight, "L-T! I got some weird shit here!"

The darkness of the room seemed to ripple, to move with purpose. In the rafters above—far above, higher than Horn's flashlight had yet reached—large shapes began to descend. Silently. Purposefully. With the patience of predators who knew their prey was already trapped.

The hum from the metal monolith grew louder, building toward something terrible.

Sergeant Horn turned his attention back to the room and did another sweep with his flashlight—this time angling upward, following the webbing to its source in the rafters.

That's when he saw them.

The spiders were massive, each one the size of a large dog. But they weren't just large—they were wrong. Mutation had twisted them into creatures that shouldn't exist outside of nightmares. Too many eyes, compound and gleaming. Mandibles that clicked and dripped with viscous fluid. Legs that ended in hooks instead of feet, hooks that had already embedded in the ceiling rafters and were now lowering the creatures down with terrible, alien grace.

There were dozens of them. Maybe more.

Horn barely choked out an "Oh, fuck me!" before stumbling over himself to turn and flee the doorway. But he was too late.

A large freakish spider leapt from directly above the doorframe—it had been waiting there, patient as death, knowing that prey always looked into rooms before looking up. The creature landed on Horn's face with enough force to snap his head back, eight legs wrapping around his skull, smothering his mid-yell cry of "Lieuten—"

In place of finishing his warning, there was a horrible crunch—the sound of a human skull compressing under hydraulic pressure, bone fragments splintering, gray matter mixing with acidic venom. Horn collapsed limp to the ground, his finger still on the trigger of his M4 carbine, letting loose a long burst of gunfire that stitched across the wall and ceiling in a random pattern.

The muzzle flash lit up the corridor like a strobe light, revealing in freeze-frame horror what was coming.

The other spiders poured out of the room like a flood, their movements unnaturally fast, their hisses filling the air with a sound like steam escaping from a ruptured pipe. The team members nearest to Horn's position opened fire immediately, but shooting something that moved like water and thought like a pack hunter was nearly impossible in the confined space and poor lighting.

In the chopper, Graven strained to make sense of the chaos that had erupted over the comm. "Lieutenant? Report in. Lieutenant!"

He could hear the gunfire through the comm, that clicked on and off in the team's frantic attempts to communicate, could hear the screams—grown men screaming with a terror that bypassed training and went straight to primal panic. "Lieutenant!"

Over the comm, through the sounds of chaos and dying, Graven could make out Lieutenant Morrison's orders to his team, his voice still professional despite the horror, "Everyone move out! Abandon building! Fighting retreat! Go, go, go!"

Inside the mill, the spiders' loud hisses turned the men's blood cold and their minds to blind hysteria. The creatures chased after the retreating team with predatory intelligence, cutting off escape routes, herding the humans like sheep toward killing zones. The tactical team sprayed bullets carelessly behind them as they ran, hitting only a random few spiders—and even those seemed to just keep coming, dragging themselves forward on broken legs with a persistence that defied biology.

The creatures pounced on the ill-fated team members taking up the rear. The howls of the dying men were quickly reduced to wet gurgles and then silent, grisly death. Bodies dropped in the darkness, torn apart by mandibles that could shear through tactical vests like paper.

Morrison and three other team members burst out of the main entrance, firing back into the building, trying to provide covering fire for anyone else who might still be alive in there. But no one else came out.

The large, rusty metal monolith in the industrial area started sparking, emitting frenzied hums as electrical streams discharged from its top. The sound built to a crescendo, a scream of tortured physics preparing to unleash something that should never have been created.

In the chopper, Graven watched in horror as a high-powered energy wave mushroomed out from the steel mill in an expanding sphere of violet-blue light. It moved like a living thing, like God's own judgment rippling outward from ground zero.

Objects in its path fluoresced, giving off a faint, hazy blue-violet glow before evaporating into mist. The tactical vans disappeared first, metal and rubber and electronics all reduced to their component atoms. Then the ground itself began to glow, concrete and earth and stone all converting to energy and light and nothing.

Morrison and his three survivors stood frozen for a half-second, watching their death approach at the speed of light. Then they were gone, not even time to scream, just there one moment and transformed into luminous mist the next.

"Get us out of here!" Graven shouted at the pilot, his voice cracking.

The pilot didn't need to be told twice. He banked hard and executed a high-power climb, pushing the helicopter to its limits. The engine screamed with the strain. Below them, the steel mill appeared to vibrate at the particle level, every atom shaking itself apart, existing in two states at once—solid and energy, matter and light.

Then it froze in time for one impossible moment.

And imploded.

The building collapsed into itself with the grinding shriek of a thousand car crashes happening simultaneously, sucking the energy wave back toward a fiery crater. The implosion created a vacuum that pulled at everything around it—trees bending toward the void, debris flying inward, the very air rushing back to fill the space where the mill had been.

The edge of the wave slammed into the chopper before retreating, catching them just as they climbed. Sparks showered upward from the instrument panel like fireworks. Alarms began screaming. The smell of burning electronics filled the cabin. The pilot fought the pedals hard to autorotate, his hands moving with desperate precision on controls that were half-dead.

"Brace for impact!" the pilot shouted, his voice tight with concentration.

Graven grabbed the overhead handles, planted his feet, tried to remember everything he'd learned in helicopter crash survival training. Below them, the Pennsylvania countryside spun in lazy circles as they descended in an uncontrolled spiral.

It was the last thing Graven heard before the blackness overcame him—the pilot's steady count as he tried to manage their descent: "Three hundred feet... two hundred... on e-fifty..."

Then impact. Metal screaming. The world tumbling. Pain blooming like fire across his ribs and shoulder. The taste of blood in his mouth.

And finally, mercifully, darkness.

Later - Unknown Time

Graven woke to the sound of sirens in the distance and the smell of aviation fuel. He was still strapped in his seat, hanging at an angle that suggested the helicopter had rolled onto its side. His head felt like someone had used it for batting practice. Blood dripped into his left eye from a cut on his forehead.

The pilot slumped over the controls, not moving. Graven couldn't tell if he was alive or dead.

Through the cracked windscreen, Graven could see the crater where the steel mill had been. It glowed faintly in the gathering dusk, still radiating energy, still burning with an inner fire that defied conventional physics.

The anonymous tip had been exactly that—a tip. A lure. A trap designed to eliminate the pursuers, to send a message, to demonstrate just how far ahead of them Filibert Austerlitz really was.

Graven tried to move, winced at the pain in his ribs. Probably broken. He reached for his radio with shaking hands, managed to key the mic.

"This is... this is Agent Graven," he said, his voice hoarse and weak. "We need... medical evac. Team is... team is gone. All of them gone."

As he waited for a response, as the sirens grew closer, Graven stared at the glowing crater and understood with terrible clarity that they weren't hunting Filibert Austerlitz.

He was hunting them.

And he was always three moves ahead.

And somewhere flying across the Atlantic, a monster born from Nazi atrocities and Cold War paranoia prepared his next move to reset the clock on decades of secrets.

The clock struck half past one.

Always half past one.

Forever.

The pursuit had begun.

Eighteen

Pursuit and Prey

NATO Joint Warfare Centre, Stavanger, Norway

The storm clouds over Stavanger looked apocalyptic—dark purple and bruised, pregnant with rain that hadn't yet decided to fall. Graven stood in front of the reflecting pool outside the NATO Joint Warfare Centre, watching the taxi that had brought him from the airport disappear back toward the city. The building before him was modernist functionalism at its finest with form following function. A five-story structure focused on sustainability and modern training capabilities. Large brushed stainless-steel letters over the entrance announced the facility: JOINT WARFARE CENTRE. The flags of member nations in the distance crackled and flapped in the wind, swivel snaps clanged, ringing out a promise of the coming storm.

He'd been traveling for fourteen hours. His ribs still ached from the helicopter crash three days ago. His mind was full of the impossible images he reviewed from the Bismarck incident—a figure moving at superhuman speed, electromagnetic interference that preceded violence, a dead senator with a wound that shouldn't exist.

And now he was here, chasing ghosts and Cold War secrets in a country where he had no jurisdiction, following leads that Rune had fed him with suspicious precision.

The revolving entrance door whispered as it rotated and escorted him inside. A man waited in the lobby—sixtyish, average height, the kind of face that disappeared in crowds. Bureaucrat written in every careful gesture.

"Felix?" Graven asked.

"Mr. Graven, I assume." Felix's English carried a refined European accent—educated, cosmopolitan, the voice of a man who'd spent his career navigating the gray spaces between nations. "I must say, your presence here required considerable... diplomatic creativity."

"Yeah, well, dead senators have a way of opening doors." Graven followed Felix through security, past guards who watched with the carefully neutral expressions of men who knew something irregular was happening but had been ordered not to care.

They moved through corridors that could have been any government building anywhere—fluorescent lights, industrial carpet, the smell of coffee and human activity lingering behind the sterility of bureaucracy. But something felt wrong. Graven had learned to trust his instincts over three decades in government service, and right now those instincts were screaming.

Felix walked too carefully. His eyes darted to corners, to ceiling-mounted security cameras, to closed office doors. A man expecting something. A man afraid.

"How may I assist the Director of Homeland Security?" Felix asked as they reached his office. The door was heavy wood, out of place with the modern aesthetic. Inside, the space was larger than Graven expected—wood-paneled walls, high ceilings, and in the corner, a suit of medieval armor complete with a wicked-looking poleaxe.

"Nice decorating," Graven said, taking the offered chair. Felix moved behind his desk and sat on the edge of his tufted leather chair. His hands kept moving—touching papers, adjusting his computer monitor, drumming fingers on the polished wood surface.

"Family heirloom," Felix said. "My grandfather—"

"Let's skip the small talk." Graven leaned forward. "As you know, I'm here about the assassination of one of our state senators."

"Yes. Barbaric. Rumors, of course, but I understand Al-Qaeda is implicated. You can imagine my surprise when rules of international diplomatic policy were bent—even broken—for you to be in my office right now."

"Really?" Graven challenged, upping the pressure he was willing to apply on this bureaucrat. "Last I knew the United States was the major financial contributor to NATO—by far. Not thinking it was a hardship for me to see you."

Felix smirked, "How little you understand old world money and politics."

There was an odd pause—as the standoff increased in weight. Felix's fingers continued their nervous drumming. Graven noticed the swelling around his left eye, the split lip, bruising spreading across his cheekbone.

"Auto accident?" Graven asked, pointing to Felix's face, easing the tension.

"Yes. Minor really. I'm fine."

He wasn't fine. Graven had interrogated enough frightened men to recognize the signs. Felix was terrified, operating on the ragged edge of control.

"An event of this magnitude—" Graven started.

"I'm afraid I'm wasting your time." Felix's voice sharpened with what might have been desperation or defiance. "I know nothing about these matters."

"You're too modest. Your name's been tied to our investigation—a lot. Almost spoon-fed to us with a trail of dirty corruption crumbs leading me straight here."

"Truly?"

"Yeah, truly." Graven's sneer was involuntary. He pulled out a plastic evidence bag from his jacket. Inside was the fragment of Kort's armor—biological material that looked like carapace, part shell, part something that shouldn't exist. He tossed it on Felix's desk.

"Let's cut the shit. I'm not here about how you've been lining your pockets with international funds. I'm here about Dr. Filibert Austerlitz, a Cold War project called '19.5,' and this."

Felix stared at the evidence bag. His hand moved, and Graven realized with a cold jolt that Felix was holding a pistol—had been holding it the entire conversation, between his legs, one finger on the trigger guard.

"Oh, you Americans..." Felix laughed—a nervous, high-pitched sound that belonged in a psychiatric ward. He rubbed his sweaty forehead with the pistol barrel, leaving a sheen on his skin.

"Hey, take it easy with that." Graven scooted his chair backward, putting distance between himself and the gun.

Felix stood up, gesturing wildly, spit spraying from his mouth as his voice increased in volume. "Everything starts and ends with you. You people have no idea what's going on—been going on. You sit on your isolated continent, content with your third-rate culture, and poking your nose in things bigger than you."

"Why don't you put that gun down and dispense with the Euro-trash talk, okay?" Graven kept his voice level, the way you'd talk to someone standing on a ledge. "I realize this is bigger than I know. That's why I'm here—to figure this thing out."

"You stupid fuck! You're not here to figure anything out, don't you get it?" Felix was shouting now, coming around from behind his desk, waving the pistol erratically. "You're here to be silenced along with me."

Graven stood, moved with measured steps to stay opposite of Felix. "Don't do anything stupid."

The office lights flickered.

Felix startled like a prey animal sensing a predator. His eyes went wide, fixed on the overhead fluorescents as they strobed once, twice, three times. In the outer office, Graven could hear the buzz and snap of electronic equipment cycling on and off.

"It's him," Felix whispered. Then louder, pointing at his battered face: "He's coming. See this? They tried to beat secrets out of me. Now I'm bait for the both of us."

He waved the pistol at Graven. "We'll see about that."

Felix's free hand thumped the laptop on the edge of his desk with manic intensity. "Oh, they'll get their secrets once I expose them to the world! I'm not going down alone!"

"The fuck are you talking about?" Graven demanded.

"You want answers? You talk to that son-of-a-bitch Mathias. He's the foundation of this perversion. Him and Filibert," he was sputtering and wild-eyed now, "...both of them crazy! Oh, yeah and Filibert's former assistant Zahra—she's a witch, a witch straight from Hell!"

The lights flickered wildly now, accompanied by a low electronic hum that seemed to come from everywhere and nowhere. The building's electrical system screamed from the erratic load.

"He's here!" Felix shrieked.

He waved Graven away from the door and leveled the pistol at it. The door handle turned slowly—metal scraping against metal in the sudden, terrible quiet.

"Now just hold on—" Graven started.

The door began to open.

"Go to hell!"

Felix fired—three shots, four, five—the muzzle flash strobing the room in freeze-frame images. Through the doorway, Felix's assistant collapsed, her chest blooming red, mouth open in an O of surprise that would never close.

"Jesus Christ!" Graven ran toward the body, instinct over-riding tactics.

"No—it can't be..." Felix's voice had gone hollow with horror.

Behind Felix, the window exploded inward.

Safety glass showered into the room like crystalline rain and then fell like fine dust. Kort burst through—not climb-ing, not jumping, but moving through the space as if physics were suggestions rather than laws. He grabbed Felix by the throat mid-flight and hurled him across the room. Felix's body hit the wall with enough force to crush and splinter the wood fibers in the expensive paneling.

With a mighty push, Kort slid Felix's massive desk toward Graven. The desk—solid mahogany, easily three hundred pounds—moved like it weighed nothing. It smacked against Graven, pushing him against the wall, but mercifully not cutting him in half. Air exploded from his lungs and the muscles of his upper thighs screamed in pain.

Kort turned his attention to Felix, who was crawling on the floor toward the dropped pistol, whimpering with each movement. Kort stood over him with a menace that transcended physical threat—this was something beyond human violence, beyond human anything.

The modifications were obvious up close. The armor wasn't separate from the skin—it grew from it, emerged from it, biological and artificial merged at some fundamental level. Where joints should bend, there was instead fluid integration. The face mask cold and menacing—hiding all intent. And the way he moved—liquid mercury, adaptive, perfect.

"Fuck you, Filibert! You hear me, you bastard?!" Felix screamed at the ceiling, at God, at whatever controlled the thing standing over him.

Graven gulped for air, the crushing pain in his legs short circuiting rational thought—he could only act. He flopped forward onto the desk while wriggling himself out from between the desk and the wall. The medieval armor display was within reach. He slid off the desk, legs barely able to support him, and grabbed the poleaxe—the weapon heavy and ancient and completely inadequate.

THWAP!

He cracked it across Kort's back with every ounce of strength he had left. The impact jarred his arms, sent vibrations up to his shoulders. It felt like hitting a steel beam wrapped in rubber and shock-absorbing gel.

Kort whipped around, giving Graven his full murderous attention.

Graven stumbled backward. "Oh, shit...!"

Kort lunged. Graven clutched his chest with both hands, gasping, and dropped to his knees in an apparent heart attack. He played it up—the pain wasn't hard to fake with cracked ribs and genuine terror.

Kort approached slowly, tilting his head with predatory curiosity. He leaned in close, reached out, palmed Graven's head as if to crush it between his fingers like an overripe melon.

Graven struck—a knife-hand chop to the throat, all his training and desperation focused into one point of contact.

THWAK!

Kort lunged backward, grabbing his throat. He shook his head, released his grip, and the protective covering on his throat shifted.

Beneath it, a second mouth—the toothy, circular maw of a lamprey eel—opened and let out a horrific hiss that wasn't made by human vocal cords. The teeth were arranged in concentric circles, each one needle-sharp, designed for latching onto prey and not letting go.

"Oh, fuck..."

CRACK!

Felix fired from across the room. The bullet hit Kort in the shoulder with a wet thud and the crackle of fragmenting armor. Biological material sprayed. Kort turned on Felix.

Felix fired again before Kort grabbed his gun hand and, with a casual twist, snapped his wrist. The bone broke with a sound like green wood splitting.

"Ahhhhhhh!"

The gun clattered to the floor.

Kort's head snapped up in response to security guards bursting into the waiting room. He picked up the poleaxe—the medieval weapon looking almost quaint in those modified hands—and met them head-on.

The first guard didn't have time to fire before Kort sliced his throat open with a single stroke. Blood fountained. Kort crashed into the group, armor absorbing their panicked shots, the poleaxe turning the confined space into an abattoir. The sounds were terrible—screams and gunfire and the wet slicing of the ancient blade doing its work.

"Move!" Graven grabbed Felix under the arm, hauled him toward the shattered window. Felix resisted long enough to scoop up his laptop. Behind them, the sounds of security guards dying filled the office—impact, gurgling, the thud of bodies hitting floor.

They ran across the restricted staff parking lot. Felix cradled his laptop against his chest with his good hand, using the broken wrist as a brace and whimpering with each step. Behind them, flashes and pops of gunfire continued to emit from the broken window. A security guard's body sailed out and hit the pavement with a sickening crunch.

Felix stopped at his car—a dark sedan that looked governmental and anonymous.

"Wait!" He fumbled for keys with his uninjured hand, tossed them to Graven with a desperate underhand throw. They scrambled inside—Graven behind the wheel, Felix clutching the laptop like a lifeline.

"Get me out of here and I'll tell you everything. Everything! It's all here!" Felix's voice was ragged with pain and terror.

Graven started the car, threw it in reverse. Felix grabbed his arm.

"Stop!"

Two vehicles blocked the parking lot exit—a black BMW and a matching van, positioned on either side of the row with military precision. Professional. Coordinated.

"Mathias' men," Felix said.

"Good—they can help."

Felix hugged the laptop tighter. "They're not here to help."

CRASH!

Through the floorboard, Kort's hand broke through metal in an explosion of torn steel. He grabbed Felix's leg—grabbed it and pulled. The foot went through the floor with a snap of breaking bone.

"Noooo!" Felix howled and struggled to stay in the car. "Let go! I know where she is—that's what you want to know! I know where she is! Let go!"

Graven reached over, tried to pull Felix back up, but it was like trying to win a tug-of-war with a hydraulic press. The car rocked. Windshield wipers activated randomly. Headlights flicked on and off. The horn bleeped in staccato bursts—electrical systems going haywire from electromagnetic interference.

Through the BMW's windshield, Graven saw two NATO agents step out, pause at the front of their vehicle, watching the impossible scene unfold.

Kort lunged through the floorboard, his shoulders somehow compressing and flowing through an opening that shouldn't accommodate anything larger than a head. With his chin pointed up, the lamprey mouth on his throat opened and Kort slammed it down hard on Felix's thigh.

Felix convulsed. Blood and chunks of muscle spurted and sputtered out of gill-like slits on the sides of Kort's neck—the modified respiratory system processing the consumption of tissue with terrifying efficiency. Felix went pale and drawn, his face aging a decade in seconds as his body was literally drained.

With his last strength, he tossed the laptop into the back seat.

"Son-of-a-bitch!" Graven threw the car into gear and stomped on the accelerator.

Kort and Felix disappeared through the floorboard as the car lurched forward. Metal screamed. Sparks flew. The undercarriage scraped against pavement.

Graven didn't look back—couldn't look back. The car skidded down the soft incline from the parking lot to the lower road. He punched the car through the barrier arm at the front gate, breaking the arm in half. A shower of debris fell behind the car as he cranked the wheel, caught the road leading away from the NATO compound, and tore through the 10 kilometers into Stavanger proper.

The streets of Stavanger had transformed from orderly European boulevards into a gauntlet of death. Graven drove Felix's sedan like a man possessed, weaving between cars, jumping curbs, running red lights while pedestrians dove for safety. The early evening traffic was thick with commuters heading home, families out for dinner, normal people living normal lives who had no idea that something from a nightmare was hunting through their city.

"Okay, easy, easy. Take it easy," Graven muttered to himself, hands death-gripping the steering wheel. His knuckles were white, his ribs screaming with each sharp turn, his thighs protesting every gas and brake pedal push as he navigated the traffic. Blood from Felix still stained the passenger seat—a reminder of what waited if Kort caught him.

The hole in the floorboard gaped like a wound. Metal curled inward where Kort had torn through steel as if they were tissue paper. Through it, Graven could see the road rushing by and the occasional spark when the undercarriage scraped against something solid.

His training kept cycling through his head: *Assess the threat. Identify escape routes. Maintain situational awareness.* But training hadn't prepared him for this. Training assumed human opponents with human limitations. What was behind him wasn't human anymore.

Traffic slowed ahead. A blue dump truck several vehicles ahead seemed to be the source of the congestion. Graven checked his rearview mirror compulsively, every few seconds, looking for that distinctive silhouette.

Nothing but traffic. Cars. Taxis. A bus filled with what looked like tourists, their faces pressed against windows, cameras ready to capture scenic Stavanger.

He glanced down at the hole in the floorboard—ragged metal and the smell of Felix's blood still strong in the confined space.

The dump truck cut in front of him suddenly, no signal, no warning. Graven yanked the wheel right, avoiding collision by inches. The sedan's tires squealed and burned. A pedestrian on the sidewalk shouted something in Norwegian—probably profanity.

"Fuckin' foreign drivers," Graven gasped, regaining composure. His heart hammered against his cracked ribs. Every beat was agony.

Traffic stopped completely. Red brake lights stretched ahead like a river of blood. Somewhere in the distance, he could hear sirens—police or ambulance, responding to the chaos at NATO headquarters. They'd find the body of Felix's assistant. The security guards cut to pieces. Evidence of something that would defy explanation.

Graven looked over his shoulder, peering out the rear window into the darkened clouds that fought against the soft, golden light of Norwegian dusk in the fall. The storm finally made good on its threat. Rain started to fall—fat drops that exploded against the windshield, turned the road slick and treacherous.

Movement on the dump truck.

It took Graven's mind a second to process what he was seeing. A shape—humanoid but wrong—gripping on the side of the blue dump truck like a rock climber. The adaptive camouflage either failing or Kort had stopped caring about stealth. His body was an off-blue color that rippled and shifted, trying to match the truck's paint job but unable to fully commit.

Through the front windshield Graven saw him come. Kort scrambled up the dump truck's side to the top like gravity was optional, picked up speed with each stride, then launched himself through the air. His body was horizontal, parallel to the ground, covering impossible distance.

Graven gunned the engine and pulled hard left. The sedan's tires found traction on wet pavement. The engine roared. And Kort crashed through the front windshield in an explosion of safety glass that filled the car like diamond dust.

The velocity of Kort's body was tremendous—he rocketed through the interior like a missile, missing Graven by inches because of the left turn. Past the passenger seat, through the car's cabin, and out the rear window in a shower of glass.

But he didn't fall. Kort's hands caught the frame of the shattered rear window, fingers—impossibly strong fingers—gripping the metal edge.

He held on as the car accelerated, his body sliding side-to-side on the trunk as momentum tried to shake him loose.

The car jumped the curb onto the sidewalk. The impact jarred Graven's teeth, sent fresh waves of pain through his body. Ahead, pedestrians scattered. A man dropped his briefcase. A woman grabbed her child. An elderly couple froze like deer in headlights.

Graven yanked the wheel, threading between civilians and storefronts. Behind him, Kort was trying to drag himself back into the car through the rear window, his modified body compressing and flowing in ways that violated every principle of human anatomy.

"What the hell are you?" Graven shouted—not expecting an answer, just needing to hear his own voice to confirm he was still human, still sane, still somehow alive.

A woman appeared ahead—young, maybe thirty, walking with a group of children. School uniforms. A field trip or after-school program. Six kids, maybe seven, clustered around her like ducklings. Their faces turned toward the oncoming car—eyes wide, mouths opening to scream.

"Oh, fuck!"

Graven careened off the sidewalk and into the street. The sedan went airborne for a heartbeat, wheels spinning uselessly in air, then crashed back down onto pavement. Missing the woman and children by feet—close enough that he could see the teacher's face frozen in horror, could see a little girl's dropped stuffed animal on the sidewalk.

The sudden motion put the car into a power slide. Physics took over. The rear end came around, momentum overcoming friction. The sedan slammed rear-first into a parked car—a Volvo station wagon that crumpled under the impact.

Kort was hurled off. His body rolled violently across the street—once, twice, three times—then smacked into a brick wall hard enough to leave cracks in the masonry. But instead of staying down like anything mortal should, he bounced to his feet with the fluid grace of a gymnast and dashed back toward Felix's car.

Around them, Stavanger erupted in chaos. Pedestrians screamed and scrambled away. Car horns beeped and honked in protest—drivers angry first, then terrified as they saw what was chasing the damaged sedan.

Graven's vision blurred at the edges. The impact had rattled everything—his brain, his bones, his already-injured ribs. He struggled to focus on the image of Kort closing in, moving with that terrible fluid precision that spoke of enhancement beyond human capability.

A shadow fell across the car. Graven looked up through the shattered windshield and saw NATO agents—two of them, emerging from that black BMW that had been blocking the parking lot. They wore tactical gear. They carried weapons. But their faces showed the same thing Graven felt: This was beyond them. This was beyond anyone.

One of them raised a hand—stop, or help, or something. Graven never found out which.

His vision tunneled. The edges of the world turned gray, then black. The last thing he saw was Kort's silhouette against the sky, rain falling around him like judgment day, and the certainty that he was about to die.

Then darkness took him, and the world went away.

When consciousness returned, it came in fragments. Blurry vision. The smell of chemicals—something sprayed in his face. A hood pulled over his head. Voices speaking Norwegian. The sensation of being moved.

Graven came fully awake in the back of a black limousine. He slumped in his seat across from two men—one distinguished and patrician, seventyish, with the bearing of someone who'd spent a lifetime in power. The other was Rune.

"Well, what a surprise," Graven said, his voice hoarse. "Rune, isn't it? That'll teach me not to take roll call. Newly assigned historian my ass."

He turned to the older man. "And you are Mathias Sørensen. I recognize you from the video conference and photos on the paper trial that led me here."

Mathias nodded an acknowledgement. "Rune here is my assistant at the research department. I'm sorry about the deception, but you see, we are all allies."

"You have a funny way of showing it."

"We had to take precautions—you understand."

"Felix mentioned your name before..." Graven let the implication hang in the air between them.

"Yes, I'm sure he did. You're lucky to be alive."

"Yeah, guess so, since he also told me I was being set up to be... How did he say it? Silenced. Know anything about that, Mathias?"

Mathias's expression didn't change—the practiced neutrality of a career bureaucrat. "We recently found out Felix had been embezzling NATO funds and distributing classified research information. Highly... classified... information."

"Information I may have been getting too close to—is that it?"

"I assure you I had nothing to do with his death."

Rune leaned forward. "Trust me, you were merely at the wrong place at the wrong time."

"Maybe. But trust is a rare commodity. Not easy to come by." Graven looked between them, trying to read what wasn't being said.

"Agreed," Mathias said.

Military security opened the limo doors. Through the window, Graven could see they were at the Sola Air Station section of Stavanger Airport, on the tarmac. An E-3A Sentry AWACS aircraft waited, engines already spinning up.

"Join us—we can talk more on the way to Oslo," Mathias said.

Graven climbed out, his ribs screaming with each movement. "Do I have a choice?"

"We all have choices, Mr. Graven. The question is whether we have good ones."

The AWACS aircraft was a flying command center. NATO staff members buzzed around technical equipment and computer terminals that lined the walls. Graven, Mathias, and Rune sat in a small passenger area while the operation hummed around them.

A female staff member approached with a beverage cart.

"So, Mr. Graven—"

"Just Graven."

Mathias nodded acknowledgment. "Tell me what you have discovered in your investigation?"

Graven smirked. "Tell you? Just like that? How about we build some trust first?"

Mathias smiled—thin, professional, revealing nothing. "Fair enough."

"What the hell was that thing? Is it connected to Dr. Filibert Austerlitz? And who is he anyway? I have a dead state senator, a dead tactical team, and a big hole in the ground, for chrissakes."

"I share your urgency, I assure you. We both want an end to this barbaric activity. After all, it's not how civilized people act, now is it?"

"No, we're usually more discrete about our killings. Or at least make up a good backstory."

"Spoken like a true nihilist." Mathias turned to the staff member: "*Te med sukker, vennligst.*"

"Yeah, well, I'm an American—we call it being pragmatic." Graven nodded to the staff member "Coffee, miss. Black."

Once they had their drinks, Rune continued: "Dr. Austerlitz is a dangerous man, Graven. We've been trying to flush him out of hiding for years, and now he appears to have taken the offensive."

"Great—another nut wanting world domination."

"He doesn't want world domination—that's not what he's after."

"Oh? Then what's his major malfunction?"

"Tsk, tsk, Mr. Graven. You're not taking turns," Mathias chided gently.

Graven sighed, the exhaustion of the last week catching up with him. "Okay. Felix had a laptop he was very nervous about. Said it contained secrets. Talked about not going down alone."

"What was on it?"

"Never got a chance to find out. Last I saw that thing reached in and took the laptop." Graven paused. "Wait. No. Felix threw it in the back seat. Before..." He trailed off, not wanting to describe what had happened to Felix.

Mathias and Rune exchanged a glance—quick, loaded with meaning.

"We'll need to recover that vehicle from the local authorities," Mathias said quietly to Rune, then turned back to Graven. "No matter—we will continue to Oslo."

"What's in Oslo?"

"We've picked up intel suggesting Oslo is a likely target for Dr. Austerlitz and—he may have a safe haven established there."

Graven glared at Rune. "I hope your intel didn't come from an anonymous caller."

Rune fiddled with papers in a folder, absorbing the hostility without reaction.

"The Royal Norwegian Air Force operates an air station out of Oslo Airport," Mathias explained. "Transport and electronic warfare operations mainly." He managed a corporate smile and gestured to Graven. "And hosting VIPs."

Graven tossed Mathias an incredulous glance.

"Sabotage is a likely motive," Rune added, "but we can't rule out Austerlitz tapping into the electronic warfare systems and starting an international incident."

"What the hell is going on here, Mathias?" Graven leaned forward, ignoring Rune entirely. "And don't give me any bullshit about sabotage. I know this is bigger than whatever that thing is that's killing people. Austerlitz booby-trapped his hideout with some energy wave—I watched the whole thing disintegrate and take my men."

Mathias's expression finally showed something—maybe respect, maybe resignation. "Dr. Austerlitz used to work for NATO back in the 1960s, bioengineering combat gear. He also had an obsession with Nikola Tesla. I'm sorry to say, you saw a version of that play out with your men."

Graven gave him a grim nod, remembering the crater in Pennsylvania, the way matter had simply ceased to exist.

Mathias continued, diplomatically piecemealing out the information. "That was just one version of weaponizing Tesla's theories. What you saw was a localized version that disintegrated matter in a confined circumference."

He had Graven's complete attention.

"My team has studied Dr. Austerlitz notes and work from the late 60s. Material I'm not quite sure he knew I obtained. The application we suspect he means to use here in Norway is not localized. He needs a central location that can hit multiple targets causing destruction that will make the Dresden bombing raid of 1945 look like a kitchen fire."

Graven listened to the words as they mixed in with images of his team evaporating, the energy wave that had swatted the helicopter out of the air like an insect—the empty smoldering hole. Not able to contain the anger heating up inside him, Graven spat, "Damn you, Mathias. Are you saying you knew what he was capable of for decades and did nothing?"

"Not nothing—we searched for him and investigated every anomaly reported."

Graven stood up and declared, "Incompetence!"

For the first time, the diplomatic demeaner gave way to the darkness that lay beneath Mathias's polished persona. He glared and growled at Graven, "And how much forewarning and reams of evidence did your government have and still failed to comprehend or stop the September 11 attacks on your country?"

The words hit Graven like sucker punch to the gut. He shook with a sharp intake of air, trying with all he had not to lunge at Mathias and throttle him. The men remained locked in combative, malignant staring.

Rune started to pale and look for the staff member with the beverage cart—craving something stronger than tea.

Mathias was first to soften, his air of professionalism returning. "Forgive me, Graven, I was out of line."

Graven softened also and sat back down, drained from the energetic surge of emotion. "I was out of line as well, I am sorry."

The two men sat in silence recovering. Both feeling the weight of men charged with the safety and security of the citizenry and both living with the unrelenting guilt of multiple failures to meet their responsibilities. Failures that cost lives—so many goddamn lives. And the loss of thousands of more seemed at hand.

"That 'thing' that attacked you means he has a soldier prototype," Mathia said, restarting the conversation. "Very similar to what he worked on for NATO."

"So what does he want—why is he creating all this chaos?"

"When his NATO position was terminated, he did not take it well. I'm afraid he's harbored a long hatred against NATO and me." Mathias's voice carried what might have been genuine regret. "After he disappeared, I received regular threatening letters—then they stopped. And now—all this."

"So that's it? A thirty-five-year-old grudge match? Jesus."

"It's more complicated than that," Rune interjected. "Project 19.5 wasn't just about combat gear. Austerlitz was working on human enhancement—biological integration of technology at the cellular level. The ethical concerns—"

"Were significant," Mathias finished. "But the work had potential. Military potential. After the project was shut down, Dr. Austerlitz smuggled out—stole—classified NATO research materials and disappeared. We thought he'd given up. We were wrong."

Graven looked between them, pieces falling into place. "And now he's got a supersoldier running around killing people."

"Not just any soldier," Mathias said quietly. "From what we can gather, that's Kort Sokolov. He was one of Austerlitz's first test subjects—a French Foreign Legion soldier, and former U.S. Green Beret, who volunteered for enhancement in Algeria in the 1960s."

"Volunteered to become that thing?"

"To survive," Rune said. "The original enhancements were meant to help soldiers survive extreme combat conditions. But Austerlitz kept improving the design, kept pushing the boundaries. And now—"

"Now you've got a weapon that can't be stopped." Graven finished the thought.

The aircraft banked, beginning its approach to Oslo. Through the window, the city spread below—lights glittering against the darkness, a city unaware that something post-human might be moving through its streets.

"Can it be stopped?" Graven asked.

Mathias was quiet for a long moment, staring into his tea. "Every weapon has a weakness. Even one as sophisticated as Kort Sokolov."

"You sound like you know him personally."

"I've studied him for years. His enhancement profile, his combat history, his psychological markers. In a sense, I know him better than he knows himself." Mathias looked up, and there was something cold in his eyes—the detachment of a scientist discussing a specimen. "But knowing and stopping are different things."

"What about Zahra?" Graven asked. "Felix mentioned something—before everything went to shit—about Austerlitz's research partner."

"Dr. Austerlitz's former research partner, Zahra, is at a secured underground NATO lab in Ålesund," Mathias said carefully. "She's been trying to replicate his work. But something's missing. A key component only Filibert knows."

"And you think that's his target? His endgame?"

"Zahra, the research, the proof that his work succeeded—" Mathias spread his hands. "Everything Austerlitz has done has been leading somewhere. Killing Senator Toresen was a message. Attacking Felix was eliminating a liability. But the real target, the real goal—that's still ahead of us."

The aircraft touched down with barely a jolt, pilots skilled from thousands of hours in the air. They taxied toward a secure area of the airport where more NATO vehicles waited—black SUVs with enough firepower to start a small war.

Or stop one.

"My men will brief you and Rune on the target locations and a possible safe haven Austerlitz may have here in Oslo," Mathias said pointing to a black SUV as they disembarked into crisp Norwegian air. "I'll be in the lead SUV tending to other matters of state. We will meet at the suspected location."

"Okay—but Mathias? If this goes bad, if that resonance weapon goes off in a populated area, this is on you. NATO, the U.S., none of the politics will matter. You'll be the man who let thousands die to protect Cold War secrets."

"If it goes that badly, Mr. Graven, we'll all be dead anyway." Mathias climbed into the lead SUV. "So let's make sure it doesn't."

Graven watched him go, then turned to Rune. "You trust him?"

Rune considered the question, took his time lighting the pipe he'd been chewing on throughout the flight. "I trust that he wants this over. Whether that aligns with what's right..." He shrugged. "In this business, sometimes you don't get to choose between good and evil. Just between different kinds of necessary."

"That's bullshit."

"Perhaps. But it's true bullshit." Rune gestured to another SUV. "Come. We have work to do."

The convoy rolled out and exited the airport. They turned south, toward an old industrial district where abandoned factories and warehouses offered the kind of space and privacy a mad scientist might need.

The radio crackled. Updates from the other teams. Nothing yet. Just empty buildings and the chilly Norwegian night.

But somewhere in this city, clocks were stopped at half past one. And somewhere in this city, the past was about to collide with the present in ways that would reshape the future.

Graven touched his ribs again, rubbed his thighs, felt the pain, reminded himself that pain meant he was still human. Still alive.

The pursuit had become something else. Graven had come to Norway hunting answers. But now he understood the truth that Felix had tried to communicate in his final moments:

They weren't the hunters.

They were the prey.

And the real predator was still moving through the darkness, patient and unstoppable, following a plan thirty-five years in the making.

The SUVs accelerated into the Oslo night. Behind them, the airport lights faded.

Ahead—darkness—and whatever waited in it.

Nineteen

Norway

Bjørvika Waterfront, Oslo, Norway – The Same Night

The warehouse stank of death and deception.

Graven pressed the crook of his elbow against his nose, trying to block the smell, but it was useless. The stench had physical presence—thick, cloying, invasive. It crawled into his mouth, coated his tongue, made his eyes water.

"Jesus! What in God's name?" he gasped.

Beside him, Mathias and Rune were doing the same futile dance—burying their faces in jacket sleeves, breathing through clenched teeth, anything to avoid the full assault of whatever rot waited inside.

Norwegian Special Forces troops stumbled out of the warehouse ahead of them, ripping off tactical masks, bending over to vomit on the concrete pier. These were hardened soldiers—men who'd seen combat, handled decomposed bodies, worked disaster sites. Whatever was inside had broken through their professional detachment.

A team leader approached Mathias, wrapping his mouth and nose with a cloth. His eyes watered above the makeshift mask.

"The building's clear, sir," he reported in Norwegian. Graven's grasp of the language was minimal, but Rune translated quietly. "No equipment. No indication of what would cause the energy surges. All we found was..."

He gestured helplessly toward the warehouse entrance.

Graven followed Mathias and Rune inside. The smell intensified—rotting fish mixed with something chemical, something deliberately engineered to offend. Huge warehouse lights popped on with industrial clanks, illuminating the source.

In the center of the warehouse floor, piled eight feet high, was a mountain of fish. Herring, thousands of them, rotting in the confined space. And splattered across the pile, painted in broad, mocking strokes of red paint was one word: **RED.**

"Explains the strong heat signature we picked up," the team leader said, his voice muffled by the cloth.

Graven stared at the pile, understanding dawning with sick certainty. "Duped! Goddamned duped!"

"Bloody red herring!" Rune's laugh was bitter, humorless.

They stumbled back outside, coughing and gagging. Graven bent over, hands on knees, sucking in clean air. His ribs screamed with each breath—the cracked bones grinding together, inflamed by the exertion.

"All right, gentlemen, let's not lose our heads." Mathias's voice was controlled despite his own obvious discomfort. "That tells us nothing of importance."

"Could Austerlitz know?" Rune asked carefully, his tone suggesting implications beyond the words.

"Know? Know what?" Graven straightened, looked between them. The air crackled with unspoken information.

Mathias and Rune exchanged a glance—the kind of look career bureaucrats perfected, conveying volumes in a flicker of eye contact.

"Don't politic me," Graven snapped. "What's going on?"

Mathias sighed, the sound of a man accepting inevitable disclosure. "I told you that Dr. Austerlitz's former research partner, Zahra, is at a secured underground NATO lab in Ålesund."

"Yes, I remember."

"What I didn't tell you is she is more than that. She was a co-founder and contributed vital processes Austerlitz couldn't figure out on his own." Mathias let that hang for a moment.

"She is also Kort Sokolov's wife. She's the only person who understood Filibert's work well enough to continue it. And, I hope, the only one Kort won't kill no matter what the mission parameters are." Mathias pulled out his phone, showed Graven a satellite image. "The Atlantic Sea-Park. Public aquarium on the surface. Classified NATO research facility underneath. She's been trying to replicate Austerlitz's enhancement protocols."

"And you left her exposed? Used her as bait?"

"We didn't know Austerlitz's location. We still don't." Mathias's voice carried the weight of calculated risk, necessary sacrifice. "But if he knows where she is—"

"Then that's his target," Graven finished.

"Not Oslo. Ålesund."

Mathias spoke a truth out loud into the night: "Don't rule out Oslo as a target. He damn well knows I'm here." And with disdain he spat, "He put me here."

"But when will he strike?" Graven asked.

"That is the critical question," Mathias answered, the confidence in his voice wavering. "A day? A week? Does he have things in place or in process? If we react too soon with a show of force, he can recalculate the target. Leaving us resource poor in the impacted area."

Mathias nodded at Rune.

Rune worked his phone. Made a connection. Gave calm instructions in Norwegian. He covered the phone and said to Graven, "Instructing to secure assets, lowest-profile, highest alert."

But even as Rune coordinated the response, Graven knew the truth that showed in Mathias's eyes:

They would be too late. Whether a day or a week—they would be too late. People were going to die.

Whatever Filibert Austerlitz had planned was already in motion. They were playing a game of catch-up and playing it badly.

Abandoned Smelter Factory, Odda, Norway – Early the Next Morning

Filibert stood before the Tesla Death Ray with something approaching religious reverence.

The device dominated the factory's tower floor—a massive assemblage of copper coils, transformers, and crystalline resonance chambers that extended through the cut-away ceiling into the cool light of the morning Norwegian sky. It hummed with building energy, harmonics that made the metal floor plates vibrate beneath his feet.

Forty years of work. Forty years of refinement, calculation, obsessive perfection. Building it piece by piece in secrecy for the last decade.

And now, the moment of proof.

"What problems?" Iniko asked from behind him, out of breath from climbing the tower stairs. She stared at the weapon, her face showing the first real understanding of what Filibert intended. "What are you doing?"

"Solving them," Filibert replied. His fingers flew across the control panel, entering sequences he'd calculated decades ago. "Revealing what a true weapon of war can deliver: victorious devastation without dangerous isotopes compromising the environment for decades."

"You're going to destroy a city."

"Cities. Plural." Filibert didn't look away from his work. "Oslo and Ålesund simultaneously. The dual resonance will create confusion, split their response. And in the chaos Kort will reach Zahra. To complete his promise."

"The people—"

"Are acceptable losses in service of a greater purpose." He paused, turned to face her. "This was always the plan, Iniko. Surely you understood that?"

Her face showed she hadn't. Or perhaps she'd allowed herself not to understand, to live in comfortable denial about what she'd been enabling.

"Kort won't last long," Filibert continued, turning back to his controls. "Have to get him close to Ålesund. That's where the fortified NATO laboratory is—that's where Zahra and my research is. They'll have bigger problems to deal with. Kort will walk right in."

"You're not thinking clearly. The lab will be destroyed as well."

"No, Iniko," he grinned horrifically at her.

Iniko's stomach twisted in response to his use of her name.

"I've set this for surface destruction like a high-yield air burst."

The weapon's hum intensified. The harmonics shifted, found resonance, began building toward cascade.

"And the world," Filibert whispered, "will never be the same."

Atlantic Sea-Park, Ålesund – Later That Day – 1:15 PM

Zahra watched the school bus through the glass doors. It sat idling—a rhythmic, heavy *chug-chug* in the silence—surrounded by the emptiness of the parking lots. The school had not received the message of the closure. The regular park staff instructed not to report to work today. A morning shift called in to feed the exhibits early had long gone home. Only a trusted few lab assistants remained with Zahra, they were quartered on Sub-basement Level 1 of the classified NATO research center under the sea park. Six Norwegian Special Operations soldiers appeared at 3 AM and wasted no time taking charge.

Mathias's doing. She had no doubt. But he hadn't bothered to brief her on the threat. Typical. She returned her attention to the bus.

Children pressed against the bus windows—maybe twenty of them, young faces full of disappointed excitement. They'd come to see the aquarium. They'd come to learn about marine life. They had been met with Norwegian Special Operations soldiers denying entrance. A young woman, the schoolteacher, hopped off the bus and strode with conviction towards a soldier, while an older woman behind the wheel plopped her face in a bored hand and shook her head.

No one at the park had any idea they were standing in a blast radius of an unconventional weapon.

Her phone rang. An unknown number. She answered warily.

"*Hallo?*"

"Zahra?" The voice was female, accented, strained. "This is Iniko."

Zahra took in a sharp breath and braced herself. "I expected to hear from you. Been following you and your master's handiwork on the news."

"Please, Zahra, listen. You don't have much time."

"I have time to hear how you betrayed me. How when it was time to sneak Kort out of the lab, you sounded the alarm. After you promised to help me—to help us."

"I know, that's a sin for another time. But you must listen to me now. He's activated the weapon. Oslo and Ålesund. Simultaneous strike. You need to get inside now. Underground. The deepest level you can reach. He's targeting landmarks and major attractions—Ålesund Church... and the aquarium will be in its path. You have ten minutes."

The rest of the information Iniko provided came fast, hit Zahra like a crashing wave, stalled her breath.

The call terminated.

Zahra's eyes went wide, phone falling like a dream from her hand. She had known security was on high alert, but not why. Not that it was due to a pending catastrophic event—and not now—not in ten minutes! She turned, looked through the doors at the Norwegian soldier arguing with the schoolteacher, at the waiting bus and empty lot, at the children—

Oh God, the children.

"What? This can't be!"

She was already moving, running out of the entrance. "Officer! Get those children inside now!"

The soldier looked at her, confused by the urgency, the terror in her voice.

"Now!" Zahra screamed. "*Alle! Alle inni!*"

Whatever he saw in her face convinced him. He grabbed his radio, started barking orders. The teacher's confused protest died as soldiers moved toward the bus. The driver sat up, her eyes registering the sharp change in the situation, and started waving the children off the bus.

Zahra looked to the sky. Clear. Blue. Beautiful. Giving no hint of what was building in the atmosphere above.

Her attention snapped back to the priority at hand. Following the school group being hustled inside by soldiers, she waved them to a secluded elevator at the end of a hall off the entrance way.

She punched a speed dial button; an assistant picked up on the first ring. Zahra instructed, "Take shelter in the surgical suite on level three. I'll be in the aquarium observation room with a group of school children." She ended the call without need to get confirmation. She said it—it would be done.

The sign on the elevator featured a pictogram of a figure holding out a halting hand inside a red circle with diagonal slash. The bilingual sign said: *Adgang forbudt—Kun for autorisert personell* Access prohibited—Only for authorized personnel.

Zahra eased through the huddling children and swiped her card. The reader beeped and the doors opened. She ushered the school group in, pushed the U3 button—Sub-basement Level 3—and to the soldiers said, "Patrol sub-basement two. Come for us when the all clear is given." As the doors closed, she added, "Or if level three is compromised."

NATO Offices, Gardermoen Air Station, Oslo - 1:20 PM
The makeshift control center buzzed with controlled chaos. NATO staff members hunched over computer terminals, coordinating responses, tracking energy signatures that were spiking across two cities. A desperate race to pinpoint the source. F-16 fighters from Bodø Main Air Station had already been deployed, holding air space, waiting for a target.

A technician jumped up from his seat, "Orientation signature locked in—Odda! Coordinates: "Sixty degrees, five minutes, eighteen point six seconds north, six degrees, thirty-two minutes, nineteen point eight seconds east!"

On the heels of the announcement, an officer shouted into a red phone: "Target acquired. Authorization code: Alpha-Niner-Seven. Prepare to receive coordinates: "Sixty degrees, five minutes, eighteen point six seconds north, six degrees, thirty-two minutes, nineteen point eight seconds east."

A staff member tapped a handset. "It's Zahra."

Mathias grabbed the phone. "Zahra, what's your status?"

Her voice came through compressed by digital transmission but thick with fear. "He knows. Filibert knows where I am. I'm tracking spiked energy readings. Harmonics building. It's going to be big, Mathias—cataclysmic!"

"Evacuate to the underground levels. Seal the facility." He smothered the mouthpiece; nodded curtly to Rune. "Alert the FSK team to lockdown. Highest vigilance." He returned his attention to Zahra.

"There are children here. A school group. I've gotten them below to level three but—Mathias, if this is what I think it is, the underground might not be enough. Did you know this was in motion? Mathias—did you know and not warn me?"

Mathias looked at Rune, at Graven. His face showed the calculation of a man weighing acceptable losses against strategic necessity. The burden of it threatened to break him.

"Do what you can," he said quietly. "We've isolated the source in Odda. We scrambled F-16 fighters from Bodø Main Air Station. If we can hit the site in time—"

"It won't be in time," Zahra cut him off. "Iniko called me. Ten minutes she said. Ten minutes!"

"They are en route. We calculate twenty minutes before weapon employment."

"Then pray your calculations are more accurate than Iniko's," Zahra snapped, and disconnected.

Graven moved closer to the large screen in the underground command center. He braced himself for the inevitable horror that would soon unfold. Then his face registered the thought that had been brewing and only now manifested. He turned to Mathias and Rune. "Wait—if the weapon projects concentrated, high-energy particle beams over vast distances as you said, it must arc in the atmosphere to get there."

"That is correct," Mathias responded.

Rune added, "Specifically in the stratosphere and bordering on mesosphere."

Graven felt annoyance at the technical and irrelevant correction. "Then won't it just smash into those F-16s?"

Rune piped in again, "Technically yes, but..."

"But they have orders to fly low and under the atmospheric disturbance of the energy," Mathias explained, finishing Rune's thought.

Graven nodded with only limited relief. There was still plenty for his gut to be tied in a knot over.

"Hard to imagine a man capable of this," Mathias half mumbled.

"I've seen what he's capable of," Graven replied. "No doubt he'll level a whole city to get what he wants."

"Contact in fifteen minutes!" the technician called from across the room.

Fifteen minutes until the weapon fired. Fifteen minutes until two Norwegian cities were hit by an energy weapon that would spread a wave of destruction.

Fifteen minutes that would determine if this was the opening move in a larger war, or the final act of a madman's revenge. But the calculation fell short.

The Attack - 1:30 PM

It began with vibrations.

For visitors at Oslo's Vigeland Sculpture Park—the famous installation of human figures in stone, hundreds of sculptures celebrating the human form—the day had been full of art, wonderment, and camaraderie until the vibrations. Tourists and locals stopped mid-stride, looking around with confusion as the ground beneath their feet began to hum. Sculptures trembled. Water in the fountain rippled in concentric circles. Birds exploded from trees in panicked flight.

In Ålesund, the historic Ålesund Church clock's minute hand moved to half past one, and the building started to shake. Behind the church, by an old cemetery, the memorial sculpture *De falne til minne*, In memory of the fallen,—honoring fallen Norwegians during World War II—vibrated with increasing intensity.

Then the harmonics hit.

The air itself seemed to scream—a sound beyond hearing, felt in bones and teeth and the fluid of inner ears. Glass windows shattered simultaneously across both cities. Car alarms triggered in cascading waves. People collapsed, clutching their heads, bleeding from ears and noses.

And then the energy discharge.

In Oslo, the Vigeland sundial sculpture exploded—stone vaporizing into plasma, the shockwave radiating outward in visible concentric circles. The fountain disintegrated to rubble-dust. Sculptures within a three hundred-meter radius simply ceased to exist, matter torn apart at the molecular level.

In Ålesund, the memorial sculpture *De falne til minne* turned to vapor. The Ålesund Church crumbled in on itself. And the energy wave continued, heading directly toward the Atlantic Sea-Park.

Two F-16 fighters screamed across the Odda sky, breaking the sound barrier in their low altitude approach, the wake turbulence chewed up the landscape and battered abandoned buildings. With a precision few pilots could execute, they maneuvered a high-g pull-up instantly after missiles away. The missiles hit true, penetrating the abandoned smelter factory in Odda that NATO's intel had finally located. The factory erupted in a fireball visible for kilometers.

Zahra had been right—destroying the Odda weapon didn't come in time to stop the Oslo and Ålesund strikes. The energy, though cutoff from its source, rushed out from the center of origin, spreading its radius and would not dissipate until more damage had been done.

The energy wave hit the Atlantic Sea-Park. No longer fully energized, the wave still caused destruction with a mixture of evaporation of matter and flying chunks of twisted and melted concrete and metal. The school bus crumpled like tinfoil. Trees ignited from the sheer energy release. The aquarium's water flashed to superheated steam.

But below ground, in the heavily reinforced NATO laboratory, Zahra waited with the teacher, the bus driver, and twenty terrified children in the aquarium observation room on Sub-basement Level 3. Beyond the wall of aquarium glass, the dimly lit water showed no signs of life. Scattered children's sobs sporadically cut through the heavy dread in the air and were met with reassurances by adults who didn't believe it themselves.

Then the building shook. Lights failed. Emergency systems kicked in—red rotating warnings, klaxons screaming, the sound of stressed metal and fracturing stone. The air pressure suddenly spiked from the initial shock wave followed by painful depressurization.

And then silence.

The kind of silence that comes after apocalypse.

Somewhere deep in the structure generators roared to life, settling into a rhythmic *thrum-thrum* of alternative power. A sharp, metallic tang of ozone from shorted circuits permeated the air. The klaxons did not return; computers rebooted—desperate in displays of error messages and warnings; emergency red lights returned to flood the hallways—catching the dust hanging in the air like a nuclear winter; various offices flickered, straining to engage the fluorescents.

Zahra stood slowly, her ears ringing, tasting blood. "Everyone all right?"

Small voices answered—frightened but alive. The teacher cried, clutching two children. The bus driver attempted a stoic composure—that was failing. But they'd survived.

Above them, Ålesund burned.

The Infiltration

Kort emerged from the devastation like something birthed from apocalypse itself.

The ruins of Ålesund stretched in every direction—buildings reduced to skeletal frameworks, vehicles melted into abstract sculptures, the ground covered in white phosphorus ash that fell like toxic snow. The over-charged atmosphere crackled with residual energy, lightning arcing between clouds that glowed orange-red with reflected fires.

His armor was scorched black, cracked in a dozen places, the adaptive camouflage system glitching, leaking the gray lithium gel that served as his synthetic blood. The protective plates on his chest showed impact damage from the Tesla weapon's energy wave—deep gouges where matter had begun to sublimate before he tossed a manhole cover like it was a paper plate and took refuge deep in the sewer system.

The power core in his chest cavity pulsed weakly, its bio-luminescence fading from bright blue to sickly yellow. He could feel systems shutting down, non-essential functions sacrificing themselves to preserve the mission.

Inside his faceplate, warnings scrolled in urgent red:

POWER CORE 2%. POWER FAILURE – 1.5 HOURS. TIME TO TOTAL SYSTEM FAILURE: 78 MINUTES. MAGNESIUM FAILSAFE ARMED.

One hour to complete the mission before going into the critical zone with degraded functioning. To reach Zahra. To fulfill the promise he'd made to Filibert forty years ago in an Algerian desert—though the memory of that promise was fragmenting now, dissolving into scattered data as his neural systems prioritized survival over history.

Time ebbing away until the magnesium self-destruct implant incinerated him from within, ensuring that no one could reverse-engineer Filibert's work from his remains.

If he didn't reach the rendezvous point with the staged emergent stabilization equipment—Kort Sokolov would be no more. If he even existed now, whatever an existing "self" even meant anymore.

He emerged from the sewer and scanned the devastated landscape, his enhanced vision cutting through smoke and ash. The Sea-Park's surface structure was gone—utterly eradicated. But his sensors detected electromagnetic signatures below. The laboratory. Intact. Shielded.

And Zahra.

The iron air vents jutted from the rubble like mushrooms after rain—industrial exhaust ports designed to cycle air through the underground facility. Kort found the nearest one, knelt beside it. The opening was perhaps thirty centimeters in diameter. Designed for air, not human passage.

He thrust his head into the opening. His shoulders followed. Too wide. The human clavicle couldn't compress enough.

Except his wasn't human anymore.

The bones buckled, reformed, angled inward. His shoulder blades flattened against his spine. Ribs that were reinforced with bio-ceramic alloys bent like rubber. Internal organs shifted position, redistributed through his abdominal cavity to allow passage through the impossible space.

His entire body flowed into the vent like water finding a crack in concrete. Behind him, the vent shaft collapsed from structural stress, sealing shut.

Inside the duct, he moved through pitch darkness. Forty-five degree bends proved a tighter fit to push through. His skull compressed—the modified bone structure that Filibert had engineered decades ago shifting, plates sliding over each other like tectonic movement. The sound was wet, organic, wrong.

No light reached this far below ground. But light was unnecessary—his modified biology read electromagnetic fields, thermal signatures, the subtle vibrations of movement carried through metal walls.

Ahead, voices. Norwegian soldiers. Armed. Professional.

Kort moved faster. The mission narrowed to a point: reach Zahra.

Everything else was noise.

Two teams of three each of the Norwegian Special Operations soldiers advanced through Sub-basement Level 2 corridors lit only by emergency wall units. Red rotating lights painted everything in shades of blood. Their C8SFW assault rifles swept corners, covered angles, maintained tactical spacing.

The team leader, decorated, fifteen years of experience, spoke quietly into his headset: "Team Two. Are you in the west corridor? Team Two? Respond."

Static crackled. Then something worse than silence—a high-pitched squeal that cut through the radio frequency like nails on a chalkboard. The pitch rose, became unbearable. All three soldiers grabbed their headsets, trying to rip them off as the sound seemed to bore directly into their skulls.

The team leader recovered first, peering down the red-lit hallway. A shadow. It darted between cover positions—fast, impossibly fast—vanishing into the Level 2 Pool Room.

"Team Two—be advised, possible sighting, consider level two compromised." He motioned his team to enter the room. Their mounted tactical lights sliced through the central access pool room; they bounced off the water, throwing rippling ghost patterns on the walls.

Kort exploded from the darkness like a predator that had been patient long enough.

The fight lasted 47 seconds.

A younger Norwegian soldier fired first—controlled burst, center mass, exactly as trained. The rounds hit Kort's chest armor and penetrated damaged sections. Gray gel spurted. Kort didn't slow.

He covered twenty meters in less than two seconds. Grabbed the younger soldier's rifle, twisted it out of his hands with such force the soldier's trigger finger broke. In the same motion, Kort used the rifle as a club, caught an older soldier across the jaw. The impact sent teeth flying.

The team leader jumped on Kort's back, wrapped his arm around what should have been a vulnerable throat. His other hand plunged a combat knife into Kort's sternum—between armor plates, seeking something vital with a twist.

Kort reached back, grabbed the soldier, and threw him off with a bone-breaking crack against the concrete wall.

The older soldier, jaw shattered but still fighting, swung a maintenance pulley on a heavy chain. The metal weight caught Kort across the side of his head with a wet smack. His faceplate spider-webbed. Visual systems glitched, showed static, struggled to compensate.

As Kort stumbled backward, disoriented by the impact, he grabbed the younger soldier—the one whose finger he'd broken—and they both went over the edge into the central access pool.

They plunged through ten meters of murky water into the aquarium observation room one floor below—in Sub-basement Level 3.

In the water, buoyancy changed everything. Kort sank—his enhanced density, the metal and ceramic components of his body, pulled him down like an anchor. The soldier kicked upward, straining against Kort's grip on his foot. Desperate for air, he pounded against the glass wall that separated the aquarium from the observation room.

Behind him, in the darkness of the tank, something large moved.

The giant Pacific octopus had been agitated by the energy weapon's resonance—its sensitive nervous system scrambled by harmonics, its natural intelligence twisted into aggression by pain and confusion.

Eight hundred pounds of muscle and fury uncoiled from out of the darkness.

Arms—each one as thick as a man's thigh—wrapped around the drowning soldier. He didn't even have time to scream out the last of his air before he was jerked out of Kort's hand and pulled backward into the unlit depths. Brief struggle. Crunch of bone. Then stillness.

Finding the equilibrium of the water, Kort floated, suspended in the murky water. His visual systems cycled through spectrums—infrared, ultraviolet, electromagnetic. Nothing detected in the darkness.

He pulled the combat knife from his chest. Gray lithium gel oozed out, mixed with the water, created bioluminescent swirls that cast faint light.

Not enough to see by.

But enough to be seen.

The octopus struck.

Reunion

In the aquarium observation room, Zahra and the school group startled as the bodies plunged into the tank, agitating the water. The children screamed. Through the glass—a floor-to-ceiling window into murky, red-lit water—they watched a Norwegian soldier hammer helplessly against the transparent wall.

His mouth open, air forced out in big bubbles. Screaming, probably. But no sound reached them through eight centimeters of reinforced acrylic.

Then long limbs—each one covered in hundreds of suckers, each sucker ringed with sharp chitinous teeth—darted from the unlit water and pulled him back into darkness. Brief thrashing. A bloom of blood washed up against the glass. Then nothing.

The giant Pacific octopus. Eight hundred pounds of highly intelligent, highly aggressive predator that Zahra had been studying for three years. Gentle with her, responsive to training, curious about its environment. But right now, confused by the energy weapon's effects, in pain, frightened—it was apex predator incarnate.

Then slowly emerging from the dark, towards the glass, a figure floated limp in the water.

"*Travelt! Travelt!*" Zahra pointed the group toward the side emergency exit, her Norwegian sharp with command. Get them out. Get them safe.

As crying children were rushed out of the room—one little girl clutching a stuffed seal, a boy looking back with wide traumatized eyes—Zahra hit the wall intercom with shaking hands: "Team to observation room! Level three compromised—I repeat compromised!"

Then she turned back to the tank, unable to look away.

Kort floated suspended in the cloudy water, pulling the combat knife from his chest with mechanical precision. Gray lithium gel oozed out, mixed with the water, created phosphorescent swirls that cast faint bioluminescent light through the tank's darkness.

His faceplate turned toward her.

Even through the water, through the glass, through years of separation and technology and everything that had transformed him into something post-human—Zahra saw recognition.

Not just visual recognition. Not computer systems identifying a target.

Recognition.

As he made his way to the tank's glass wall, her breath caught. Fifteen years. Fifteen years since she'd escaped out of Filibert's secret laboratory, unable to watch what her husband was becoming, unable to save him, to spare him of this. Fifteen years of guilt and grief and wondering if any part of him remained.

"Kort..." The whisper caught in her throat.

In the tank, Kort's body language shifted. The predatory crouch softened. One hand—still recognizably human despite the modifications—pressed against the glass. Palm flat. Fingers spread.

The gesture of their first real date after stolen moments in Algeria following his rescue of her. Though he always thought of it as her rescuing him from a soldier's lonely life. New York City, 1964, when he had secured some R&R. Standing outside in the rain, hands pressed against opposite sides of a coffee shop window, laughing at the absurdity of paying for overpriced coffee when they were both broke.

Tears blurred Zahra's vision.

Then the octopus struck.

It came from below—survival instinct honed over 300 million years of evolution. Eight massive cephalopod arms wrapped around Kort, jounced him violently like fishing lure. The creature's body—a bulbous mass of muscle and neural tissue—pulsed dark red, the color-changing chromatophores expressing aggression, warning.

The octopus slammed Kort against the glass hard enough to pulverize a normal human. Kort's body went loose, absorbing the blow as the octopus drew him back like casting a fly rod—second slam. Third.

Zahra's body jumped with each inaudible impact, releasing throaty gasps.

Then the creature's beak—parrot-like, designed to crush crab shells and crack open tough prey—crunched into Kort's exposed abdomen where armor plates had been torn away by the energy weapon.

More gray gel gushed out, mixed with the water in phosphorescent clouds.

Zahra let out an anguished yowl and bit hard on her hand.

He brought his lamprey throat-mouth—that horrible modification that had disturbed her dreams for years—down on one thick arm. The circular teeth latched on. Octopus blood spewed and sputtered from Kort's neck gill-slits as he processed the consumption.

The octopus tightened its grip, trying to crush him, its three hearts pumping furiously, its distributed brain processing pain and anger through neurons spread throughout its body.

Helpless as her husband fought for his life, she screamed and pounded her right fist into her thigh.

It should have won. Eight hundred pounds of muscle versus a power-core running at two percent, systems failing, structural damage compromising integrity.

Except Kort had one last trick.

An electrical charge burst from him—massive, uncontrolled, draining his power core from two percent to one. The water lit up blue-white—began to boil.

The intense light triggered a deep flight response in Zahra, her body instinctively jerked around and propelled her toward the side emergency exit door.

The octopus's neurons—so efficient, so precisely wired—became conductors. Its brain tissue cooked. Muscle spasmed once, violently, then went slack.

The creature was dead in seconds. It and Kort started to float up to the observable top half of the tank.

Kort held out his palm toward the glass—a cone of agitated particles in the water spewed forth. A circular distortion of the glass, two meters in diameter, wobbled and buckled with a glowing hum at the top of the tank.

The water exploded through the void where the glass had been.

Zahra slammed into the panic bar on the exit door, tumbled out of the room.

Kort and the limp octopus crashed into the observation room on a tsunami of seawater and salt stench spilling out of the hole in the glass. The brunt of the gush slammed against the opposite wall with the force of a semi-truck collision. Zahra was through the side door, spared a fatal impact, but the surging backwash still swept her off her feet. Her head hit the floor. Stars burst across her vision.

She shook off the stunning blow, crawled back into the observation room, struggled to her feet. Water drained through floor grates with mechanical efficiency, emergency pumps roaring into action, over 35,000 liters from the second floor to the bottom of the hole.

In the observation room, Kort crouched before her. His power core had drained from one percent to point-zero-five.

He was wrecked. Protective plates torn away, showing the gray synthetic tissue beneath. Chunks missing from the octopus attack—ragged tears where cephalopod limbs had literally ripped flesh-analogue from his frame. One of his arms hanging at an unnatural angle, the joint clearly dislocated or broken. His faceplate spider-webbed, showing only fragments of the face beneath.

His eyes—those eyes that still held some spark of the man she'd loved—focused on her face with terrible intensity.

"Kort. Do you remember, my love?" Her voice broke on every word. "It's Zahra. See me."

Team Two burst through the door. Zahra raised a hand without looking at them: Wait.

"See me," she repeated, taking one step forward through ankle-deep water.

Behind Kort's shattered faceplate, his visual systems flickered. Data inputs went berserk—recognition software conflicting with combat protocols, mission parameters colliding with memory fragments, forty years of conditioning fighting against something deeper and more fundamental.

His systems were failing. But in that failure, something broke through.

Then Kort's body convulsed.

He flopped to the ground on his back, spine arching, limbs splashing in the water, jerking in uncontrolled spasms. Gray gel leaked from a dozen wounds. The power core in his chest sputtered, dimmed, fought to maintain even minimal function.

Memory flashed through his failing systems:

Nineteen-year-old Zahra in that Algerian compound, covered in dust and fear but alive, so beautifully alive, those playful green eyes that seemed to say: "You belong to me now."

Thirty-three-year-old Kort and twenty-seven-year-old Zahra kissing in the rain in New York City after his discharge, their first apartment upstairs, their first real life beginning, everything ahead of them pure with possibility.

Forty-five-year-old Zahra in the shower of their suburban house, water streaming down her graying hair, still beautiful, looking at him with love despite everything: "I love you, Kort."

The convulsions stopped. Zahra rushed to his side, dropped to her knees in the water, grabbed his hand—ignoring the gray gel that coated it, the synthetic tissue that felt wrong against her skin, all the technology that had consumed the man she loved.

"Kort... I'm sorry I left you there." The tears came now, unstoppable. "I'm so sorry you had to live this hell. Forgive me, my love. I can make it right. I can set it back to the start, back to what you wanted."

Behind his faceplate, new text scrolled in fading red:

TOTAL POWER FAILURE.
SELF-DESTRUCT SEQUENCE INITIATING.
MAGNESIUM CORE ACTIVATION: 20 MINUTES.

Kort sat up slowly. The movement took tremendous effort—every system fighting entropy, trying to hold together just a little longer. He hung his head, showed his palms in surrender.

The gesture meant: I'm done fighting.

His outer layer turned sad blue—the damaged adaptive camouflage system flickering one last time, expressing what his voice could no longer say. Not aggression. Not combat readiness.

Grief. Acceptance. Love.

And beneath that, something that might have been relief.

Zahra understood. She looked away, couldn't watch them carry him off. "Take him."

She released Kort's hand—felt the synthetic skin one last time, the warmth that came from engineered biology rather than human blood. Felt it slip from her fingers like all those years had slipped away.

The soldiers moved in with smooth efficiency. Two soldiers supported Kort's weight. The third maintained weapons discipline, covering angles, following protocols.

They followed Zahra to the surgical theater, where she hoped to bypass the self-destruct system—a last resort contingency she'd known about since the design phase. She would spend the next six hours to first deactivate the self-destruct mechanism and then to save what remained of her husband.

Twenty

Aftermath

Norwegian Sea, 24 Nautical Miles Off the Coast of Ålesund

The kicked-up waves from the Ålesund blast had violently rocked the fishing trawler, sending loose equipment clattering across the deck in a discordant symphony of metal on wood. The disturbed gray Norwegian Sea heaved and churned, angry and violated, white caps exploding against the hull with percussive force as the energy blast sucked back to its source like a reversed film reel. Each wave hit with enough power to remind those aboard that nature—even wounded nature—still commanded respect.

In the background, Ålesund smoldered. What had been a picturesque Norwegian coastal town was now a blackened wound on the landscape, smoke columns twisting into the overcast sky like dark serpents ascending to some unholy heaven. Orange flames flickered through the destruction, refusing to die, casting hellish reflections on the churning water that made the Norwegian Sea look like it was bleeding fire.

The smell reached them even here, carried on the wind: burning wood, melted plastic, something chemical and wrong that made the throat tighten and the eyes water. Hundreds of people had been in Ålesund when Filibert's

Tesla weapon had torn reality apart. Now they were ash and memory.

Cutting through the treacherous waters, three NATO patrol boats converged on the trawler, their engines growling through the aftermath of destruction. They moved with military precision, forming a triangle pattern that left no escape route, no possibility of flight, closing in with an abundance of caution, but closing in all the same.

Filibert and Iniko sat in the cramped wheelhouse, both looking pale and hollow-eyed. Their breathing was labored, recovering from the thrashing of the waves and the weight of what they'd just witnessed. The trawler captain worked the helm with the practiced efficiency of a man who'd weathered countless Norwegian Sea storms, helping to further steady the boat as it rode the subsiding swells.

The smell inside the wheelhouse was a nauseating mixture—diesel fumes, salt spray, and something else. Fear. The kind of fear that clings to skin and soaks into fabric.

All three jumped at the loud crackle of the radio cutting through the flatness of the moment, shattering the terrible silence that had settled over them.

From the radio, a NATO officer commanded in Norwegian through the squelch, his voice distorted but unmistakable in its authority: "Come aft with your hands up and prepare to be boarded!"

The Captain reached forward to adjust the squelch control, his weathered hand trembling slightly.

But Filibert gave a sharp command that froze him mid-motion. "*Stanse!*"

The Captain withdrew his hand from the knob as if it had burned him and turned slowly toward Filibert, his eyes widening as he found himself staring down the barrel of a pistol. The weapon looked almost delicate in Filibert's hand, but the Captain knew enough about firearms to recognize a 9mm Luger when he saw one. An old weapon. A weapon with history.

Filibert's hand was steady, his face expressionless. He waved the pistol in the direction of the wheelhouse door with a gesture that might have been polite in another context. "*Forlate*," he ordered.

The Captain grimaced, his jaw working silently as he considered his options. Then, wisdom winning over pride, he stepped away from the helm, turned the ignition key off with a defiant flick, and left without a word, his footsteps heavy on the metal stairs leading to the deck.

The wheelhouse fell silent again except for the groan of the boat and the distant roar of approaching patrol boat engines. Through the salt-streaked windows, they could see the Norwegian coastline—or what remained of it. The destruction was total. Systematic. Precisely what Filibert had calculated.

Iniko stared out at the devastation, her hands clenched in her lap. Her knuckles were white, tendons standing out beneath the skin. When she finally spoke, her voice was flat. Dead. "It's over."

Filibert said nothing. He rested the pistol on his thigh, his finger alongside the trigger guard rather than on the trigger itself. Exhausted.

"Kort has failed," Iniko continued, still not looking at him. "He's not bringing Zahra. They will not be at the rendezvous point. His power core will fail. He will be incinerated." She paused, and when she spoke again, her voice cracked. "People killed for nothing."

Outside, the patrol boats drew closer. Iniko could hear in the distance shouted commands in Norwegian.

Filibert eyed her with the cold calculation of a chess master studying a failed gambit. He already knew the answer to his question, had probably known for hours, maybe days. But he asked it anyway, his German accent thickening with barely suppressed rage. "And how do you know that?"

Iniko turned to face him for the first time since the Captain had left. Her eyes were red-rimmed but dry. She'd cried out all her tears somewhere between Pennsylvania and here, between the laboratory and this moment of reckoning. The tears had come in the dark of night, in moments when Filibert wasn't watching. But now there were no tears left. Only a terrible, crystalline clarity.

"I warned her," she said without hesitation, without a hint of regret. The admission hung in the air between them like smoke. "I betrayed you."

The words should have been harder to say. Should have caught in her throat, should have required courage to force out. But they came easily, almost with relief. After years of complicity, of watching Kort float in that vat, of calculating dosages and adjusting parameters and pretending she was just a scientist following orders—after all that, the truth was the easiest thing in the world.

She'd called Zahra from the Skansekaia pier, her hands shaking so badly she could barely hold the phone. She'd told her everything: the deployment, the target, Filibert's plan to send Kort to capture her and force her cooperation to work with him again, and most damning of all—where to find her and Filibert at sea. She'd given Zahra just enough time to get to safety, to mentally prepare to save Kort from following his programming to its terrible conclusion.

It hadn't been enough to stop the destruction. The Tesla weapon had still fired. Ålesund and Oslo still burned. But it had been enough to save Zahra. Enough to give Kort a choice. And perhaps, Iniko thought, it had been enough to save something of her own soul.

Filibert's jaw tightened with a sneer crawling up his face in an all too familiar, grotesque way. He wasn't surprised—she could see that clearly now—but swallowing the bitter truth was hard all the same.

The confirmation of what he'd suspected felt like glass in his throat. "You know this will end badly for both of us?" His voice dropped to barely above a whisper, more dangerous in its quietness than any shout. "Your treachery will turn on you and devour you."

"I deserve it to," Iniko replied immediately. There was a strange peace in her voice now, the peace of someone who'd already made the hardest decision and found relief on the other side of it. "I should have betrayed you long ago when Zahra asked me to help her get Kort out of the lab." She looked down at her hands, filled with the shame of that day in the laboratory when she'd chosen Filibert's vision over Zahra's desperate plea. "I didn't, and my soul has been dying ever since."

"Your soul." Filibert sneered, and the expression transformed his face into something inhuman. "You are a scientist. Don't insult me with all that sentimental foolishness."

The boat rocked as a larger swell passed beneath them. Through the windows, the patrol boats were close enough now that Iniko could make out individual figures on their decks—NATO security personnel in tactical gear, faces grim and professional, the metallic sound of weapons being readied.

"Yes," Iniko replied, her voice gaining strength. "I am a scientist and a human as you once were." She paused, studying him as she might study a specimen under glass. "But now, now I don't know what you've become. You're post-human, transformed into a monster like Kort."

"Shut up," Filibert growled. The pistol shifted slightly on his thigh.

But Iniko couldn't stop now. The words had been building inside her for years—since the laboratory "accidents," since the first time she'd seen Kort floating in that vat and understood what they'd truly done. "Only," she continued, noting the pistol in Filibert's hand as it shifted toward her, "yours was a mutation of the soul, twisted by hate and suffering."

"Shut up!" he commanded, thrusting the barrel directly at her chest. His hand trembled now, just slightly. The first crack in his composure she'd seen in years.

Unperturbed by the threat, Iniko kept hard eye contact and moved slowly toward him across the cramped wheelhouse. The floorboards creaked beneath her feet. The radio crackled with another Norwegian command, but neither of them acknowledged it. They were locked in their own private reckoning now, a moment forty years in the making.

"And as a scientist," Iniko said, each word deliberate and clear, "I warned you there was something wrong in Kort's new biology." Her eyes never left Filibert's face, watching for the moment of recognition she knew would come. "He went off mission with Zahra just like he went off mission in Bismarck. He disobeyed you, disobeyed orders, exercised his free will that you failed to account for in all your brilliant calculations."

The words hit Filibert like physical blows. She could see it in the way his shoulders sagged, in the sudden looseness around his eyes. The tension drained from his face like water from a broken vessel. He lowered the pistol, resting it in his lap as the crushing truth of a critical miscalculation set in.

The great Filibert Austerlitz, the genius who'd rewritten the rules of human biology, had forgotten the simplest truth: love was stronger than programming. Kort had chosen Zahra. Was always going to choose Zahra. And all of Filibert's nano-implants and behavioral conditioning couldn't override that fundamental human reality.

Iniko gently reached over and took the pistol from Filibert's limp grip. The weapon felt heavier than it should, weighted with the gravity of what it represented. She stepped back to the wall, the cold metal pressing against her spine, and said quietly, "It's over."

Defiance flickered back into Filibert's eyes, that stubborn spark that had driven him from the orphanage to Columbia University to the black sites where they'd created monsters in the name of progress. He spat the words like venom: "Nothing's ever over—it just mutates and survives."

It was pure Filibert. The eternal optimist of horror, always believing he could evolve past failure, adapt past consequences, survive past judgment.

Iniko felt a sad smile touch her lips. "Perhaps you will go on, continue your work," she said. "But I will no longer be on this journey with you." She paused, letting the weight of her next words settle. "Face it alone."

"I always have," Filibert muttered, and for just a moment, Iniko saw not the monster but the six-year-old boy from war-torn Berlin, standing over his mother's body, already alone in a world that had taken everything from him.

Filibert's eyes drifted from Iniko's face to the nautical clock embedded in the console. Its brass face was tarnished with age and salt air. The black hands stood at two-thirty. He stared at it with an intensity that seemed to transcend the present moment, his finger rising to point at the clock face.

He started making small, counterclockwise circular motions with his finger, the same gesture Iniko had seen him make a thousand times before—in the laboratory, in his bedroom surrounded by clocks, in moments of stress when the weight of what they'd done threatened to crush him. Always counterclockwise. Always trying to turn back time. Always trying to return to that moment in Berlin when everything changed.

"I always have," he whispered again, lost somewhere in memory, somewhere in the past he could never quite escape or recreate.

Iniko turned the pistol barrel on herself, pressing the cold metal to her chest just above her heart. She could feel it through the fabric of her sweater, could feel her heartbeat against the muzzle—steady, calm, ready for this to end.

She thought of Zahra, of that moment in the laboratory when she'd refused to help. Zahra had begged her: "Help me get him out. Help me save my husband." And Iniko had chosen Filibert's vision instead. Had chosen the promise of scientific advancement over basic human decency. That choice had haunted every moment since.

She thought of Kort, floating in the vat, his humanity stripped away piece by piece. The first time she'd seen him after the transformation, she'd vomited in the hallway. Not from the grotesque biology of it—she'd seen far worse in her years at the laboratory—but from the look in what remained of his eyes. The confusion. The betrayal. The echo of the man who'd once dreamed of being a better soldier, not a post-human weapon.

She thought of Ålesund burning on the horizon, of all the people who'd died because she'd been too weak to act sooner. Children in school or out on a class trip. Shop owners maintaining their shops—the backbone of the community. Elderly couples walking by the harbor. All gone because she'd told herself that she was just a scientist, just following orders, just trying to survive. She'd ignored that small voice that persisted, cried out for humanity. A voice from her own war trauma in Nigeria. Watching politically backed thugs machete-hack her parents and sisters to death. Her home set ablaze as she hid down the street with her aunt's hand over her mouth, dragging her away. A voice, a memory successfully evaded—until now.

She'd ignored it for too long.

Not anymore.

"Face it alone," she said again, softer this time.

The gunshot was intense and sharp, impossibly loud in the confined space of the wheelhouse. The crack of it seemed to split reality itself, a sound that would echo in Filibert's memory forever, another ghost to join all the others.

But Filibert didn't register it in the moment. The sound failed to penetrate the fortress of his interior world. He remained lost in himself, lost in time, his finger still making those small counterclockwise circles as if he could actually turn back the clock, could return to half past one, could undo everything that had brought them to this moment.

Nor did he register the sound of Iniko sliding down the wall, her body leaving a blood trail down to the floor—a crimson streak that looked almost artistic in its terrible simplicity. Her body crumpled at the base of the wall, her head tilted at an angle, eyes open but seeing nothing.

Nor did he register the shouts of the NATO team that had boarded the trawler, their boots pounding on the deck, their voices urgent and commanding as they secured the vessel.

Filibert sat alone in the wheelhouse, staring at the clock, his finger making those endless counterclockwise circles. Two-thirty. Always two-thirty. The time when everything ended or began, depending on how you measured it.

Outside, Norway burned.

Inside, Filibert Austerlitz sat with the body of the last person who'd known him before he became what he was, before the desperate experiments, before the obsession, before the hatred calcified into purpose.

He sat alone with his clocks and his memories and his terrible, unwavering belief that somehow, someway, he could still set things right. Could still turn back time. Could still return to the start and make different choices.

The NATO officers burst through the wheelhouse door, weapons drawn, voices shouting commands in Norwegian and English. They took in the scene in an instant—the woman's body against the wall, the blood, the pistol on the floor, the strange man sitting motionless at the console, staring at a clock and making small circular motions with his finger.

"Hands up! Now!"

But Filibert didn't respond. He was somewhere else entirely, somewhere in the past, somewhere in a world where clocks ran backward and the dead could be restored and six-year-old boys didn't have to watch their mothers die.

Two NATO officers grabbed him roughly, pulling his arms behind his back. The handcuffs clicked shut around his wrists with cold finality. Still, Filibert's eyes remained fixed on the clock.

Two-thirty.

Always two-thirty.

The time when Iniko's soul finally found the courage his never could: the courage to stop running, stop surviving, stop mutating into something new and terrible just to escape the weight of what they'd become.

As they dragged him from the wheelhouse, Filibert turned his head one last time to look at the clock. His lips moved, forming words no one else could hear:

"I always have."

And somewhere in the distance, Ålesund continued to burn, the smoke rising into the gray Norwegian sky like a monument to the terrible price of trying to play God with the human condition.

Stavanger, Norway - Three Days Later

The cafe was quintessentially Norwegian—clean lines, minimalist decor, windows facing the harbor where fishing boats bobbed in post-storm swells. News played on a mounted TV, volume low, showing aerial footage of Oslo and Ålesund's devastation on repeat. The international media had descended like vultures, speculating about terrorist attacks, Al-Qaeda connections, geopolitical implications.

They were all wrong. And they would stay wrong, because the truth was too dangerous to acknowledge.

Graven sat across from Mathias in a corner booth, as far from other patrons as possible. His left arm rested in a sling—dislocated shoulder from the Oslo blast. Mathias wore a neck brace, the white collar stark against his expensive suit. They looked like what they were: survivors of something that shouldn't have been survived. The energy-wave had lost power by the time it brushed past the makeshift NATO control center, but impacted it enough to toss personnel and office equipment around like so much flotsam.

The waitress approached—young, blonde, her Norwegian accent lilting as she asked: "Anything else?"

Graven looked up from his untouched coffee. "Yeah, how's the apple pie here?"

"Is good."

"I'll take a slice." He glanced at Mathias, who shook his head. The waitress left with efficient Nordic courtesy.

They sat in silence for a long moment. On the TV, a Danish expert was explaining how terrorist organizations were increasingly targeting civilian infrastructure. Another expert—this one from MIT—discussed theoretical directed energy weapons that might exist in five or ten years.

If they only knew.

"So what happens now?" Graven asked finally.

Mathias stirred his tea with deliberate precision—the practiced movement of a man who'd spent decades in meetings, negotiations, the careful dance of international bureaucracy. "Our research will continue. Now that we have the final piece... we can move forward. Kort's biology was the missing key to creating modification acceptance."

"More killing machines."

"Better specialized soldiers for special needs." Mathias set down his spoon, aligned it precisely parallel to the table edge. "And progress in organ transplants and prosthetics. Bio-integrated limbs that function better than natural ones. Tissue that doesn't reject. Organs that last lifetimes instead of decades."

He paused, met Graven's eyes. "You don't think Zahra would stay on just to create assassins, do you?"

Graven said nothing for a moment. They both knew the truth—once technology existed, it would be used. For good and ill. For healing and killing. The distinction between medical advancement and military application had always been paper-thin.

"The death toll," Graven said quietly. "Final numbers?"

"Oslo—four hundred thirty-seven dead. Mostly from the Peace Park area. Another thousand injured, many critically. The resonance wave's effects on human tissue..." Mathias trailed off. "Ålesund was worse. Eleven hundred dead. Maybe more—they're still finding bodies in the rubble."

"Fifteen hundred people." Graven's voice was flat, clinical. If he let himself feel the weight of that number, he'd break. "Because of a Cold War grudge."

"Because Filibert Austerlitz couldn't accept that his work was deemed too dangerous. Couldn't accept oversight, ethical constraints, the basic acknowledgment that some knowledge shouldn't be pursued." Mathias's voice carried an edge now—anger breaking through diplomatic composure. "We gave him resources, funding, the best facilities. And he abused it all. Created horrors that violated every principle of human dignity."

"So you shut him down. Took his research. Left him with nothing."

"We tried to contain a threat." Mathias leaned forward. "Would you have done differently? When a scientist starts treating human beings as raw materials for experimentation? When his 'volunteers' start dying in agony because their bodies reject the modifications?"

Graven thought about the files he'd read during the flight from Washington. Four enhanced soldiers dead—most before age thirty. Aggressive cancers. Organ failures. Bodies literally tearing themselves apart as synthetic and biological systems warred for dominance.

Four dead.

And one survivor.

"Kort Sokolov," Graven said. "What makes him different? Why did he survive when the others didn't?"

Mathias smiled—the expression carrying no warmth. "That's the fifteen-hundred-dead question, isn't it? Something in his genetic makeup, his immune system, his cellular structure—something made him compatible with Filibert's modifications in ways the others weren't. We've been trying to isolate it for decades."

"And now you have him. Or what's left of him."

"Now we have the answer."

The waitress returned with apple pie—generous slice, whipped cream on the side, the presentation precise and appealing. Graven looked at it without appetite.

"The world is a messy, complex place, my friend," Mathias continued after the waitress left. "Its security has always fallen on the few to do what needs done."

"That's the kind of thinking that created this mess."

"Perhaps." Mathias sipped his tea. "But it's also the thinking that will contain it. Filibert is in custody. His weapons are destroyed. His network—such as it was—has been dismantled. Iniko Aneke is dead. Shot herself right in front of Filibert I'm told. What passed between them in those final moments will likely not be known. And we have Kort's genetic material, which means we can finally move

Project 19.5 forward without the instability that plagued earlier attempts."

"You're going to make more of them."

"We're going to give soldiers a chance to survive impossible situations. We're going to heal injuries that would end careers, ruin lives. We're going to push human capability beyond current limitations in ways that are stable, controlled, ethical."

Graven laughed—harsh, bitter. "Ethical. Do you actually hear yourself?"

"I hear a realist acknowledging that technology marches forward whether we like it or not. The Chinese are working on enhancement programs. The Russians never stopped. Private corporations in Silicon Valley are experimenting with neural interfaces and genetic modification. The genie is out of the bottle, Graven. Has been since Filibert first proved it was possible. Our choice isn't whether enhancement happens—it's whether it happens under oversight or in secret. Under international law or in the shadow laboratories of a mad man."

"And NATO gets to be the arbiter of what's acceptable?"

"Someone has to be."

They sat in silence again. Outside, Stavanger continued to function post-national disaster and unthinkable tragedy—people going to work, tourists visiting historic sites, life asserting itself against recent horror. The human capacity to normalize, to adapt, to move forward even after apocalypse.

"Filibert," Graven said. "What happens to him?"

"High-security detention. Psychiatric evaluation. Trial, eventually, though it will be closed to the public. No one will know of his crimes—national security concerns."

"He'll never see daylight again."

"Would you prefer he did?" Mathias's voice was sharp. "After what he's done? After fifteen hundred bodies?"

"No. I just wonder if locking him away makes us any different than him. If we're just perpetuating the same cycle—secrets, lies, revenge."

"The difference," Mathias said carefully, "is that we acknowledge oversight. Accept constraints. Recognize that some prices are too high to pay, even for progress."

"Do you? Really?" Graven pushed his pie away untouched. "Or are you just better at hiding what you're willing to do?"

Mathias didn't answer. Which was answer enough.

Ålesund, Norway – Zahra's Laboratory, Six Hours Post-Attack

The surgical suite gleamed under lights that never changed—day and night meant nothing three stories underground in a super-hardened facility that had saved them from Filibert's weapon.

Zahra stood at the stainless-steel table, surrounded by the lab assistants who'd stayed behind with her, who'd been with her for years. They knew not to speak unless necessary. Knew to hand her instruments before she asked. Knew that what they were doing would never appear in any journal, never win awards, never be acknowledged by history. Knew they welcomed the distraction from the reality that above them much of what they knew was dead or dying. Greif was for later. In private rooms. Deep in bottles.

Before her, on the table, lay what remained of Kort Sokolov.

She'd spent six hours removing the magnesium self-destruct unit—delicate work, requiring precision that would have been impossible if her hands shook. They didn't shake. Couldn't shake. Not when this was the last thing she could do for him.

The bypass had worked, shorted out the countdown from reaching zero and incinerating Kort. From the complete destruction of forty years of research, of genetic material that held answers to questions researchers had been asking since the beginning of Project 19.5.

But the power failure had been total. The consciousness that was Kort Sokolov—husband, soldier, enhanced weapon, complicated human being who'd existed in all those identities simultaneously—was gone.

What remained was biology. Enhanced tissue. Modified organs. A spine containing genetic sequences that held the key to stable human modification. A brain that might still hold memories, if preserved correctly. If technology advanced enough. If enough years passed.

If she was willing to wait that long.

Zahra extracted the brain with movements she'd practiced on cadavers, on animal models, but never on someone she'd known. The tissue came away cleanly—Filibert's modifications had integrated deeply enough that standard anatomical boundaries no longer fully applied. The brain, the spinal column, the major organs—all were networked in ways that transcended normal human biology.

She placed the brain carefully in a preservation vat. Custom-built, filled with suspension fluid that would maintain cellular integrity indefinitely. Or as close to indefinitely as current technology allowed.

The label read simply: **KORT - NEURAL TISSUE.**

Clinical. Professional. Giving no hint of the grief that threatened to crack through her composure if she let it.

Next, the spine. This was the critical piece—the structure Filibert had modified most extensively, integrating neural pathways with synthetic enhancement channels that allowed for the kind of adaptation Kort had demonstrated. The spine came away in sections, each one carefully catalogued, prepared for analysis.

A laboratory assistant withdrew fluid from the spine with a syringe—genetic material, cellular samples, the building blocks that would inform the next generation of enhancements.

Behind her, visible through the surgical suite's observation window, four larger vats stood in a row. Each was seven feet tall, filled with nutrient solution that glowed faintly blue from bioluminescent additives. Each contained a subject in various stages of assembly—bodies reconstructed from preserved tissue, from genetic material salvaged from failed enhancements four decades ago, from the bleeding edge of bioengineering that had killed them the first time.

Now they would have a second chance.

Each vat bore a name etched into a steel plate at the base:

JEAN

HANS

D'ARCY

RAZO

The team cleaned up and she dismissed them to rest. She needed to be alone and take in the breadth of what had happened—how it all began.

The four legionnaire soldiers who hadn't survived Filibert's first generation of enhancements. Zahra had known them well in the brief years between her rescue and their deterioration and discharge from the Legion into hospitals and then the grave. Kort's love for her was all they needed to take her into their tight-knit brotherhood. She was treated like the kid sister by them, complete with good natured ribbing and teasing. And she was the one who began their care when things went wrong after she joined the lab at Sidi Bel Abbès.

D'Arcy had died first—brain cancer, aggressive and inoperable, inducing severe paranoia and hallucinations. He'd lasted four years post-enhancement. D'Arcy, the quiet one, always reading—philosophy, science fiction, anything that helped him understand what they were becoming, what it meant to be more than human but less than human simultaneously.

Razo and Hans had survived longer—eight years, the last of which they spent languishing in a French hospital.

Razo, who'd written poetry in his native Dutch when he thought no one was watching—verses about transformation and loss and the price of transcendence, hidden in notebooks that were never found until his death. Razo wasting away as his immune system attacked the synthetic tissue, unable to distinguish self from foreign.

Hans, who'd been terrified of heights but jumped anyway because legionnaires didn't refuse—who'd conquered his fear through sheer will only to end up in the same hospital as Razo. He succumbed to aggressive muscular dystrophy—the modified muscle tissue breaking down faster than his body could repair it.

Jean was the last, refusing to die in hospital. Jean, who'd loved to sing—American jazz standards, incongruous coming from a French soldier, but he'd learned them from Armed Forces Radio and sang them constantly until he was too weak to do so, then just hummed. Found weeks after his death in his slum of an apartment. The filtering systems that processed Filibert's lithium gel compounds weren't compatible with normal renal function. He'd died in agony, the gel backing up into his tissues, poisoning him from within.

Filibert always believed he could fix any unintended genetic effects no matter how catastrophic. Could make it work, could prove that human enhancement was not just possible but inevitable. And now, with Kort's genetics—with the stable integration patterns that his unique biology had demonstrated—Zahra could try again.

Could resurrect her husband's dead comrades and give them what they'd wanted the first time: enhanced capability without the death sentence. Military effectiveness without the horror.

Or she could create exactly what Filibert had created: weapons that wore human faces and forgot their humanity.

The choice, now, would be hers.

Weeks Later

After allowing herself recovery time, cut briefly because her racing thoughts dragged her back to the lab, she and her team set to the task of analyzing Kort's tissue and organ samples using the latest techniques and equipment. In the early morning hour, in her office adjoining the laboratory, Zahra stood before a massive whiteboard covered in formulas. Chemical structures. Genetic sequences. Integration patterns mapped across decades of research.

This was Filibert's work and her work and Kort's sacrifice all tangled together into something that might save lives or end them, depending on application.

She wrote out a new sequence—combining Kort's genetic markers with modified enhancement protocols that incorporated what they'd learned from four decades of failure. Her hand moved with automatic precision, muscle memory from years of iteration, calculation, endless refinement.

The formula stretched across six feet of whiteboard:

$\Delta G = \Delta H - T\Delta S$ (modified for biological integration) $\kappa =$ (cellular acceptance) × (synthetic compatibility) / (immune response) Integration threshold: 94.7% (Kort baseline) Failure threshold: <87% (Jean, Hans, D'Arcy, Razo historical)

Below that, she'd mapped the genetic markers that made Kort unique:

HLA-B*57:01 (enhanced compatibility) CCR5-Δ32 (modified immune response) ACTN3 R577X (enhanced muscle fiber adaptation)

Plus seventeen other sequences they'd identified, each one contributing to his body's ability to accept modification without rejection. Without the kidney failure that had killed Jean. Without the muscular dystrophy that had destroyed Hans. Without the brain cancer that took D'Arcy or the autoimmune diseases that ended Razo.

Seventeen genetic markers that had saved Kort's life while his brothers died.

And now she was going to use those markers to bring them back.

Behind her, through the glass wall separating her office from the laboratory proper, she could see the vats. See the subjects floating in their nutrient solution, breathing through masks attached to their faces. Not quite alive. Not quite dead. Something in between.

Waiting for her to decide if this resurrection was mercy or madness.

She turned back to the board, added another variable, crossed out a section that wouldn't work. Started over. The mathematics were elegant—biological systems following rules that could be predicted, controlled, optimized. Remove the emotional component and it was just engineering. Just problem-solving.

Just science.

But she couldn't remove the emotional component. Not when she remembered Jean's laugh. Hans's nervous habit of cracking his knuckles. D'Arcy's quiet intensity when he read. Razo's poetry, verses about home and honor and the weight of what they were becoming.

Not when she remembered Kort's face the last time she'd seen him before she had to flee Filibert's lab at the mill the night Iniko was supposed to help her get Kort out. But Iniko had betrayed her and Zahra had to go into hiding. She had found her way to NATO, to Mathias—to her last chance to save Kort from what he had become.

Now she was completing the process. Taking what remained of him—genetic material, tissue samples, the preserved brain that might hold his memories—and using it to create more enhanced soldiers.

More weapons.

More men who would lose themselves in modification.

Her phone buzzed. She ignored it. Buzzed again. On the third time, she answered.

"Doctor?" Mathias's voice, transmitted through multiple layers of encryption. "How is the work progressing?"

"We have viable samples. The genetic sequences are stable. I can begin integration within the month, but it will take time to produce anything tangible."

"Excellent. The NATO council is very interested in your timeline. We have... situations developing that would benefit from enhanced capability."

Situations. The euphemism made her jaw clench. Situations meant missions. Missions meant combat. Combat meant men like Kort being deployed into scenarios that would kill normal soldiers, betting their lives on modifications that had killed four out of five test subjects the first time.

"These are people, Mathias. Not tools. Not weapons. They deserve to be brought back with dignity."

"Of course. No one is suggesting otherwise." His voice carried the smooth assurance of a career diplomat who'd spent decades saying things he didn't mean. "But you understand the importance of the work. The applications for soldiers in hostile environments alone—"

"I understand perfectly what you want. What I'm trying to determine is whether what you want is worth the cost."

Silence on the line. Then: "What cost would be too high, Zahra? How many soldiers' lives are too many to save with enhancement? How many critical missions should fail because we lacked capability? Where, exactly, do you draw that line?"

She didn't have an answer. She had been wrestling with that question since she'd first agreed to continue the project. Since she'd decided that Kort's sacrifice shouldn't be meaningless. That something good could come from all the horror.

But the question kept expanding the more she thought about it. If enhancement could save soldiers' lives in combat, could it also save cancer patients? Burn victims? People with degenerative diseases? Where did military application end and medical treatment begin? And if the technology existed for both, did refusing to use it make her complicit in preventable deaths?

Or did using it make her complicit in creating weapons?

"Zahra." Mathias's voice changed, dropped to a controlled, firm, authoritative tone, like a parent preparing to scold a child. "The lie you told me has come to light. My years of suspicion has been confirmed."

On her end of the call, Zahra winced, had been preparing for this moment, but hadn't expected it now. Not now. Not at this critical moment. But then again, what else did she expect from Mathias? What else but a masterful ambush.

"You knew where Filibert and Kort were all along. When you came to me fifteen years ago, scared and desperate, saying Kort had vanished, thinking he ran off to join Filibert at an unknown location—that was a deception. A *doublé* as it were in our little fencing game. Tsk, tsk, tsk. You knew. I dare say, you probably engineered some of the final stages. You share in the responsibility for what has happened. You understand that, yes?"

Silence.

Then Zahra's measured response, "I'll have preliminary results in three months. Full integration will take longer. You can't rush biology, Mathias. Not if you want it to work."

Silence. Zahra could feel the sadistic smile that certainly was forming on his face, savoring the leverage he had on her. Bastard.

"Of course. Take the time you need." A pause that felt loaded with unspoken implications. "How are you holding up? Personally?"

The question surprised her. Mathias wasn't known for personal concern—NATO's interests were his interests, and individual wellbeing rarely factored into strategic calculations. What was the game now?

"I'm fine."

"Zahra—"

"I said I'm fine." She cut him off, couldn't have this conversation, couldn't acknowledge the grief because acknowledging it meant confronting it and confronting it meant breaking down and she couldn't break down. Not yet. Not while there was work to do. Not while four men were waiting in vats for her to give them another chance at life. "Three months, Mathias. I'll send reports."

She hung up before he could respond.

Through the glass, the vats hummed with circulating fluid. The subjects floated, suspended, waiting for her to give them life. Or something like it.

That's when it hit her.

Not a notion that emerged slowly enough to process in digestible bits. No, it was a brutal truth that thrashed her core. She felt dizzy and sick from the cramping in her gut.

Betrayal. All around her—betrayal.

The betrayal of Russian soldiers who came to liberate Berlin from the Nazis only to ravage it and kill Filibert's mother. The betrayal of nations promising peace after war tore the world apart, only to dominate and continue violence-for-profit philosophies. The betrayal of universities and NATO who funded research that produced untold wonders only to steal it away from its creators. Filibert's betrayal of Kort, turning him into a mindless assassin. And Filbert's betrayal of himself from his vision of improving the life of those who served only to succumb to an obsession with revenge for his personal pain.

The betrayals of nations throughout time and time to come of those who stepped up to keep the watch, bracing the cold, allowing the rest to slumber warm and protected and unbothered. The betrayal of soldiers like D'Arcy, Hans, Razo, and Jean and countless others who gave their all—giving still—and too many thanked by languishing alone in hospitals, dying from the aftermaths of their service, ending in silent graves. Betrayals all of it. It started coming closer to home. Iniko's betrayal of her when the time came to take Kort from the lab at the mill and away from Filibert. And now—she felt like vomiting—wasn't she continuing the cycle of betrayal? Reestablishing the program, reactivated those who had already given so much—too much. She punched her right thigh in rapid succession and sucked back hard the flood of sobs and tears that were straining to break through.

"No." she commanded.

No. Betrayal is part of the process. She must see that. Does the teen not betray the dreams of the child, and the adult of the teen, and the elderly of the adult? Does one generation not betray the former one by creating their own visions? Change is the only constant she had been taught and had come to know. And change is a betrayal of the past. The difference might be if the betrayal is in the service of something better. But who could know if better will be the outcome? And better for whom and worse for whom?

"No." she repeated with cold resolve. "This is just. My cause is just." The distress, the dizziness, the gut twist, abated.

Zahra returned to her whiteboard, wrote another sequence, checked it against Kort's baseline data. The mathematics aligned. The biology should work. In theory.

Theory had been wrong before.

But science was iterative. Failure led to understanding. Understanding led to success. And success meant that Kort's death—the end of the man she'd loved—would have meaning beyond tragedy.

Would have to have meaning.

Because the alternative was unbearable.

She wrote faster now, filling the board with calculations that might save lives or end them, with formulas that could heal or kill depending on application, with the accumulated knowledge of four decades spent trying to perfect what Filibert had started and she'd tried to stop.

And in the vats behind her, four men who'd died for science waited to see if science could return the favor.

Epilogue: Half Past One

NATO High Security Prison, Brussels – One Year Later

The cell was sparse but not cruel. Concrete walls. A narrow bed. A desk and chair. A toilet behind a privacy screen. A window too small to climb through, overlooking an interior courtyard where nothing grew.

Filibert Austerlitz sat at the desk, his fingers moving in small circles against the wood surface. His lips formed a quiet narrative—equations, calculations, theories that no one could hear and wouldn't understand if they did.

He hadn't spoken since his capture. The psychological evaluators had tried—endless sessions where they asked questions and received only silence and that continuous finger movement, tracing counter-clockwise circles like a broken record.

The official diagnoses, rendered out of professional frustration, a hodge-podge of the best guesses of NATO psychiatrists and psychologists as nothing really fit: Delusional Disorder, Grandiose Type with comorbid Selective Mutism, Stereotypic Movement Disorder, and obsessive-compulsive features. Trauma response to capture, to failure, to the realization that his grand plan had been thwarted.

They were wrong, of course. Filibert wasn't mute or locked into a fantasy world or lacking purpose in his movements. He was calculating, hyper-systemizing in his engagement with the world. Working through problems in his head that required years of mathematics, decades of theoretical physics, generations of biological engineering.

He was designing the next iteration.

The clock on the wall showed 2:47 PM. He looked at it, and his finger movements intensified. 2:47. Too late. Always too late. If he could just turn it back to 1:30...

The cell door clanged open.

A guard's voice: "I'll wait right here, sir. Protocol."

Filibert didn't acknowledge the visitor. Kept muttering, kept calculating, kept staring at the equations only he could see projected against the concrete wall.

"*Hallo*, Doctor Austerlitz."

Mathias's voice. Cultured. Controlled. Carrying the same patronizing tone it had carried in 1970 when he'd first shut down Project 19.5.

Filibert kept moving his finger in circles. Kept muttering.

"The team has gone off mission and are missing. Something has gone wrong in the formulation. You know these men, they were your men. I need your help—Zahra needs your help."

The finger stopped.

The muttering stopped.

Filibert's head turned slowly toward Mathias. And he smiled. Really smiled.

Not the trauma response the psychologists had documented. Not the broken mind giving up on reality.

The smile of a man who'd just been told that his work had succeeded beyond his wildest dreams. That his creations were out there, doing what they were designed to do. And missing what Zahra didn't know. What Iniko had identified, but Filibert had ignored until it became his undoing. A free will manifesting randomly.

The smile of a man who'd just learned that his revenge was incomplete. That there was more work to do. More worlds to reshape. More time to turn backward.

Mathias stood in the doorway, briefcase in hand, the weight of NATO's desperation making him willing to bargain with the devil who'd killed fifteen hundred people.

"We can discuss terms," Mathias continued. "Your cooperation in exchange for—"

Filibert raised one finger: Stop.

Then he pointed at the clock on the wall.

His lips moved: "Half past one."

And Mathias understood, in that moment, that Filibert Austerlitz had never been broken by capture. Had never given up on his obsession. Had simply been waiting for exactly this moment—when they would need him badly enough to compromise every principle.

When they would prove that he'd been right all along about the corruption, the moral bankruptcy, the willingness to embrace any horror if it served strategic interests.

"We can work together," Mathias said carefully. "Limited consultation. Oversight. Ethical guidelines—"

Filibert's smile widened.

Because they both knew that "ethical guidelines" meant nothing when enhanced soldiers were missing. When NATO's newest weapons had gone rogue. When the only person who understood the technology well enough to fix it was sitting in a cell, smiling, waiting for the world to beg him to continue the work they'd tried to destroy.

"Terms," Filibert said. His first word in a year. His voice rusty, cracking, but clear enough. "I want everything. All the research. All the data. Complete access to Zahra and her laboratory."

"That's not possible—"

"Then Jean, Hans, D'Arcy, and Razo will keep killing—that's what they're doing, isn't it? Selecting their own targets? Making their own moral decisions of what is justice? Yes, they will keep killing until their power cores fail or you destroy them. And everything they know—everything I taught them through Kort's genetic memory—dies with them." Filibert leaned forward. "You need me, Mathias. You've always needed me. You just couldn't admit it until the cost of refusing became too high."

Mathias's jaw tightened. "Limited access. Supervised consultation. No independent research."

"Complete access. Unsupervised work. And I want Kort's brain."

"What? What makes you think we have... Why?"

Filbert lobbed Mathias a derisive smirk. "Because he's my brother. Because I promised him peace. Because you took everything from me once and I'm not letting you take this."

They stared at each other across thirty-six years of history—two men who'd shaped a secret program that killed and saved in equal measure, who'd created weapons and healing technologies from the same research, who'd drawn different conclusions about the same fundamental question:

How much humanity can you sacrifice in pursuit of progress?

"I'll need to consult the council," Mathias said finally.

"You do that." Filibert returned to his finger circles, his muttering, his broken-clock routine that was no longer broken but calculated. "I'll wait. I've gotten very good at waiting."

Mathias left. The cell door clanged shut. The guard returned to his post.

And Filibert Austerlitz sat alone, moving his finger counter-clockwise, smiling at equations only he could see, knowing that the cycle was starting again.

Knowing that time always moved forward, but if you were patient enough, if you were clever enough, if you were willing to sacrifice everything—

Sometimes you could make the clocks turn backward.

Sometimes you could return to half past one.

Sometimes you could resurrect what was dead and give it new life in ways the world wasn't ready for.

The clock on the wall ticked forward—2:48, 2:49, 2:50.

But in Filibert's mind, it was always 1:30 PM, Berlin, 1945.

Always the moment before everything changed.

Always the moment he was trying to return to.

Always the moment when his mother lay dying, when Russian soldiers violated everything he loved, when time itself fractured and left him obsessed with turning it backward, resetting it, making the world obey his will the way clocks should but didn't.

And now, with Mathias's desperation giving him leverage, with four enhanced soldiers running loose carrying Kort's genetic memory, with Zahra's laboratory waiting and NATO's oversight crumbling—

Now he had his chance.

Not just to continue the work. To expand it. To prove that his original vision—humanity enhanced, perfected, transcended—wasn't madness but prophecy.

He thought about Kort, floating in that vat in Pennsylvania. Healing. Recharging. Preparing for deployment. His brother in all but blood, the one person who'd understood from the beginning what they were trying to accomplish.

Kort had kept his promise for forty years. Had endured modification after modification, had sacrificed his humanity piece by piece, had become more weapon than man because he'd promised Filibert they would finish the work together.

And even now, even reduced to tissue samples and genetic material and a preserved brain that might never wake—even now, Kort was keeping that promise.

Because his genetics had resurrected Jean, Hans, D'Arcy, and Razo. Gave them the stability he'd achieved through genetic accident and four decades of refinement. And now would create a new generation of enhanced soldiers who wouldn't die young, wouldn't reject the modifications, wouldn't suffer the cancers and organ failures that had plagued the first attempts.

Would succeed where Filibert's original work had failed. Would succeed because in the past year, he had solved the free will problem. The problem Zahra was ignorant of. Dangerously ignorant.

The door opened again. Not Mathias this time—a different guard, younger, carrying a meal tray. Standard prison food: bread, soup, protein of indeterminate origin. Designed for nutrition rather than enjoyment.

The guard set the tray on the desk, careful not to get too close to the prisoner. Filibert ignored him, kept moving his finger in circles, kept muttering equations that the guard couldn't hear clearly but found disturbing anyway.

"Eat something," the guard said in French-accented English. "You haven't eaten in two days."

Filibert didn't respond. The guard waited a moment, then left, locking the cell behind him.

Alone again.

Filibert looked at the food, at the clock, at the concrete walls that were supposed to contain him but couldn't contain what mattered—his mind, his calculations, his absolute certainty that everything he'd done was necessary and right and would be vindicated by history.

Fifteen hundred dead in Oslo and Ålesund. A tragedy, yes. Collateral damage in service of a greater purpose. The price that had to be paid to demonstrate capability, to prove that his work had succeeded beyond NATO's most optimistic projections, to force them to acknowledge that enhancement was inevitable.

They called it terrorism. Mass murder. Crimes against humanity.

He called it demonstration. Message. Proof of concept.

And now they needed him. Would bargain with him. Would give him access to everything they'd tried to keep from him because the alternative—enhanced soldiers running loose without oversight, without control—was worse than making deals with the devil who'd created them.

Filibert smiled at the ceiling, at cameras that recorded his every movement and transmitted them to analysts who tried to find patterns in his obsessive behaviors.

Let them watch. Let them analyze. Let them think him broken.

He wasn't broken. He was patient. Had been patient for six decades, since Berlin fell and his world ended and he decided that if he couldn't save his mother, he could at least prevent future tragedies by making humanity strong enough to survive anything.

Strong enough that a six-year-old boy would never again have to hide behind a couch while his family was destroyed.

Strong enough that time itself could be controlled, commanded, forced backward to moments of safety.

The clock struck 3:00 PM.

Filibert's finger moved in circles.

Half past one.

Half past one.

And halfway to two.

Forever and ever, amen.

TO: Research Oversight Committee, NATO Special Projects Division

FROM: Dr. F. Austerlitz, Biological Enhancement Research, Sidi Bel Abbès

DATE: 17 November 1957

RE: Theoretical Framework for Directed Genetic Modification in Combat Personnel

~~CLASSIFICATION: TOP SECRET~~

I. EXECUTIVE SUMMARY

Recent advances in molecular biology, particularly Watson and Crick's elucidation of DNA structure (1953), have opened theoretical pathways for direct manipulation of genetic material at the cellular level. This memorandum proposes a framework for utilizing these principles to enhance combat effectiveness through targeted biological modification.

While current technology limits practical application, the theoretical foundations established herein may prove relevant to future military research initiatives. I submit this framework for archival purposes and potential long-term development.

II. THEORETICAL FOUNDATION
A. DNA as Modifiable Code
The double helix structure revealed by Watson and Crick demonstrates that genetic information is not immutable

destiny but rather a *code*—and codes can be rewritten. Each base pair represents a discrete unit of information. In principle, targeted modification of these units could alter protein expression, cellular function, and ultimately, organism-level capabilities.

Current limitations in precision do not negate the theoretical validity of this approach. What cannot be achieved in 1957 may prove routine by 1967, 1977, or beyond.

B. Evolutionary Templates in "Junk" DNA

Preliminary analysis of genomic sequences reveals extensive non-coding regions—colloquially termed "junk DNA"—whose function remains unclear. I propose an alternative hypothesis: these regions represent *dormant evolutionary programs*, silenced during species development but potentially reactivatable under appropriate conditions.

Consider: Human embryonic development recapitulates evolutionary history (Haeckel's biogenetic law, though disputed in details, suggests deeper truth). Embryos temporarily exhibit gill-like structures, tail formations, and other ancestral characteristics before subsequent development suppresses these features.

Question: If developmental processes can temporarily activate ancestral traits, could targeted intervention activate them *permanently* in adult organisms?

C. Marine Organisms as Biological Templates

Certain marine species exhibit capabilities absent in mammalian biology:

Lampreys (*Petromyzon marinus*): Unique oral structure capable of powerful suction; anticoagulant proteins in saliva; extraordinary resistance to bacterial infection

Octopi (*Octopus vulgaris*): Distributed neural architecture allowing autonomous limb function; rapid cellular regeneration; adaptive camouflage through chromatophore manipulation

Electric rays (*Torpedo nobiliana*): Specialized cells generating bioelectric potential exceeding 200 volts; precise control of electrical discharge

Each represents millions of years of evolutionary optimization for specific survival strategies. The genetic programs encoding these capabilities exist as discrete, identifiable sequences. In theory, these sequences could be *isolated, modified, and introduced* into mammalian genomes.

III. PROPOSED MECHANISM: TARGETED GENETIC INTEGRATION

A. Viral Vector Delivery

Certain viruses naturally insert genetic material into host cell DNA. Bacteriophages demonstrate this principle in bacterial systems. Theoretically, modified viral vectors could serve as delivery mechanisms for desired genetic sequences.

Challenges:

Viral vectors currently lack precision targeting

Host immune response typically destroys modified cells

Integration sites are random, potentially disrupting essential genes

Success rate would likely be <1% with current methods

However: These are *technical* limitations, not *theoretical* impossibilities.

B. Enzyme-Mediated Sequence Modification

Recent work on restriction enzymes (Lederberg, 1952; Luria, 1953) demonstrates that certain proteins can cut DNA at specific sequences. The theoretical inverse—proteins that could *insert* specific sequences at targeted locations—would enable precise genetic modification.

Such "molecular scissors and paste" do not yet exist. But the biochemical principles suggest no fundamental barrier to their eventual development.

I propose the existence of naturally-occurring enzyme systems capable of targeted DNA modification. They remain undiscovered, but discovery is merely a matter of time and systematic investigation.

C. Integration Timeline

Assuming successful delivery and integration:

Days 1-7: Viral vector infection; initial genetic integration in target cells

Weeks 2-4: Modified cells begin expressing new proteins; initial phenotypic changes

Months 2-6: Systematic tissue modification as altered cells replicate

Years 1-5: Full organismal integration; stabilization of modifications

This timeline assumes *ideal* conditions. Practical application would likely require significantly longer adaptation periods.

IV. MILITARY APPLICATIONS

A. Enhanced Combat Effectiveness

Theoretical modifications could produce personnel with:

Accelerated wound healing (octopus regeneration)

Enhanced sensory capabilities (electric ray electroreception)

Improved physical resilience (lamprey infection resistance)

Extended operational capacity (modified metabolic efficiency)

B. Operational Advantages

Modified personnel would require:

Reduced medical evacuation

Decreased recovery time from injuries

Lower susceptibility to environmental pathogens

Enhanced performance under extreme conditions

C. Strategic Implications

Nations achieving practical genetic modification technology would possess decisive military advantage. A single modified soldier might accomplish missions currently requiring entire squads. Casualty rates could decrease substantially. Operational capabilities would expand dramatically.

This is not speculation. This is logical extrapolation from established biological principles.

V. ETHICAL CONSIDERATIONS

A. Informed Consent

Any practical application would require:

Full disclosure of procedures and risks

Voluntary participation from subjects

Reversibility of modifications (if technically feasible)

Long-term medical monitoring

B. Unintended Consequences

Genetic modification carries inherent risks:

Unforeseen physiological complications

Psychological effects of biological alteration

Potential heritability to offspring (creating permanent genetic changes in human populations)

Unknown long-term health impacts

These concerns warrant serious consideration but should not prevent fundamental research.

C. Moral Boundaries

There exist modifications that, while technically feasible, would violate human dignity. I propose the following ethical constraints:

Modifications must preserve human cognitive capacity and emotional range

Modified individuals must retain reproductive compatibility with unmodified humans

Modifications must not create permanent dependency on external support systems

The individual must remain recognizably human in appearance and psychology

Within these boundaries, enhancement serves human flourishing. Beyond them lies the creation of something no longer human—an outcome to be avoided.

VI. CURRENT RESEARCH LIMITATIONS

A. Technical Constraints

No method exists for precise DNA sequence modification

Viral vectors lack targeting specificity

Immune rejection destroys most modified cells

Integration success rate insufficient for practical application

No reliable method for testing modifications without human subjects

B. Theoretical Gaps

Incomplete understanding of gene regulatory mechanisms

Unknown interactions between introduced sequences and existing genome

Uncertain effects of activating dormant evolutionary programs

Unpredictable long-term stability of modifications

C. Resource Requirements

Practical development would require:

Advanced molecular biology facilities

Decades of systematic research

Test subjects willing to accept significant risks

Substantial financial investment

Institutional commitment despite uncertain timelines

VII. RECOMMENDATIONS

A. Immediate Actions

Establish dedicated research program for molecular biology fundamentals

Investigate enzyme systems capable of DNA manipulation

Study marine organism genetics to identify transferable capabilities

Develop theoretical models of genetic integration

B. Medium-Term Goals (5-10 years)

Achieve reliable viral vector targeting

Demonstrate successful genetic modification in mammalian cell cultures

Identify and characterize dormant evolutionary sequences

Develop methods for controlled gene activation

C. Long-Term Vision (10-30 years)

First successful human genetic modification

Stabilization of enhancement protocols

Deployment of modified personnel in limited operational contexts

Refinement based on real-world performance data

VIII. CONCLUSION

The theoretical framework presented herein is decades ahead of current technical capability. This memorandum will likely appear speculative, perhaps even fantastical, to contemporary review.

However, I submit that history demonstrates the rapid pace of scientific advancement. What appears impossible in 1957 may prove routine by 1977. The nation that begins theoretical development now will possess decisive advantage when technical capability catches up to theoretical understanding.

The question is not whether genetic modification of combat personnel will occur. The question is which nation will achieve it first.

I recommend NATO begin systematic investigation of these principles immediately.

Respectfully submitted,

Dr. F. Austerlitz
Research Director, Biological Enhancement Division
Sidi Bel Abbès Research Facility
17 November 1957

[STAMP: ~~CLASSIFIED - TOP SECRET~~]
[STAMP: PROJECT TERMINATED - 12 APRIL 1965]
[HANDWRITTEN NOTE: *"Theoretical only. No practical application. Recommend archive and discontinue funding. - M. Sørensen, 14 April 1965"*]

EDITOR'S NOTE:

The above document was allegedly recovered from NATO archives during research for this novel. Its authenticity remains unverified. Certain technical details align suspiciously well with CRISPR-Cas9 technology developed in 2012—fifty-five years after this memorandum's purported date.

Readers may draw their own conclusions about whether Dr. Austerlitz was a fictional character, a prescient scientist whose work was suppressed, or something else entirely.

— END OF DOCUMENT —

Acknowledgements

This book exists because of people who believed in stories about broken soldiers, obsessive scientists, and the price of transcending human limits.

To my family, who tolerated years of me muttering about lamprey modifications and bioelectric fields at dinner—thank you for not staging an intervention.

To the beta readers who told me when the science went off the rails and when the emotional beats landed—your honesty made this book what it is.

To the veterans who shared their stories, their tactical knowledge, and their understanding of what service costs—Kort and his brothers exist because you showed me what loyalty looks like.

To the scientists who patiently explained cellular biology, genetic cascades, and why my initial enhancement protocols would absolutely kill someone—any remaining errors are mine, probably because I thought the science was "close enough."

To the researchers and historians who document the French Foreign Legion, NATO's Cold War programs, and the uncomfortable truths about military experimentation—your work provided the foundation this fiction is built on.

And to everyone who ever wondered what would happen if we could actually become more than human—this book is my answer. It's probably not the answer you wanted, but it's the one that kept me awake at night.

The clock always shows half past one. That moment before everything changes. Before we become what we were always meant to be, or what we should never have tried to become.

Thank you for reading.
MCKENNA/PLOUFFE

About the Authors

Kris McKenna | KA Ploufffe

Kris McKenna is an American inventor, filmmaker, and law enforcement professional whose multidimensional career shapes the authentic grit and scientific imagination behind his stories. A certified Law Enforcement Officer with over two decades of experience, McKenna has served on the front lines of real-world investigations and crisis response, grounding his fiction in the sharp realism of tactical decision-making and human behavior under pressure.

Beyond his criminal justice background, McKenna is an accomplished product designer and entrepreneur. His patented technologies—some approved for integration into Department of Defense eyewear specifications—bridge advanced materials science with practical field applications. This fusion of science, engineering, and operational insight informs the speculative frameworks of his writing, including the Gothic series: *Rectified.*

As a storyteller, McKenna has written nine feature-length screenplays and produced award-winning short films. His scripts have earned high professional marks, with his dramatic thriller *Sculpted* receiving praise ranging from "9 out of 10" to "this needs to be made." His work blends cinematic pacing, emotionally driven characters, and grounded scientific intrigue.

McKenna is also the founder of Tactician Fragrances, a creative brand known for its equipment-inspired designs and storytelling-driven marketing, demonstrating his unique ability to merge entrepreneurship with narrative vision.

He currently focuses on expanding his intellectual properties—across literature, film, and product innovation—while continuing to develop new theories, designs, and stories that explore the intersection of human resilience, science, and the unknown.

K. A. Plouffe is a retired Air Force member serving in security and behavioral health specialties with assignments at nuclear missile sites, Air Force Survival School, and Cuban refugee camps in Panama. He has rank in a variety of martial arts and unarmed and armed combatives. He has paraprofessional and professional experience in mental health partial hospitalization and substance abuse treatment programs, community and police-based mobile crisis, county jail, home-based family, school-based, and office-based therapy. He holds a BS and MS in Psychology and a MS in Counseling.

K. A. Plouffe is a writer with ZERO|END™ productions, contributing to a number of completed full-length film scripts as well as finishing a musical stage play. He contributed two peer-reviewed journal articles on trauma to the professional field. He is the winner in the Visionary Fiction Division of the 2013 Beverly Hills Book Awards for the fantasy novel *Annie's Odyssey*. He has provided numerous editorial contributions and magazine articles. He continues to serve the community through his work in the mental health field and lives with his wife in Maine.